AFTER DARCY

Also by Joanna Nadin

The Double Life of Daisy Hemmings
The Queen of Bloody Everything
The Talk of Pram Town
The Future of the Self

Books for Young Adults

A Calamity of Mannerings
Birdy Arbuthnot's Year of 'Yes'
My Teeth in Your Heart
Joe All Alone

AFTER DARCY

JOANNA NADIN

First published in the UK in 2026 by Bedford Square Publishers Ltd, London, UK

bedfordsquarepublishers.co.uk
@bedfordsq.publishers

© Joanna Nadin, 2026

The right of Joanna Nadin to be identified as the author of this work has been asserted in accordance with the Copyright, Designs and Patents Act 1988. All rights reserved. No part of this book may be reproduced, stored in or introduced into a retrieval system, or transmitted, in any form or by any means (electronic, mechanical, photocopying, recording or otherwise) without the written permission of the publishers.

Any person who does any unauthorised act in relation to this publication may be liable to criminal prosecution and civil claims for damages.
A CIP catalogue record for this book is available from the British Library.
This is a work of fiction. Names, characters, places, and incidents either are the product of the author's imagination or are used fictitiously, and any resemblance to actual persons, living or dead, businesses, companies, events or locales is entirely coincidental.

ISBN
978-1-83501-406-6 (Paperback)
978-1-83501-407-3 (eBook)

2 4 6 8 10 9 7 5 3 1

Typeset in 11 on 13.5pt Adobe Caslon Pro
by Avocet Typeset, Bideford, Devon, EX39 2BP
Printed and bound in Great Britain by
CPI Group (UK) Ltd, Croydon CR0 4YY

The manufacturer's authorised representative in the EU for product safety is Easy Access System Europe, Mustamäe tee 50, 10621 Tallinn, Estonia
gpsr.requests@easproject.com

For all my chosen sisters

WINTER

DECEMBER

Sister Act
Jane, Lizzy, Mary, Kitty, Lydia

~Lydia Bennet
happy new year!
13:34

~Jane Bingley
Wrong day. It's not even 3pm in Paris, for heaven's sake. Unless you're in Australia. Oh God. Are you in Australia?
13:36

~Lydia Bennet
gare du nord, bitches. i'm coming home!
13:36

[Missed voice call]

~Jane Bingley
Really? Does Mum know? Please don't get drunk.
13:37

~Lydia Bennet
too late. and no. surprise! DO NOT TELL HER
13:37

~Jane Bingley
Please don't get any more drunk.
13:37

~Lydia Bennet
okay, mary
13:39

~Jane Bingley
It's Jane.
13:39

~Lydia Bennet
hard to tell
13:39

~Kitty Miller
OMG! Seriously? Why? How long for? Call me when you get here! Or just come to the Dragon. Dave's playing. Off to drop Bridge at Mum's now. Also Mary isn't even in here.
13:57

~Lydia Bennet
yes she is. she just doesn't post. she lurks. LURKER! got to go. train boarding. love you.
13:58

~Jane Bennet
Lyds, please don't drink any more. I'm serious. Not today.
13:58

[Missed voice call]

~Jane Bennet
Lyds?
14:01

JANUARY

It is a truism, frequently invoked by the members of the Meryton Women's Guild, that one is only ever as happy as one's unhappiest child. So, with five daughters and four grandchildren, it was a miracle Mrs Hester Bennet ever raised a smile. At best, she was only ever tentatively pleased, and even then understood that her contentment rested on the edge of a gaping precipice into which she would inevitably tumble the second Kitty or Lydia (it was almost always those two) messaged in the clutches of yet another existential crisis.

She wasn't asking for a lot, was she? For them all to be married and happy, the one following the other in her mind like port after cheese. Of course, Lizzy and Jane had started the ball rolling nicely – wed within a month of each other and to best friends who had both gone to Cambridge. Cambridge, no less! If only those silly boys— She cut the thought off. No use crying over spilt milk; they'd done enough of that yesterday. No, one had to move on, even if, as in Jane's case, it was with George Wickham. Still, even he seemed to have grown up since that silly business with Lydia, and he was obviously besotted, doted on Grace as well, which took some doing (fifteen was never the easiest of ages with girls). So, good on Jane, really. And Kitty hadn't let the disaster that was her ex-husband (and Bridget's biological father) stop her. Dave might only be a postman, but he had a good head of hair, his own flat, and was handy with mechanics, and, really, that wasn't to be sniffed at, not these days.

Lizzy might take a leaf out of her sisters' books and at least make an effort to find another man, instead of burying herself in birth canals at work. She was still solidly attractive, financially stable (though private gynaecology would surely pay better) and forty-three was no age these days. Not with HRT and Spanx. Besides, having a C-section will have helped *down there*. No little accidents. Not like the time Mrs Bennet had been persuaded onto the new trampoline by Kitty and Bridget. Still, at least Bridget had been young enough then to blame it on. Though she might feasibly have picked Kitty, given the heft of Bridget when she came out. Eleven pounds could do untold damage. None of hers had been more than seven-three, but then the quantity contributed as much as volume, she supposed.

Mary was another matter. About as sexual as a jellyfish, that one. Kitty had dropped into a WhatsApp conversation that she was probably 'ace' (Mrs Bennet had had to google that). Well, perhaps she was, but she didn't seem happy about it: veered like a pinball between irritation and disgust. Mrs Bennet wouldn't even mind if Mary was a lesbian. Barbara Clyde's eldest was married to a woman and was on the ladies' golf team, and look at Charlotte Lucas and that potter she'd run off with in lockdown. Much happier by all accounts, unlike poor Colin who'd had to move back in with his aunt at the age of forty-three. Mary might still be living at home, but that was different. Mary had never left in the first place. And, besides, you couldn't compare Mrs Bennet with Carole Burghley, not even on a bad day.

She wasn't dreaming of white dresses and St Saviour's nave bedecked in cherry blossom; she wasn't under those delusions anymore. She'd be perfectly happy with a civil whatsisname at the register office, or even living in sin, like Kitty and Dave. Just as long as they were all settled before... you know. Not that she or Gordon were planning to pop off any time soon, but they were both sixty-seven, and Renee Nesbitt had dropped down dead in the chemist's at sixty-eight, so one never knew. Still, at least the girls would all be under one roof for once, and on this – the trickiest of days. At which thought, she trotted up the dogleg staircase and started along the threadbare hessian of the landing to check on Lydia.

Of course, what began as single-minded, determined, purposeful, quickly segued as Mrs Bennet found herself distracted by what appeared to be yet another patch of damp on the ceiling between Lizzy's old room and Mary's current one. The roof then. Again. Lawks, if it wasn't one thing with this place it was another. It was all very well, living in eighteenth-century splendour on the edge of Meryton, with its feature fireplaces and flagstone floor and whatnot, but sometimes she would give her right arm for one of those retirement flats over near Fowlmere. Swimming pool. Gym. Restaurant on site. On site! No more wondering what to cook for dinner and settling on mince, yet again. Though of course, that raised a question as to where the grandchildren would sleep when they came to stay. Or Mary, who would no doubt come with. Or Lydia for that matter, who ping-ponged from location to location like a drunk swallow but always, somehow, landed back at Longbourn—

Lydia! Mrs Bennet snapped to and hurried the last creaky steps to her youngest and most vexing of daughters' childhood bedroom, pushing the sticker-stippled door cautiously. The girl had shown up at the station at some godawful hour in some godawful state, and with no cash for a taxi (as usual). Thank heaven Gordon had only had one sherry at that point and could be sent to fetch her. Heaven knows what had led her to abandon Paris, but it would all come out in the wash, she supposed. It always did with Lydia.

As if to concede the point, Lydia belched, pulled her duvet (the Spice Girls one she'd begged for for an entire year) over her head, then continued her snoring. Mrs Bennet sighed. One was supposed to find it pleasing watching one's offspring sleep, but she had rarely found that the case with her youngest. Hence, instead of giving a contented smile, she rolled her eyes and nudged the bucket (still, thankfully, empty) a little closer to the edge of the bed. It was tempting to throw back the curtains, open a casement window to counteract the muggy fust of unwashed hair and the God-knows-how-much-a-bottle perfume Lydia insisted on wearing to cover it, but it was hardly worth the argument. She would send Bridget in to wake her up in a bit. That would do the trick.

As she backed out of the room and pulled the door to, Mrs Bennet checked her watch for the seventh time that morning: less than three hours until everyone else was due to arrive, so she'd better get on with the ham, hadn't she? Perhaps she'd WhatsApp Jane as well: check if Grace had declared any unhelpful resolutions regarding meat or dairy again. Last year's quiche (bacon, eggs and cream all verboten) had been a disaster. Thankfully that phase had lasted mere weeks, but one never knew with teenagers (or Kitty and Lydia) when fads would rear their silly heads again.

Yes, better to check.

* * *

To do:
- George – who picking up whom?
- Grace – shoes
- ~~Pudding. Flan? Pavlova?~~
- ~~Decent cheese~~
- Resolutions – make some

Three miles along the Cambridge road, or two across the fields as the crow (or occasionally, in the past, a wasted Kitty or

Lydia) flies, Jane Bingley sat at the kitchen table (sanded antique pine, legs in Farrow & Ball 'Dropcloth') at Netherfield Lodge, contemplating lists. Lists, she had found in the wake of... everything, helped. They chivvied things, made sense of them, distracted from the stark fact of it all. There was a satisfaction in the ordering of life into a series of tickable 'to-do's, and then the sharp, if brief, relief when one crossed something off. Of course, George helped as well. At that thought, she raised her eyes to the ceiling, as if she might see through the cornicing ('Slipper Satin'), the polished oak floorboards and the Persian rug to the iron-steaded king-size above, in which, at this very minute, he was sleeping off a bottle of '96 Chateau Latour that she had – willingly, she admitted – been persuaded to dig out of the cellar (one of the many pleasing features that had persuaded her to say yes to the red-brick Regency doer-upper) and open.

'What were you saving it for anyway?'

She had shrugged, trying to close off the memory of a delighted Charley on his thirtieth birthday, the bottle in his hand. 'A rainy day, I suppose.'

'Well, good,' said George. 'It's pissing down.'

And then he had kissed her, and now... here they were again. As they had been, every weekend for, what? More than two years now? Well, when Timon wasn't on exeat. And actually, now that she thought about it, often when he was. Of course it made perfect sense: the Meryton flat was cramped in comparison, it saved on endless petrol and taxis, and (though she would never voice this aloud) it gave Grace someone else on which to focus her substantial ire. Not that she blamed Grace, not really. Adolescence was miserable enough, without your father being snatched away so... so cruelly.

The worst thing, Jane thought occasionally, was that it – the accident – had been so desperately unremarkable. They hadn't been rushing to a birth or a wedding or an airport. They weren't trying to rescue anyone. They weren't stepping up to prevent a crime. It was a run-of-the-mill run-in with a jackknifed lorry on a wet stretch of the M1. There had been something up with the trains — a drivers' strike — that meant it was the only way the boys could get up to Pemberley in time to see New Year in. The rest of them — she and Lizzy, Grace — twelve, then, and only edging on reticence — the twins — just months old, barely teething — had been there for days: airing, decorating, hoovering up woodlice and spiders — nature's annual invasion between their summer stay and this winter one. But Charley and Fitz had both had work — this and that at the charity and solicitors that they couldn't (or wouldn't) get out of — so she had extracted promises to at least leave mid-afternoon, to be there by supper. And, a lasagne in the oven (from the Ocado delivery that Fitz had insisted on: 'I'm not having either of you buggering about like Jamie sodding Oliver. It's a holiday, for God's sake') they had played board games while they waited. And waited.

And waited.

Her mother was right. It did seem impossible: that two such astonishing men could meet their end in such mundanity. But, then again, few deaths were newsworthy, really, to the unrelated anyway. Though, it was true there were tweets at the time (mostly complaining about the traffic build-up; it had taken five hours to clear the motorway) and write-ups in the *Cambridge Evening News* and *Herts and Essex Gazette*. None of the broadsheets thought to run an obituary — Charley's brief celebrity when he left the Bar for Greenspace had long since waned and Fitz loathed the limelight — but the funeral was announced, on Mrs Bennet's insistence, in *The Times*.

'You know he hated that paper,' Jane had pointed out to her mother at the time. 'They both did.'

But Mrs Bennet's acquaintances treated it as the pious might a bible and so *The Times* it was.

Though, she was thankful now, of course — she cast her eyes ceiling-ward again. As George had pointed out, several times since, if the notice hadn't been posted, he might never have known about the tragedy, might never have been there to help. To *rescue* her. Not that *she* used that word, at least not to the others, but *he* had, hadn't he? He was the one who had known what to do when the boiler had suddenly given up the ghost that first winter. The one who had found Socrates – poor Socrates, locked in a shed, his greyhound legs trembling – when he'd gone missing in spring. The one who had told her, again and again, that with him by her side whenever she needed him, everything would be fine, until she believed it.

And it was, wasn't it? Fine? More than, at times, especially… in bed. At that, her pale cheeks flashed crimson as a memory of him flickered unbidden: of his fingers inside her, pushing and pushing her over an edge to a place she thought she'd long abandoned to night feeds, then tantrums, then panics about SAT tests. Had happily abandoned, if she was honest. Not that they hadn't still had sex, she and Charley, but even before it was never… never quite… this. And what did it matter if George Wickham wasn't her first love, her 'one'. There had to be others, didn't there, whatever Lizzy believed? Besides, she realised now, him being here neatly solved another conundrum. And with an almost-smug flourish, she crossed off another to-do from her list.

★ ★ ★

'Can we do swimming?'
  'Gooses can swim.'
  'Can we have a goose?'
  'Can we?'
  'Is you sad?'
  'Is you, Mummy?'
Ten miles from Netherfield Lodge, in the veritable centre of Cambridge, Lizzy snapped to, saw the concerned faces of Milo

and Arden — mirror images of their dark-haired father, right down to the frown — and quickly flicked the television onto CBeebies. 'Oh, look.' She rummaged in her Mary Poppins bag for 'enthusiasm', pulled out 'fixed grin'. '*Bluey*! Just half an hour, then we'll be going to Ganny's.'

The twins squealed with delight, and began the habitual squabble over who got the inexplicably coveted left-hand side of the sofa, while Lizzy's brief relief as she slunk into the study and sunk into the club chair was punctured by swifter guilt. *Television isn't a babysitter,* said the Jane in her head— No, it wasn't fair to blame Jane. Lizzy had said the same words herself; *he* had. It was one of the myriad things they agreed on, both in the first flush after marriage, when their imaginary children had seemed practically tangible; then in the difficult decade and more after when they slipped into almost-impossibility and these 'rules' for their future were the only things that kept inflated a small balloon of hope. But then neither of them had imagined this: a life in which she relied on a nanny five days a week, not merely for childcare but for actual sanity; in which her conversations veered between perineums and Play-Doh with nothing in between; in which any minutes for just… thinking, for *him*, had to be greedily snatched. And — oh, God — today of all days, she needed to think of him. It wasn't the twins' fault, of course. They were three; they didn't know what today meant — not the idea of a new year, nor the grim anniversary that fell on it. Well, fell last night, but it was gone one in the morning when they'd both been declared dead…

She pincered. That word: *dead*. So decisive. So final. And yet, was it? Was he? She still felt his presence in every room of 27 Ledbury Road — the three-storey Victorian terrace they'd bought as an avocado-suited eighties relic and turned into something, if not quite Netherfield Lodge, with its Instagrammable kitchen and wet room, then so very 'home'. She still smelled him and the Diptyque cologne she had bought him every Christmas (still bought; another bottle spritzed in his wardrobe only last week). She still heard him in the tuneless piano that hogged the morning room. And, even without the snapshots on the mantelpiece, she still saw him in the deep petrol blue of the boot room that he'd conceded to and secretly grown to adore, in the shelves of biographies and glossy historical hardbacks that lined their shared study, in his beloved Crombie – his father's before him – that hung by the front door and retained his shape, his heft, as if he might have shucked it off only a moment ago; as if he might slip it on again soon—

With a sharp intake of breath, she tamped down her anger and sorrow – that godawful concoction – picked up her pen and opened a three-quarters-full journal to where she'd left off last night.

Dear Darcy, she began.
Why the fuck aren't you here?

I suppose I should chivvy, Lizzy conceded, nearly fifty minutes later. *Apparently Lyds turned up drunk at silly o'clock. And I know I should be glad she's here at all, but am almost a hundred per cent positive she'll have done something – or do something – to fuck it all up. There'll be a man involved of course. Fingers crossed this one's not married. Also I have a horrible feeling about Wickham. I mean, worse than usual.* She paused, an image of George needling her, his feet – quite literally – under the table at Netherfield Lodge, his Cheshire-cat smile deceptively benign. He'd always glommed on to people, to the ones 'most likely', but this was different. This was Jane. *And if Charley were here, this would never have happened. If Darcy—*

She sighed, steeled herself. *I'm still livid with you,* her pen scratched. *Till death do us part wasn't meant to be yet. It was meant to involve slippers and dicky hips and grandchildren, for God's sake.*

But I love you, she finished. *I still bloody love you.*

* * *

Back in Meryton, in a flat above Ladbrokes, Kitty Miller blinked awake in a bed that smelled of something worryingly soupy, and reached for her phone. Two missed calls – both from her mother – and four WhatsApps, increasingly heated in tone, demanding she ring. The last one entirely in caps.

'Fuck,' she muttered.

'Bridget okay?' Dave, fresh from the shower, pulled up his boxers and snapped the elastic against his waist with a frown.

Kitty made a non-committal noise.

'She'll be fine. She's with her nan, what's the worst that could happen?' He looked down at his paunch and patted it sadly. 'Cheese, that is. All cheese. That's the first thing I'm giving up. After lunch, anyway.'

'"Granny", not "Nan", how many times? And isn't that Lent?' she said, clicking on voicemail. 'Giving stuff up?'

Dave shrugged. 'Dunno.' He flexed a forearm in the mirror. 'Jesus.'

As she listened to her mother witter on, not about Bridget but Lydia, Kitty assessed her – what was he? 'Partner'? God, no. That was too businesslike. Too Alan Sugar-y. 'Boyfriend', then, she supposed – she assessed her boyfriend as one might do a bull at a market (or horse for slaughter): good head of hair (as her mother often pointed out), nice shoulders ('like that swimmer'), bit of a dad-bod, admittedly – well, stepdad-bod – the kind she'd maligned in her twenties as 'cringe'. But everyone she'd ended up in bed with had been coke-thin back then, and she'd given that bollocks up when she got pregnant with Bridget (or, rather, two months in, when she *realised* she was pregnant with Bridget) and she wasn't exactly whippet-like herself these days. No, Dave was objectively all right. He was fine. If they weren't going to Longbourn for lunch, she might rouse the will and libido to drag him back to bed. But at the thought of, she assumed, food (the alternative – to have gone off sex – was unthinkable), a wave of nausea caught her and sent the room on a tilt-a-whirl.

As she lay back under the musty covers, clinging to her pillow, Kitty's only consolation was that Lydia was absolutely guaranteed to be in a worse state than her.

★ ★ ★

Lydia might be forgiven for thinking she was still drunk or dreaming, given that the first thing she saw when she opened her eyes on New Year's Day morning was a life-sized cut-out of Katy Perry (in her 'Roar' era). The second thing, though, was a bucket – red, plastic, its Homebase sticker intact; the third, an earnest-faced and eight-year-old girl.

'Are you dying, Aunt Lyds? Mummy says she's dying when she looks like that, but she never is.'

Lydia did some rapid maths – taking in the decor, the slight aroma of damp, and the pitch of beamed ceiling – and came up with Longbourn. She'd obviously done— oh, God. What had she done? She tried to snatch at it but her memory was soup-like: a minestrone of Rue des Martyrs, too many pain au chocolats at Gare du Nord and that argumentative guard all floating in a broth of duty-free vodka and – oh Jesus – those individual bottles of Liebfraumilch, which had been all that was left in the M&S at Liverpool Street – a travesty even the cashier had agreed with. As if in protest, she belched, and then vomited loudly and copiously into the expertly placed bucket.

'Oh, fuckity fuck,' she said, wiping her mouth on what appeared to be a ballgown, then remembered she had company. 'God— sorry, Bridge. Don't tell Kitty.'

'Mum says fuck all the time,' replied Bridget, now sitting on the end of the bed. 'But I'm not allowed. Not at school or in the Co-op or' – she appeared to rack her memory – 'or to Granny. And I haven't been sick for eight months and two weeks because

I don't eat prawns. Have you eaten prawns? You shouldn't. You're probably allergic like Mummy.' Her brows beetled under her aggressively bobbed hair — Kitty's work, no doubt.

'Your mum's not—' But she cut herself off. If that's what Kitty wanted her kid to believe then who was Lydia to argue? 'You're not missing out,' she segued. 'Disgusting things, prawns. They live on dead things and poo. Oysters, though, now they're a whole different matter—'

But with that, the soup in her head seemed to part — Red-Sea-like and she Moses — and in its centre appeared not a path but a snapshot of a bar on Rue de Buci: of her in vintage Givenchy, drinking Veuve Clicquot; of *him* feeding her huîtres à la sauce mignonette. Jesus, what *had* she done this time?

'Oh, fuckity fuck,' she repeated, then promptly threw up again.

'Prawns,' said Bridget decisively, and sighed.

★ ★ ★

While, upstairs, Lydia continued to vomit intermittently, and Bridget dutifully fetched for her, in turn, a cold flannel, a glass of squash (not lemon barley!), and a packet of beef Monster Munch, downstairs the rest of the resident Bennets continued about this 'trickiest' of mornings in their habitual manners: Mrs Bennet by turning the thermostat up to 21 (it was brutally cold, even for January), clattering pans and frantically WhatsApping (variously Jane, Lizzy, and the Meryton Women's Guild 'Kitchen Tips' sub-group); Mary by embarking on the second of this year's resolutions, to alphabetise the bookshelves along the scullery corridor (the first resolution — to tolerate Lydia — she had already ticked off several times by 7am); and Mr Bennet by ignoring everyone and everything except direct questions (and sometimes even those) and retreating into the drawing room with yesterday's papers, having turned the thermostat back down to an acceptable

19.5. He had said his piece when he had advised against a 'big do', given the likely state of several family members the morning after, but had been told it wasn't 'a do' and that 'those poor girls' needed to be with family, and so his role was, as he understood it, already played out. Well, that, bar—

'Door!' called Mrs Bennet. 'It'll be Jane with the thingy!'

Mr Bennet put down the paper (he had learned many years ago that dallying bought him nothing) and trudged into the hallway in the manner of the condemned heading gallows-ward. 'There's a key under the frog thing,' he muttered as he fumbled with the Chubb lock. And didn't the girls still have their own?

But when he swung open the heavy oak that still creaked in its jambs no matter how many times he WD-40'd the hinges, it wasn't one of the girls on the frosty doorstep. It wasn't even one of their men. It was—

'Colin!' pronounced Mary, manifesting as if from nowhere. 'Come in. Come in.'

While Mary chivvied in the wretched Colin Burghley, Mr Bennet, seizing his opportunity, retreated back to Radio 4 and *The Times* while he still had the chance. God knows why Hester had invited him, given his many and varied food intolerances, and general intolerances (cats, rabbits, fabric conditioner to name but three). Probably felt sorry for him still, Charlotte having run off with 'that lesbian'. ('That lesbian' being a celebrated ceramicist with an MBE, a fact that seemed lost on most of Longbourn and Meryton.) Still, Mary seemed pleased. But then she would. Odd girl. But each to their own; live and let live and all that. Live and let live.

* * *

Mary *was* pleased. Firstly because, whenever he was present, Colin tended to bear the brunt of her sisters' alleged 'wit' (she rarely understood the funny side) and was a useful foil in general, and secondly, being a theologian, he understood books, and the importance of order.

'Oh, this looks interesting,' he declared, having taken off what can only be described as a 'practical' jacket and hung it on the 'guest' peg. 'Dewey decimal or...?'

'Alphabetical, predominantly.' Mary's tone was apologetic. 'Daddy wouldn't let me put stickers on. But' – she cheered up – 'as you can probably see, they're split into fiction and non.'

Colin nodded (she beamed), then frowned (her stomach plummeted).

'What is it?'

'Well, I see you have Charles Dickens in the same section as John Donne, and I wonder... it's just that... shouldn't there be a separate poetry section?'

Far from feeling punctured or stung, Mary ballooned with that satisfaction when one's mind meets its like, as it often did in Colin's presence. 'Of course you're right,' she said. 'I was lumping them together as pre-twentieth century, but this makes much more sense.' She began de-shelving the Shelley, the Wordsworth, the Donne.

'Let me,' said Colin, re-shelving them together on the bottom right. 'We can always shunt them up if there's room.'

'Oh, there won't be room,' said Mary without a hint of sarcasm. 'I measured.'

The pair continued in this happy manner for more than an hour, Mary asking questions when they occurred to her, regardless of relevance.

'Will you move back to London.' (I doubt it – house prices, you know.)

'How is your aunt?' (The usual, the usual.)

'Do eggs count as dairy?' (No, but they are related, as animal produce, and allergies can often overlap, as I'm sure you know.)

When the door went again – Jane this time, finally, with

Grace and that idiotic Wickham – Mary found herself peeved at the interruption, a mood from which she wouldn't recover until well after lunch.

★ ★ ★

The meal was, in edible terms, a success. Grace's single proscription was swede, and only on the grounds of it being 'like, gross'; Colin was pleased with his individual dairy-free tart (he said he would overlook its processed nature 'just for today'); and no one commented on the fact that Jane's coffee pavlova was more chewy than usual (Grace had gone out 'somewhere' during its preparation, and so Wickham had seized the day (and Jane), thus temperature and timing had gone slightly awry).

Lydia wolfed down two plates of ham, salted pork products, she explained, being 'nature's own cure-all'. Kitty gratefully left Dave to her mother and plonked down next to Bridget, fielding a flock of queries about ducks (she was determined to acquire one), which Mary (her usual ally in these matters) was unavailable to answer, seated as she was next to Colin. And Jane, when she wasn't nudging Grace to buck up and muster a smile, had eyes only for Wickham, which Lizzy, had she been more than vaguely present at the table (rather than living in her head as usual i.e. a hundred miles away in Derbyshire), might have thought 'pitiful'.

It was Mrs Bennet who raised it – resolutions, and who was doing what and whether or not they had any chance of achieving them. 'I'm taking up Zumba,' she announced. 'With Bad Karen.' (There were two Karens: one five foot ('Little'), and one who had once been caught speeding on the A11 near Newmarket ('Bad').) 'And working my way through Delia Smith. The *Complete Cookery Course*; something new every day!'

'Oh, joy,' muttered Mr Bennet, whose chief requirement for food was that he had tried it before and knew it to be 'fine'.

'What about you, Grandpa?' Bridget frowned at him. 'I'm going to get a pet for my resolution. A duck or maybe a sheep. You could have sheep here. They'd mow the lawn. Or a horse.'

'God, no,' said Mr Bennet. 'Not again.' At this he eyed Jane, whose affection for all God's creatures, particularly the afflicted, had blighted an entire decade.

'We're not getting a pet.' Kitty sighed. 'Bridget, I explained—'

'So, what *will* you do, Grandpa?'

Bridget was patient, expectant — a look he found hard to ignore, and an idea brimmed in him — one he'd nurtured for months — and spilled over. 'Sell up,' he blurted. 'Move to the country.'

There was a brief silence, fat and hard enough to slice.

Mrs Bennet broke it within seconds. 'I do beg your pardon?'

Then the cacophony started. 'You can't!' chorused Kitty and Lydia.

'Where will we do Christmas?'

'Where will I *live*?' asked Mary.

'More to the point,' added Mrs Bennet, 'where will *I* live?'

'You're already technically *in* the country,' added Colin. 'Unless of course you mean somewhere significantly less populous. The North Yorkshire moors, for example.'

Mr Bennet, who had burgeoned for that moment, found himself wilt again. 'It was just an idea. A joke.' It wasn't. But the fight wasn't worth it.

Mrs Bennet snorted. 'Lawks! Well, thank goodness for that, Gordon. You know what I think about moving. Look at the Braithwaites!' Bob and Norma had sold their four-bed on Haycombe Park for a tidy sum (despite the attics being in a frightful state) and poured the profit into a villa in Malaga, only to end up buggered by Brexit and the health system, and forced back to a bungalow on an estate north of Sawbridgeworth, which might as well be Essex, quite frankly. 'Anyway, who's next? Resolutions.'

Jane put up her hand. 'I'm going to do ten thousand steps again. Oh, and get the back bedroom wallpapered.'

Grace mumbled something, which may or may not have been scathing.

Kitty smirked. 'Lyds can learn to pack a suitcase.'

Lydia, who had tipped up her Birkin just two hours earlier to find only a tulle Molly Goddard, assorted condoms and three pairs of knickers (not even clean, though they were Agent Provocateur at least), had been forced to resort to the remnants of her teenage wardrobe – in this case, a pair of low-slung cargo trousers and a fluffy Ragged Priest crop top in an improbable shade of orange.

'I was in a rush,' she protested.

'Because… ?' prompted her mother – her fourth attempt to wheedle out reasons for this apparently inexplicable visit.

'Because I was… being spontaneous,' she managed – not even a lie, if by 'spontaneity' one meant desperation, humiliation and 'nowhere else to go'. 'And you said it was important. To be together today. So here I am.'

Mrs Bennet, though often worryingly gullible, was wise to this particular child and mustered only a 'hmmm', which Lydia knew from old was a holding pattern until such point as she could be pinned down (potentially literally, if Kitty were involved) and forced into confession.

'How long are you intending to stay?' asked Mary, interested not in gossip but facts.

'I…' Lydia trailed off. Should she admit at least this? Get it over with? Yes, fuck it. 'I don't know yet,' she said. 'I just needed a… a fresh start. Paris wasn't… it wasn't *challenging* me. So' – she pasted on her out-to-please face – 'here I am!'

Mr Bennet was not the only one around the table whose bright new year hopes – in his case, of peace and quiet, preferably far away from Meryton – were suddenly punctured. 'Well, er, lucky us.'

'I call bullshit,' said Kitty.

'Kitty!' Jane protested. 'Language. Bridget and Grace are here!'

'Fuck's sake,' muttered Grace. 'I'm not five.'

'And I know *all* the swears,' added Bridget.

Jane winced. 'The twins then!'

Lizzy, dragged reluctantly from the Pemberley in her head, snapped to. 'What about them?'

'They're fine,' drawled Wickham. 'Fuss over nothing. Contrary to popular belief, swearing *is* big and it *is* clever. Timon knew the c-word by seven.'

'I'm quite sure he did,' said Lizzy. 'But perhaps let's just… not.' She went for her wine glass then, remembering she was driving, detoured to the grapes.

'Balls of sugar,' said Colin. 'Grapes, nutritionally I mean. You might as well eat aniseed balls.'

Lizzy grimaced. 'I'm not sure—'

'It's fascinating, when one looks at it,' Colin went on. 'That whole five a day thing—'

'We're giving up drink,' Dave interrupted, to everyone's relief, bar Kitty's.

'Are we?' She looked more than mildly put out.

'Yeah, dry January.' He grinned, which sent a spasm of irritation through her. 'We agreed last night, remember?'

'You've both had wine,' said Mary. 'And a beer in your case.' (Well, he had.)

'Starting tomorrow,' he said. 'No alcohol at all. Kits?'

'No alcohol *or* prawns,' said Bridget.

'Or cheese,' added Dave, patting his belly again.

'You've had four helpings of Stilton.' Mary frowned.

'Tomorrow, Mary,' he said. 'We're starting tomorrow.'

'I'll do it if Lydia does it.' Kitty side-eyed her sister. 'Lyds?'

Lydia, who had been clinging to her glass of Riesling through lunch as one might a crutch, blanched.

'Come on. You always say it's the drink that makes you f—' Kitty corrected herself, 'mess things up. So give it a miss for a bit.'

'She'd need to give it a miss for a year not a month,' said Mrs Bennet, rather unkindly, if truthfully.

'A year? Not a chance,' laughed Wickham. 'I give it a week. Two, tops.'

Lydia bristled. If there was one thing guaranteed to make her do something, it was someone — especially Wickham — telling her she couldn't (see also the box splits, passing her French GCSE, and getting off with Harry Bradshaw.)

'A year,' she said. 'Watch me. I shan't drink at all. Not even a… a chocolate liqueur.'

'And the drugs,' hissed Kitty.

'What drugs?' Mr Bennet frowned.

'Nothing.' (Kitty and Lydia in chorus.)

'Ooh, you could have therapy as well.' Mrs Bennet was seized by the idea. 'It's all the rage at the Women's Guild. Bad Karen swears by it — all that offloading. Says she's not felt this unburdened since her impacted colon got fixed six years ago.'

'I'll pass,' said Lydia, knowing full well she couldn't afford it. Besides, the one time she had tried counselling (after the whole *Love Shack* debacle on Channel 5, in which her dream of television fame was snuffed out when she was caught on camera giving Olly Ronson [a car dealer and part-time model from Stockport] a blow job, and the viewing public turned on her and voted to 'sack her from the shack' after only a week) she had spent the entire forty minutes blaming her mother and crying, and she could do that for nothing with Kitty. 'Just the drink for now.'

'Good, good,' said Colin. 'Alcohol is, statistically, behind most unprotected intercourse, you know. So you're also reducing your chances of herpes, antibiotic-resistant gonorrhoea and all manner of sexually transmitted diseases. Although if you completely abstained from sex—'

Kitty exploded with laughter. 'As if.'

'What?' demanded Lydia. 'I could... abstain, if I wanted.'
'You absolutely couldn't,' Kitty replied.
'I could!' She scanned the table for back-up. 'Mum, couldn't I?'
But Mrs Bennet pulled the face she favoured when confronted with someone with cancer or a recently deceased dog: abject pity.

Fuck it. She wasn't giving them sex, but she would concede the other two. 'Fine. Drink and drugs. Sorry, Mum' – she pulled her apologetic face – 'a year. I'll bloody show you.'

'That's excellent,' said Colin. 'Facing up to one's addictions—'
'Oh, I'm not addicted,' insisted Lydia swiftly. 'I just *like* them. There's a big difference. Huge.'

Thankfully, before anyone challenged her, Jane moved the conversation on. 'Anyone else? Lizzy?'

Lizzy shook her head. 'The whole thing is pointless. If I want to do something I'll do it whenever, not on some arbitrary date.'

'What about Pemberley?' asked George.
Lizzy went cold. 'What about it?'
George looked pointedly at Jane.
'I thought...' Jane pinked. 'You told me you'd think about selling it.'

'I... yes, well I...' Lizzy, usually so sharp, so deft with her words, was losing them like peas from a split bag. 'I've thought about it and it's not... it's not the time. We can't all just... just put things on a list and tick them off as if they're no more than chores.'

'I didn't...' Jane found herself flailing; George – dear, dear George – caught her hand.

'It's all right, darling,' he told her. 'It's a...' he paused, '*significant* day.'

'Perhaps I should wash up,' said Mr Bennet, seeing his escape route.

'What about my turn?' Wickham, again. 'Don't I get a resolution?'

'Oh.' With an air of dejection, Mr Bennet sunk back down, as Wickham stood.

Then knelt.

Oh fuck.

The air in the dining room was tauter than it had been the time William Lucas called Mr Bennet a 'traitor' for voting Lib Dem. While Jane, well, she thought she might faint.

'Is he?' whispered Kitty.

'I think so,' said Lyds.

'Jane…' began Wickham.

At her name, it was as if a horde of bees awoke in her, began humming. Oh God. He was going to do it, wasn't he? Had he even asked for permission? She glanced at her father, but Mr Bennet seemed as perplexed as the rest of them. Or, more accurately, stunned.

'…I know this day will forever be tied to Charley. May he and Fitz rest in peace—'

At that Lizzy let out a mew, which might have been protest or mere shock, but Wickham ploughed on, oblivious. 'However, I would like to change it, from one of pure sorrow, to something closer to bliss.'

'Christ on a bike.' Kitty nudged Lydia.

'Girls!' Mrs Bennet glared at the pair of them.

'Jane Hester Bingley,' Wickham continued, projecting as if he were on the main stage at the Barbican, not a mid-sized dining room in North East Hertfordshire, 'will you please, *please* be my wife?'

The room held its breath as Jane scanned frantically for an answer: Lizzy was clearly not pleased; Kitty and Lydia's faces were contorted in what might have been awe, but more likely hangovers and bafflement; Mary was, as ever, unreadable; Colin was busied with the ingredients list on a packet of Matchmakers; and Grace – Jane dared not even look at her own daughter, knew her face would be plainly enraged, but then, when wasn't it these days? Instead her eyes turned back to George, who was beaming below her: his teeth almost perfect; his eyes practically guileless; his hair, chestnut, thinning on top, she saw now. And it was that, conjuring in her that same unconquerable pity that she suffered on stumbling across an injured bird, or a sick kitten, that nudged up her answer.

'Yes,' she said. 'Oh, darling, yes.'

Justice for Jane
Lizzy, Kitty, Lydia, Mary

Lydia Bennet created group 'Justice for Jane'

~Lydia Bennet
what the holy fuck? wickham?
14:32

~Kitty Miller
IKR. He carries a bottle of Sriracha around like it's a fucking character trait.
14:32

~Kitty Miller
On the plus side he'll probably jilt her.
14:34

~Kitty Miller
Or murder her a month after the ceremony.
14:34

~Lizzy Darcy-Bennet
Please don't joke about things like that.
14:34

~Kitty Miller
Sorry. You're right. Probably. But he is a massive knob.
14:36

~Lydia Bennet
or has one
14:36

~Kitty Miller
MY EYES!
14:36

~Lydia Bennet
sorry not sorry
14:37

~Kitty Miller
Although, you'd know, wouldn't you?
14:37

~Lydia Bennet
fuck off
14:37

~Lydia Bennet
Lizzy kissed him too. Ask her.
14:37

Lizzy Darcy-Bennet left the group.

★ ★ ★

Of course it was all the majority of Bennets could talk about, a fact that brought some relief to Lydia, at least, who had been bracing herself for a post-lunch character assassination and forensic interrogation of her motives for staying. Instead she found herself abandoned to the drawing room with Colin and Mary (and an interminable game of Monopoly), while in the kitchen her mother tried to gee Mr Bennet into something approaching enthusiasm.

'She's violently in love with him!' insisted Mrs Bennet. 'Violently!'

'That's the sort of idiotic thing Lydia would say. And about someone she's known for a matter of hours.'

Mrs Bennet's already florid face reddened. 'What *are* you talking about? Jane's known Wickham almost as long as she's known Charley and Fitz— Knew,' she corrected herself. (Three years was forever in some things, and yet no time at all when it came to correct tenses.)

Mr Bennet smiled wanly. 'And yet she chose Charley.'

'Yes, well.' Mrs Bennet flapped a hand. 'Look how that worked out.'

'That's hardly a reason—'

'Just because you haven't got a romantic bone in your body, don't wish that on Jane.' She had pulled out her trump card and both of them knew it. 'She's happy, and God knows she deserves that!'

The argument was won, and Mr Bennet conceded, as he usually did, with a 'Yes, dear' and a swift retreat to his study, while Mrs Bennet went off to message Kitty to catch up on whatever gossip she'd manage to elicit from her sisters (who had, she had no doubt, been WhatsApping for hours on the matter).

★ ★ ★

Well, except Lizzy, perhaps, who had decided to depart to Meryton Rec within minutes, citing the twins' need for exercise.

'Like dogs,' she'd explained. 'Or they won't sleep tonight.' But if she had hoped for some peace, she was to be left sorely wanting.

'I'll join you,' said Jane. 'I could use some fresh air.'

Bugger. 'There's no need—'

'No, really. Grace is somewhere with Bridget, and George says it's all right.'

George says. But she wouldn't rise to it. Not this time. Not now.

However, the pact she had made with herself – to stay out of Jane's business – lasted only as long as the mile-walk to the swings and other chipped equipment in a corner of an awkward oblong that was otherwise mostly home to generation after generation of teenagers, desperate for somewhere to drink and whatever else away from the prying eyes of their parents, and moles, doing what moles do and ruining the turf for Herbert Jones, who drove the local authority mower.

As the pair watched the twins fling themselves with happy abandon down the same filthy slide all the Bennet girls had played on as children, Lizzy turned on her sister. 'Are you really so incapable of being alone?' Guilt pricked her the moment the words left her mouth. But she couldn't retract them; left them hanging in the air like static. Fat and accusatory.

'That's incredibly unkind,' Jane managed eventually.

'You're right. I'm sorry. It's just… it feels too soon. Like a… a rebound.'

'Three years,' Jane pointed out. 'That's hardly a rebound. And I don't want to end up… closed off.'

Lizzy flinched, and stabbed back quickly. 'I'm not closed off.'

Jane grasped her arm, her suede gloves tight around the brown wool of the Crombie. 'I was going to say Mary.'

She let Jane's hand stay for a moment, then thrust her own into a pocket, a movement designed to force an uncoupling. 'Do you love him? I mean, really?'

Jane paused. Long enough for Lizzy to believe she might have uncovered a chink in her sister's armour. But—

'I do,' she said, matter-of-factly. 'I really *do* love him. I mean, not… the same as I loved Charley, but that's to be expected. And enough in any case.'

'Enough?' Unbelievable. 'Enough to marry him? This isn't the 1950s. You can have sex without walking down the aisle.'

'It's not about that!' Jane swung at her. 'It's about… stability. For Grace, more than anyone.'

That was an absurd excuse. 'Wickham is the least stable person I know, bar Lydia,' she said. 'And Grace is nearly sixteen.' Again she regretted her words. Though all of them were true.

'What is this really about, Lizzy? Do you still…'

Jane appeared to steel herself, and Lizzy's insides lurched as if being driven too quickly over a humpback bridge.

' …I know if I hadn't insisted on Charley being there that night, Fitz could have come up earlier.'

Lizzy spasmed with embarrassment. 'It's not that.'

It was that. Well, a little. But it was more; it was Wickham himself. He was just… just so very wrong for Jane. Wrong for anyone. Yes, Lizzy had kissed him once. Just once – New Year's Eve more than two decades ago under the mistletoe at Longbourn. Or rather he had kissed Lizzy and she had let him. And only in a ruse designed to egg Fitz (whom Bingley had brought back after Michaelmas term for the second year running) to declare something other than his dislike of crisps and hope that Tony Blair might stop 'buggering about playing Bush's lapdog'. And it had worked: within the hour they were snogging in the scullery to the unlikely strains of East 17's 'Stay Another Day' (a song she regretted at the time and could now no longer listen to); within two they were in bed. A mere three years later they'd moved in together – at first to a rental in Chesterton, then, after the wedding, to Ledbury Road – but still George had pursued her. Had flattered her, flirted, insinuated himself into her life, much to the ire of Fitz, who had begged Charley to ditch him. But he wouldn't of course; like Jane, he was a fool for any creature in need, and orphanhood (and some bad luck with the stock market) secured it. Wickham had slunk off eventually of his own accord – got involved with Calypso (Silly Calypso). But then, after the... accident, he'd resurfaced and hit on her. Not Jane at first but on she, Lizzy. Lizzy he'd hugged that moment too long at the funeral. Lizzy he'd offered to drive home, to sit for the twins, to help with 'his paperwork'. It was only when, in desperation, she'd slapped him that he'd slunk off to try Jane. Or maybe he'd been playing them both all along.

'If you just even began to look for someone, you'd realise—'
Lizzy snapped to, bristled quickly. 'No. Really, no.'
'I just mean—'
'We don't all need a man to prop us up.'
Jane seemed to flinch and her pale eyes pooled.
Lizzy wilted; it was her turn to clutch at her sister. 'God, I'm sorry. It's just... today. I can't talk about... this stuff *today*.' She paused. 'I should go.' She chivvied the twins, who were red-cheeked and filthy and highly delighted about it.

'It's fine. Really. I... I should get back as well. Heaven knows how Grace is taking it. I do wish... well, I just wish he hadn't put me on the spot like that. Had given me a chance to talk to her. As it is, she probably feels rather ambushed.' Jane laughed as they walked, but it was a taut, forced thing.

Lizzy rallied, in spite of herself. One had to with sisters. 'I'm sure she'll get over it. I'd be more worried about Silly Calypso.'

Calypso de Witt – a slip of a thing when Wickham had met her, straight off the books at Storm Models – had moved swiftly on from cocaine and Stoli and weekends at Babington to tramadol and valium and extended stays at various Priories. Timon (a briefly 'happy' accident following several missed pills – Calypso claimed they caused weight gain) had been shipped off to Millfield at seven 'for safekeeping' and since then only saw his mother on her rare good days, and his father under both their duress. Jane rather liked him: six foot three, and most of it limb; dark, diffident curls that he peered through accusingly; a string of eclectic obsessions — beetles, Frank Auerbach, Prince's earlier work. Grace dismissed him as 'weird', but then she dismissed everything these days.

'It must be terribly difficult, being so… so ogled at all day,' Jane concluded, 'and from such a young age. I think perhaps she just wasn't ready for it. Marriage, you know. A child.'

Lizzy rolled her eyes. 'God, Jane. You never see a fault in anyone. The whole world is agreeable in your eyes. You'd find something nice to say about Piers sodding Morgan.'

'Well, he always looks smart. What?' Jane frowned. 'He does!'

'You're not even doing it for your own gain. You genuinely believe it, don't you?'

'Isn't that better?' asked Jane.

Lizzy paused. How could she put it without bruising? 'Not everyone deserves the benefit of the doubt.'

But Jane was a peach and purpled at even the slightest words. 'You mean George, of course.'

'I didn't say—' Lizzy tried.

'You didn't need to.'

They walked the rest of the way back to Longbourn House in disagreeable silence, each rigid with cold and the conviction that they had been the one to be slighted. Unusually, it was Lizzy who softened first.

'I am happy for you,' she insisted as they crunched up the pea gravel pathway (herding the twins around the extensive cat shit Mr Bennet had warned his wife about before they laid the thing, to no avail). 'But I've had my "great love". I don't need another. Besides, I couldn't stand the comparisons. They'd all come up wanting.'

Jane was quite sure this was another dig at George, albeit unconsciously, but chose, as was her way, to rise above it. 'I think you'll surprise yourself and us all. When the time is right.'

'Perhaps,' conceded her sister.

But if Jane thought it was more than a sop she was wrong.

Dear Darcy, Lizzy wrote the moment she got home. *You will not believe what that idiot Wickham's done this time.*

★ ★ ★

'Can you believe the audacity?' Kitty snapped at Dave as they undressed for bed at an uncharacteristically early ten thirty. 'What a twat.'

'I thought it was romantic.'

Kitty bristled. 'You think belching the national anthem's romantic.'

Dave grinned, gave himself an appreciative grunt and took a deep breath.

'Jesus. Don't even think about it.' Kitty yanked on a T-shirt and threw herself into bed, pulling the stale, soupy duvet over her head in case he'd ignored her.

Though a windy rendition might have been preferable, she would think only moments later, as she felt the familiar bulk spoon around her, his breath in her ear – a prelude to the sort of lazy sex they'd fallen into of late: no kissing required, no moving on her part.

'Babe,' Dave muttered.

'I'm too tired,' Kitty protested, pushing his thankfully still-panted groin away.

'I wasn't going to,' he insisted, pushing it back again. 'Just... How about it? You and me?'

'How about what?' Kitty swung onto her back, thwarting, she thought, any further attempts at entry.

'You know,' Dave's arm snaked under her T-shirt, landed on

her left breast, began a rhythmic stroking that only served to irritate her further, 'marriage. The whole "I do" shenanigans.'

'Yeah right. Are you high?'

Dave's hand stilled. 'You know I'm not. I barely even drank. How do you think we got home?'

Despite lying flat, Kitty seemed to list, at that moment, as if on a ship, unsure if she might topple or vomit. 'Jesus, you're serious.'

'Maybe. I mean, we've been together for more than four years. Bridget likes me.'

Bridget loves you, she thought. But Bridget wasn't the problem. 'I just,' she flailed for an excuse, any excuse. 'Is that the best you can do? "How about it?"?' She sat up, snapped on the light, faffed with the glass of water he'd insisted on bringing her. It wasn't even forced – her ire; the more she thought about being short-changed like this, the more incensed she became. 'Everything's so— so half-arsed with you. You just… you just settle.' She warmed to her theme, disappointment inflating her like a balloon. 'It's like the music. You were going to DJ raves when we met. Play Glastonbury. Latitude. You run a mobile fucking disco and gig at the Legion. And what happened to ditching Royal Mail? Running your own business? You're still up at four in the morning and selling knock-off microwaves down the Crown.'

'Don't hold back, will you.' Dave held up his hands.

'I…' she trailed off. Her conviction – that she was right, was entitled to this – was slipping, slowly deflating her.

'You done?'

She nodded, her hot anger gone; now she was just cold and nauseous and sorry for herself, and bracing for a – frankly justifiable – torrent in return.

But there was none. Of course there wasn't. Because Dave was a fucking angel.

'So this is about place, yeah? Timing? If I'd done the whole shebang – flash mob, big ring, down on one knee – you might have said yes?'

No. God, did he not know her? That this was the last thing she wanted? She and Lydia – they weren't made for this life. This... this provincial thing. They were supposed to be on the beach in Ibiza – *had* been on the beach in Ibiza till she'd fucked up with Bridget— No, that wasn't fair. Bridget was the best thing that had happened to her. It had just meant she'd had to come home once the knobhead of a father had fucked off back to Queensland. At least Lyds still had a choice; could have stayed away, stayed in Paris, for God's sake. What was she thinking?

'Kits?'

'Huh?' She frowned. 'Oh, that. Maybe,' she lied, and turned off the light. 'I need to sleep now, yeah? I feel shit.'

★ ★ ★

So what *was* Lydia thinking? Why *had* she returned after two decades away?

In truth, she hadn't been – thinking, that is. It had all happened so rapidly: one minute she'd been sleeping off the Champagne and huîtres in her attic room above the Atelier Perlot at Notre-Dame-de-Lorette, the next she'd been the target for an appetiser volley of discarded shoes, handbags, and unwashed laundry being flung at her (admittedly all hers, and her bad for not clearing the floordrobe) followed by the entrée of accusations of philandering with Madame Perlot's own husband. Lydia hadn't even tried to deny it. And, if she were minded to paint it with positive spin, the whole debacle gave her a much-needed get-out clause, given the previous evening he'd declared his intentions to leave Mme P – an unthinkable twist on Lydia's part, given her belated discovery of his habit of picking his toenails whilst watching the telly, plus the unfavourable prenup. And the job itself was hardly a calling – assistant to a brittle stick of a woman who, at first glance, made Anna Wintour resemble a CBeebies presenter. And yet, at the outset, when she'd first landed in Paris, with her faux LV suitcase and real Louboutin heels (a gift from the last one, also tragically married) it had all seemed, as it tended to in Lydia's myopic eyes, so hopelessly romantic.

It wasn't even Lydia's fault, not really. Men just tended to fall for her — moths to her substantial flame — before deciding the peak of the crazy/hot matrix was not a long-term prospect (being at the peak of the hot/misogynistic one themselves). And she was fine with that, she'd decided this time — who wanted a life of clearing up socks, and squeezing their blackheads and wondering who else they were fucking, when they showed up late for bloody supper?

Lizzy had once told her she chased drama, cultivated it where there was none. But Lydia was merely (as she frequently reminded herself), the troubled youngest child, a victim of benign neglect, her sisters' deliberate brilliance, and the Dick Whittington promise of Instagram. So no, she wasn't sad to leave Paris, not really. Her only regret at this very minute was agreeing to give up the (admittedly quite substantial) drinking and drugs, thanks to bloody Wickham.

She jinked when she thought of him down on his knee in the dining room. And for Jane of all people. Not that Lydia ever thought it might be her, not really. So what if she had loved him once? In truth he was the only man on whom she'd ever truly bestowed that deepest of feeling (though she willingly threw those three little words around like confetti and almost meant them as well) but she'd been sixteen and silly then and so of course she was drawn to him. He'd been at a party at Magdalen thrown by Charley — or was it Fitz? Well, whoever, he had been there and she, heavily in her Heathcliff meets Heath Ledger phase, had fallen for his not insubstantial charms over too many vodka and Red Bulls and spent the next four hours doing the sort of things she'd only heard of in porn. He'd taken, that night, her innocence, and (though she'd deny it if you asked her) her heart. And despite the fact their 'relationship' comprised no more than a series of drink-and-pill-fuelled hook-ups she could count on two hands, she had adored him with a conviction and intensity she'd been chasing ever since.

She shook herself, eyed the drinks cabinet slyly. Could she sneak a quick snifter of Jameson? A tot of the port? It's not like her father would notice, nor anyone care. Then again, *she* would know, and more than that, it would mean Wickham had won, wouldn't it? And if there was one good thing that had come from today, it was the chance to best Wickham.

Not three seconds later, her mother bustled in – the deciding factor – for an improbable nightcap Campari. 'Still up, love?' she noted. 'I'm surprised, given the state of your stomach this morning. Half a litre there was in that bucket. Your father said we didn't need another one, still less one with measurements, but I said it might come in handy and voilà!'

Lydia winced at the memory. 'Jesus, Mum. You worry me.'

'Me? It was Bridget who checked it. I'm just glad I was right and your father had to eat his ill-chosen words.' And she swept from the room as triumphant as if she'd just proven that Carole Burghley had cheated at whist.

Besides, protest Lydia might, but the delight her mother took in small victories was the example she needed. And, for only the third time since her seventeenth birthday (the other two being bouts of norovirus and an appendectomy) she fell into bed sober, didn't bother to masturbate, and dreamt of nothing at all.

★ ★ ★

The only one who was truly untroubled by the events of the day as she settled in bed was Mrs Bennet. Though she often complained, and loudly – about the mess, the expense, the

Rorschach patterns of hair stuck to the shower wall in the morning – she had missed the happy chaos of Longbourn when all five girls were at home, or at least within visiting distance. In truth, she was nervous of being left with no one but her husband to talk to. Lovely man – kind, wise, reliable (in bed and with finances) – but he'd never been one for gossip and, well, everyone knew that gossip, along with a Campari and soda, was her main solace in life. So the double blessing of Lydia – her own prodigal daughter – fresh back from Paris, and Jane getting engaged, well, she was frankly in clover.

Of course Mr Bennet had questioned it: What was the state of his bank account? Where would they live? Wasn't it a bit ghoulish, his lickspittling of Charley and now of his wife?

'You could take a leaf out of Jane's book,' she'd said in the end. 'Try to be positive, instead of looking for the worst in everyone.'

'That's Mary.' He sighed. 'She's the pessimist. I just see things rather more clearly. Warts and all. No rose-tinted spectacles.'

But she refused to be bowed. 'Well, I for one am delighted. I do love a wedding. Such a shame about Jane's *hysterectomy*.' She mouthed the word as if it were explicit. 'Though forty-four's a bit old to get pregnant.'

'Good God, woman. You've already got four grandchildren. Five if you count Silly Calypso's boy.'

'Janet Hudgell has got nine. Nine!'

'It's not a competition, dear.'

Mrs Bennet, who regarded most of life as a competition, said nothing to this.

'Still,' Mr Bennet, despite being a realist, did try to find a bright side occasionally, 'that's one off your hands. Though I'm sure Lydia will amply fill the space with whatever it is she's done this time.'

Mrs Bennet bristled again. She might be allowed to dispense with every insult about her daughters, but coming from other mouths — even her husband's — she regarded it as a personal slight on her parenting. 'Perhaps she just missed Meryton. Or... or her sisters. Or us!'

There was a long, meaningful silence, before, 'Perhaps,' said Mr Bennet.

It was a small concession but she took it as a win and smiled to herself as her husband clicked off the lights.

Something, though, still niggled her. A flea in her nightgown; a mite on her skin. 'You didn't mean it, did you?' she said into the thick, familiar fust of the master bedroom — the bedroom they'd slept in for more than forty years, had made babies in, and *had* babies in, in Kitty's and Lydia's cases. 'About selling up?'

But the answer, when it came, was only a snore. Mr Bennet, in his wise reliability, had gone straight to sleep lest he be pestered again.

FEBRUARY

Sister Act
Jane, Lizzy, Mary, Kitty, Lydia

Resolutions:
Kitty
- ~~No drinking until February~~.

Lydia
- No drinking or drugs until next January.

Lizzy
- Think about dating (no pressure to actually do it, Liz, but thinking is a start).

Jane:
- Ten thousand steps.
- Get back bedroom wallpapered.
- Grace GCSE revision.
- Arrange wedding.

Mary:
- ?

~Jane Bingley
I'm attaching a group checklist for New Year resolutions. I thought it might be fun for us to encourage each other. I'm trying to work out how to put in little tickboxes. It's terribly validating.
08:31

~Lydia Bennet
duck off
10:17

~Lydia Bennet
no. ugh. duck off.
10:17

~Lydia Bennet
oh for duck's sake!
10:17

~Kitty Miller
Just because you've failed already, Lyds.
10:18

~Lydia Bennet
i haven't actually. nothing stronger than diet coke has passed my lips since new year.
10:18

~Jane Bingley
You know diet soda is associated with type 2 diabetes?
10:19

~Lydia Bennet
thanks mary
10:19

~Jane Bingley
It's Jane. As well you know.
10:19

~Jane Bingley
Actually, @**Mary** – can you add your own? I don't remember what you resolved for this year – sorry, all a bit distracted, for obvious reasons. Is it something to do with books again?
10:20

~Lydia Bennet
mary could do lizzy's for her
10:22

~Kitty Miller
She isn't here. I keep telling you. And anyway, I told you, she's probably ace.
10:22

~Lydia Bennet
she IS here kitty. how many times? i'm adding it. officially: mary: get laid
10:22

~Kitty Miller
She probably has 'make love to Wickham' on one as well, with a little tickbox next to it.
10:25

~Kitty Miller
FAAAAARK. SORRY. Wrong group. Only joking, Jane.
10:28

After Darcy

~Kitty Miller
@Jane ?
10:29

★ ★ ★

'You learn nothing from television!' had been a constant refrain in the Bennet household during Lydia's childhood, invoked by both parents at various points in ill-fated bids to nip in the bud bingeing on *Dawson's Creek* (Lizzy and Jane), *The OC* (Kitty and Lydia), and *Taggart* (Mary). It was hogwash, of course. Lydia had learned several essential life lessons from the small screen: how to Dutch braid her hair (*Tracy Beaker*), the trick to a decent martini (*Sex and the City*), the symptoms of chlamydia (*Holby City*). This very morning had come the revelation that Colin was probably right, and it wasn't merely drink and drugs that she... liked a little too much, but love itself.

According to *Morning Glory*'s resident sexpert, Dennis Plemons, her history of failed relationships stemmed from endlessly chasing the chemical hit one got from that first flush of falling for someone. Or, in Lydia's case, when one first fell into bed. It wasn't the sex she craved, of course (so Dennis informed her), it was the adoration, but they tended to come together with men, and it was so very hard to say no when someone so obviously wanted you. Lizzy had told her more than once that if she didn't know a man's surname then they weren't to be granted entry to her genitals (she had actually said 'genitals', rather than any of the traditional Bennet euphemisms of 'foofoo', 'tuppence' and, inexplicably, 'minky'). Of course, Lydia had promised this faithfully, but in truth had allowed more than one man, and woman (she was, if nothing else, indiscriminate in her sexual incontinence), unfettered access without even knowing their first name, let alone their second.

'True love,' insisted Dennis on the garish velvet sofa, 'doesn't need sex to verify it. Not at first. Some of my biggest success stories have been celibate for months before going to bed with the partner they eventually wed. More than a year, in several cases.'

The presenters, along with Lydia, and indeed Mr Bennet (also at a loss for things to occupy his time these days) expressed a deal of disbelief at this. It was only Mary, who had happened to glance up from a battered copy of an Ursula Le Guin at precisely the right time, who nodded along with a grunt of self-satisfaction.

Mr Bennet, who hadn't been aware of his middle (and most judgemental) child's presence until that moment, stiffened with a mix of indignation and guilt. 'Ah, Mary,' he said. 'What new observation of threadbare morality have you for us today?'

'There is far too much emphasis on sex,' she announced, putting her book down decisively. 'The world is obsessed with it.'

'Well, not everyone,' Mr Bennet suggested, all too aware that his own sex life had dwindled even further of late, post-menopause (he wasn't sure which was worse: the hot flushes or the fixation on Channing Tatum), his own occasionally tricky issue *down there*, and, of course, the ever-present Bridget at weekends. Plus now, of course, there was Lydia, who had regressed into her habit of wandering into the master bedroom and flinging herself across the end of the divan like a consumptive war widow. He had attempted to fit a lock on the door, to no avail – Mrs Bennet (egged on by Bridget) being paranoid about emergency egress in the event of a house fire, an invasion of snakes, or a zombie apocalypse.

He segued (a tested tactic with Mary). 'Shouldn't you be at work?'

Mary – a part-time librarian in Meryton's children's department – checked her watch, and then the carriage clock on the mantelpiece for good measure. 'I'll leave in six minutes.'

Which she did, the room almost static with anticipation during the wait.

'Thank God for that.' Mr Bennet exhaled as the front door shut with a clunk. 'Now,' he popped on his spectacles, checked the *Radio Times*. 'Yes, after this we can watch *Bargain Hunt*, and then *Doctors* at two.'

But Lydia wasn't listening; she wasn't even watching the telly anymore (Dennis Plemons now replaced by a camp man in a plaid shirt demonstrating a gravy fountain). She was making some swift calculations. Dennis Plemons had cited one of his trickiest 'customers' – a now thirty-six-year-old woman who had totted up an impressive (or depressing, depending on your outlook) seventy-two lovers in less than two decades before, after eighteen months of celibacy, finding true love. Seventy-two was, however, peanuts compared to Lydia's roster, which topped off in the late one-hundreds. And what happiness had that brought her? Precious bloody little, beyond the obvious.

But she'd been sober and straight now for thirty-two days; celibate for thirty-three. Could she manage to give up all three of them? For a year? Well, possibly, if she stayed in Meryton. The boredom admittedly made not drinking an issue, but her father had hidden the whisky, leaving only Campari and advocaat, and she wasn't that desperate. Not yet. And as for the sex: it wasn't as if there was a plethora of eligible men, plus her wardrobe was still very much late-nineties focused so unless someone had a Sk8ter Girl fetish she was pretty much buggered. So, she could turn that into an advantage, and fix herself for the sake of love. It would give her something to focus on. She could draw up a chart, tick off little boxes like Jane. Plus it might even be romantic – like a regency novel. She could have a chaperone; make guest appearances on telly as the former *Love Shack* slut turned born-again virgin. She could monetise it. Men would fling themselves at her then – actors and musicians and perhaps even Wickham—

She stalled. Okay, perhaps not him. No, definitely not him. God, what was wrong with her? This is why she needed the celibacy! She had to stop chasing this… this impossibility. This idiocy. She didn't want Wickham. She just wanted what Jane had: she wanted true love. And if that meant giving up sex as well as everything else, well, she would do it.

Masturbation didn't count though, did it? She googled 'does celibacy include masturbation dennis plemons'. And then 'dennis plemons wife?', and then 'henri perlot celine perlot' for good measure.

Well that was conclusive. She could (and would) fantasise all she wanted.

She just couldn't act on it.

★ ★ ★

Mary, meanwhile, in a chilly side room off the main library between the newly gender-neutral lavatories (*that* had caused a ruckus, much to Mary's incomprehension) and near (too near) the communal computers with their irritating 'tick tack' keyboard noises and their users' heavy breathing, was reshelving a sticky copy of the sixth Wimpy Kid book. Why didn't parents ensure their children follow the rules? she wondered silently (of course). Why didn't *they* follow the rules themselves for that matter? Rules, she reminded herself, as she did regularly (and often vocally) were there for a reason. They made things fair, just as boundaries made things manageable. At which thought, her mind turned to Jane's resolution checklist. Much as she had derided it at first, it might actually prove useful, if only the rest of the Bennets could be relied upon to stick to it.

As a child, Mary had felt keenly the injustice whenever one of her sisters (usually Kitty or Lydia) tried to impose hastily conjured 'house rules' on Monopoly, Cluedo, or even Connect 4, in order to favour their own limp ability. 'Play it right!' she would shriek, quoting the Hasbro instructions, and, when they refused, would go wailing to her father who would sigh and remind her, 'It *is* just a game, Mary.' Eventually, she had refused to join in any Christmas Day board games, card games and even sardines until each sister signed a sworn affidavit that they would not even think about cheating. That had held until Boxing Day when she caught Lydia (of course, Lydia) peering through her fingers from her vantage point at the landing bannister. The ensuing ruckus had left a taint on festivities that was still very much palpable in January, while Mary, at her wits' end with her sisters, had retreated into what had seemed a far safer environment at the time, rules-wise: Harry Potter.

The obsession lasted decades. She could quote entire passages, place any character and indeed any person in their correct house (she was, she would admit without shame or pride, for it was a matter of neither, but rather mere fact, Slytherin), and argue at length why no, Harry should not have ended up with Hermione. It was briefly derailed by Lydia, who had convinced Mary that the Weasleys lived in Catmere End, a village a good four miles from Meryton, necessitating a lengthy cycle ride, and resulting in hoots of derision from passers-by when she asked where she might find the family and their pale blue Ford Anglia. Still, she had not given up the passion. It was only relatively recently, in the wake of a rant from Kitty on the rights of trans and queer people, which – when one extracted the swearing, and the brief diversion into Holliday Grainger's accent – made perfect sense, that she had finally abandoned that fandom and turned instead to Tolkien, who, if a little verbose, was dead, and therefore less likely to disappoint her.

Online, she found communities that at first fanned her passion, but it was rules, again (or other people's inability to stick to them) that ruined it for her. She could not, she found, hold with 'shipping', with 'head canon', with the reams of overenthusiastic and adolescent fan fiction that played merry hell with such a precise, tightly managed world. One might as well try to defy gravity here in Hertfordshire as Bilbo 'just throw away the ring' in Middle Earth, as she tried to explain to her mother.

On Mrs Bennet's encouragement she tried a fantasy reading group at her local bookshop, but again found their loose interpretations (of the word 'fantasy', as well as individual series) an affront. It had been the same in her brief stint in the Meryton Regency Re-enactment Society – too many silly women thinking it was enough to stick on something empire-line from Primark when everyone knew polyester wasn't invented until the mid-twentieth century. All of which was serving to remind Mary exactly why dating was too fraught with potential irritants to be in any way advisable. Because it involved Other People, and Other People, in her experience, were invariably wrong.

Contrary to popular opinion in the Bennet household, Mary was not a prude, though there was a general obsession with sex that felt both unnecessary and a personal affront, considering she hadn't had any. For a long time she'd suspected she might be, as Kitty so bluntly put it, 'ace'. She was, after all – as with her namesake (or rather unlike her namesake, who clearly didn't understand science) – a virgin. She had never even kissed a man. Oh, she had suffered a series of 'fixations', as her mother called them as a teenager and since:

Jeremy Paxman

Jeremy Bowen (leading Mrs Bennet to assume it was the 'Jeremy' bit to which she was attracted, until an experiment with a photograph of Jeremy Clarkson proved this moot.)

Mr Dent-Beston, who did the boiler

Billy Pritchard

Only one – Billy Pritchard – had resulted in an actual encounter. He had, having asked nicely, felt her left breast on a camp-out near Chelmsford, albeit through a gilet, a sweater and a thermal vest. So simultaneously bored and appalled was she (it was as if she were biscuit dough and he kneading her) that she had quit Scouts immediately, sacrificing her Backwoods Cooking badge and an imagined career as the next Baden-Powell.

She had, at least, had more luck with the men of her imagination, having masturbated (following the usefully detailed online guide OMGYes) with varying degrees of success to Richard Madeley, Gillian Anderson and the vicar, so she knew that she worked on a mechanical level. But imaginary bedfellows were not the same as real people. Real people annoyed her. Even the vicar. Especially the vicar. In fact the only person she could tolerate at any length was Colin Burghley, and since he had told her, in May 1998, when she was a mere thirteen, that he fully intended to marry her sister, Elizabeth, one day, and then proceeded to wed Charlotte Lucas, he was obviously off-limits still, despite the divorce. And then, there was her own appeal, which was categorically lacking. In the past she had been compared to 'a house elf' (Kitty), 'Carole Burghley' (Lydia) and 'a glass of milk – the thin insipid sort' (Carole Burghley). The whole project was doomed, then.

And yet – there it was, on the list (albeit an addendum). And lists were – Jane was right – so very compelling.

★ ★ ★

Lists were ridiculous, Lizzy told herself as she marched past the car park at Addenbrooke's hospital, checking her Fitbit as she went (3,453 steps already, and it was barely 8am), as was the very concept of dating, let alone trying it now, at this age, in this... predicament. It was so very mercenary, so transactional: filling in forms and tickboxes – more bloody tickboxes – as if both disliking wine or having a passing interest in kickboxing or... or being a Leo might somehow bring about a match to rival Rhett and Scarlet, Heathcliff and Cathy, she and Fitz. The thought of all those stilted conversations, awkward dinners, fraught walks, all the while trying to tally compatibility as if it were a calculable thing. Surely one had as good a chance of happiness sticking to the old-fashioned way: bumping into someone slightly drunk down the pub or at a party — like Jane had done; like she.

Not that she wanted anyone else, however they might meet. She was managing perfectly well — well, she and Delilah were (thank God for Delilah, and the very notion of au pairs). Anyone else in the mix would be disruptive for the twins, who were going through a difficult stage in terms of sharing as it was. Yes, the twins needed stability. And they had plenty of positive role models, albeit mostly women. Although on reflection, perhaps only Jane and Delilah were really all that positive. But still, look how Grace had started acting out since Wickham had bludgeoned his way into the lives of the Bingleys. Of course, she'd been a bit tricksy in the past — who wouldn't with Jane as a mother? Perfect, impeccable Jane. But Charley had balanced Jane's more obsessive tendencies in a way that Wickham just… didn't. He was flashy, brash, and his hedonism was matched only by Lydia's. Which was all very well in their twenties but now seemed borderline tragic. Of course he swore he'd given that all up years ago, but Lizzy had her doubts. And in any case, his worst vice, which had always been idleness, was still very much in evidence. No wonder Timon, all of sixteen, was having an identity crisis. No— she corrected herself. Societal norms were not at Wickham's door. But he was just so try-hard alpha, so *Made-in-Chelsea* wide boy, and Timon was… not. Anyway, all of it served to reinforce her point, which was — God, what *was* her point?

Oh yes, dating. Dating was disruptive, time-consuming and frankly unnecessary. She had the twins for hugs, a perfectly serviceable vibrator for anything else, and two seasons of *The Crown* to catch up on. Thank God for box sets. And her job, obviously.

She hurried across the hospital lobby towards Obstetrics, nodding at colleagues while gesturing at her AirPods, as if she were already trapped in conversation, rather than merely avoiding it. As she hung up her bag and coat on the back of the door and sat down at her desk she checked her wrist again: 4,298 steps. She'd be done by lunchtime if she went up to the ward a few times, which Jane had surely known when she'd given her a Fitbit for Christmas. Or would have, if her head had been less giddied by Wickham. Perhaps she'd pass the thing on to Lydia, who could more than use the exercise. According to their mother, she'd not left the house since she'd arrived more than a month ago, she and Daddy forming some sort of 'redundancy club' in the front room, where they mostly watched quiz shows and *Loose Women*.

'He's obsessed with that Nolan woman,' Mrs Bennet had declared only yesterday. 'I'd be put out, but she looks quite like me in the right light.'

Lizzy hadn't answered. 'If you can't say something nice, then best say nothing' had been Fitz's motto in later years. Of course, as a result, he'd been overwhelmingly silent.

If only her mother and sisters could try the same.

★ ★ ★

'Lydia,' came the yell from upstairs again. 'Door!'

This time she rose from the sofa, her groan matching the creak of the seats, which had been reupholstered at least three times in her own memory (one minor fire, one incident with indelible ink, one with indelible sick). 'I don't see why it's always me,' she muttered as her father, not three feet away, shook his paper with emphasis.

In truth she saw exactly why it was her, and had been for the past week, given the doorbell now rang up to four times a day and not, as Mrs Bennet had quickly discovered, with meter readers, Jehovah's Witnesses (her speciality) or the sort of gossip that could only be passed on over tea and custard creams, but with the weary faces of ASOS and Vinted delivery men.

'I don't know where she gets the money,' Mrs Bennet had complained to Mr Bennet only yesterday.

Mr Bennet, who had wandered into the kitchen for some peace and a slice of illicit cheese (his cholesterol was teetering in the 'of concern' area, so naturally Mrs Bennet was convinced death was imminent and was depriving him accordingly) retreated swiftly, while Mrs Bennet went back to doing something inventive with mince, and no more was said on the matter. And likely wouldn't be until the credit card bills arrived. Lydia, in a fit of pique about her depleted wardrobe, and with no intention of either heading back to Paris to retrieve the rest of it or following her mother's advice to 'get something sensible' from any of the five charity shops that lined Meryton High Street, had had to resort to another method. That method being using her father's credit card, the details for which, she discovered, were stored without thought for security on the Longbourn laptop – a communal brick of a thing that had survived through two changes of government, and considerably more spilt gin.

It was hardly her fault, when you thought about it, or rather, she deserved a treat given all she was suffering, what with the break-up and the not drinking and not having sex. Plus, frankly, they owed her, given the whole Arthur debacle.

Not long after the 'giving up everything' thing, she had been dispatched to the chest freezer in the garage to fetch a bag of pork chops (more Delia) and had opened the lid to uncover the frozen body of a dead dog looking up at her – her parents' dead dog, to be precise, who had died four years ago. Unsurprisingly she had yelled loud enough for all Meryton to hear, and her mother's explanation had done nothing to assuage her.

'Why didn't anyone warn me?' Lydia had managed, once words rather than mere strangulated sounds had finally come to her again.

'We forgot,' came the breezy reply.

'Forgot?' she snapped. 'It's an Alsatian cross!'

'Honestly, he's been there so long, we don't notice him anymore.'

Which was, Lydia thought with some understanding, likely, given Mary was alive and they barely noticed her half the time. Still, it was hardly an explanation. 'I just... why is he even there?'

'Oh your father and I couldn't agree where to bury him. And then the roof needed doing and then there was that hoohah with Bridget, and, well, there he is.'

There, indeed, he was, all three foot of him, rigid and grinning toothily. Needless to say, Lydia didn't eat the chops that night. Nor the defrosted lamb casserole the following day. And when the chance had come to use the card, she took it as deserved recompense.

And now, again, here were the fruits of that fuck-up.

'Thanks,' she mumbled through a curtain of decidedly unstyled hair, as she scrawled an 'L' on the postman's little handheld thingy.

'Trying to fill the hole of sadness, I see.'

She bristled, deigned to look up, saw the raised eyebrow and angular face (or the kind that had once been angular, but was now slightly blurred at the edges, as if time had taken a rubber to it) of someone she vaguely recognised from school but couldn't place. Chances were she had kissed him, or belittled him, and judging by his smirk, it was the latter.

'Compulsive shopping,' he continued. 'Classic move.'

'All right, Judge bloody Judy.'

'What is it then? Break-up? Sacked? Cancelled?'

Was this actually happening? 'You do know I could report you? And anyway, maybe I'm reviewing them. Maybe I'm' – she clutched at a straw – 'an influencer.'

'A sex toy influencer?'

She felt her cheeks heat and a rush of panic followed by an

aftershot of pure indignation. 'How do you even know? They said "discreet wrapping"!' She snatched the package, turned it over. 'Have you opened it?'

'See that number?' He pointed at a corner. 'It's a code. Porn stamp we call it. Every postie knows it.'

She wilted. 'Oh, marvellous.' At least it wasn't Dave though, she supposed, thankful his round kept him the wrong side of Meryton.

'Don't be embarrassed,' said the man. 'Very sex positive, me.'

A flicker of something licked at her as she considered his intentions, reconsidered his face. It wasn't all that bad, actually. Decent cheekbones, nice eyes – a flecked greeny-brown – stubble a bit gingery, but then wasn't every middle-aged white man's? God, perhaps she *had* got off with him?

'I'm not embarrassed,' she said eventually, and she wasn't – at least, not at that, though she felt keenly the playground shame of being caught wearing last season's jeans and a sweater (one of her father's cast-offs) that could be described, at best, as retro and, at worst, as gagging for landfill. 'I'm just busy.' She Lydia-ed herself, as Kitty once called it – pasting on her wry smile, and pulling up her posture so that her back arched and her neck lengthened. 'Got a Love Button to road test. Enjoy your' – she flapped a hand at him – 'walk.' And then shut the door, the triumph washing through her almost as pleasing as an orgasm.

Later, having completed the 'road test' (does what it says on the tin, five stars, would recommend) she wracked her memory and realised she did remember him – Denny something or other. In Kitty's year, or the year below that. Had dropped out of sixth form to join a band – some grunge-meets-punk lot, semi-famous, but the hair was unbearable, and as for the trousers. Well, *that* had obviously not worked out, had it. Not that she cared. He wasn't her type, even if she had been 'in the game'. Dropouts weren't really her thing (a trait in which she saw not a shred of hypocrisy), unless they had a tragic backstory, of course.

Perhaps he did have a tragic backstory? Perhaps he had fallen prey to… to an unscrupulous manager, or… or had an affair with Courtney Love and the whole thing had broken him. Or—

She stopped herself. No, the needy were Jane's bag; Lydia wanted them independent, and preferably independently wealthy as well. A Hertfordshire postie was hardly a catch.

Not that she wanted to catch him, or anyone.

The fact that she washed her hair the next morning, dug out an eighties Dash sweater dress and put on some new Air Max trainers was purely a matter of hygiene, of self-esteem, of decent arch support.

Nothing more at all.

Sister Act
Jane, Lizzy, Mary, Kitty, Lydia

~Jane Bingley
George and I are having a little engagement do on Saturday. Not enough time for paper invites (I have checked with Pritchards, so if Mum tries to suggest it, do remind her of this) but please regard this as official. Netherfield at 7.30pm. Bring a bottle. (Catering arranged – thank heaven for Chaters!)
19:01

~Kitty Miller
Dave says can the band play a set? I'm sure you'd rather chew tinfoil, but he saw the message and is making me ask.
19:32

~Jane Bennet
I'll check with George.
19:32

~Jane Bennet
George says yes, just a short one, as long as it's gratis. What are they called now? I'll put it on the schedule for nine.
20:01

~Kitty Miller
Duck knows. It was Frivolous Pigeons but I think it's changed again. Hang on.
20:05

~Kitty Miller
Listless Biscuits (don't ask). Just be glad he got overruled or you'd be announcing Three-Layered Rat Hammock or Incognito Meat Bag. Also yay! A party! @**Lydia** There will be men!
20:06

~Lydia Bennet
i don't need a man
20:07

~Kitty Miller
Says the Longbourn shag champion.
20:07

~Lydia Bennet
did you just slut-shame your own sister?
20:08

~Kitty Miller
I didn't say you should be ashamed. Just that you shag a lot. Which you do.
20:08

~Lydia Bennet
i haven't had sex in 38 days
20:09

~Kitty Miller
The fact that you're counting proves my point.
20:10

~Lydia Bennet
well we can't all be happily shacked up with a postman
20:10

~Kitty Miller
Define 'happily'.
20:11

~Lydia Bennet
sliding into your DMs…
20:11

* * *

A party! On Valentine's Day! Mrs Bennet could barely believe her luck, it effectively killing two birds with one stone: one, her inevitable disappointment when Mr Bennet failed to arrange anything vaguely romantic, and two, a chance for the unattached girls to mingle with eligible men and pick someone. Of course, Jane had called it a 'little do' but all Meryton would be there, and half of Hertfordshire too – perhaps even some of the Cambridge set. Surely there must be *someone* eligible amongst Wickham's friends. But there would need to be preparations: facials, make-up, new dresses! At least for Mary and for herself. (Lydia, despite acquiring an entire wardrobe-full in the past fortnight, would probably show up in something more akin to underwear, and

Mrs Bennet had long since given up trying to tame or constrain her; why bother when Mary lived for policing?) And yes, she had several dresses that would 'do' but 'do'ing wasn't enough for the mother of the bride, was it? Besides, she could hardly wear the mauve Debenhams set, not since she and Philippa Baxendale had had their colours done and half the spectrum had become verboten. But when she suggested a trip to Cambridge to address the glaring vacancy, Mr Bennet was less than effusive.

'Do we have to? There's snooker on at two.'

'Since when have you liked snooker? And don't say "redundancy club". You're retired, not redundant, and she's… God knows what she is.'

'The traffic on a Saturday will be murder,' he tried. 'And as for parking…'

Mrs Bennet narrowed her eyes. 'I might die tomorrow,' she said, invoking one of her favourite threats, 'and then you'll be sorry.'

'I doubt it,' he muttered. 'You're like Tupperware. You'd survive the apocalypse.'

But he knew when he was defeated and so the car keys were fetched, and Mrs Bennet and Mary ferried to the hallowed passage of Grand Arcade, where they bought a forgiving Mint Velvet shift in cobalt blue (Mrs Bennet) and the new R. F. Kuang novel (Mary, who had already decided to wear her Cats Protection League T-shirt and black leggings, and there was no persuading her otherwise) before dropping in on Lizzy and the twins for tea, because the queue at John Lewis was akin to 'the black hole of Calcutta' and in any case the scones were always on the dry side.

'Kolkatta,' Lizzy corrected, as she doled out fig rolls and darjeeling. 'You know this.'

'I do, I do!' Mrs Bennet confessed. 'It's like Marathons, though, isn't it.'

'You mean Snickers.'

'Exactly,' her mother said, with an air of having successfully predicted a Grand National winner. 'It's so hard to keep up. Anyway, appaz—'

'Please don't use appaz. You sound like a teenager from the noughties. Or Lydia. Just say apparently.'

'Do I?' Mrs Bennet shimmered briefly. 'Anyway, *appaz* Charlotte and The Lesbian will be there, and of course Colin is coming, so heaven knows what sort of hoohah that will induce.' This said in the expectant tone of someone who very much enjoyed hoohah, at least when it related to other families.

'It's all perfectly amicable, from what I hear,' Lizzy replied. 'Sorry to disappoint.'

But if Lizzy thought she'd served advantage, she was mistaken.

'Well, then she won't mind if you and he… you know.'

Lizzy did know, and nettled. 'No thanks. And I'm not even sure I can make it. Delilah's got some "thing" and can't sit that evening and the rest of you will all be at the party, so…'

She trailed off before stating the obvious, a rookie mistake, she realised quickly, as it left an opening into which Mrs Bennet deftly inserted herself.

'You can put Milo and Arden down at Jane's and either take them back later or all stay the night at Netherfield. There or at Longbourn. We'll be leaving by ten to ferry Bridge back as it is.'

'Will we?' Mr Bennet looked up gloomily from his fifth fig roll.

Mrs Bennet ignored him. 'So there. It's settled.'

They departed soon after, Mrs Bennet brassy with success, which was only slightly tarnished when they had to turn back at Chrishall, having realised they'd left Mary looking at kitchen bins in homeware two hours ago, and quite forgotten about her.

Justice for Jane
Lizzy, Kitty, Lydia, Mary

Lydia Bennet added Lizzy Darcy-Bennet to the group.

~Lydia Bennet
Game plan? Brave faces? Or do we stage some kind of intervention and persuade her she's mad?
14:40

~Kitty Miller
If we do stage anything can it wait until Dave's played?
14:42

~Lydia Bennet
i thought you hated the band? you said they were, and i quote, 'the worst kind of dad rock'
14:43

~Kitty Miller
They are. But they've got a new bassist. Ex-some Grammy-winning band. Ticks lots of boxes. And he's hoping that bloke Wickham knows from Sony will be there, so
14:45

~Lydia Bennet
wanky simon? i doubt it. he moved to manchester
14:45

~Kitty Miller
How do you know?
14:46

~Kitty Miller
?
14:48

~Lydia Bennet
duck off. it was once. and i'm serious. are we just accepting this now? or do we wait until the vicar asks for objections?
14:49

~Kitty Miller
Perhaps you can honey trap him, Lyds?
14:50

~Lydia Bennet
totally up for that. as long as you promise to bear witness that it wasn't my fault when we do the big reveal
14:50

~Lizzy Darcy-Bennet
For God's sake, let her have her party. The engagement won't come to anything. They'll stay as they are for a year or two and then he'll do what he always does and go back to Calypso.
14:51

~Kitty Miller
Silly Calypso.
14:51

Lizzy Darcy-Bennet left the group.

★ ★ ★

To do:
- ~~Cheeses~~

- ~~Flowers~~
- ~~Glass hire~~
- Grace – shoes

Jane gazed across the stage of what, not six hours ago, had been her kitchen-diner and felt the knots of tension in her neck give a little. The flowers – winter jasmine and daffodils (nothing out of season) – were exquisite; the buffet an artfully arranged table of artisan cheeses and meats (Socrates had been shut in the boot room, and everyone under strict instructions not to let him escape); the lighting warm and inviting, but not so bright it would discourage dancing. Everything was perfect, just perfect. Or as good as, with a nearly sixteen-year-old.

Grace had been in a vile mood since Friday, though Jane put this down to her hair. She'd come home with a wodge of chewing gum in it (again) and the freezing-it-out trick hadn't worked this time; instead they'd had to cut it with the kitchen scissors, which might have been fine had it been near the ends but, given it was not two inches from her crown, was, well, rather conspicuous. The obvious solution would be to cut in a fringe, but Grace, apparently, 'would rather die'.

'I wish you'd tell me how it happened,' Jane had urged her, as she tried to fashion a waterfall plait to disguise it.

Grace had snatched her head away. 'God! How many times? It was an accident.' And she'd put on her headphones and stormed to her room and that had been the end of that discussion. She was still in there now, refusing to put on a dress, or even come down. Though George – darling George – had gone off to talk to her.

She noticed a sprig of the jasmine escaping its arrangement, went to re-twine it. Then decided to redo the daffs so they looked a little more artfully rustic. But as she fussed over them she heard him. 'Who cares?' he whispered, his breath a kiss on her neck. 'They're here for you, not the botany.'

Charley?

She swung round, to be faced not by her deceased husband – of course not; how stupid! – but by George, his smile cat-wide, his eyes bright with something.

She shook herself, metaphorically anyway. 'Darling! Is Grace okay?'

'All sorted,' he said. 'Anyone who says there are some things that money can't buy has never dealt with a teenager, clearly.'

'Oh.' Jane tried not to wilt. 'How much?'

'I told her fifty, but if you give her forty I think she'll be fine.'

'But I...' No, no point in spoiling things.

'She'll be down in an hour,' George went on. 'And Timon's train's not due until seven.' He turned her around, so they could see themselves reflected in the wide French windows. Which means we've plenty of time to...'

He let his words trail off as his lips, pressed against her shoulder, bare but for a shrug to compensate, comfort-wise, for the strapless Westwood she'd rented – probably a foolish choice in February, but the stylist was right: it really did flatter her. She felt practised fingers undo the covered buttons, one hand slip inside the corseted, watermarked taffeta, begin stroking her breast; breath quickening, felt herself sink into it, this... this dizzying spell he cast over her.

'Darling, we can't,' she panted. 'What if someone comes early?'

But even she knew she didn't mean it. And so when he pulled up the structured skirt, pushed her down into the Reblochon, she let him.

★ ★ ★

'I thought Jane was wearing Westwood?' Kitty said, as she stuck a breadstick into a smeared wheel of cheese that had clearly seen better days. 'That tartan thing. She showed us a picture.'

Lydia, idly puffing on a pickle as if it were a Cuban cigar, shrugged. 'Maybe she put weight on. Or lost it. God knows. Where's Dave?'

'Why do you want to know?' Kitty frowned. 'The band are all twats, in case you were thinking of tapping one of them. Well, not total twats, but you know. Middle-aged men who still think they're Stone Roses. Though half of them are married, so you'll probably love them.'

'Fuck off. Besides *you're* married to one of them,' Lydia pointed out. 'Remember?'

'Not *actually* married, thanks.' Kitty shuddered, and not for effect.

Lydia, who recognised juice when she saw it, swallowed the cornichon and widened her eyes. 'That bad?'

It was Kitty's turn to shrug. 'Oh, it's fine,' she conceded. 'You know. It works well enough. And Bridge thinks he's Wolverine, which is… useful.'

Lydia frowned. 'Wolverine?'

'Highest compliment currently. It used to be Monty Don, so this is an improvement.' She squinted, picked a hair off her cracker, before putting the entire thing in her mouth, and washing it down with a mouthful of Chardonnay. 'Where are you going?' she sputtered as Lydia turned to head off to the hallway.

'Nowhere,' lied Lydia. 'The loo.'

In fact, she was off to seek out Caroline Bingley-Hicks, who for some inexplicable reason (guilt, perhaps? Duty?) Jane had decided to invite, an arrival that Lydia protested at first, but in which she now saw the advantage. If there was to be an ally in her plan to take a cleaver to the whole Wickham idiocy, Caroline was it.

In fact, though, Caroline was rather more blasé than Lydia had expected, repeating Lizzy's belief that the whole thing was an expensive diversion, and that Wickham would be gone before the month was out.

'The nothingness and self-importance of these people,' she went on as she observed both Wickham's friends from the ad agency and some of the Meryton lot, dancing (admittedly poorly) to 'Mr Brightside'. 'And what about you?' She turned to Lydia. 'Why are you even here? Last I heard you were in fashion. In Paris, no less.'

'Yes, well...' Lydia dithered. 'It didn't quite work out.'

'I am all astonishment,' said Caroline, clearly nothing of the kind.

This had been a mistake, Lydia realised, excusing herself, and planning on a cheeky fag in the back garden but bumping straight into her mother, who exhorted her to find Lizzy immediately.

'She needs to rescue Colin,' Mrs Bennet explained, in frantic tones. 'Mary's got him stuck in a corner, probably boring him to death about hobbits or goblins. This is a real chance for Lizzy! Colin's got a fortune coming to him once his aunt pops her whatsits. And he's a professor. A professor!' She shrieked the word the second time, as if she were declaring him King.

Lydia glanced at Mary, and at Colin, who seemed more than happy to be rapt by whatever tedium Mary was inflicting upon him. 'He looks fine to me,' she announced, then slid off again quickly, thinking she was being quite the covert, taking a shortcut via the boot room, where she mightn't be seen so easily. But as she clicked round the handle, slid through the gap, who should she see but Wickham, rolled-up note in his hand and his head thrown back.

He swung round at the interruption, eyes glistening then widening in alarm.

Coke, then.

'Fuck,' he exploded. 'What happened to knocking?'

She tamped down the flush of want that had brimmed in her, replaced it with indignation. 'Right. So you're off your tits and I'm the one at fault?'

He thrust the note back in his pocket, smeared a sleeve across the top of the scrubbed oak shoe rack. 'Just because you can't handle it, you don't need to police the rest of us.'

Lydia let out a snort. The wanker. Well two could play at that game. 'So Jane's aware of this, is she?'

'Jane accepts me with all my flaws.'

'There's enough of them.'

'Well, you'd know.' His smile quirked on one side.

The pair faced each other, the air taut, Lydia all too aware that this was how it had started, how it always started: a spat, then that passion, a tide of it, which – God! – she wanted to ride. Only—

'We can't do this. You're marrying my sister.'

'Do what?' He walked towards her. 'This is flirting. A bit of fun.'

They were inches apart now; she could feel the heat of him, measure his breath, smell his fragrance: not Kouros anymore but Tom Ford, Tobacco Vanille. Not even knock-off. Fuck.

Lydia set her shoulders, dropped her eyes. 'I don't think Jane would agree.'

She felt his fingers tuck a lock of hair behind her ear, his face tip forward the better to whisper. 'I don't think she'd believe you, do you? You're the one who fucks anything still, remember?'

Lydia balled her fists. She would not rise to this. Would not look at him. Could not—

His lips grazed her ear. 'If you ever want…' – he paused – '… anything. You know where I am.'

Then he turned on his heel (Loakes, she had noticed) and sauntered out of the boot room, leaving Lydia bereft in the centre, looking for all the world as though she'd seen a ghost.

'Are you okay?'

Lydia came to, yelped, then heaved in relief. It was the

postman from the other day – the sarky one, with the vibrator. What the feckity hell was he doing here?

'Side hustle,' Denny replied when she asked him. 'Catering.' His face cracked at Lydia's reaction. 'Joking. I'm in the band.'

'Oh, right,' she managed. *He* was the new bassist. Of course he was. She pictured him and Dave, sorting letters alphabetically – or whatever it was postmen did – side by side whilst discussing E strings. And G strings, no doubt.

'Wasn't that the groom?' Denny nodded at the door.

Lydia nodded. 'Yes. Worse luck… God, sorry. I don't mean that.'

'Yes you do,' he said, his face focused on her in a way that made it somehow impossible to lie.

'I do, actually. He's an irredeemable twat.' She segued, which was the next best thing in the absence of being able to fib. 'So, you're still playing bass then.'

Denny frowned, but not unkindly.

'Denny Lennox. You wore a lot of eyeliner and then joined Slitchicks,' Lydia prompted. 'In sixth form.'

'Blimey. Word gets around.'

She shrugged. 'You were two years above me at school. It was all anyone talked about. Well, until Lewis Henderson shat himself in RE.'

He laughed. 'Well, yes, that's me then. Second most exciting after self-soiling. And less, I don't know… "look at me" these days?' He gestured at understated black trousers, CDG T-shirt. 'But, you know, same old muso really.'

'I prefer you now actually,' she said without thinking. Fuck. Rescue it! Rescue it! 'Better… hair?'

'I'll take that,' he said generously. 'And if we're doling out compliments, I like your dress. Very retro.'

She beamed. 'Vintage actually. McQueen Fall 2003. Got it for a song on Depop. Well, about two hundred, but when you think what it would have been new, that's practically giving it away.'

'Practically. Anyway, it suits you. Though I was quite partial to the fisherman's jumper thing.'

'Ha ha.' But she smiled anyway, allowed herself a second to assess Denny. 'You driving then?' She nodded at the Lucky Saint.

'I am as it goes. Driving I mean. But, well—'

He hadn't been about to trail off, but Lydia finished it for him anyway. 'You're an alcoholic,' she realised.

Denny snorted. 'Don't mince your words, will you.'

Lydia grimaced. 'Shit, sorry. It just comes out of me sometimes. Word vomit.'

'It's fine really. How about you?' Denny nodded at Lydia's Diet Coke. 'Or is caffeine your latest addiction?'

'I'm not an addict,' she said quickly. 'I just… *like* it. Amongst myriad other things apparently. Drink. Drugs. Sex.' That last one hadn't been meant as a test but as soon as it was out it sounded provocative and Lydia winced.

But if Denny noticed he didn't let on. Instead he nodded almost reverently. 'That's quite the collection. Plus there's the internet shopping.'

Lydia pulled a face again. 'Sorry. Like I said, word vomit. How about you?'

'How about me what?'

'You never answered. It's not just because you're driving, is it. The no drinking, I mean.'

'Oh, that.' He nodded, took another swig. 'Doesn't mix with meds, sadly.'

Lydia squinted. 'Let me guess. Citalopram.'

'That obvious?'

She shrugged. 'Single man in his forties.'

'Almost forties. And how do you know I'm single?'

Oh. Good point. How *did* she know? She frowned. It was one of those things she could just sense. Like having gaydar, or knowing when an egg was past its best. 'No ring? No hickeys?' she tried. No rank desperation, she didn't add.

'Who the feck has hickeys at our age?'

'Your age. I'm two years below you, remember?'

'"Below". We're not at school anymore, Lydia Emerald Bennet.'

She winced again. 'Oh God. How did you know my middle name? Are you stalking me?'

'Postal worker, remember? We know everything. Like God. But with a uniform.'

Lydia bristled. 'Right. And you'd be surprised about the hickey thing. It's rather transgressive. Which is pleasing in itself. Also, you have that smell.'

'Pardon me? What smell?'

The smile had faded now, and Lydia felt a brief stab of regret. 'I just mean… it's clothes that haven't quite dried properly I think.' She knew. 'Though I suppose it shows you don't still live with your mother at least.' She braced herself.

But Denny's lips quirked upwards. 'My mother's grand, I'll have you know. And pot kettle, with the living at home.'

'Touché.' Lydia found herself smiling. 'Circumstance, and all that.' She was about to launch into an explanation that toned her misdeeds down slightly and painted her in a rather more tragic light than was true, or even believable, when, from the kitchen-diner, Wickham clinked his coupe glass with a knife rather pointedly.

'Oh God, they're going to announce something.' She sighed. 'Come on.'

Denny followed her through. 'She's not pregnant is she? Your sister?'

Lydia shook her head. 'Can't be. No uterus.' She started. 'God, sorry. Word vomit again. And TMI.'

'It's fine.' He waved a dismissive hand. 'I'm totally au fait with all problems of the lady area. Been there, got the T-shirt.'

'"Lady area"?' Lydia snorted. 'Seriously?'

'What do you call it then?' Denny was genuinely interested.

Lydia considered this, was about to admit to 'minky', when Wickham rattled his coupe again. 'Ladies and gentlemen, while you're all gathered here. Our dear friends, and beloved family…' At this he looked pointedly at Timon, who rolled his eyes and skulked further behind a curtain.

'He thinks he sounds like a vicar,' Kitty hissed to Dave. 'When he actually sounds like a bell end. Jesus! What was that for?' She put a hand to her ribs, which had felt the full force of Dave's elbow. 'I said it quietly.'

'Not quiet enough,' Dave whispered, nodding at Mrs Bennet, whose eyes were sharp as daggers and pointed at Kitty.

'As I was saying,' Wickham continued. 'We wanted to take this opportunity to thank you for all your support. Didn't we, darling?'

Jane, her hair slightly mussy, her face as flushed as the rose-pink shift she wore, nodded.

'And as long engagements are so outré these days, and we're not getting younger' – pause for amused disavowment – 'no, no, it's true. And as you're all here, we thought we'd tell you today that we've set the date already.' He looked at Jane again, as if prompting her.

Jane came to, gave a broad smile that only the most observant of her sisters could have known was rather more mustered than unstoppable. 'We have,' she confirmed. 'It's December. This year.' She glanced at Lizzy, her mouth quivering almost imperceptibly. 'The thirty-first, actually.'

'New Year's Eve!' clarified Wickham.

'New Year's Eve,' confirmed Jane, her gaze on her sister unwavering as Lizzy fled from the room.

★ ★ ★

'I really don't see what the problem is,' said Mrs Bennet to her husband, having given up placating Lydia, and sent her off to sort out Kitty, who had had far too much plonk (Dry January but a memory) and was last seen engaged in an argument with Dave about shackets. 'Winter weddings are all the rage these days. Dresses with sleeves, which are more flattering for Jane's age, and the men can wear velvet. Well, not you. Not after last time. But the church will look lovely, very festive.'

'I don't think it's the weather that's the issue, dear,' said Mr Bennet.

'Well, yes. But isn't this better? To have something positive to focus on instead of traipsing to the graves in the blessed rain and then feeling sorry for ourselves?'

'When you put it like that,' Mr Bennet said blisteringly, 'it's hard to see what all the fuss is about.'

Not for the first time, his sarcasm fell on selectively deaf ears. 'Precisely. Now, time to fetch Bridge. Drink up.'

She chivvied her husband, who was stuck on the Nosecco, which would only repeat on him later, and keep him up half the night given it was mainly green tea, but it had been thrust into his hand for the toast, and it was easier, he had found after this many years, to just do as he was told.

In the end it was both Bridget and Kitty they bundled into the car, Lydia having given up on reasoning with her sister, and Dave busy with dismantling the drums.

'Keep her head out of the window,' instructed Mrs Bennet to Bridge. 'Like a dog. At least if she's sick it will wash off the paintwork.'

Lydia would have rather taken up Denny's offer of a lift, but knew that came with far too many risks. Not from him – he seemed entirely trustworthy. Gallant even. A sort of anti-Wickham. No, it was herself she was wary of. Back seats, and even front seats, of cars from Ford Escorts to Porsches had played a major part in several of her teenage undoings, and she wasn't about to fall at the first hurdle. Instead, 'Give us your phone,' she'd said.

'What for?'

'So I can put in my number.'

'Bold,' said Denny, grinning.

Lydia shrugged as she took it. 'I like talking to you,' she admitted. 'Plus you'll need someone to sniff-test you. Clearly your mates can't be trusted.' She handed back the iPhone. An SE, but pristine, unlike her cracked Samsung.

He'd nodded, gave her a handshake good night (which she tried not to find charming), then texted her ten minutes later, as the Bennets' Volkswagen Passat pulled up on the driveway at Longbourn. A date and a time. And her heart – her foolish heart – shimmered until she realised what it was: not a date, the next AA meeting.

Well she wouldn't go, obviously. She wasn't an addict, for God's sake. She didn't need to hang out with a bunch of sad old alkys. But the texting – that was good wasn't it? This was just what she wanted. Needed, in fact: a friendship. An old-fashioned friendship. Entirely sexless. The sort she'd only ever had with gay men (most men – and women – either hated her, or slept with her). Denny could help her with the whole Wickham thing. Post him menacing letters or something. Or at worst take her side. Yes, this, she insisted, as she pulled off her dress, and crawled under the Spice Girls duvet (she really had to buy bedding), was progress. Perhaps she'd text Lizzy. She, at least, would be pleased with her.

★ ★ ★

Even if Lydia had called her, Lizzy wouldn't have answered, still less conceded. She was far too incensed with Jane to start concerning herself with Lydia's idiotic reasoning.

'New Year's Eve?' she blurted. 'Really?'

Jane, who felt cornered enough in the scullery, without Lizzy having shut the door behind them, braced herself. 'I wanted something good to mark, instead of...' She trailed off, tried again. 'It's just too depressing to have it wrapped up in... that.'

'Depressing?' Lizzy, who had tried to remember her breathing exercises, had urged herself to 'keep calm', blistered with indignation now. 'God, Jane, "that" was your husband. *Mine*. It's— it's devastating and so, yes, that day is shitty and miserable but you don't see me trying to throw parties to distract myself.'

Jane felt the words as keenly as if they were a slap, and tears brimmed, threatening her Victoria Beckham Kajal eyeliner for the second time that day. 'You think I don't know that? You think I don't miss him with every cell of me? Every second?'

Lizzy's flapped her hands in the air. 'So why marry Wickham then?'

'Because he's not coming back, Lizzy!' she snapped. 'Charley is gone and I have to move on. I don't want to live like a... a salmon in aspic. I'm sorry. I know that's not what you want to hear, but it's true.'

Lizzy bristled again, then remembered herself. This wasn't the time. It wasn't *her* place. 'God, I'm sorry,' she said, pulling her sister into a hug. 'I only...' She pulled back, looked at her. 'I'm happy for you. Honestly I am. I'm just tired. The twins aren't sleeping and I think Delilah might have applied to university, which means, well, back to square one.'

Pity swiftly swilled out ire and Jane squeezed Lizzy's shoulders. 'I'm sure that won't happen. And if it does, well, we'll fix it. But in the meantime, why not just give it a try. Dating I mean. I know you don't believe me, but second loves can be as rewarding. Look at George and me. Look at Charlotte!'

The latter, at least, was true – Lizzy had never seen her childhood best friend as happy as she was with Flavia. 'You know what's what with vaginas,' Charlotte had told her over the smoked hummus and celery sticks. 'So much easier than penises, in many ways.'

Lizzy hadn't argued, but in truth desired neither right

now. 'The trouble is,' she said to Jane, 'I think men are terrible.'

Her sister frowned. 'Lizzy, that's… that's an awful thing to say. And it just isn't true.'

But to Lizzy, who frequently saw them at their most utterly redundant — in the delivery suite — it was close enough to it. She shrugged. 'Most of them then. They're all just too… difficult.'

Jane, bruised, countered gamely. 'Not even Fitz was perfect,' she pointed out.

But the blow fell short. 'Oh, I know,' Lizzy conceded. 'He could be moody, brutal even — in his assessment of other people at least. But he was clever, loyal, and he adored me. And I couldn't love anyone half as much, not even close. So why bother?'

'I thought so too,' said Jane. 'Until George.'

There was a silence then, which Lizzy failed to fill.

Instead, Jane, in the spirit of 'in for a penny' seized the chance for another confession. She touched her sister's arm lightly, bit her lip. 'I need to tell you something.'

Lizzy felt her insides slip. Oh God, was Jane dying? Was *that* what this was? Was Lydia right? Was this all a bid for inheritance on Wickham's part? 'Jane?' she prompted, placing her hand over her sister's. 'What is it?'

The weight of Lizzy's hand steeled her. 'I want—' Jane began, then stopped herself, adjusted. '*We* want a baby. George and I have decided—'

The room seemed to tilt and Lizzy had to clutch on to the butler sink to steady herself. A baby? Was that better than death? Yes, it was better — she shook herself — of course it was. But when? And more importantly how? 'Jane—'

'Not yet,' Jane blurted, anticipating every question (having drawn up a list) that Lizzy might muster. 'I've said I want to wait until after the wedding. But then we'll need to get on with it, obviously, given our age.'

'Jane,' Lizzy repeated. 'What's going on? Is there something missing? Is that it?'

'No,' Jane replied quickly. It wasn't that. It really *wasn't*.

'Sorry,' said Lizzy. 'I didn't mean...'

And so, unable to concede the brutal truth, Jane fashioned something close to it. 'There's just... it's the hope a baby brings, I think. And... and making something together. He'll be moving into Charley's house, inheriting Charley's things, Charley's kid. I want something— *we* want something that's just *ours*.'

'And he wants this? You're sure of it?'

'He wants what I want.' And then out it slipped. 'I'm scared, Lizzy. That without it, it won't measure up. I won't, or he won't, or—'

Lizzy felt herself tense again. 'If that happens it won't be because you don't have a child.'

'I know. But I've thought and I do want this. I really want this.' Jane's gaze was beseeching. 'You know Charley and I planned to have five once upon a time, but then...'

Lizzy's imagination flashed with the memory of her sister on the delivery bed, blood gushing from her in a torrent that she had known at the time meant only one thing. 'So what will you do? Adopt?'

But Jane shook her head. 'Surrogate, I think. Will you help me?'

'I... well, there are agencies, and I can look into it. But Jane, are you sure?'

'I am,' she replied. 'This will be good for us. For Grace and Timon as well. It will knit us together, won't it?'

It shouldn't have come out as a question, and didn't strictly require an answer, but Lizzy gave her one anyway. Not the 'if you say so' that tricked about her lips, but something more... Jane. 'Better to be kind, than be right' rang in her head, and perhaps it applied this time, even if it went against everything about Wickham that Fitz had instilled in her, that she had instilled in herself.

'Of course, darling,' she told Jane. 'This is all... such very good news.'

SPRING

MARCH

March slunk in and hid in the corner, a recalcitrant cat, trailing with it a gush of floods, which closed the top road for a week; an infestation of a) nits for Bridget (and, inevitably, Kitty) and b) mice in the kitchen at the irritatingly hipsterish Koffee Kup, which precipitated a flurry of custom to the smug (and correctly spelled) Meryton Kettle; and the surgery's announcement that Dr Ogden (enormous hands, perpetually stained waistcoat, obsession with kidneys) was to retire (albeit unwillingly), and that unless a replacement could be found to take over his list, the practice would be forced to close or merge with Royston, a possibility that sent Mrs Bennet into a spiral of self-pity from which she was only just recovering when Denny delivered the credit card bill.

'But I don't understand how!' was her first proclamation, until Kitty (dropping off a freshly washed Bridget) demonstrated the lack of security by commandeering the laptop and almost buying a caravan, a Prada jumpsuit and a full set of Le Creuset pans in a matter of minutes.

'Oh,' Mrs Bennet replied contritely, in a brief, reflective moment, before her substantial imagination took hold again. 'Perhaps we've been hacked by a gang of identity thieves. Bad Karen says the Russians are everywhere. They hacked her Facebook and changed her status to an advert for por—' – in the nick of time she remembered Bridget – 'portaloos.' A courtesy she instantly regretted as Bridget launched into a lengthy dissection of the many disadvantages of portable toilets, while Kitty patiently explained that international criminals probably had better things to do than hack the Bennets' John Lewis credit card, but if they had, she was pretty sure they wouldn't be spending quite so much on Depop or Brand Alley.

All eyes turned ceilingwards, to where Lydia was languishing in bed, under recently acquired gingham linen top sheets, and in satin pyjamas.

'Leave this to me,' said Mr Bennet, who had stayed out of discussions until this point, other than to add a not-quite-silent 'I told you so' as regards the storing of passwords on a sheet of paper sellotaped to the laptop. 'I shall deal with it.'

Loath as she was to miss out on drama, Mrs Bennet did get a thrill when Mr Bennet flexed his authority. There would be *relations* later, she thought, as she bustled upstairs. Best shave her legs.

'Lydia!' her father thundered from the kitchen. 'Get down here now!'

Lydia, who had been flicking idly through that month's *Vogue* (£24 for the first six copies; a veritable online bargain) whilst simultaneously weighing up the pros and cons of gym membership versus a Sky subscription, went cold. She knew that tone. It was the tone invoked when she had flooded the back bathroom aged eight (trying to recreate *Titanic*), set fire to the dining room curtains aged thirteen (the Yankee Candle phase), and allowed various men to drain her father's Lagavulin (ages sixteen, twenty-one and thirty-three).

'Feckity feck,' she muttered, as she swiftly debated feigning death or disease.

'And don't pretend to be dead!' he yelled.

So, with a groan, she pulled on her Piglet in Bed dressing

gown (forty per cent off in the January sale), pushed her feet into Uggs (children's, i.e. no VAT, so practically a giveaway), and plodded downstairs.

It became clear, surprisingly quickly, that her usual ploys (declaring absolute ignorance, blaming Kitty, or crying loudly and snottily) were not going to wash this time.

'For God's sake, Lydia, you're not a child anymore,' he went on. 'You need to start taking responsibility for things.'

'But, Daddy—'

'No!' He held up a hand. 'Do not "Daddy" me; it won't wash. You're getting a job, and that's final.'

Lydia went rigid again. 'Oh, Daddy, no!'

'It's for your own good,' he said, thrusting the *Herts and Essex Gazette* into her hands, pages open at 'Situations Vacant'. 'You need to... to start contributing if you're going to live here. Mary pays us two hundred a month and she does the dishwasher and hoovering.'

Lydia clutched at that straw. 'I could wash the car?' she tried. 'Or... reorganise the "bugger it" drawer!' The 'bugger it' drawer being the top left in the sideboard, home to, amongst other things: forty-six Allen keys (but never the right one), fuses (both new and used), two screwdriver sets, a home pregnancy test (out of date), a stack of paper napkins, superglue, various stain removers (wine, ink, engine oil), dog wormer, cat flea treatment, a cake piping set, a jam thermometer, a rectal thermometer, blue shoe polish (unused since Lydia left primary school), a jar of buttons (still awaiting their day of usefulness), four train tickets, a token for the car park at Waitrose, and a box of indoor fireworks, use-by date 2005.

'You're not a Brownie on a bob-a-job,' her father pointed out. 'Chores are on top of normal employment. Even your mother still works. Though God knows I've told her to stop now.'

It was true; Mrs Bennet did two mornings a week as a receptionist at Meryton Vets, for the company rather than the money. She'd have preferred Dr Ogden's (medical gossip being of much higher currency) but this one came with free tea and biscuits, and an endless supply of cats, so she had decided not to look this particular gift horse in the mouth and was now reluctant to give it up, especially while Janet Carolgees' Burmese Kenneth (Jammie Dodgers habit, no filter – Janet, not the cat) continued to be a frequent flyer.

Lydia changed tack. 'Can't I add it to my IOU?'

Of course Lydia knew very well that IOUs in the Bennet household tended to exist in metaphorical terms only, and that any debt would, like the cost of the whisky, the fire and flood damage, and the myriad times she had promised to pay him back for taxis from obscure places at unspeakable times, be quietly written off.

'You already owe four thousand five hundred and seventy-six pounds,' came a voice from the corner.

'Jesus Christ!' Mr Bennet and Lydia swung round in unison to see Mary eating a bowl of Rice Krispies and peering over yesterday's Culture section.

'And eighty-three pence,' she added.

'Have you been keeping a tally?' Lydia was seething.

Mary nodded, without trace of either pride or embarrassment. 'Kitty owes almost the same,' she pointed out, matter-of-factly, 'because of Bridget's pills, and the deposit on that flat she pulled out of, and the flights back from Ibiza.'

Lydia paled, which was quite a feat given that her complexion at this time of year tended to resemble a glass of milk as it was.

Her father, though, was unmoved by either her plea, or Mary's clarification. 'A job,' he repeated.

'What about an allowance?' Lydia tried. 'Just until I find something?'

'My pension won't stretch to that. Not in this house with,' he waved generally, 'all of you women. And with a wedding coming up.'

'Isn't Wickham paying for that?' asked Mary.

Mr Bennet sighed. 'Apparently his assets are not exactly liquid right now. But anyway, none of this is the point. The point is' – he jabbed at the jobs pages again – 'you need work.'

Lydia pouted – a last-ditch appeal for clemency. 'But I'm not qualified for anything.'

But her father had already left the room, and Mary, who liked nothing better than a challenge, especially when it involved Lydia, had put down the review of a Tarantino film (pleasingly critical) and picked up a red pen.

* * *

Of the five girls, only Lizzy had made good on the promise they'd all exhibited to one degree or another at Meryton Grammar. She'd never veered from her desire to pursue medicine, gaining straight As in all her sciences and graduating cum laude from King's straight onto the wards at Royal Free and then back to Addenbrooke's, where she was now well-respected and highly sought after.

Compare that to Jane, who had a first-class honours in Law, but had managed barely two months at the Bar. It was, as Bingley had pointed out at the time, a job entirely unsuited to someone who saw the best in everyone, and who abhorred all conflict to the point of self-deceit. She had worked briefly for the NSPCC, before falling pregnant with Grace and happily abandoning the commute for Gymboree and Singalong Tots in the village hall. Now she did two days a week at Citizens Advice Bureau, a voluntary job that added nothing to the coffers and tested her limits of patience, but, as she told Wickham whenever he complained, if she could help just a tiny bit, it was worth it, wasn't it?

Kitty didn't think so, but as she had veered from ski season to Ibiza and back again, only settling on hairdressing when she, too, fell pregnant, she could hardly throw stones. Besides, Meryton had its advantages, in terms of babysitting at least. Not that Lydia could see any of them right now. Nor her own. She had, of course, planned on a long and lucrative career in television, but after the untimely, and admittedly explicit, end to her reality TV appearance, the endorsement work she'd anticipated had not been forthcoming. She'd played a season of panto in Margate and had a brief stint on a shopping channel (graveyard shift – she lasted three days), but the modelling work she'd been living on until then had dried up quicker than spilt milk in a heatwave. The only bonus was that she'd used a stage name to enter, so that if anyone recognised her, she could swiftly disavow them by producing her driving licence. Not that that had happened in years. Largely because she had moved to Paris, where the French were either above franchised Channel 5 reality shows or were generally more laissez-faire about anything sexual.

'Pilkins Fish are looking for an assistant,' Mary said, biro poised.

Lydia rolled her eyes. 'Oh, God, no. Imagine the smell. And you have to wear a white coat. White drains me.'

Mary, to her credit, did not contest this, merely moved on to the next advertisement. 'Waitrose in Saffron Walden.'

'Tabards? Fuck no.'

'Cleaner at Meryton Grammar. Five mornings a week.'

'Jesus Christ.' Lydia shivered, both at the humiliation of having to skivvy at their alma mater, and the thought of getting up before seven. 'Can't we just look on Indeed?' she continued. 'I mean, who advertises in papers anymore? Saddoes and hasbeens, that's who.'

Mary frowned. 'You're banned from the laptop,' she pointed out. 'You could use your phone, only Dad's turned the Wi-Fi off and I don't suppose you have the data.'

Lydia bristled at the insult, before conceding that this was, sadly, true. 'Fine,' she sighed. 'What else?'

'No,' Mary said, scanning the pages. 'No, no and no.'

'What?' demanded Lydia. 'At least let me be the judge.'

'They're all graduate jobs,' Mary replied. 'And you haven't even been to university.'

Lydia bristled. 'I could have, though,' she protested. 'I mean, I had the grades.'

This was true, and an irritant to Mary who felt that the just deserts for someone with Lydia's disregard for revision, for tests, for education in general, should be abject failure, and a dance card of life-chances as empty as Mary's was socially. Instead, Lydia had notched up three Bs at A level, an insult when one considered how hard Mary had had to work for her A, two Bs and a C (a C she had appealed against, convinced of marking malice or slapdashery, to no avail). At least Kitty had had the decency to achieve exactly what she deserved: Ds at every level.

'Yes, well, you took more exams,' placated Mrs Bennet, who was still of the opinion that quantity very much trumped quality when it came to most things. 'So you won.'

But try as she might, it would remain a considerable fly in Mary's ointment throughout her time at the University of Hertfordshire, and for the almost two decades since. It was, then, to both sisters' relief that the doorbell went, and Lydia, despite still being dressed for bed (albeit at a boutique hotel), ran to answer it.

'That had better not be more shopping!' her father called from the study.

Lydia stared at the caller. 'It's not,' she replied.

At least, it didn't seem so. Because, while it was, indeed, Denny in front of her, instead of a parcel, he was proffering an armpit.

'Smell me,' he said. 'Go on.'

To be fair, Lydia had had stranger requests, and hesitated for only a second before pressing her nose against his shirt. 'Linen fresh.' She nodded with appreciation, sniffing again. 'With a hint of Lynx. Nice. If a bit adolescent.'

'Thanks.' Denny smiled, a dimple appearing in his left cheek. Lydia was a sucker for dimples – had attempted to fashion her own with a pencil and perseverance at one point – and had to try very hard to drag her eyes away. 'I appreciate the honesty,' Denny went on. 'Both times. When I get a pay rise that comes close to Eau Sauvage, I'll let you know.'

'Too obvious.' She let a smile dimple her left cheek. 'Plus Johnny Depp's a knob. It's all about Santal 33 these days, don't you know.'

Denny raised an eyebrow. 'I do not, but I'll make a note for my butler.'

His voice snapped with sarcasm, but was he peeved, or flirting? Not that it mattered, it was just nice to know. 'I haven't seen you for a bit,' Lydia tried.

Denny tilted his head, his greying hair falling across his face, a look that sent him from weirdly cute to absolutely shaggable. 'Did you miss me?'

Flirting then. Definitely. Lydia had to stop herself loosening the robe to better suggest cleavage. 'Only because I've a load of parcels for collection. Or I will have, when I pack them.'

'Buyers' remorse?' Denny asked.

'Buyers' skintness,' Lydia admitted.

Denny nodded. 'Been there. If you're looking for a job, there might be something at the depot.'

'At Royal Mail?' Lydia screwed up her face. 'God, no. Do I look that desperate?'

Denny pulled a face. 'None taken. And actually, yes.'

Fuck. But also fuck him. Lydia opened her mouth to tell Denny exactly that, but by the time she'd peeled her eyes away from the dimple, the dip of his collarbone, and the silver St Christopher pendant that rested on it, and stopped wondering whether and how much he trimmed his pubic hair, Denny had carried on chatting.

'I was on annual leave, since you asked. Went to Scotland.

Walking, you know? Clears the lungs. And the head.'

Lydia did not know, but found herself very much wanting to know, a state she recognised as fatal, particularly given her dislike of outdoor clothing and the very concept of bothys.

'And I've family up there. Edinburgh.'

God, she bloody loved Edinburgh though. Had once got so drunk in Bannerman's on the opening night of the Fringe she woke up in the bed of a TV comedian and didn't leave for three weeks, when his American girlfriend surprised him with a visit, and found Lydia giving him head while he watched videos of his own Channel 4 appearances.

Right, that was it. Cut it off at the source. 'Well, thanks for...' Fuck. What could she thank him for?

'The lively repartee? The on-pointe outfit?' Denny paused. 'The hot body?'

Denny's eyes were on Lydia's, and did not even blink. She felt her insides shimmer, the gusset of her linen pyjama bottoms get slick.

Fuck. She had to stop this. If nothing else, she wanted to return the sodding pyjamas and lady juice probably voided the terms. 'If you haven't actually got any post, I should go,' she said, in as Mary a manner as she could muster. Then slipped into Lydia again. 'Unless it's another credit card bill for my dad, in which case, is it illegal to bin it? I'm already persona non grata as it is.'

Denny frowned. 'Understood,' he said. 'And no.' He leafed through a sheaf of envelopes. 'Gas for your dad. Conservatory brochure for one Hester Bennet. And a catalogue from Lovehoney. That's yours.'

Lydia's face pinked, but she wasn't letting him win. 'Well, if men weren't such a let-down.' And she snatched the catalogue and slammed the door before her face could give away what she'd really felt when she'd stuck her nose into Denny's armpit, when he'd mentioned Lovehoney, when his eyes had bored into hers – desire. Pure desire, hot and wild.

A desire that only sharpened when, five minutes later, her phone pinged:

'£230 a bottle? I'd have to run Royal fecking Mail for that.'

'should have stuck to music' Lydia replied. Then, as an afterthought, added an 'x'.

It took Lydia less than an hour to slip into her Dad's old office, turn on the Wi-Fi, log on to Facebook, and search through the eleven Denny Lennoxes to find her one— No. Not *her* one. Just the one who lived in Meryton. Or so she tried to tell herself, as she clicked on his profile picture and felt the swoop of disappointment on finding that the cover photo featured a skinny, if short, woman with a neat French bob and that attractive Madonna-gap that she and Kitty had once tried to manufacture by wedging increasingly wide strips of cardboard between their front teeth.

She was almost glad when her father realised her subterfuge, stormed into his study, and pulled the plug from the router.

★ ★ ★

Like any family, the Bennets took idiosyncratic approaches to social media, some more successful than others. Mrs Bennet's sole account (Facebook) was a source of endless mirth or embarrassment, depending on your empathic capacity, it largely consisting of a string of messages to friends that she still hadn't realised were public, and complaints about supermarkets. Like their father, Jane and Lizzy mostly avoided it, Jane's presence on Instagram being purely to monitor Grace's account (or at least, the one she knew about). Kitty's profiles were a whirligig of selfies, at increasingly flattering angles, through increasingly flattering filters. Lydia's pictures were, if more naturally posed, entirely chaotic, portraying her in varying states of non-sobriety, in very little clothing. Her 'friends' list was also notable for its reliance on the company of strangers, the bulk of her IRL acquaintances having blocked her at one point or another, Lydia having slept with their husband/partner/BFF's partner, or, in one case, their father. Her lack of access, then, should have been freeing, but as days progressed, the frustration spilled into indignation, which in turn boiled over into her actually getting a job, albeit temping as a receptionist at the dog food factory on the Royston road. With her first pay packet, she bought herself a 12GB bundle of data, and, installed on the mustard chaise (a mistake, upholstery wise, but time had been kind and faded it from Colman's yellow to a French muddy brown), began her stalking in earnest.

So, Denny Lennox had a girlfriend – one Juniper Weeks. Or at least he had done two years ago, when he had last accessed the account. Whatever their status (which was, Lydia kept telling herself, no business of hers), and despite her aggressively 'look at me' name, Juniper was undeniably hot. What was worse, though, was that she looked *interesting*. See here, Juniper laughing behind the *Guardian* on a Saturday morning, light filtering prettily though the jar of homemade (natch) marmalade; see Juniper reading Sartre (and probably bloody understanding it) on a punt (for fuck's sake); see her caught candidly, pulling on wellingtons – probably to go and dance in bloody puddles, or make snow angels, or rescue a bear. Okay, not a bear, but something more thrilling than Lydia might manage. 'Oh, God,' she thought loudly. 'Am I boring?'

'I wish,' said Mrs Bennet, who had apparated in the manner of Mary, and was suddenly very *there*, holding a glass of orange squash and a bottle of pills. 'Now, have you seen Bridget? It's time for her tablet, because if I have to listen to one more monologue about poultry I will not be answerable for my actions.'

It was an empty threat – Mrs Bennet doted on Bridget as much as she had doted on her own daughters, even Lydia – but Lydia sent her garden-ward anyway (she had seen her niece through the leaded glass of the drawing-room window, flinging herself around the trampoline wearing a crash hat and swimming goggles) and settled back into her stalking— No, not *stalking*, 'information gathering', which, she told herself, is what any decent researcher would do, when faced with someone they had absolutely no intention of sleeping with. Oh, look! Six-year-old Denny with a gap in his teeth, and a cowlick. Adorable! Now, what about holiday shots… preferably topless.

★ ★ ★

'Hello, Lydia.'

Lydia, who had just been trying to enlarge a picture involving Speedos, jumped. 'For fuck's sake, Mary, can you not just… knock, or warn me?'

Mary, who had actually been humming the first violin solo from Pachelbel's Canon as she stomped down the now-entirely-alphabetised library corridor, ignored her. 'What are you doing? Is that porn? Or are you on Bumble?'

Lydia pinked. 'Fuck off. No.' Hang on a minute. 'What do you know about porn? Or Bumble for that matter?'

Mary's face gave nothing away, but her usual blunt enunciation betrayed a slight stammer. 'I— That is, I know *something*.'

'Mary Bennet, you dark horse!' Lydia grinned, unfolded her legs, and patted the space next to her. 'Tell me everything. Now.'

Until recently, there was little to tell, as Mary's activities on the internet had been limited to Tumblr, Pinterest, and a Mastodon silo for fantasy fans, plus she was the password holder for a now-defunct Rupert Grint stan account. However, since New Year and all the resolution hoohah (and Mr Bennet's threat of selling up, however empty) she had decided to broaden her education, her relationships, and, perhaps, her living arrangements, and had signed up to several dating sites.

'I finished Hinge,' she said, with the air of someone who had finally unclogged a toilet, or removed a plug of hair from the drain. 'And Bumble.'

'What do you mean, you "finished" it?'

'I swiped left on everyone.'

Lydia frowned. 'You swiped left on the whole of Hinge?'

Mary nodded. 'Within ten miles. With a postgraduate degree. Who doesn't own a cat or a dog, or a corduroy sofa—'

'What?'

'The texture is upsetting,' Mary explained, then went on. 'Or who takes selfies in a toilet. Or their car. Or anyone else's car.'

'Jesus—'

'Or who smokes,' continued Mary, who wasn't nearly finished. 'Or uses drugs. Or misuses apostrophes or semicolons. Or uses "LOL" at all. Or says they went to the "University of Life", which isn't a place, or that they're "comfortable in their own skin"—'

'Fair—'

'Or who actively wants children, or actively doesn't want children—'

'So, child ambivalent?'

Mary nodded sagely. 'And who didn't go to Meryton Grammar.' She smiled, finished at last.

'And that left?'

'About twenty people.'

'And they were?'

Mary considered this. 'Unsuitable.'

'Right.' This was going to be more difficult than Lydia had imagined. 'Give me your phone.'

Mary, wisely cagey about the prospect of this, having been fleeced by her sisters on myriad occasions, clutched it to her buttoned-up cardigan. 'What for?'

Lydia looked genuinely put out. 'Because I'm going to help you,' she said.

Mary wasn't the best at reading people, an issue that had landed her in mishaps and spats on several occasions, but something in Lydia's expression — no smirk, no set jaw, no fingers surreptitiously crossed underneath her thighs — suggested she actually meant it. Mary handed the phone over, and Lydia opened up Bumble, adjusted Mary's parameters to be slightly less oppressive, and awaited an influx of princes.

What she got, of course, was frogs — a plague of them.

'Jesus Christ on a penny farthing,' she said. 'We're doomed.'

Aside from a brief stint on Tinder in her twenties when she and Kitty had signed up for the 'likes', Lydia had managed to avoid dating apps, even for hook-ups, relying on her tried and trusted method of getting drunk somewhere public in a corset top. So to stumble upon the array of men on offer to women approaching middle-age, and living in rural East Anglia, was like lifting up a rock in the garden and watching bugs scuttle.

'Why are so many called Terry?' she wondered aloud. 'Why can't they spell "holiday"?'

'Or rotate a photo?' added Mary.

'Or just not be cunts?'

Mary flinched at the c-word, but had to admit, given the heft of evidence set before her, that her sister was right.

'This one might be okay.' Lydia squinted at the screen. 'Oh, wait, no. He's not wearing socks. Or *is* wearing trainer socks. Which is worse.'

Ten minutes, and a hundred and twenty-seven profiles later, Lydia was forced to concede that they were playing a long game. 'This is good,' she decided. 'It gives us time.'

'Time for what?' Mary asked, rightly hesitant.

Lydia held up Mary's own profile, which, if one was being generous, was at least accurate, and if one was being honest, rendered her about as appealing as a young Margaret Thatcher. 'You're going to get a makeover,' she said. 'And then, we're going to get you a man. Or a woman.'

'A man,' said Mary, decisively. 'Unless it's Emma Watson.'

Lydia, who was rather enjoying being helpful for once, bit down the obvious insult. Instead, she nudged her sister. 'I don't think Emma Watson is going to be on Bumble. In Hertfordshire. Looking for a forty-one-year-old children's librarian. But, good to aim high.'

★ ★ ★

The makeover phase had lasted for several years in the Bennet household. Seeded by readings of a battered Ladybird *Cinderella*, and then fed and watered by a DVD of *She's All That* and TV repeats of *10 Years Younger*, *The Swan*, and Mrs Bennet's favourite (and Mr Bennet's nemesis), *How To Look Good Naked*, Kitty and Lydia, and even, occasionally, Lizzy and Jane, had spent many rainy Sundays restyling each other's hair and wardrobe, and perfecting the invisible make-up look (which requires, as all women know, more time and product than the very visible kind) before presenting each other with a loud 'ta-da!' to their ecstatic mother, tolerant father, and an entirely indifferent Mary.

Even at the tender age of eleven, Mary knew the pursuit of beauty to be both a fool's errand and beyond her reach, and so declared it facile and shallow, thus alleviating herself of considerable burden and cost, as well as the humiliation of feigned praise from her mother, whom, she had discovered from an overheard telephone conversation with Bad Karen, thought of her as the 'plain' one. However, having clicked a few preferences on Bumble in order to peruse her competition, it was clear she needed to do... something. Her hair, cut into the same shapeless lob since her twenties, hung listlessly when down, and so was most often clipped back in the manner of a wartime four year old. Her clothes... well, they fit her, but were designed for a different decade, and often gender, and not in a fashion-forward androgynous way, more in a 'there was an emergency so I'm having to wear my dad's cast-offs' way, as Kitty pointed out when she was summoned to Longbourn the following day.

'You just don't do yourself any favours,' she concluded. 'Not with those tits— Sorry.' She had clocked Bridget. 'Breasts.'

Bridget, who had been busily lining up her twenty-six Jellycat animals along the windowsill, looked up. 'Cows have udders,' she said ominously. 'Why don't we have udders?'

'Your aunt Mary does,' Lydia whispered, then felt a needle of guilt as it became clear that a comment meant for Kitty had filtered further afield.

'They're 32H,' said Mary. 'Nothing I can do about that.'

'Yes there is,' said Kitty. 'When did you last get fitted for a decent bra?'

It transpired that the last time Mary had got fitted for anything, or indeed shopped for clothes beyond Age Concern and the sale at Marks & Spencer, was 2004.

'Road trip!' Kitty yelled triumphantly. 'Or London. We could go to London!' Her eyes lit up as if she were suggesting a flight to Dubai, or a night at the Ritz.

'I've got a piano lesson at four,' Mary pointed out.

Kitty shrunk, as London became, yet again, a distant memory, an imagined fling. 'Cambridge then. At least we can park at Lizzy's.'

★ ★ ★

'What the blazes have you done to Mary?' Mr Bennet gawped as, several hours later, Lydia and Kitty paraded their sister through the front door, as if bringing home a trophy.

In truth, she did look like a new woman, and that woman was Zooey Deschanel meets Amélie by way of Weird Barbie, the sisters having settled on an angular dress from Cos, matched with a chunky perspex necklace, black tights to replace the

Rohan golfing trousers ('Not orange! You look like you teach art at fucking elf school!'), and Dr Martens platform brogues (Mary would not consent to anything with a heel, it being a tyranny against women, but this elevated her beyond five foot for the first time in her life). Add to this the radical haircut Kitty had delivered in Lizzy's kitchen, and the whole effect was quite astonishing.

'You look like Joan of Arc,' said her father.

'But in a good way,' prompted Lydia.

'*Is* there a good way?'

'I think she looks marvellous,' said Mrs Bennet. 'Like that funny little woman on *Sewing Bee*.'

'Esme,' said Bridget, who had once named a plush squid after her.

'Quite so,' said Colin, who had dropped in to offer Mary a lift to the lesson. 'But younger, despite the grey hair. Hair dye is full of carcinogens,' he added, looking pointedly at Lydia, whose bleach was still very much in evidence, then Kitty, who balayaged on a three-monthly basis.

'So is coleslaw,' said Bridget. 'It said so on telly.'

Colin, who had eaten the same in a sandwich not three hours ago – albeit homemade – paled.

'Ignore her,' said Kitty. 'She's trying to find reasons not to eat vegetables.'

'Shall we go?' said Colin quickly. 'Or the Hugginses will worry.'

Mary, unsure whether the sum of the reactions was overly positive or not, picked up her sheaf of sheet music, and stumbled towards the door (those soles would take some getting used to after Hush Puppies).

'Photoshoot later!' Lydia reminded her, in a tone that verged on mild threat. 'Bumble, here you come!'

'What's Bumble?' asked Colin as he ushered her out. 'I've been thinking about keeping bees you know. Although the risk of allergic reaction in someone like me is quite high.'

Mr Bennet slammed the door, pointedly, and rather too violently.

'Why she persists with those wretched lessons is a mystery,' said Mrs Bennet, to no one in particular. 'It's not as if she ever improves.'

'If she enjoys it, does it matter?' asked her husband.

She looked at him as one might look at a dog with two heads, but decided for once to ignore him. 'A shame you didn't bring Lizzy back with you,' she said instead to the girls, bustling them into the kitchen. 'Colin could be the tonic she needs. So very sensible.'

'Jesus Christ,' muttered her husband.

'I heard that,' Mrs Bennet snapped.

'You were meant to, dear.' He smiled, thinly. 'I wouldn't wish Colin on Liz if he were the last man alive.'

Kitty opened the fridge, picked at the cheese. 'Perhaps she'll meet someone at this dance class.'

'What dance class?' Mrs Bennet slammed the door, banishing the light and filling the room instead with her vivid presence. 'What are you talking about?'

'I...' Kitty, who had been sworn to secrecy, trailed off.

Bridget, who had been eating a flapjack at the time while challenging the twins to see who could headbutt her the hardest (and for whom secrecy was a physical impossibility), continued for her. 'She's going to dance class with Aunt Jane. For the wedding. Because Wickham's too fucking busy.'

★ ★ ★

Lizzy was indeed – against all better judgement, and despite vehement arguments with Jane delineating myriad reasons why she could not and would not, ranging from the plausible (work, childcare arrangements) to the mildly ridiculous (a dicky ankle, an intolerance of Santana, an allergy to polyester) – going to dance class. Specifically, Latin and Ballroom for Beginners (Senior), on a Tuesday night in a draughty church hall off Mill Road in Cambridge.

'At least it's walking distance for you,' Jane reminded her. 'I have to drive eleven miles.'

Lizzy pulled a face as they plodded down Gwydir Street in the drizzle. 'Yes, and you signed on for this, so suck it up, sis.'

Jane, who had conveniently forgotten that part, smarting as she still was that George had somehow wriggled out of attending, despite it being his idea, made a non-committal grunt.

'How is he, anyway?' asked Lizzy, more out of habit than actual interest, knowing as she did that the 'kidnapped' or 'abandoned me' she hoped for was woefully unlikely.

Jane shrugged. 'Feeling sorry for himself, actually,' she admitted. 'I think I've hurt his feelings.'

'How? Did you tell him Lydia noticed the combover?'

'Oh, ha ha. No. I paid Timon's school fees.'

Lizzy came to an abrupt halt outside number forty-two and grasped Jane's arm. 'You did what?'

Jane stared at her sister's gloved hand on the sleeve of her Whistles coat, pulled pointedly away. 'There was a letter from school,' she said, walking purposefully the last few yards to the hall. 'What else was I meant to do? He's weeks away from GCSEs.'

'Oh, I don't know,' snapped Lizzy, catching up with her. 'Tell Wickham to pay?'

It wasn't meant as an actual question but Jane chose to answer it. 'He's had cashflow problems. Silly Calypso, I think. It's the least I can do. Not that he seems to appreciate it.'

Actually he had been vaguely grateful, once he'd exhausted his rant about the school's and his son's myriad failings ('Boarding was supposed to toughen him up. If anything it's made him more fey than ever. He's completely weird.') and once she'd apologised several times. A gratitude he'd shown by giving her two orgasms within five minutes, an anatomical first. Now, though, he was using the excuse of needing to clock in some overtime at the agency to avoid dance, which she could hardly deny him, could she?

'Oh look, we're here,' she said, signalling the end of that conversation, and the start of an hour and a half of what Lizzy knew would be torture.

The class was run in an airless room that had that determined Scout-hut smell of bleach and braised meat, by a slender woman of indeterminate age wearing a leotard, swing skirt, and a set of gold character shoes of the kind the girls (bar Mary, obviously) had once begged Mrs Bennet for during a brief but intense *Strictly* phase. As they clumsily one-two-three'd across the worn parquet, Lizzy glanced around the hall and noted that several of the other 'ladies' (only 'gentlemen' and 'ladies' danced, apparently; God forbid anyone non-binary should choose to take up the foxtrot) were wearing the same combination, in stark contrast to her 'uniform' of ankle-cropped culottes (anything longer risked trailing in God knows what in the hospital toilets) and ageing New Balance 327s, complete with a smear of something that might be blood, faeces, or cupcake mix.

'Ow!' protested Jane, and not for the first time, as one of them galumphed onto her brand-new jazz shoes.

'You're more than welcome to lead,' Lizzy replied.

'You know I can't do that,' said Jane. 'The whole point is that George will be leading.'

'I don't see how,' Lizzy pointed out, 'if he won't even come to lessons.'

'Oh he can already dance,' Jane lamented. 'School, I think. Or some university society. This is all for my benefit.'

Lizzy rolled her eyes over Jane's shoulder, accidentally catching the eye of another awkward waltzer – a bearded man in a Breton top and round tortoiseshell glasses (so very try-hard), dancing with someone clearly young enough to be his daughter. He seemed to 'tut' back at her — a gesture of empathy? In any case, Lizzy ignored him — the dirty old perv — and tried to focus again on her feet.

'"Every savage can dance",' she said, as they executed a less-than-professional fleckerl past the refreshments hatch.

'Pardon?' Jane asked.

'Fitz used to say it, remember? To justify why he wouldn't even mosh at concerts. As if it would be lowering himself.'

'He was a terrible snob,' Jane pointed out, quite fairly.

'He was,' agreed Lizzy, though her tone was less condemning than wistful.

At that, the music (not, thankfully, a clunking piano, but a bluetooth speaker booming out the godawful 'Kiss from a Rose', so swings and roundabouts on that front) came to an end and Gloria (of the gold shoes) clapped her hands in the air in a gesture so affected Lizzy actually emitted a scoff.

Jane elbowed her.

'Sorry,' she muttered. 'What's she on about?'

'Wife swap,' sighed Jane. 'And yes she actually said that. I suppose we just shuffle round one?'

As Jane stepped gracefully towards an elderly gentleman in a slightly-too-shiny suit, Lizzy scanned frantically — memories of country-dancing trauma as fresh now as they were when she had to partner Peter 'smells of stew' Foster aged six — to find a blur of blue-and-white stripes in front of her. She looked up into a beard and hipster glasses and winced.

'God, is it that bad?'

'I just… you're very tall, aren't you? Sorry, I know that's rude to comment on people's height or weight or whatever. It's only' — she peered desperately for someone — anyone — other than cradle-snatcher man, but everyone was paired up — 'that I'm not. Tall, I mean.' God, shut up, woman!

'I can stoop?' he offered.

She went to snap at him, but when she looked up, he seemed serious.

'My daughter's not much taller,' he added, nodding towards the girl he'd been dancing with previously. 'So I'm used to it. Though she would say it doesn't show in my dancing.'

'Your daughter!' Lizzy blurted. Why was that a relief? Why did she care? He was still… actually, no, he wasn't *still* anything, and she should shut up and dance.

His hands on her back were massive, and she realised it was the first time any man, aside from her father, whose grip was, at best, vague, had held her so closely since Fitz.

'She's getting married,' he went on. 'Wants me to do some bloody ridiculous father-daughter thing. All the rage these days, she says. TikTok or something. And, well, I could hardly say no, could I?'

'I suppose not.' Lizzy thought of Milo and Arden, and the absurd lengths to which she would probably go – already did go – to placate them.

'I'm Saul, by the way. Like the Bible.' This, clearly, a practised line. But useful, she had to admit.

'Lizzy. Like, well, nothing,' she replied, then promptly trod on his foot. 'God, sorry. I was leading before.'

'Your girlfriend?' He nodded towards Jane, who was already resembling an accomplished celebrity, mindfully guided by Anton Du Beke. Clearly Lizzy had been holding her back.

She snorted. 'My sister! I'm not—' Did it matter? Who cared anyway? She segued. 'She's getting married,' she explained. 'Again. But her fiancé is…' She paused. Actually, fuck it. 'He's a bit of a dick, so here I am.'

'We have much in common, then. Luella's fiancé is a colossal knob – actually thinks Bitcoin is genius – but if I tell her this, it'll be me that gets dumped.'

'What does her mum say?' She wasn't fishing, really she wasn't. It was a genuine question.

'If she were around she would say, "Jesus Christ, can't we knock him off?" But she died, five years ago. So Luella's pretty much it.'

'I...' Lizzy felt a swerve of something come over her – that tenderness when Milo's bottom lip would quaver, or Arden's eyes fill with tears. 'I'm sorry,' she managed.

She felt his shoulders shrug up and down, felt too (but resisted) the urge to squeeze them. Then promptly trod on his foot again. 'Bollocks. Sorry!'

But he laughed, shook his head. 'At least you make me look half-decent.'

And there it was again, that... burgeoning, not quite maternal, but something atavistic perhaps – an empathy for bereft men. Pathetic. And when Gloria clapped her hands again, Lizzy thanked Saul's feet, then hurried back to Jane with the frantic passion of a lost child.

Dear Darcy, she began later that night.

Dance class was far worse than I imagined. They are all absolute savages with improbable shoes. You would hate it. I—

She paused. Had she hated it? She certainly hated how she had felt when Saul had nodded to her as they left, and she had smiled tightly, then evaded twenty questions from Jane. But those hands...

No.

I hated it, she wrote. *Worst hour and a half of my life. Well, since you chose to leave me.*

APRIL

Sister Act
Jane, Lizzy, Mary, Kitty, Lydia

~Jane Bingley
@**Kitty** have you decided what you're doing for your 40th?
10:37

~Kitty Miller
Botox and Profhilo.
10:40

~Jane Bingley
I'm serious.
10:40

~Kitty Miller
So am I. Stacey booked me in for the Saturday morning. Do you want anything? There's a discount if she does all of us. Mum's having filler and IPL on her foo-foo.
10:41

~Lydia Bennet
stop frittering our inheritance on mum's vag. it's like putting

fairy lights up in the arctic – who even gets to see it?
10:41

~Kitty Miller
@**Lydia** Dad? Also pot kettle re: inheritance. Anyway let me know by tomorrow.
10:42

~Jane Bingley
Please cease and desist regarding Mum. I can't believe you roped her into this. I'm calling a meeting. Tomorrow. 7pm at Netherfield. All sisters to be present. @**Lizzy** Grace can sit for the twins if you need to bring them. She owes me a favour.
10:44

~Lydia Bennet
seriously? you're calling a meeting about mum's foo-foo?
10:45

~Jane Bingley
No. That discussion has ended. This is about Kitty's birthday, and another matter I need to discuss with you all.
10:45

~Lydia Bennet
omg have you and wickham split?
10:45

~Lydia Bennet
???
10:45

* * *

Justice for Jane
Lizzy, Kitty, Lydia, Mary

Lydia added Lizzy Darcy-Bennet to the group.

~Lydia Bennet
is this it? do you think it's all over? her and wickham? what do you suppose he's done?
10:47

~Kitty Miller
I doubt it. It'll be about flowers or cakes or table arrangements or something else no one gives an actual about.
10:47

~Lizzy Darcy-Bennet
It isn't.
10:50

Lizzy Darcy-Bennet left the group.<MS/>

* * *

To do:
- ~~Socrates – worms~~
- Surrogacy
- Timon – shoes

Though Jane was only serving non-alcoholic cocktails and a few biscuits for nibbles, and only to family, by seven the table at Netherfield was set as if for high tea at Claridges – an assortment of floral shortbreads (lavender, rose, geranium) alongside an arrangement of early anemones from the garden (garish, but Grace had once loved them, and she found she could not bring herself to dig them up). It was perfect. Quite perfect. But as the clock struck, and she heard Lizzy pull up on the drive (Kitty and Lydia would be predictably late) she had to steel herself, clutch the back of an Ercol chair in the hallway before opening the door.

It wasn't all over of course – her and Wickham. In fact, it was nothing to do with the wedding at all, but everything to do with the marriage and whether or not one of her sisters might help it bear fruit in the shape of a baby.

Kitty was the first to explode. 'Surrogacy? From one of us? Are you an actual madwoman?'

Jane's insides, already eelish, slip-slid around more. 'I've talked it over with Lizzy.' She glanced at her sister, but if she hoped for a smile of encouragement, she was left wanting; there was, at best, resignation. 'The thing is, going through official channels is prohibitively time-consuming and, well, we would be unlikely to make it to the top of anyone's list, given our age and the fact we both have children already.'

'So, adopt.' Kitty stated the obvious.

'George isn't keen,' admitted Jane. 'He says you can't be sure what you're getting, genetics-wise. He's worried they could be… you know, unstable or something. Or— or have a massive head.'

Lydia snorted. 'Seriously?' Lizzy shot her a look, which she ignored. 'So what's the plan then? The full *Handmaid's Tale*? He services one of us while you stand there judging—'

'Lydia!' Lizzy snapped. 'Don't.'

'But—'

'Listen to your sister,' said Lizzy. 'For once.'

Kitty frowned. 'So his sperm and one of our eggs then?'

'Oh. My. God.' Lydia made a vomit noise.

Jane fanned herself, to no avail. 'Yes. Sort of. Lizzy is going to deal with that sort of thing. The medical aspect. I just… I wanted to ask if either of you might be willing?'

Kitty frowned. 'Either of us? What, me and Lyds?'
Jane nodded.
'What about Liz? What about Mary?'
Jane, at a loss, beseeched her sister say something.
'I'm too old,' offered Lizzy. 'And Mary—'
'That would literally be the virgin birth,' Kitty scoffed. 'Nothing goes in, nothing comes out.'
'That's Willy Wonka's chocolate factory,' pointed out Lydia.
'Oh God. The imagery.' Kitty grimaced.
'I *am* here,' Mary pointed out. 'But… I have an inhospitable womb. Lizzy already checked.'
'What? You would have done it?' Lydia looked incredulous.
Mary shrugged. 'Nothing else to do.'
Lydia frowned. 'Dating not going well then?'
'What dating?' asked Lizzy.
'Nothing,' replied Mary and Lydia in unison – a rare moment of agreement.
Jane, who felt she had lost the room before they'd even begun, steeled herself. 'Can we get back to the subject?'
'Well don't look at me.' Kitty held up her hands. 'My vagina was a war zone after Bridget. I've got more stitches down there than a needlework sampler.'
'Please don't exaggerate,' said Lizzy.
Kitty rounded on her. 'You had a C-section, so you do not get to comment on the state of my vag!'
Lizzy was unmoved. 'I spend a large proportion of my working day staring at vaginas. I can assure you, yours is not even close to a "war zone", which, by the way, is fairly offensive to several countries suffering right now. You could have ripped your entire perineum. You could have prolapsed—'
'You're not exactly selling it,' blurted Lydia.
'Like you'd offer,' said Kitty.
Lydia bristled. 'I might.' She wouldn't.

'Is she even allowed?' asked Mary.

Lydia slammed down the can of Diet Coke she'd been clinging to. 'What's that supposed to mean? Because, what? I've shagged a lot?'

As ever, Mary did not read the 'stop' signal. 'That. And you've had two abortions.'

'I—'

'And then there's the history of drug abuse.'

'But—'

'And the alcohol.'

'I haven't had sex, drugs or one fucking drink since New Year!' Lydia railed.

'And you're handling that so well.' Kitty grinned.

'Fuck off.'

Kitty rolled her eyes. 'Jokes. Anyway, as if you'd say yes. You don't do anything unless there's something in it for you. Actually, scratch that, unless it's solely for your benefit.'

No one said anything for a second, the room filling with a frantic kind of static.

It was Lydia, in the end, who punctured it. Having been slapped with a painful truth, and being sober enough for once to be contrite about it rather than argue, she shook her hair, took a sip of her drink, and said, 'That was the old Lydia. I'm different now. I've... grown up.'

Still no one else said anything.

Fine. Well, she'd prove it then. 'Ask me,' she dared Jane. 'Go on. Ask me again.'

'I...' Jane looked at Lizzy for guidance, but she seemed fixated on a stain on the travertine floor tiles. She was on her own, it seemed. And, yes, she'd hoped it would be Kitty, who at least had a track record of carrying a pregnancy to term, but beggars and all that. And perhaps... Yes! This wasn't just about Jane asking a selfless favour of someone. This was doing Lydia one too. Giving her purpose. An understanding of the meaning of life. A chance to share in something miraculous. She seized on that bright diamond of hope. 'Would you?' she asked.

Lydia took a breath. 'I might,' she said. 'I might.'

It was equivocal – the 'yes' – of course it was. And rightly so. There was a lot for both of them to think about, Jane told herself as she slipped between the sheets (five hundred thread count, a new thing; George said any less risked hives) later that night. And she'd need to discuss it with George more – the how's and the when's. And with Lizzy, who had agreed to handle the… whatever it was called – not a turkey baster, exactly, but not dissimilar, she'd said. Jane hadn't thought about it too hard, or the implications became too gruesome. And as for telling Grace… well, anyway it was all a long way off. Nine months off, ironically, at least. Or was that actually irony? She could never remember, and that Alanis Morissette song only confused things. Whichever, that hump was over for now, and she could get on with the wedding itself, which of course George thought was taking up far too much headspace, but as she'd told him, she liked that – being occupied. Having a lot to think about. Because if she stopped for a second, looked around, took it all in, everything that had happened since— No. She just couldn't do it. Best not to dwell. For once, Lydia was a decent role model: go in swinging, and never look back.

And with that, she turned off the original Anglepoise lamp, turned her back to the expanse where Charley would once have been, and fell swiftly and deeply asleep.

★ ★ ★

Lydia, on the other hand, lay rigid on her single bed, staring up at the white eyes and gleaming teeth of Katy Perry, as if the singer might impart some wisdom in the manner of a scantily clad deity. What the fuck had she done? A baby? She didn't even like babies. Not really. Such loud, sticky things, and so needy, so entirely reliant on someone else, which was the ultimate ick. Children were fine. Delightful, even, at times. Bridget, for example, was fascinating, and the twins, hilarious, but babies? No thank you. Obviously she wasn't required to do anything with the baby itself, just incubate it, which, again, what the fuck? She'd be ruining her body – stretch marks, haemorrhoids, a belly that would never look good in a bikini again, not without surgery, and that's before you even got near the undercarriage. Lizzy might dismiss it, but Lydia was the one who'd dealt with Kitty's messages after Bridget. 'Like a kebab dropped on the pavement,' she'd called it. 'I can't walk without pissing myself.' She'd sworn she'd never have sex again, and while that turned out to be patently untrue, was it ever really as good? I mean, how much could one feel when one had pushed out something the size of Bridget, whose head was still disproportionately large, so much so that she'd been known as 'the swede' for years, until someone had to explain to Dave that it referred to the vegetable, not the country, and it was decided it was probably time to retire the joke.

Then there was Wickham. What was she thinking? That this would endear her to him? That he'd be indebted forever and thus do her bidding? What bidding, for God's sake? No, she was so totally over him – a state Jane should be chasing, rather than… this.

Although, perhaps that was the key to it all: go back to Plan A, i.e. break up the couple, ergo the whole thing becomes moot, ergo she won't have to face letting Jane down. Was it 'ergo'? It always sounded intelligent, so she'd used it liberally over the years, scattering it about conversation with the same blitheness with which she smoked and swore. She should probably look it up. In fact she might google it now. After she'd checked 'pregnancy side effects' and 'worst birth stories' and 'what does selfless really mean?'.

★ ★ ★

Twenty minutes and several rabbit holes (and other holes) later, and Lydia might be slightly wiser, but was no more convinced of the right thing to do in this situation. She clicked open her phone messages, opened up Denny's thread.

'do you think i'm selfish?' she wrote. 'be honest'

Three dots appeared quickly. Then, 'It's one in the morning, and I have to be at work at five, so on that alone, I'd say yes. But what's up?'

Fuck. 'nothing' she replied. 'sorry to wake you'

Except, it was hardly her fault, was it? I mean, who kept their phone on all night unless they were in love or asking for trouble? 'you should turn off notifications' she added. 'ergo you won't get woken' (She'd been right all along.)

'Or you could stop (selfishly) texting. Ergo I won't wake up.😉'

Winkies usually gave her the ick (along with tongue-out — she might not have a degree, and she might like sex a little too much for her own good, but she wasn't a salivating moron), but this time she found herself smiling. 'i'm stopping' she wrote.

'I can tell' Denny wrote back.

Now, usually, Lydia would have continued this conversation merrily until it descended into sexting, and then, around three in the morning, FaceTime masturbation or an IRL booty call. But this was New Lydia, remember, and she wasn't into Denny that way, nor anybody. So she put her phone down on her bedside table (on top of a Hello Kitty sticker), went back to staring at Katy, and felt only minor deflation when Denny didn't reply again either.

As for the Jane thing, she would do what she always did when she'd agreed to something on the spur of the moment (climbing Snowdon, a silent retreat in a monastery, a threesome with a Championship footballer and his brother) and then, in the cold light of the early hours, realised she didn't actually fancy it that much after all: strenuous denial, and if that failed, crying.

* * *

If Mrs Bennet wondered why her youngest had ditched a third temping job in as many weeks, she did not articulate it beyond, 'Buck up, Lydia, dear, it'll give you wrinkles.' She had, thankfully, been kept firmly out of the loop as regards surrogacy (on Jane's insistence, not because her mother might be against it, but because the last thing Jane needed was the entirety of Meryton reviving discussion of her hysterectomy, or demanding details on the extraction of Wickham's sperm).

Besides, Mrs Bennet had a plethora of other things with which to occupy herself: the new vet, her husband's increasingly erratic bowel habits, and an answerphone message from Charley's irritating sister, asking if she might 'drop in' one Sunday.

'Drop in?' Mr Bennet protested. 'From Gloucestershire?'

She had admonished him out of habit, but in truth his ominous tone was warranted. Caroline Bingley-Hicks was trying at the best of times, and this, Mrs Bennet suspected, was not even close to anything best. Caroline had barely tolerated Jane marrying her beloved younger brother as it was, and blamed the Bennets firmly for his untimely end. ('Who,' she had wailed, 'chooses to drive to Derbyshire on New Year's Eve?' The implication being they should have decamped to her place at Daylesford; the fact they'd been making excuses not to do so on a yearly basis not cutting any mustard with her.) Now she monitored her sister-in-law's decisions with the critical eye and inherent bias of a spurned thirteen-year-old.

'Perhaps it's about Grace,' Mrs Bennet suggested to placate him. 'She is Caroline's niece, after all. And Millfield might be an idea, given the *hoohah* at school.' The hoohah being the appearance in Grace's iPhone messages of a picture of an erect penis, owner unknown. Grace's defence had mainly rested on the facts that a) she couldn't stop people sending her stuff and b) Jane shouldn't have been snooping in her phone in the first place. Unsurprisingly, neither washed with Jane. But nor did Grace's subsequent begging to move schools, preferably to one with boarding.

'Timon gets to board,' she had wailed. 'Why not me?'

She had then, apparently, played what she assumed was her trump card, i.e. that 'even Aunty Caroline agrees' – one of Caroline's long-standing complaints about Jane being her refusal to send Grace away to be educated, as was tradition with the Bingleys (her own children were at Oundle and Stamford – good, healthy distances from the Cotswolds, meaning exeats were possible but unlikely). Jane, of course, had merely doubled down and arranged an appointment with the headmistress of Meryton Grammar after the Easter break to get to the bottom of the whole penis debacle, a threat that had sent Grace into her room in a funk for a fortnight, emerging only to make toast and roll her eyes.

Mr Bennet was characteristically pragmatic. 'You don't mean that about Millfield. You'd hate it if Grace left. Besides, the whole' – he waved his hand – 'willy thing will blow over.'

Of course Wickham had said something similar, pointing out that it wasn't as if anyone had actually *done* anything. 'For God's sake,' Jane had wailed. 'What if she sent... *something* back? She's fifteen. She could end up on the Sex Offenders Register!'

'Men!' Mrs Bennet had complained when Jane had relayed this information. And complain she did again now, loudly, as she flounced from the room to busy herself with the more gratifying issue of one Mr Hindon Lydiard, MRCVS, and the latest addition to the Meryton practice, after Bob Churston's ill-timed decision to have a stroke in the middle of an episode of *Love Island All Stars*.

So far she had ascertained – through a potent mix of googling, supposition, and unashamed interrogation – that this Mr Lydiard was forty-something, single, had two young sons who lived with their mother (with whom he was on amicable terms) on the continent but visited him on occasional weekends and school holidays. He also owned a basset hound called, improbably, Dorothy, had rented the Nugents' old cottage on Frog Lane, and was partial to cheese and Branston sandwiches, milk chocolate Tunnock's wafers, and the word 'marvellous', which he used as enthusiastically and indiscriminately as Lydia employed 'fuck'. Most importantly, though, what all this added up to was the fact that he was *eligible*, hence had taken precedence over both Caroline Bingley-Hicks' visit and Mr Bennet's back-end issues, a hitherto unimaginable situation.

'Of course, I suspect he's out of Mary's league,' she told Bad Karen, over chai lattes (like spicy Horlicks) and a shared slice of coffee and walnut cake at the Meryton Kettle (they had eschewed the Koffee Kup even before the mice had moved in, in what they saw as a protest against both trendy spelling and communal tables). 'Even with the makeover.'

'She looks like that funny little woman off *Sewing Bee*,' pointed out Bad Karen.

'Esme.' Mrs Bennet nodded. 'Of course, it's got her nowhere. Not a single right-swipe, she's had. And you should see some of them. I wouldn't touch them with your bargepole.'

'Makes me thankful for Laurence,' agreed Bad Karen. 'Even with the you-know-what.'

Mrs Bennet smiled through hastily gritted teeth, managing not to reveal her true feelings on Bad Karen's second husband – that the you-know-what was only the tip of a similarly limp iceberg, which she would not want to touch with anyone's bargepole, even if he were the last man on earth.

She took a sip of her chai latte. 'Pity he's not really Lydia's sort of thing,' she segued. 'It's the checked shirts. And the cords. She says it's as if he's "cos-playing a Tory". Lizzy, though. Now she'd be ideal. More tolerant, if a bit older. But decent legs, even at her age. She's taken up ballroom, you know. Quite the dancer. Oh!' – she snatched at it – 'Perhaps he could partner her! I'll suggest it to him' – she let her fertile imagination bloom – 'over Sunday lunch. When Caroline comes!'

Yes, that would soften whatever blow Mrs Bingley-Hicks was hoping to land on them. Safety in numbers, after all. And, if she invited Kitty and Bridget as well, Lizzy would appear quite the rose among thorns. Of course she'd have to keep Jane away, for everyone's benefit. Being perfect was a curse, it really was. But Lizzy was presque perfect. Presque everything in fact. And, while Jane was taken, Lizzy, like Hindon Lydiard, was so very, very *eligible*.

★ ★ ★

Lizzy, of course, had a different opinion.

'I'm not on the market,' she insisted for what felt like the umpteenth time, as she and Jane danced a passable quickstep to 'Despacito'. 'And even if I was, which I'm *not*, a vet is the last person I'd pick. Bar Colin. If I wanted someone medical, there's a mildly attractive anaesthetist who has made his availability and interest patently obvious.'

In fact, Hugh Sellers – fifty-two, divorced, baritone in the hospital operatic society – had laid his cards on the table ('Drinks. Dinner. A quickie in the sluice room. Whatever you want really.') the previous September, after a charity performance of an *HMS Pinafore* medley. Lizzy had declined his 'kind offer' with the same seething demeanour with which she slid past the furtive glances of the rotating juniors on what they called 'cougar patrol', or batted off the wandering hands of various senior oncologists.

'I just worry,' Jane tried again, 'that if you leave it too long, then you'll be… beyond all that. After a while they just stop looking, you know. Men, I mean. We become invisible.'

Lizzy, who knew that Mrs Bennet had, only last March, fended off the owner of an egg-bound canary despite their respective ages adding up to more than seven score, ignored this. 'The whole Sunday lunch thing is a farce in any case. You know Caroline is coming?'

Jane stiffened slightly in Lizzy's grip. 'I assumed that's why I'm not invited. So she can work on Mum to get this wretched prenup. I've already said I'm not doing it, but she won't let it lie. You know what Caroline's like when she gets the bit between her teeth.'

The equine metaphor was not unwarranted: an unfortunate state of dental affairs that both Mrs Bennet and Lydia had commented on several times in the past. Lizzy, however, was above that. And far more concerned with Jane's recalcitrance when it came to her financial arrangements. 'I don't see what the big problem is. It's no different to a will and you've got one of those. It makes sense for everyone involved.'

Jane tripped slightly, righted herself. 'Not for poor George it doesn't. It's like telling him I think he might murder me in my sleep. Or— or divorce me on some spurious whim and take half of— of...'

'Charley's money,' Lizzy finished for her. 'So you can see why Caroline is concerned.'

'But it isn't *his* now, is it,' Jane bristled. 'Charley's, I mean. I wish it bloody was but he's— he's gone, and pretending otherwise isn't healthy for anyone.'

'Jane...' Lizzy tried, but her sister refused to be drawn further.

The truth was, Jane *had* raised it with George, having taken advice from Charlotte – a solicitor specialising in family law (hence her own swift and uncontested divorce) – who told her it was merely a 'sensible' precaution.

'But "sensible" isn't terribly... romantic, is it?' she had replied.

'Nor is penury,' replied Charlotte.

But when she had mentioned it to George that evening over

Chateaubriand at the Chop House on King's Parade – their 'place' in Cambridge – his response had shocked her. 'Do you really think so little of me?' He laid down his knife and fork, his eyes seeming to glisten in the candlelight.

'I... No, darling.' She had clutched his hand, which had lain sullen, still for a moment, before he slipped it out to pat hers.

'Good,' he said. 'Then we don't need something so cold. So... mercenary, do we.'

The rest of the meal had passed in a pleasant haze, while the inevitable sex (Barolo always fired him up) had been especially tender and attentive, and so she had happily shut the subject in a box and pushed it to the back of a cupboard, and did not need her mother or anyone else rummaging around in there now.

'Have you spoken to Kitty?' she segued now. 'I've told her I'm happy to host but she hasn't given me an answer and I don't want her to end up down the Dragon again.'

You mean *you* don't want to, thought Lizzy – Jane having never taken to their Meryton local (all those awful horse brasses, and suspiciously sticky carpet) – but bit her tongue in favour of a non-committal grunt, and a very committed wondering as to when the awful Gloria might call 'wife swap, please' and thus end this unfortunate episode.

★ ★ ★

Aside from her aesthetics appointments, and a veto on Bridget baking a cake in the shape of Boba Fett, Kitty had done as little as possible to engage with the fact she was turning forty, or as she thought of it: the overwhelming evidence that she was hitting middle age. She had not booked a table for twelve at the Mad Hatter, as suggested by her mother, had refused Dave's suggestion of a 'dirty weekend in Brighton' (the last thing she felt like right now), and had failed to reply to any of Jane's exhortations to let her host a 'do' at Netherfield, a situation that would only highlight the gargantuan gap between her sister's version of adulthood and her own. A chasm that Dave seemed determined to widen on a daily basis by his mere existence.

'I'm sick of it!' she had wailed only yesterday evening, as Dave tried to persuade her to a gig by some sixteen-year-olds he 'had a feeling about' (having decided he should branch out into band management).

'Sick of what?' Dave swept off the pastry crumbs that had fluttered like dandruff down his Stone Roses T-shirt.

'This!' She was flailing around, Lydia-like, and knew it. But knowing it couldn't stop her. 'It's embarrassing,' she clarified. 'Traipsing down the Scout hut like we're still teenagers.'

'But it's my job, Kits,' said Dave.

'It isn't though, is it,' she ranted. 'Your job is being a postman. This is just another... whim. Like when you got all those foot spas off Mad Harry to sell on eBay, only they're still in your mum's garage.'

The foot spas, along with the microwaves that had preceded them, and the fake Air Force 1s that had come after, were a sore point; raising them was tantamount to a declaration of war.

'What do you want to be doing then?' Dave waved his Ginsters at her. 'Getting pilled up at Glitterbox still? Or is it dinner at the Ritz?'

'Yes... No. I don't know.' It wasn't Dave's fault. Or not entirely his fault. It was just... 'Everything is so small-town,' she told him. 'I hate it.'

'Well, I hate to mansplain, but Meryton *is* a town. And arguably not as large as Royston or Walden—'

'Oh, fuck off.'

Dave held up his hands (still clutching a pasty) in surrender. 'No one's forcing you to come,' he conceded.

So she hadn't. She had stayed in with Bridget, watched seven episodes of *Friends* whilst they both marinated their feet in lavender bath salts, and contemplated how she had ended up with someone so... lacking in ambition, so wretchedly content, in the first place.

They'd met at a party he was doing for a friend's thirty-fifth birthday, two years after she'd skulked back to Longbourn, overly tanned, nominally married, and with a six-month-old Bridget in tow. Back then, a night out – any night out, even in Meryton – had seemed spangled with the same glamour that had sent her and Lydia giddy at their first school disco, their first house party, their first Hooch-fuelled trip to Cinderella Rockefellers. And Dave had been one year above her at the grammar, a status that, despite time and all manner of shags, had not lost its allure. She'd asked him to play Carly Rae Jepson and he'd refused, on the grounds that a) he didn't do requests and b) 'Call Me Maybe' was criminal. She said she'd make it worth his while, and promptly yanked up her tank top to reveal her bra-less 30Cs (pregnancy had not taken the toll her mother had warned it would, largely because Bridget – a stickler even then – refused to breastfeed). Dave had played the song, and didn't regret it, not when it was greeted by a series of expletives from the bar, and an open bag of cheese and onion Golden Wonder thrown into the DJ booth. They'd been together ever since, moving into his flat in a matter of months – it was closer to the salon, she'd argued when her mother had suggested she might be rushing things, and to Bridget's nursery.

Only now, ever since he'd cleared the gutters at Longbourn and procured her an almost-convincing camo Dry Robe only a month after Carole Burghley had paraded down the high street in hers, her mother had declared him a keeper, and Kitty was the one having doubts.

So many doubts.

But if she were to raise it again, he'd only ask her the same: what *did* she want? And the problem was, she really didn't know. Just... not this. Or this but... better, maybe. Slicker, more thrilling, more... Lydia-ish. Well, until Lydia had become a teetotal bore, whose highlight of the day was *Loose Women*, for which she had jacked in another job (in a call centre) claiming the earphones might give her lice. And yet, leaving Dave seemed as impossible as moving away from Meryton. It wasn't as if she was being taunted by other options in either case. Besides, she had Bridget to think about, at least for another — she did some quick maths — ten years. She'd bide her time until then, perhaps. By which point she'd be — Jesus, fifty. At least that made forty seem less depressing, she supposed.

She pulled focus back to the now. She'd better muster something up for the birthday, hadn't she. Or it would get mustered for her, and that would almost certainly be worse. She picked up her phone and clicked open WhatsApp.

Sister Act
Jane, Lizzy, Mary, Kitty, Lydia

~Kitty Miller
Saturday night. Drinks at the Dragon. Then cabs to Labyrinth.
20:32

~Lydia Bennet
after filler? are you sure? what if you end up like shrek?
20:33

~Kitty Miller
Stacey's a professional. The thing with the Botox could have happened to anyone.
20:34

~Jane Bingley
I'll have to drop out after the pub, I'm afraid. Unless you want to switch to something at Netherfield?
20:35

~Kitty Miller
Thanks (again), but the Dragon's just easier.
20:36

Kitty Miller added Lizzy Darcy-Bennet to the group.

~Kitty Miller
Liz? Drinks at Dragon on Saturday then cabs to Labyrinth.
20:38

~Lizzy Darcy-Bennet
Definitely not Labyrinth. I don't know about the pub. I'll have to check with Delilah.
21:15

~Kitty Miller
Mum can have the twins. She's got Bridget so two more won't matter.
21:16

~Lizzy Darcy-Bennet
Says the mother of a single child.
21:17

~Mary Bennet
Can I bring someone, please?
21:17

~Lydia Bennet
OMG mary! you're alive!
21:18

~Kitty Miller
Is it Colin?
21:18

~Mary Bennet
No.
21:18

~Kitty Miller
Then yes.
21:19

~Lydia Bennet
is it a man? *@Mary* – i am coming to see you immediately
21:20

~Mary Bennet
Please don't. I am on the toilet.
21:21

~Lydia Bennet
was it the eggs? dad's been in the downstairs lav for an hour now
21:22

Lizzy Darcy-Bennet left the group.

* * *

Who, then, *was* Mary considering bringing to the Dragon?

'It *will* be Colin,' insisted Lydia, as she and Jane stared somewhat disconsolately into their second orange juice of the evening. Lydia for obvious reasons; Jane because she had offered to be designated driver to the club in Cambridge (no later than ten!) before fetching Grace from Longbourn (persuaded into babysitting so

Mr and Mrs Bennet could come to the pub). The nudes hoo-hah had, as George predicted, 'blown over' after Grace confessed that someone called Marina Pill had catfished her into the whole situation by pretending to be sixth-former Brandt Castro, who claimed to fancy her and sent the engorged proof, which in turn turned out to be an image pilfered from Marina's sister's Tinder, and belonged not to Brandt, but to a welder called Terry. Marina had been duly hauled up in front of Mrs Wilfred at Meryton Grammar, and after her 'it was just bantz' defence failed, swore it wouldn't happen again. Still, Jane didn't like to leave Grace unsupervised for too long as she was clearly easily led, sext-wise, plus Bridget knew an awful lot about penises for an eight-year-old, admittedly pertaining to livestock but one couldn't be too careful.

'Colin's at choir,' their mother pointed out. 'Devoted he is. And a lovely voice. Practically Aled Jones.'

'I bet Aled doesn't live on fucking mung beans,' muttered Lydia.

'Lydia!' their mother snapped. 'We're in public!'

'Oh God. Are you worried Bad Karen might report you to Carole Burghley and you'll be jettisoned from Meryton Women's Guild for having a wayward daughter.'

Mrs Bennet raised an eyebrow, or would have, had the Botox not frozen her into perpetual serenity. 'If that were a criterion for membership, I would have been blackballed decades ago.' Point made, she spotted Donald Hawkins and hauled poor Gordon off to prove another one about conservatories (she very much for; Mr Bennet against; Donald the owner of one with bifold doors and an indoor water feature).

'Whoever it is, be kind,' said Lizzy.

'Well he can't be up to much,' Lydia replied, 'because she refused to show me his picture off Hinge and besides, he swiped right on Mary and, well...'

'Mary is a perfectly attractive woman,' said Jane. 'With specific opinions.'

'This is like Piers Morgan all over again,' said Lydia. 'I'm going to the bar. I need peanuts.'

She did not need peanuts (no one *needs* peanuts). Rather Kitty, Dave, Stacey of filler fame, and several members of Listless Biscuits, including Denny, were lurking near the dart board, while Kitty berated the state of her presents.

'Vouchers!' she protested. 'All of them! Cheese. Books. Since when do I read? I got one from Mum for a therapy session. What happened to *present* presents? You know, actual things in boxes.'

'Pandemic,' said Denny, his face peeling into a grin the minute he saw Lydia – a change that did not go unnoticed, at least by Kitty.

'Watch yourself,' she told him. 'My sister has a thing for musicians.'

Lydia bristled. 'I… what? No I don't.'

'The drummer of some shite indie band,' Kitty reeled off. 'Then the bassist. Then the A&R guy at a gig they did at Brixton.'

'I…' Lydia stared at Denny, willing him to ignore Kitty.

Denny, either a mind-reader, or entirely uninterested in her sexual preferences, obliged. 'I'll take the cheese one if it's going spare. Vouchers, I mean. Unless there are others you want to offload?'

Lydia, who had given Kitty an IOU for 'FUN TIMES' (finances were tight again since she'd dropped the call-centre job) decided to steer the conversation into less choppy waters. 'What did Dave get you anyway?'

Kitty mustered her best Oscar-runner-up face. 'Hotel voucher.'

'Nice,' said Denny.

She glanced at her partner, who was thankfully deep into a discussion on the possibility of overuse of a wah-wah pedal. 'Premier Inn,' she added. 'Yay me.'

Denny shrugged. 'Decent mattresses, though. I've got one at home.'

Bed. Denny was mentioning bed. Was this a hint? Lydia stared at him for clarification, but came there none.

'He says there's something else,' Kitty went on. 'But he's saving it until later.' She sighed.

'Dinner at Harvester?' suggested Lydia.

'More likely a strap-on,' said Kitty without thinking. She snapped to when Denny's eyebrow shot up. 'Shit. TMI, sorry.'

Denny shook his head. 'Unshockable, me. And nah,' he said. 'Not delivered one of those. So unless he got it knock-off—'

'Which he would have done,' said Lydia.

At this, Kitty did what she always did when faced with a brutal and depressing truth. She decided to drink through it.

Which meant she missed the arrival of Mary and the fifty-two-year-old anaesthetist she had finally swiped on (surmising that someone who chose to spend most of their time with almost-dead bodies might be tolerable), whom Lizzy had greeted with a 'God, not you' and who had disappeared out for a fag with Stacey fifteen minutes later, never to return.

'He's a knob,' Lizzy told her sister in uncharacteristically frank language. 'Not your sort at all. You'd be better off with Colin. And that's saying something.'

'What's wrong with Colin?' snapped Mary.

'Nothing,' placated Jane. 'And I thought he had nice eyes.'

'And bum,' said their mother.

'For heaven's sake!' Lizzy protested. 'You're supposed to be on Mary's side here.'

Mary did not need persuading, however. Hugh would have been for the chop even had he not run off, having ticked several boxes on her red-flag checklist (an actual list, kept in a black Moleskine notebook) for wearing a gilet (they made no sense – arms needed heat just like every other body part), smelling of petrol (potential terrorist), and misusing the word 'disinterested'.

And if she was concerned at accidentally rendering herself the centre of Bennet attention, it was to be short-lived. One of her little sisters was about to eclipse her in that regard. And for once it was not Lydia.

★ ★ ★

In Kitty's defence, she had made it clear to Dave, after the whole Wickham thing, that she just wasn't into it. Or at least she thought she had. But as he asked for quiet at the bar, told her he hoped she was ready for her main present, she had a sudden, awful sense that she hadn't been adamant enough about marriage.

Wickham – of course sodding Wickham – tapped his glass.

Oh God, this was happening. And in fucking public. What should she do? Try to make light of it to buy time, she decided. Maybe throw in an insult to put him off. 'It had better not be knock-off,' she said, her fake laugh an octave too high, 'whatever it is.' Don't let it be a ring, she willed. Don't let it be a ring!

Dave pulled out a grey velvet box, about an inch and a half square, and began to drop to one knee.

'Oh, fuck no!'

Dave's face fell, and there was a collective intake of breath to match the grimaces.

'Kitty!' wailed her mother.

Five Jäger shots and a sambuca pitched in her innards and she wished, for once, she had listened to Dave when he'd told her to line her stomach and offered to make her some Supernoodles.

'I said that out loud, didn't I,' she whispered. 'Shit. Dave, I didn't mean…' She *had* meant, though, hadn't she. 'Can we go somewhere? To talk?' She gestured frantically at him to get up, then held out her arm to help him.

Dave stood, ignoring her hand and brushing off the ones of Denny, Beef McKenzie (keyboards), and Sticks Kimble (drums, clearly). 'I give up,' he told her, and promptly walked out.

There was another collective intake of breath, and yet again, it was her mother who broke the tight silence. 'Kitty, you idiot!' she wailed. 'You need to go after him! Lydia, make her go!'

Lydia knew there was no making Kitty do anything, but equally there was no refusing her mother under such circumstances, and so she apologised to Denny (for what she wasn't sure, he just seemed to warrant it), grabbed her sister, who was fast dissolving into a vat of self-pity and hauled her out of the Dragon and onto the High Street.

'What the fuck?' said Lydia, as they sank onto the steps outside the Conservative Club (forgetting, evidently, their own political allegiances, as well as the numerous times Lydia had been sick or got fingered on them).

'I know, right,' agreed Kitty. 'What was he thinking?'

'Are you serious?' Lydia said, surprising even herself at this point, given her habitual support of any and all waywardness.

'What?' snapped Kitty. 'Why would I want this? I'm sick of it.' She warmed to her theme, not unaided by alcohol. 'Same dick every night,' she went on. 'Well, not every night. Fridays and Saturdays. Sunday mornings when Mum has Bridget for the weekend.'

'Mum always has Bridget for the weekend.'

'Exactly. It's predictable. It's just so… small town,' she repeated her phrase from her previous spar, 'so boring. All of it.' That, at least, she knew Lydia would sympathise with.

But Lydia continued to fight against type. 'Boring?' she snorted. 'A stable job? A kid who adores you? A man who loves you enough to want to marry you? And who you love back?'

'Whom,' said Kitty automatically (she had been corrected by Mary enough times to distinguish these days). 'And I know. But… what if there's something else out there? Something better.'

'You mean some*one*. And trust me, I've looked at Bumble:

there isn't. Unless you want Mary's sloppy seconds. Well, thirds now Stacey's been there.'

'What if I'm gay?' tried Kitty. 'Or… or heteroflexible? It's like not knowing you're actually a potential Olympic pole vault champion because of lack of access to… to poles.'

'It really isn't like that and you've had plenty of access to… poles. You're straight. So stop waiting for a shinier penis to come along and buck up and be glad Dave can even get it up at his age, and not just to dwarf porn.'

'Jesus. Who haven't you slept with?'

Lydia, who did not have a good answer to this, ignored it. 'But if you don't want to marry him, tell him.'

'I…' Kitty was going to say 'did' but the more she thought about it, the less convinced she was that she had. 'I should go home,' she realised.

'You *should* go home,' agreed Lydia, standing and holding out her hand. 'Come on, I'll walk you.'

Kitty let herself be hauled to standing. 'Can we get a kebab on the way?' she pouted.

'Only if you're paying.'

Kitty knew when she was defeated, bought them both a doner, and Dave a shish chicken, and slunk up to the flat with her peace offering.

It took forty minutes to persuade Dave to turn down Pink Floyd and come out of the bedroom, by which point the kebab had gone cold and sat congealing between them.

'So you see,' she continued, 'it's not that I don't want to be pinned down—'

'You make it sound like I'm the Taliban!' he protested.

Bollocks. She tried another tack. 'It's just I don't *only* want to be Mrs Pickens.'

'You don't have to be Mrs Pickens at all,' Dave replied. 'I never said you had to change your name. You could double barrel. Be Miller-Pickens. Or triple barrel: Miller-Pickens-Bennet?'

Jesus. 'It's not about the name,' she explained, more truthfully this time. 'It's about me. I don't just want to be Kitty the wife. Kitty the mother. I want to be...' She pitched into her imagination. 'Kitty the, I don't know, influencer. Or Kitty the celebrity hairdresser. Or just... Kitty the piss artist.' Okay, that one was ridiculous.

Dave went with it though. 'And you can. I'm not stopping you doing those things. Well, maybe the excessive drinking. But only for health reasons. I want you to be whatever you want.'

'But do I have to get married to do it?' she said.

Dave slumped, picked up the kebab, and bit into it. 'I don't know,' he said between mouthfuls. 'I guess not.'

And so it was, the least romantic proposal in the history of the Bennet family, outflanking even Mr Bennet's 'Shall we?' as he and the then Hester Gooderham watched the Lucases walk down the aisle in 1975, came to an even less romantic end. But at least Kitty and Dave were staying together, a decision they cemented with performatively vigorous make-up sex, a perfunctory vomit (in both cases), and a dose of cystitis for Kitty two days later.

MAY

May came, and a strange air of discontent settled over Meryton and Netherfield, despite the clement weather. Mr Bennet's was bowel-related: what was, for years, a reliable 8am toilet call, had, since Christmas, been rationed out over several visits, each stretching upwards of half an hour. On the positive side, it gave him ample opportunity to browse the World Wide Web, and imagine himself in other countries, pottering about other landscapes, and using other toilets, which were less plagued by women demanding to be let in because they need tweezers/tampons/*Hello!* magazine.

Kitty's irritation was similarly anatomical, though in her case, rather more penis-shaped. She had absolutely taken on board everything of which Lydia had accused her on the night of her fortieth – well, the bits she could remember – and was trying hard to appreciate what she *did* have, rather than covet what she didn't, and stop speculating how green the grass might be anywhere but Meryton, and quite how thrilling the penis (and man it was attached to). And yet, as she dip-dyed Bad Karen's outgrown bob, disguised Barbara Clyde's regrowth, and waxed Carole Burghley's chin hair (Stacey was in Portugal for a fortnight with the anaesthetist) it was to Other Penises she kept on returning.

To that end, she had set up an egg of a Hinge profile – no photo, no pithy tagline, no declaration she was an Aries, was looking for a 'partner in crime', or lived for 'wine o'clock' – purely for the privilege of flicking through the eligible men of the parish, and several other parishes besides. It was, she told herself, not in itself a problematic habit. Being addicted to window shopping wasn't the same as getting into debt over a slew of high-price purchases from Liberty, after all. Or rather more Primark, in this case. Though, being less Mary about these things, and not setting any store by academic qualifications or having an aversion to furnishing fabrics, there were at least three men she might deign to waste money on. More if one considered the under-twenty-fives as fair game – which she didn't, not even when she was 'just looking'. Although, God, the pecs on them. The promise. The absolute lack of baggage, other than a couple of bunk-ups behind McDonalds if they were lucky.

It didn't help that she and Dave had barely done anything bed-wise since the premature engagement fiasco. No protracted shags, with three acts, an expansive cast of toys, and a finale involving the sort of thing that normally got a ninety-seven per cent rating on Pornhub. No quickies in the kitchen while Bridget was at Brownies (the sole purpose of enrolling her, and begging her to stay when she complained about itchy uniforms and inexplicable rules, and everyone else's absolute lack of interest in pigeons, Taylor Swift or being able to name every Star Wars character alphabetically). Not even a lazy Sunday fucking with him spooning her and doing the work as she pretended not to read Facebook. He'd given up even touching her, unless it was to move her out of the way of the TV while he and Bridget played Mario Kart, or to test whether a batch of factory-second smart watches actually fit a woman's wrist (they did not). So, if you thought about it, it was his fault she was casting about for attention elsewhere, albeit only in theory; his fault she was dissatisfied.

* * *

Similarly, it was Kitty's eldest sister's fault that Wickham's life was so difficult right now. This, George patiently explained to Jane as they lay in the afterglow of precisely the kind of mind-blowing sex Kitty had been imagining as she flicked listlessly through Hinge.

'I'm just asking you to consider it,' he said, as he ran a finger over Jane's delicate hip bone.

'But... Grace,' she breathed. 'School.'

'She hates Meryton,' he replied. 'You know she does. If we do it soon, she can join Timon at Marlborough, or... wherever.'

'Millfield,' she sighed, reminded of Caroline. 'He's at Millfield.'

'Is he?' George pulled a face. 'Bit horsey, I thought, but I suppose it does the job. The point is, she wouldn't need to slum it in a London comp just because we've moved up there.'

Jane felt her bare flesh goose-pimple, pulled a sheet over her, as if it were the cold, rather than his plans, behind her shiver. 'But my sisters—'

'Are a fucking coven,' he finished for her. 'Sorry, but they are. They don't like me, and I'm tired of it. They don't trust me. They don't understand me like *you* do.' His hand slid up to cup her face, the flash of anger gone from his eyes, which were pleading now: a lost boy to her Wendy. 'Because you're different. You're special and generous and just, well, better.'

She wasn't stupid. She knew what he was doing: practising what Daddy always called 'cupboard love' – a speciality of Kitty and Lydia. And yet...

'Darling, I do hear you, I do,' she replied, her slight hand resting on his. 'I know it can't be easy, but can you at least think about moving in here? See if you like it? You could do it before the wedding if you wanted. Free up the rent from the flat for... whatever.' God knows where his salary went – Silly Calypso probably – but she knew from some mutterings on the phone that his finances were less than golden. Knew too that he would refuse again any offers of help, even a loan. 'I don't want to be that man,' he had told her. 'I need you to rely on me, not the other way around.' Perhaps London was his way of making this absolute.

He closed his eyes, breathed deep as if forcing down tears. 'You know I can't do that. I can't… be Charley. I *won't* be. And if I move in here I'll always feel second best. A stand-in. Even in Meryton I feel it – everyone assessing me. Comparing me—'

'No—'

'Yes. I'm sorry, darling, but they do and you know it. Pretending otherwise won't make it go away. It won't make it any easier for me.'

'I didn't ask you to move to Meryton,' she said then, bruised.

'I know,' he conceded. 'I chose it. I wanted to be near you after… everything. To be able to help you, and your sisters. I put my life, my career on hold for you. Taking a step back at the agency. Letting Hugo take that big campaign.' He paused, letting that weight be felt before his next shot. 'Now, all I'm asking is that, given you *have* no career, you put me first for once.'

If Jane had been Lizzy, she would have taken issue – would have argued that Citizens Advice might not be a 'career' as he defined it, but it was *something* nonetheless, and indeed everything to a few people, and he should think himself lucky he'd never been in a position to need it. But Jane was Jane, and so she said merely that she would think about it, then got up for a precautionary wee (urinary tract infections ran in the family) and a long, disconsolate shower. The whole thing had put her in a brutal mood, one that would last throughout the day, meaning she clean forgot to fetch the dry cleaning from Geraghty's at ten, clean forgot she was meant to be collecting Grace from 'revision camp' at five, which in turn led to an argument that meant she clean forgot that at seven she should have been, not on the sofa mindlessly humming *The One Show* theme, but on Gwydir Street with Lizzy, learning to jive.

After Darcy

✦ ✦ ✦

Lizzy would normally wait for Jane, and then abandon plans once it became apparent that she'd had some sort of mental lapse, or an emergency involving Grace, Socrates or an injured sheep that had wandered onto the Netherfield Road (these were surely the only explanations for lateness). However, a particularly violent tantrum from Milo (she wouldn't let him wear his wellies to bed) and the insistence from Delilah that logical reasoning wasn't helping a jot, meant that she had burst from Ledbury Road with all the desperate energy of a trapped cat.

Now, though, as she stood in the corner of the Methodist hall, watching the couples warm up in the fug, she rather wished she'd stayed to explain, for the fourth time, the concept of friction sores to a three-year-old. This, *this*, was when she really missed Fitz. His steady head, his ability to think clearly, to bring her back from the brink when she was livid.

'No Jane?'

'Jesus!' She swung round, found herself face to face – or more face to chest – with the ageing hipster.

'God, sorry,' he said quickly. 'I didn't mean to alarm you.'

'No, no,' she replied, swiftly trying to erase any vestiges of rage from her face. 'Not your fault. I was… elsewhere.' Was his name Paul? No, Saul, that was it. As in the Bible. He'd been missing for the last two sessions. Not that she was counting. 'And no. God knows where she's got to. This isn't like her at all.'

'Should you call her?'

At this, she bristled, apparently visibly.

'Sorry!' he repeated. 'Not trying to, you know, mansplain anything. You just seemed… at a loss.'

Something in her slumped. 'I was, rather. And don't apologise. I've left a message already, so I'm sure she'll get back to me soon. I'm sure she'll be here soon, in fact. She's probably left her phone behind. It won't be the first time.'

It would be the first time, but this way she had a chance of calming herself.

'Well, I'm a Billy No Mates as well this week if you can believe it.'

Gloria chose this moment to sound her alarming clap, call 'Positions please for the Viennese waltz!' and press play on her bluetooth speaker, which boomed out a tinny 'Hedwig's Theme'.

'Jesus, really?' Lizzy said without thinking.

'Awful, isn't it? Still, when in Rome.' Saul held out his arms. 'Shall we?'

'I…'

This was the moment she should apologise and go home. She didn't want to be here. She didn't even *have* to be here, not without Jane. And it would serve her sister right if she were to walk in and find herself partner-less.

But that sort of vindictiveness was a bit Lydia, wasn't it? And she and Jane weren't exactly on the steadiest of bases as it was, given… everything. So, 'Fine,' she said, and, with only a trace of bracing, placed her left hand on his shoulder and let his right encircle her waist before they began one-two-threeing across the floor, both trying to push thoughts of Hogwarts from their minds.

'So, where's Luella?' she asked, as they reached the drinks hatch and made a passable turn.

'You remembered!'

Bollocks. 'Don't read anything into it,' she said swiftly. 'I have a photographic memory. It's a curse, frankly.'

He laughed. 'Oh, I shan't. And malingering,' he explained. 'She's had a row with Dexter.'

'The colossal knob?'

'The very same.'

'But you came anyway?'

'Well, it's this or listen to her berate him, and if I agree with her, which I do, she'll then hold it against me the second they make up, which they will. This is the fifth time they've split in as many years. The second since they got engaged.'

'So, a hopeless romantic,' Lizzy said. 'I have a sister like that.'

'Well, just hopeless I think. But, given everything, I can't hold it against her.'

'No, you can only listen and be there when it all goes tits up.'

She felt him smile, despite both their sightlines being firmly fixed on the middle distance for fear of more shrieking from Gloria.

'Exactly.' They fleckerled, not quite impeccably. 'So, how many sisters do you have then?'

By the time they had moved on to the trickier quickstep, they had established siblings (one brother, Judd, who owned a microbrewery outside Chipping Norton), and employment history (failed sculptor, now art tutor at Anglia Ruskin, decidedly bitter about it, but open about that bitterness), before moving on to major dislikes.

'Where to begin?' he pondered.

'That many?'

'Oh, hundreds,' he said. 'Beetroot, for a start. Inexplicable stuff. Jodhpurs – the word and the trousers. Horses in general in fact. Huge brutes. Unpredictable with it. Sculptors. For obvious reasons. All forms of social media…'

At that, something in her hitched. 'You sound like someone I know,' she said, then corrected herself, if only in her head. *Knew.* When would she remember?

'Oh dear.'

'No,' she assured him. 'It's a good thing.'

'Oh, well then.' He dipped her backwards. 'Your turn.' He snapped her back up.

'Oh. Have you finished?'

'Not at all. But we'll still be here until next week at this rate.'

'Fine, then. Pride.'

'Is pride a bad thing?'

'It can be. Vanity,' she went on.

'Ah, a pointless pursuit,' he agreed. 'Ageing chases us all, and catches us too.'

An image of her own crow's feet flashed in front of her. She blinked it away. 'Quite.'

'Don't worry,' he assured her, 'we all fall for it. You've seen my jeans.'

Lizzy tamped down a smirk. 'I wasn't going to say anything.'

'Of course not. You're far too polite.'

She laughed. 'Oh, you don't know me at all then.'

'No, but I'd like to.'

Lizzy flinched, then stiffened.

As he did in turn. 'Oh, God. Have I said something wrong? I only meant…'

They had dropped their hold and come to a halt in the middle of the floor, couples about them still flicking their heels gleefully to 'You're the One That I Want'.

'I…' Something in Lizzy had tilted, was spinning. 'I just…'

'I'm sorry.'

'Chip chop!' called Gloria. 'No time for dawdling. Pick up, pick up!'

Lizzy let Saul grasp her again, followed the steps, but the rest of the dance was spent in a tight silence. And when John and Olivia had finally finished, she excused herself quickly and went to the ladies, where she sat abruptly on the cold, black plastic and shook herself.

What was wrong with her? Why had she seized up like that? He wasn't proposing marriage. He wasn't even proposing a shag, as Lydia would put it. He was just being kind. Probably felt sorry for her. Except… she had felt something. And not just on his part. The briefest flicker, the merest kindling, but *something* nonetheless. And it had been a long time since she had felt anything other than devastation, emptiness.

Perhaps she should just take her mother's advice and buck up. See what happened. Yes. That's what she would do. She would try to be open.

She stood, brushed down her palazzo pants, and flushed the loo for good measure. Then, in the mirror added a quick slick of lip gloss (Charlotte Tilbury – a present from Jane), before bracing herself, and swinging open the door.

But, as she went to step into the corridor, she heard a familiar voice – his, Saul's – and another one, a woman's.

'Shame about your daughter. She has promise. Unlike the blonde. Awfully clompy.'

Gloria then. Oh joy. And also, bollocks to her. Lizzy wasn't that bad.

'Lizzy?' he replied. 'You think so?'

'Oh, "Lizzy", is it? And yes, I do, sadly. You can do better.'

Lizzy winced. She knew she should close her ears – she had learned, in a house full of sisters, that ignorance really was bliss. And yet she felt compelled to hear his opinion of her. A compulsion she was about to regret.

'Oh, it's not like that.' He laughed. 'She's really *not* my type.'

The soft ball of whatever it was that had begun to inflate in her punctured suddenly. Well, that resolved *that* then. And she pulled the door to tightly.

Of course, if she'd lingered, she would have heard Gloria press him as to what, precisely, *was* his type. To which he would reply, 'No one. I'm really not in the market for that right now.' And, were she peeking as well as earwigging, she might have seen the lie on his face, might have realised that this was all no more than an avoidance tactic – something, as a wealthy gentleman of half-decent looks, he had had to learn swiftly in the wake of his wife's death.

But she didn't linger. Instead, she ran the taps while staring at her wrinkles in the flyblown mirror. Then, after five minutes, she decided they'd have finished their cosy little conflab, and so pasted on a tight smile, strode into the hall, and snatched up her jacket from the stack of chairs where she'd left it.

'You're leaving?' Saul pulled a face.

'Yes,' she said, steadily. 'I think I'm done for tonight.'

'But the foxtrot—'

'I'm sure *Gloria* will partner you.' More your *type*, she didn't add.

Saul frowned, his freckled forehead bunching endearingly. No— not endearingly. Like a lying… conniving… something or other. This was why she needed to stay away from men. The whole giddy tilt-a-whirl, the carousel of it all was anathema. So, she'd be closed off forever? Who cared? At least she could concentrate on the twins that way. Could concentrate on work. No wonder Lydia couldn't hold down a job when she ricocheted from fling to fling. It was sickening.

'Next session then?' he tried. Of course he did. They didn't bloody give up.

'I doubt it,' she said, her tone cold, her words precise. 'Jane will be back by then.'

He shrugged. 'I'm sorry, if it's something—'

'Not you,' Lizzy insisted. 'It's me.' Because she was an idiot for thinking this might be anything other than the usual. At which thought, she sunk a little. It really wasn't his fault. He was only human, after all. And a mere man, at that. 'Enjoy the foxtrot,' she finished.

Then, she walked out of the hall, back down Gwydir Street and onto Ledbury Road, where, at number twenty-seven, Arden was fast asleep, while Milo had finished his boot-related tantrum and was merrily watching *The Wire* with Delilah.

'One episode,' she said. 'Then bed.' It wasn't as if he could understand a word of it. Nor could she. As Fitz always said, the accents and language were unfathomable.

She paused, thought, then gathered up her journal and pen, before settling on the chaise.

After Darcy

Dear Darcy, she wrote.
You were right about dance.

* * *

There were few advantages to reaching Mr Bennet's age. A bus pass. Discount tickets to the cinema. Elasticated trousers, perhaps. But one of them, surely, was being able to eat what one liked, when one liked, and not having to pander to fads anymore, particularly those of one's children. And yet, there he was, on a rainy May Sunday, staring disconsolately at a pot of something that looked like the bottom of a hamster's cage.

'Quinoa,' Mrs Bennet said, before he could question it. 'It's very high in protein. Mary said Colin said his aunt eats buckets of it, and if she can, so can I. Plus Hindon's ever so empathetic with the animals, so even though he says he's not vegan, I think he might be inside.' She said 'Hindon' in the same strange tone with which she was known to invoke 'Keanu'.

'No one who's vegan doesn't know about it and tell you,' he complained. 'At least ten times a conversation.'

'Well, it won't do you any harm anyway,' she parried. 'Might even settle your stomach. I know it's been dicky.'

Mr Bennet made a noise of what might equally have been consternation or concession. In any case, he plodded back to his study, shut himself in with *The Sunday Times*, a cup of Kenco, and *The Archers* omnibus, before the awful hordes descended.

And hordes they were: Lizzy and the twins, Lydia and Mary (of course), Bridget, Colin, Caroline Bingley-Hicks and her husband Jonty (short, pink shirt, red face, thus resembling an overcooked prawn), Bad Karen (a last minute addition following a row with Laurence over the compost, which had somehow jumpcut into accusations of eyeing up a cashier at Scotsdale's Garden Centre, resulting in him storming off to the golf club in the Porsche, and she to Longbourn in the pink Fiat 500, complete with headlight lashes), and finally, the guest of honour, Hindon Lydiard, who had, to Bridget's and the twins' (and no one else's) delight brought his basset hound, Dorothy, who had already been forced into a ballet tutu and deely boppers, and was currently ensconced in the morning room in a blanket fort.

'Marvellous,' declared Hindon. 'Quite marvellous.'

Mrs Bennet beamed. If Hindon took a liking to Milo and Arden, then Lizzy must surely be the logical next step. Not that love should be logical, but really, what other options were on the table in Meryton for him? Lydia wasn't to be trusted with anyone, Mary was… Mary, and the only other eligible women of a certain age were Midge Painswick, whom she knew through her channels was 'totally over' sex, and Little Karen's youngest, Sapphire, who bred hamsters, despite being forty.

'Nice to be around young ones, isn't it,' she encouraged. 'I suppose you must miss your boys.'

'Oh, I do,' he declared. 'They're just so…'

'Marvellous?' Lizzy finished for him, her tone rather more acid than one would have liked, but at least she was speaking to him.

Not that Hindon seemed to notice. 'Quite!'

'Well, feel free to admonish mine,' Lizzy continued. 'Or they'll have kidnapped the poor dog before the afternoon's out. Or enrolled it at Rambert.'

Hindon looked perplexed at the mention of, admittedly, one of the more obscure ballet schools, but plunged gamely on. 'You don't have pets?'

'Too anal,' said Lydia.

Lizzy narrowed her eyes. 'Too busy,' she admitted. 'Except perhaps for fish. And God knows what the twins would do to *them*. Jane's the animal lover. Pity she's not here, you'd like her.'

'Oh, I don't think so,' interrupted Mrs Bennet quickly.

But Lizzy was not to be derailed. 'Why *didn't* you invite her?'

She eyed her mother with mistrust. 'You do know that she knows we're all here. I can't imagine she's thrilled.'

'Don't be silly,' flustered Mrs Bennet. 'She'll be busy, and besides... there isn't room at the table.'

She eyed Caroline, currently picking her way through the steamed quinoa and tahini aubergines with all the relish of a penitent on dry crackers, while her husband bored on about oil futures to Bad Karen, and Colin tried to highlight petrochemicals' contribution to the climate crisis. While Caroline had previously made her views on the 'whole Wickham thing' perfectly clear – 'I assumed she would have come to her senses by now' – the subject of the prenup itself had yet to rear its hideous head, but would surely make an appearance between dessert (plum crumble – Hindon's second favourite pudding after sticky toffee, but Waitrose had run out of dates and Mrs Bennet was still boycotting Tesco over a discontinued chicken parmigiana) and coffee.

'Where's Kitty?' Lizzy asked instead.

'Having sex,' said Bridget.

The table – even the diminutive yet braying Mr Bingley-Hicks – fell silent as Mrs Bennet reddened. 'Well, I don't... They're sorting things out. After, you know.'

'What's sex?' asked Arden.

Thankfully, before Lydia could intervene, her brother declared the need for an urgent poo, distracting everyone and removing a relieved Lizzy from the equation. Not that there was anything wrong with Hindon per se, she thought – as she watched her son picking the woodchip off the wallpaper in the downstairs lavatory (a decor 'phase' in the eighties that had yet to be addressed) and doing anything but the pooing he had declared was 'already coming out'. He (Hindon) was polite, clearly kind, financially stable. But he was also altogether too easy-going – a pushover, frankly – plus he had a penis, which in itself went against his favour, after the dancing debacle.

Jane had, she had later discovered, left several apologetic messages for her, but that didn't stop Lizzy berating her sister, in a 1am voicemail. 'It was hideous,' she had blistered. 'Humiliating. I shan't be going again, so don't ask me.' By 7am, inevitably, her anger had lessened to more of a mintiness, and her guilt ballooned, so that when Jane rang again to plead clemency, and to beg her to rethink her stance, she conceded. But only to prove Gloria wrong, she told herself. 'Clompy', indeed. She would bloody show her.

'Stop that,' she told Milo, unpicking his fingers as he readied himself to pull off an entire strip of hideous woodchip. 'Is it out yet?'

'It went back in,' he said solemnly, and then sighed with all the pathos of a defeated warlord.

'Come along, then,' she said. 'Spit spot, or you'll miss pudding.'

Milo hopped down from the lavatory with another weighty sigh. 'Will it be bits again?'

Lizzy frowned. The whole 'Complete Delia' phase was painful enough, but veganism took the biscuit. 'If it is, I have biscuits in my bag,' she promised.

Satisfied, Milo trotted down the corridor and back to the dining room, where, Lizzy was shocked, and yet unsurprised, to discover, Jane stood, her hair wet through, and her mood one of fury.

'I just thought,' she railed, in a quite uncharacteristic pitch, 'that as I'm the one under discussion, I should at least be here.'

'But I've tried to talk to you,' Caroline explained, her own tone that of a patient, if almost at the end of their tether, parent. 'And you won't listen. So I was hoping your family might help you see sense.'

'Why are you wet?' demanded Lizzy. 'Where's the Range Rover?'

Jane frowned. 'George needed it. The Audi's packed up apparently. At the garage. That's not the point.'

'And he couldn't at least have dropped you off?'

Jane held up her hands. 'No. I don't know. He's gone up to London for something.'

'This is why a prenuptial agreement is in your favour, dear,' continued Caroline. 'If and when he abandons you—'

'He's not abandoning me!' Jane rounded on her sister-in-law – ex sister-in-law. 'He's just… got a thing— Oh. What an adorable dog.'

Dorothy, assuming the ruckus was food-related, had appeared from her fort.

'Marvellous, isn't she?' said Hindon.

'Does she pick up ticks though? So close to the ground?'

Hindon reached into his pocket, pulled out a pair of fine-tipped medical tweezers. 'She does, poor sausage, but I'm rather an expert.'

'The vet.' Jane clapped a hand to her forehead. 'Of course. I'm so sorry for the interruption. It's just… family business.'

'Not at all,' he replied, for once managing to forestall before declaring it 'marvellous'.

Jane rounded on Caroline again. 'I don't want or need a prenup. And in any case it's none of your business—'

'Well, as a Bingley—'

'No.' Jane was adamant. 'I know Charley had money when we started. More money than me. But what we did, we did together. Netherfield included. It was me who retiled the bathrooms. Me who replanted the walled garden. Me who sorted the remortgage when he set up the charity. And now it's me who has to…' She trailed off, all too aware she was in danger of being dragged down that dead end that is Memory Lane. Then, suddenly, she mustered, 'It's just not happening. And that is my final word on it.'

'And that is my final word on it,' repeated Bridget, who was going through a phase of echoing everything anyone said, much to Dave's amusement and Kitty's panic.

Jane merely smiled tightly, buttoned up her coat, and pushed a hank of sodden hair behind one ear. 'Exactly, Bridge,' she said. 'Now I should go.'

'You don't want to stay for pudding?' asked her mother. 'I'm sure we can... all budge up a bit.'

Jane peered at the remnants of mains on the table. 'I'll pass.'

Hindon shot to standing. 'You can't possibly walk in this downpour. I can give you a lift.'

'No,' said Lizzy, who hadn't moved from the door as it was. 'I'll take her. Come on,' she said to her sister. 'We can talk on the way.'

★ ★ ★

For more than two decades, at frequent intervals, the two eldest Bennet sisters had sat just so – in the front seats of one or other's cars, on the gravel drive at Netherfield – dissecting whatever the universe (or more habitually, another Bennet) had chosen to throw at them: the time Charley had decided to give up the bar; Fitz's depression when they'd failed to get pregnant; Lydia's tryst with a junior cabinet minister when, to everyone's horror, she'd very much succeeded. Then that night, that bastard of a night when Lizzy had driven Jane and Grace back down from Derbyshire, one mute, one wailing, and she, numb at the wheel, praying the twins wouldn't need feeding, praying there'd been some sort of mistake, that they'd wake up tomorrow, and, like one of Mary's terminal stories in primary school, it would all be a dream.

It was impossible now, even three years on, not to feel the shape of that, the weight of that, as they sat there; impossible not to sense ghosts – of themselves, and who they might have become, as much as the men. And had they been different – had they had Lydia's impulsiveness or Kitty's flinty sense of injustice – they might have blurted that out, might have dissected that. God knows they needed to, even Lizzy recognised it. But they weren't Lydia or Kitty; they were sensitive Jane and diffident Lizzy, and so they tamped it down and swatted it off and got on with more immediate business.

'I know you agree with Caroline.' Jane clutched her damp hands in her lap. 'But you need to let me deal with this my way.'

Lizzy gripped the steering wheel. 'I know that. And I am. I just… we worry a little, that's all. You're in a vulnerable—'

'I'm not vulnerable!' Jane railed. 'I'm not weak. I'm not some hothouse flower or… or tall poppy or whatever wisp of a thing you think I am.'

'No one is saying *you're* weak,' Lizzy insisted. 'It's the situation that's difficult. And it's not just about Wickham and whether or not he might run off, which, for the record, I don't believe he will. It's just there are… other things to consider.'

'By which you mean Grace.'

'By which I mean Grace, and Netherfield itself, and what would happen to both if… if something happened to you. Not that I think it will, but…'

Jane made a hollow sort of a noise. 'No one thinks it will happen to them.'

Lizzy put a hand on her sister's. 'Exactly.'

Jane didn't take Lizzy's fingers in her own, but she didn't push her away either. 'You don't believe George would step up? Would do the right thing?'

Lizzy shrugged. 'I honestly don't know. I mean, he dumped Timon in boarding school.'

'Only because of Calypso,' Jane said. 'And because London comps are such a… a mixed bag. And it's not really "dumped". Millfield is very high in the league tables.' Her voice was getting more shrill by the minute. 'They have horses.'

'Well, yes, perhaps.' Lizzy would concede at least where Silly Calypso was concerned. 'But it's not like he changed arrangements once he'd moved to Meryton.'

'Oh, you can't move schools during GCSEs,' Jane said solemnly. 'It's an academic death sentence. Especially for a child as volatile as Timon.'

'That's not strictly true, though, is it. And Timon's not volatile; he's a teenage boy, that's all. Besides, he was only in Year Nine.'

'"Teenager",' corrected Jane. 'Not "boy". And "they".'

'I'm sorry?'

'Timon's non-binary,' Jane explained. 'They decided last week. Or realised. Or... I don't know. Anyway, George is mortified of course. He thinks it's Calypso's fault for taking cocaine when she was pregnant. Though the school is being extraordinarily supportive.'

Lizzy squeezed Jane's hand. 'And you? How do you feel?'

'I feel terrible. Poor boy— I mean, *person*. It must have been so difficult. I should have noticed. I should have—'

'No, I know you'll be fine about Timon. You're you. I mean how do you feel about George. About the wedding. About everything?'

'Oh.' Jane tried to rein in her train of thought. 'Well, I just feel... unsettled. There's this sticky business with Caroline. Grace is behind schedule with revision and miserable with it, and I'm worried she'll develop an eating disorder, because they seem so very popular in Year Eleven. Lydia hasn't given me an answer about the surrogacy and I can't bear to push her in case she says no. And now George wants to move back to bloody London.'

If Lizzy had been struggling to know where to start, that last answer brought things sharply into focus. 'Oh, Jane. You can't be serious.'

She nodded. 'I've said no. Of course. But...' She trailed off.

Lizzy knew what had been coming in any case. But she knew, too, that any admonishment risked her sister inching closer to Wickham's position. 'Please, just put yourself first,' she said. 'For once in your bloody life.'

There was a pause, then, in lieu of an answer, Jane went to open the door. 'You should get back. You're missing lunch.'

'I think I'll live. You saw what the first course was.'

'Quinoa *is* very high in protein,' Jane said, a smile – at last – on her lips, if only lightly. 'And can you please not tell Mum about Timon yet? She'll think she's won the Women's Institute bingo.'

Lizzy scoffed. 'I think you mean Meryton Women's Guild. And she did that with Bridget.'

'Oh, gender dysphoria trumps ADHD, surely?'

At that, Lizzy grinned, and grasped Jane's arm. 'Whatever happens, promise we won't become them.'

Jane nodded. 'I promise.'

Lizzy squeezed her arm again. 'Good. I'll move to bloody London with you if I have to.'

It was a lie, but a kind one. And sometimes, with sisters, buying time is far, far more advantageous than a brutal but premature truth.

★ ★ ★

As for the aborted lunch at Longbourn, and what the elder Bennet sisters had been missing, there had, actually, been more developments than one might assume. While Lydia had spent the entire time flicking between TikTok and Instagram under the table, occasionally messaging Denny reels of cockatiels doing amusing things, or hairless cats looking especially menacing, Mrs Bennet had interrogated the poor vet, and Caroline, Jonty and Bad Karen went in circles as to whether or not pashminas were common (Caroline for; Bad Karen against; Jonty confused as to what constituted a pashmina and what a poncho), Mary had managed to sign herself up to choir at St Saviour's.

Mary's voice had long been the source of open amusement and private derision in the Bennet household. Not because it was poor, precisely, but more that where she heard a mezzo soprano capable of scaling the heights of La Scala, everyone else just heard Mary. It wasn't that the notes were off, more the emotion. Thus, having been eclipsed once too often by the far more expressive Kitty, and after one too many impressions by Lydia – a po-faced plonking through Phil Collins' 'In The Air Tonight' – Mary had slammed her sheet music back in the piano stool and taken up reading instead, which, to be fair, had led to a career of sorts, and one slightly more assured than the fickle world of entertainment. But she did miss that feeling that music had given her – a sort of soaring, which, while it might not have made itself evident on her face, had lifted her insides and, once, during a particularly intricate harmonisation over something by Guy Garvey, given her butterflies and the sort of shimmering she had only ever read of, and only ever in relation to love.

And so, when Colin mentioned, over the box of Waitrose chocolate gingers that were passed around with coffee, that he had taken over as temporary choirmaster while Nicholas Biggins had an operation on his prostate, her interest was piqued.

'Hymns, I assume?' she checked – hymns encouraging the sort of plodding she was good at, and Jesus seemingly requiring far less emoting than Elbow.

'Of course.' Colin's face lit up. 'That will be my first act as master. Biggins has instigated a lot of modern nonsense – Taylor Swift and whatnot. "Rock choir" he calls it, but I shan't be persuaded. We may not be religious but we rehearse in a church, and God, if he, or *she*' – Colin was nothing if not willing to keep up with the times, at least within limits – 'exists, doesn't want to listen to anyone wittering on about shaking it off.'

Mary felt — as she often did around Colin — a sense that she was with a kindred spirit. Someone who understood that rules were there for a reason, that boundaries were helpful for everyone. 'Good, good,' she said.

'Of course Marjory Pence has threatened a walkout over the madrigal, and someone used the word "coup", but I shan't be swayed. It's all a lot of hot air that I'm sure will dispel once they realise just how enervating, how relevant, *proper* music can be. Having you there would be a boon,' he added, 'backing me against the...' He frowned as he sought the most appropriate words. 'Against the great uneducated.'

'Then yes,' said Mary, unusually energised herself, not least by being painted as an indispensable ally in an important war. That, and she had had four dark chocolate gingers, which was four more than advisable, given her sensitivity to caffeine and anything tingly.

'Excellent. It's decided!' Colin beamed, as if he had conquered Kilimanjaro, not shored up a temporary position corralling four solicitors, a pharmacist and six housewives for two hours on Tuesdays.

And Mary, having carped the diem for possibly the first time in her life, found herself beaming along with him.

* * *

Mary, though, was not the only Bennet taking her fate into her own hands. A mile and a half away, in the flat above Ladbrokes, Kitty was contemplating a form of discreet infidelity.

She and Dave had made up, which is to say, she'd chopped up mozzarella for a tricolore salad, stuck an M&S lasagne in the oven and opened a bottle of plonk, and then, two glasses in, let him go down on her in the kitchen, trying to ignore the fact she'd seen a leaf of basil stuck between his front teeth only two minutes earlier. But ignore it she did — to the point of a slightly above average orgasm — even agreeing to return the favour after they'd eaten lunch and watched two episodes of *Better Call Saul*.

It was then, as she knelt on the 'sex cushion' (a usefully washable faux velvet from Next), listening to Radiohead and trying not to let Dave's penis hit her uvula and force her to throw up two helpings of pasta, that the idea came to her: she would upgrade the egg to an actual profile. Still for research purposes. For reassurance that staying with Dave was the right thing to do. Which is what she'd say if anyone caught her — well, actually she'd probably blame it on Lydia, or say she was only helping Mary out and absolve herself of any involvement.

Besides, it wasn't really about meeting anyone. It was about the likes. Like when she and Lyds used to post bikini shots. Every 'heart' was a little hit — cheaper than a line of charlie and arguably less destructive. Then she'd promptly got pregnant and well, everything changed. Who wanted to see pictures of stretchmarks and permanent period knickers? Not even Shane Miller, apparently, who'd bolted back to Brisbane five weeks after the wedding, and five days after the birth.

So, no, she wouldn't do anything with it — Bumble or Tinder or Hinge or whichever she picked — it was just about that feeling of promise. That's what she missed. Not the doing — which would likely be little improvement on today's kitchen cunnilingus — but the possibility of it. And a little possibility, she told herself, never hurt anyone.

★ ★ ★

Back at Longbourn, however, in the downstairs lav, it was precisely this concept of possibility that was clouding someone else's already arduous Sunday.

Admittedly, quinoa and all that new-fangled shenanigans probably wasn't doing Mr Bennet's old-fashioned colon any favours, but he had almost got used to the punctuated nature of his defecating. Now, however, something more troubling had just made itself known in the form of what looked like blood in the pan of the Armitage Shanks.

His first thought was to call for Mrs Bennet, whose medical knowledge was vast and quite gorily detailed, thanks to both her appetite for gossip and the invention of Google. But she was still dealing with an incident involving Bridget and the twins and a colander, and besides, she was rather alarmist, and would probably diagnose cancer and impending death, which frankly could wait after all the hoohah with the Bingley-Hickses. Godawful pair. How Charley had ended up so well and Caroline so… trying, was one of life's mysteries.

No, he thought, as he clicked open the lid of the flushable wipes (Mrs Bennet had had issues with haemorrhoids), he would do what he always did, and give it a week or so. He might have been mistaken anyway. There might have been beetroot in with the tahini and whatnot. God, what a revolting monstrosity and all in the name of animal cruelty. What about human cruelty? What about his digestion, for God's sake?

And, in more of a hump than ever, but having decided he wasn't dying quite yet, he pulled up his trousers and flushed away the evidence, and, he hoped, any lingering memory of quinoa.

SUMMER

JUNE

In the past, the start of summer had arrived in a variety of guises. For Kitty and Lydia, it was merely an overheated version of their perpetual playtime, necessitating only a change in SPF and proximal water. For Mary, it stretched out inexorable – a flat, bland landscape to be populated with hobbits and heroes and regency bucks. For Lizzy and Jane, it meant Pemberley.

A month, if they were lucky – less for the men, who could abandon the charity and solicitors' for no more than two weeks at a time without getting hives – of long days in bracing walks across the dales; of nights spent idling with books, with music, with grand plans for all of them. Since the… incident, though, the subject had been, not forgotten, but pointedly ignored, and for obvious reasons: neither sister had a wish to relive that night, nor the drive back that had ended in two deaths and more broken hearts than one might think possible. And so the house – once the home of a great uncle, then Fitz's parents' holiday cottage, then Fitz's when he'd bought it off them – had lain empty. Not even Fitz's little sister, who lived a matter of miles away, could bring herself to visit – a fact that had played on Lizzy's mind if only from a practical point of view.

The fridge, at least, had been cleared. Mrs Briggs in the village had seen to that, along with the hoovering, the laundry, the turning down of beds. And she'd checked in every couple of months or so since: 'Just to keep an eye, mind. I'm not saying I'll be able to fix anything.' Hence a panicked WhatsApp one early June morning saying that two of the roof tiles were down, and there looked to be wasps nesting in the back bedroom, and slugs in the scullery.

'I'll deal with it,' Lizzy insisted. By which, she had meant she would ring Bill Jenkins, eventually, and pay him an inordinate amount of money for the upkeep of a house she had no intention of ever setting foot in again, but also no intention of either leasing or selling. A fact that, for the first time since… everything, struck her as rather dog in the manger. Of course it was awful – even thinking about giving Fitz's tatty cashmere to charity had given her a spasm of panic, and this was his very childhood. But could she justify, in this day and age, hanging on to property, owning a 'second home' even, when so many people lacked even one? Admittedly, it wasn't big, by country home standards – more a holiday cottage, really: four bedrooms (at a push), a bathroom, a downstairs lav with a thuggish flush, electrics that were tricky, and a heating system with a mind of its own (and a disorganised one at that). But they had loved it once, and someone else would again. And properly; not just once or twice a year.

No, she thought decisively as she climbed the stairs to Obstetrics (one lift was out again and the other contained a particularly malodorous proctologist), she could not justify it any longer. Yes, it was the twins' inheritance, but Milo and Arden had (thankfully) no memory of the place, so the money could just as well be spent on education (university, not school; she wasn't a hypocrite), put into trust, or just into something less… stress-inducing than Pemberley had proven to be. She would sell the place, get it on the market this summer if she could – let people view it in sunshine, rather than the damp and the drizzle that cloaked it for most of the year. Bill could deal with the tiles and the wasps – there was no stopping the slugs who were at the tail-end of an annual pilgrimage and would depart of their own volition by July – and she'd get an estate agent round to value it in the meantime. In fact, she'd call up this lunchtime, get the ball rolling.

Come lunch, though, she realised there was one rather more arduous telephone call pending: her sister. Not that she needed Jane's permission nor approval – though the latter would be a boon – just that it was politic to let her know. And not just that: given Lizzy would need to be there to let the wretched estate agents in, Jane might, being kind, accompany her.

'We shan't stay in the house,' she explained quickly. 'I could book a hotel. You wouldn't even need to set foot in the place. I can do that.' Though the company – and courage – would not go amiss.

'Oh, Lizzy,' began Jane, in a voice her sister recognised immediately. It was the one she used whenever a pet died, or she had another rare reason to let someone down. 'I can't. I mean… for obvious reasons I don't want to, but it's the middle of GCSEs and I can't leave Grace. She's flailing enough as it is.'

At least she was honest. Lizzy steeled herself. 'Of course.'

'If you need me to take the twins…' Jane paused, clearly thinking better of that already. 'Although obviously it would be better if Delilah could do it. The noise, you see.'

'It's fine, really. I understand. And I can take them with me if needs be.' She could not. The thought of a four-hour drive with the pair of them was unthinkable, let alone two days in a hotel. But Jane had made herself perfectly clear, and Delilah would be fine about it.

And so it was that not two minutes later, while she still had the gumption, she booked Bill Jenkins and several estate agents to come to Pemberley, and booked herself into The Hawden, which had a four-star rating, a sauna and an outdoor jacuzzi. Fuck it, if she was going to put herself through hell, then she could at least get a massage and a facial out of it, or stew herself in what Lydia insisted on calling 'human soup'. And, satisfied she was not only doing the right thing but the kind thing all round, she went back to the ward, and to two episiotomies and a suspected rectal prolapse.

By the time she left, however, five hours later, the high from having decided something had been worn steadily down by the fraught traumas of late-stage labour, the kind of persistent understaffing that left midwives and consultants alike in a perpetual state of wits' end, and the fact that the canteen had only managed a cheese and something unidentifiable sandwich, and that on its last, curl-edged, legs. This, though, was nothing compared to the scene she walked into at 27 Ledbury Road, which comprised Milo and Arden stark naked and covered in what might have been talcum powder, or flour, or potentially cocaine, and Delilah chasing them with a towel and a fishing net.

'Jesus,' she muttered to herself, along with a silent 'thank you' that this sort of idiocy (playing ghosts?) could be better dealt with by hired help, while she took a bath, fixed herself dinner, and then settled on the sofa for a quick five minutes of CBeebies bedtime hour, several kisses, and then an undisturbed evening of *Bridgerton*.

And so, when Delilah appeared – having captured and swaddled Milo ('a moth,' he explained, 'the flour is the anxious dust'), and given up on Arden, who had got distracted by a woodlouse and was in the toilet 'teaching it to swim' – and confessed she was resigning and in less than two weeks, 'not best pleased' was an understatement.

Still, Lizzy swallowed the 'Oh, for God's sake!' that threatened to emanate, and managed to corral it to a less accusatory 'Are you absolutely sure?'

'I'm sure,' said Delilah, still clutching a writhing Milo. 'Sorry.'

'Is it'– she nodded swiftly at her child – 'the k-i-d-s?'

But Delilah shook her head. 'No. They're... adorable. It's college,' she explained. 'I got on to a summer programme and it starts mid-July.'

Mid-July? But that was more than a month away. Lizzy seized on what seemed to be a reprieve. 'But you can stay until then?' she suggested, Pemberley still on her mind, as well as what the hell to do about work, given the hospital crèche was a) oversubscribed and b) a hotbed of lice.

But Delilah could not. She wanted to travel, she explained, and had booked the tickets already. She would have said something sooner, but Lizzy hadn't seemed in the right mood for bad news until today, and then this morning there had been the incident with the water pistol, and so this evening was the first proper opportunity.

'I'll clean up the moth dust,' she promised, as if that might make up for it.

But Lizzy waved a weary hand at her. 'I'll do it,' she said. 'You... relax. Have a night off.' She might as well get used to it, she reasoned: doing it all.

This is what always happened, she told herself, as she dusted down the sofa and curtains — both apparently 'moth' territory — when one tried to move on. The universe, or — given she didn't have any dealings with fate — Delilah, decided it wasn't time yet.

Yes, it was obviously a sign. Though, now she'd put her mind to it, she wasn't going to change the arrangement with Pemberley. She would just have to cancel The Hawden, and get Mrs Briggs to let Bill and the estate agents in. And telephone a house clearance company to deal with the contents. And an auctioneer to sell off anything decent. And — oh God, the enormity of it! And for a second, a blistering, hornet-hot second, she hated him. For leaving her to deal with this. For leaving her at all. How the fuck dare he?

But then, as ever, it passed.

Dear Darcy, she wrote.
It's all a bit of a pickle.

* * *

Meanwhile, in a situation one might suspect of being the kind contrived by a novelist, as Lizzy scoured the online equivalent of the back pages of *The Lady* in search of a replacement au pair, her sister Lydia was in want of a position.

Lydia had moved in and out of temp jobs with the same alarming frequency and apparent indifference she had once got through men – of course the more observant might have noticed the physically intolerable boredom that precipitated each switch, along with the turmoil that always came in its wake, but the Bennets were not these people, and as such dismissed her as a work-shy ingrate and downright flibbertigibet.

'I just can't!' she had complained only yesterday at the breakfast table, when trying to explain to her father why she had just phoned in sick to yet another seemingly promising office job – this one in Bruton and Foulks, Meryton's leading surveyors. 'It… it's itchy!'

'Wear a vest,' suggested her mother, who had nipped into the kitchen for a Yakult on her way to the vet's.

'I don't mean like that!' she wailed in reply.

What Lydia meant was that having to wear sensible clothing, having to remember a specific spiel each time she answered the phone, having to even be at work at the right time was somehow both claustrophobic and far too expansive a task. One that made her brain ache and her limbs twitch, so that, not for the first time, someone had asked if she had needed a wee, or was having some sort of seizure.

Mr Bennet had no sensible suggestions, bar a reminder of her outstanding debt, which to Lydia's disbelief seemed to be steadily rising (along with the 'sensible clothing', she had been forced to add new underwear to her tab, having put on a little weight now she was no longer on the 'Paris' diet [mostly cocaine and oysters], and she refused to sink to M&S, still less Primark). Mary, despite having suffered a similar irritability during a brief stint at Boots (the seams of the uniform were as infuriating as the idiotic customers) was also decidedly unsympathetic, suggesting 'radio newsreader' because of its brevity and variety, ignoring both Lydia's lack of interest in current affairs, and a very slight lisp.

'Well, you have to do *something*,' concluded Mr Bennet unhelpfully.

'I know!' yelled Lydia, at this point willing to do pretty much anything that didn't require her presence outside the house at an ungodly hour, a uniform, or being around alcohol (she had managed two nights at a Wetherspoon's, but every facet plus the proximity to cheap spirits, threatened to drive her to drink). But what did that leave? Sweet Fanny Adams, unless she could persuade Jane to pay her for the whole surrogacy thing. Except, she reminded herself, that was supposed to be about selflessness, otherwise why bother?

Oh God. She'd end up like Denny at this rate. Stuck in a small town with nothing to show for her life but a 5am wake-up call and a polyester uniform. Only Denny liked being outside, didn't mind the fugly shoes or the unflattering cut of the shirts, the embarrassing trousers, the fact that his job didn't reflect anything resembling ambition or achievement but was just something that 'paid the bills' – a state of play that, as a teenager, she had openly derided as 'sadsack', and even now, though at least recognising her snobbery, could not bring herself to accept. Only, what else was on offer?

And so, the scene was set, the conditions primed, for Lizzy's impromptu appearance that Saturday, the purpose of which was to complain about the paucity of applicants for her 'position vacant' and beg Mrs Bennet to step in.

'I'd love to,' her mother replied, 'but I can't. Not with Hindon being so busy, and then there's Meryton Women's Guild, and the dramatic society has auditions coming up, plus I'm thinking of running for Parish Council.'

'Please, God, no,' muttered Mr Bennet.

Everyone ignored him.

'You have Bridget,' Lizzy pointed out, literally, given her niece was in the morning room next door at that very moment, ploughing through several episodes of *Countryfile* and planning her menagerie.

'On Saturday nights,' Mrs Bennet explained, 'and two days after school. But she's very self-sufficient, and doesn't wee in the pot plants.'

That had been an unfortunate development, on both Milo and Arden's parts, though their explanation had made vague sense at the time. 'Couldn't Dad—' Lizzy began.

'No he could not,' he replied, before even finding out what it might be that he was required to do, but knowing he wouldn't be suited to it. Besides, he had done his time – forty-four years at the bank – and he had no intention of extending that, not even for one of his least problematic daughters.

Lydia, who had only half tuned in to the beginning of the conversation (because she was too busy guiding Milo and Arden through the moves to the Macarena, and had entirely missed the bit about the extensive hours and early starts) suddenly saw it in front of her: not merely a job, but her very redemption. Yes, it made sense. She loved the twins and their idiotic conversations, she could wear whatever she liked, and the whole project might make surrogacy seem less daunting.

'I'll do it,' she blurted.

Mr Bennet at least had the decency not to laugh, unlike his wife.

'Oh, Lydia, don't be ridiculous!' she hooted. 'You couldn't possibly do that.'

Lydia bristled. 'Why is it ridiculous?' she asked. 'Why couldn't I do it?'

'Well, I...' Mrs Bennet trailed off, uneasy about mentioning her youngest's reputation in Bridget's earshot (she had freakishly good hearing, and had not yet dropped the habit of repeating things).

'Liz?' Lydia pushed her sister. 'Come on. I'll be good at it. I can make fairy cakes, I actively like *In the Night Garden*, and I have almost zero shame.'

This was true, thought Lizzy, and yet... Lydia? Really?

'And they're at nursery, what, four mornings a week?' continued Lydia. 'I mean, how hard can a few hours a day be?'

'There's some evenings as well,' Lizzy explained, assuming this would be the straw that broke the self-centred camel's back.

'I can manage evenings,' insisted Lydia. 'Not like I've got anything else to do.' Which was true, unless you counted *Taskmaster* or texting Denny. Plus she was sick of listening to Mary's choir practice, which was both horribly regular and painfully extensive.

'I...' Lizzy's instinct was to decline her. But then she reminded herself she'd exhausted all alternatives, and asking her mother had been the very last resort. What else was she going to do? Give up work? And then what? Actually have to parent all day because she could no longer even afford nursery fees, and be left for hours with either endless 'Wheels on the Bus' or her own awful thoughts?

'Yes,' she said. 'Actually, that would be great.'

★ ★ ★

Lydia took to au pairing, if not like a duck to water, at least like a duck to a small, muddy puddle – one that she has led her ducklings haphazardly across a B-road to reach. That is to say, she wasn't particularly accomplished at it – she wasn't particularly accomplished at most things – but was delighted to find she mildly enjoyed it. Milo and Arden were easy company; they, too, had the attention spans of gnats on amphetamines, and were also willing accomplices in all manner of things Lydia preferred to spend her afternoons doing: eating cheese, watching *Countdown*, scrolling through the *Mail*'s sidebar of shame in the hope of coming across the #MeToo comeuppance of any of the myriad men in the industry she'd been 'persuaded' to fellate, or the cellulite thighs of a rival.

If Lizzy was disappointed to arrive home to discover the kitchen littered with breadsticks or the sofa coated in a layer of what appeared to be grated cheese, she wisely kept that to herself and was likewise reminded that it was this, nits, or penury. Besides, there was something about spending so much time within the giddying spin of Lydia's orbit that was enervating, emboldening – encouraging a let-them-eat-cake laissez-faire-ness that she hadn't experienced since childhood, or the first days with Darcy, before medical school, her residency and seventy-hour weeks, and then the grim rollercoaster of fertility treatment. So taken was she with the effect, that she decided to keep the reservation at The Hawden, having agreed to let Lydia sit for an entire weekend. A progression Lydia treated as if she'd just been handed a grade A.

'I think it'll be good for me,' Lydia explained to Denny, as they sat nursing pints of lime and soda in the back bar of the Dragon. (She might be able to avoid bar work, but pubs were a hazard of hanging out with a band, and Denny had just come from a fraught meeting with the other members of Listless Biscuits about whether or not to name an EP 'It's Still Twitter, You Shithead'.)

'Maybe it's your calling.' He tore open a packet of salt and vinegar crisps, laid them on the table between them.

'What? Nannying?' Lydia pulled a face. 'I doubt it.'

'I meant… You never wanted kids?'

Lydia flinched. This was the kind of nettling question her mother, or Carole bloody Burghley might ask. But from Denny? What did he care? Or, worse, what did he know? Had he heard something from Kitty via Dave about the surrogacy thing?

Her alarm was clearly writ large, because he immediately retracted it. 'Sorry, I wasn't thinking. I forget that's a... a loaded question for women of your—' He stumbled, corrected himself. Badly. 'Gender. Not that it's something I've been thinking about. I hadn't marked you out for a broodmare situation. Ha ha! I just...' He paused. 'I'll shut up now.'

Thank fuck. He didn't know anything. He was just a man. A standard, galumphing man. 'It's fine,' she said. 'Like I care. And not really. I mean – this is different. I get to hand them back at the end of the day, and I don't have to clear up after them—'

'I think you might—'

'And I get paid for it,' she continued, oblivious. 'Win win. Plus, it fucks up your sex life. Kitty's always whingeing. And Lizzy and Fitz hadn't done it once since the twins, and then, well, the whole death thing. So she probably hasn't had a shag in four years now.'

'I know how she feels.' There was a pause, then Denny's face dropped again. 'Sorry, I didn't mean... That was uncalled for.'

Ooh. Interesting. 'Me too. I mean, it's been' – she did some haphazard maths again – 'like, five months and a bit?'

'So absolutely comparable to four years then.'

Lydia grinned. 'Oh, fuck *off*.'

That, she had assumed, would have been the end of it. But Denny pressed on. 'So, why haven't you?' she asked. 'Had sex I mean?'

Lydia, who could add easily oversharing to her litany of unsavoury habits, was suddenly uncharacteristically bashful. 'You know why,' she told him. 'I'm a walking fucking cliché.'

'Right. The bisexual slut. Not my words,' he added. 'Just proving I know my tropes.'

Lydia winced anyway. 'Though I saw a man on television – Dennis Plemons, terrible hair – and he said it's love that I'm after. Or the promise of it. And one tends to come with the other. Love and sex, I mean. Or not, and then it all gets messed up and I'm back to square one.'

'Or perhaps you're addicted to the falling bit, not the work of love itself? Love's a doing word.'

'I'm not addicted,' Lydia insisted. Then frowned. 'Is it? A "doing word".'

'Line from a song.' Denny lifted his pint. 'Massive Attack. But yes. It isn't a state. You can't just… just fall and then expect to stay there. Suspended in joy, like it's, I don't know, jelly.'

Lydia knew the song. Had sung it, wept to it, had sex to it. But she had never paused long enough to listen to the lyrics, still less think about them. Was love work? Was she as incapable of that as she was sticking to a job long enough to get promoted, or, sometimes, even her first paycheck?

'My sisters did,' she said, defensively. 'Just stay there, I mean. Well, not Mary. Or Kitty. But Lizzy and Jane.'

'I doubt it. They'll have rowed. Been bored. Even wanted to leave at times.'

'No.'

Denny shrugged. 'But then they'll have made their minds up to *love*.'

So it *was* Lydia's fault again. She was unable to focus. To commit. No, no, no. She wasn't having that. 'It's because I'm the youngest,' she explained (having read an article on it once in *Glamour* magazine and thus being an expert). 'I was starved of attention.'

Denny pulled a face. 'Were you though? Really?'

Actually none of the Bennets could have claimed that. Mrs Bennet had had endless, if fickle, attention back then, and they spent most of their childhoods trying to escape it. But it suited Lydia to have someone on whom to blame her chaotic tendencies.

'Anyway, what about you?' she segued. 'Why are you depressed?'

'What?' Denny feigned disbelief. 'A single man in my almost forties? You really have to ask?'

'Oh ha ha.'

'I *am* joking. It's not because I'm old. Or single. Though I'm single because of it. She couldn't cope and I don't blame her. I wasn't getting myself sorted. It took her leaving for me to do that and by then, well, she'd found someone else. Married with a kid now.' Denny pulled a face. 'Anyway, he's not so bad. Decent bloke. Solicitor. Did the conveyancing on my house.'

If there was one thing Lydia could recognise – largely because it was like looking in a mirror – it was a breeziness disguising a lie. 'I'm sorry,' she told Denny, resisting the urge to place a palm on his thigh.

'Don't be.'

Lydia sat on her hand. 'How long for?' she asked. 'Have you had depression, I mean?'

'Hard to say. Maybe always? But how can you tell when you're seventeen, you know, what's normal existential dread and what's… something else. And for years I had other… coping mechanisms, you know?'

Lydia nodded. Oh she *did* know.

'But then I hit thirty and I met her and I wanted to clean up for someone. Which I did – I mean I knocked the booze and the pills on the head, anyway.'

'So why not get meds then?'

Denny laughed, softly. 'I was scared I'd get addicted to them instead.'

'And you're not?'

'Turns out it doesn't work like that.'

This seemed an impossibility to Lydia, who took Nurofen

on an almost daily basis, 'in case'. 'Well, you never seem sad,' she said.

'You never seem drunk.'

Lydia frowned. 'Because I'm not.'

'Exactly.'

Touché. 'All right Philippa fucking Perry.'

'I prefer Karamo myself.'

Lydia laughed. '*Queer Eye*.' Nice, progressive reference. She paused. Then, fuck it. 'If I were cynical, I'd say you'd worked out my weak spot is woke postmen and were making a play.'

Denny stared at her, his drink paused midway to his lips.

Oh God, had she fucked this up? Was Denny about to call her out? Walk out?

In the end, he put down the glass and shrugged. 'But that would be a poor shout on my part,' he said. 'Given you're out of bounds.'

Lydia couldn't resist it. 'For now,' she added. (It was taking all her willpower not to climb onto his lap this minute, so this was, in her eyes, a triumph.)

There was another taut pause. Then, 'What are you saying?' Denny asked her.

'I don't know,' Lydia told him. 'I honestly don't.' Then she touched his hair, just for a second, before pulling her hand away as quickly as if it had been singed. 'I should go.'

'Yeah, me too.' Denny stood in a fluster, scraping his chair and sending the dregs of their drinks slopping over the copper-top table.

In her rush for the door, Lydia noticed a man staring at her, nudging his mate. Already flatly embarrassed, and now instantly incensed, she snatched her driving licence out of her purse and flashed it at him: 'See? Lydia Emerald Bennet!' she yelled. 'I'm not who you think I am!' Then, she stormed out of the Dragon and stamped back to Longbourn, blind with rage at the irony that the only thing that might take the edge off this situation was a drink or a shag. And right now, she was entitled to neither.

*　*　*

The man in the pub wasn't the only one. Within a few days, there had been a sudden and strange spate of staring of the nudge-nudge wink-wink kind around Meryton and its environs, and at a level that Lydia hadn't really experienced since her mid-twenties side-boob phase. She began to experiment sartorially, swapping out tank tops for old band T-shirts, anything fitted for loose alternatives, and yet still, on the High Street, at the train station, even once as far as Cambridge when she was out with the twins, some perv would double-take and then, worse, make out he knew her – nodding, winking, or, worse (a mechanic at the garage on the Royston Road, when Mr Bennet was getting petrol) giving her the universal gesture for cunnilingus.

She blamed Andrew Tate, and men in general, and then reminded herself that it was not flattering, that she wouldn't fall for it – not even the silver fox out jogging, who had tripped over his own HOKA Rockets when he'd clocked her – because she wasn't on the market, and if she was, well, it wouldn't be any of them she was jumping in bed with. It would be—

No. She stopped that thought in its tracks. She was in a phase of self-improvement, which was why this recent attention was unwelcome, distracting her from her focus on 'doing good things' (which only yesterday she had demonstrated by not threatening to bring violence on Mary for singing 'Morning has Broken' at the dinner table, but rather taking her aubergine parmigiana to bed and leaving their parents to deal with the racket). In any case, Denny had been avoiding her since that night at the pub, swapping his round with a woman called Judith with a mullet and a tattoo of Ursula from *The Little Mermaid* on her forearm. Which, now that she thought about it, was just bloody rude (Denny, not Judith, who was all Lynx and cheer). Had that been all he'd wanted? A snog? And now that Lydia had made it clear she was out of bounds – even with the 'for now' caveat – he just wasn't interested? Was Denny really that shallow and Lydia that tedious? Only worth knowing for her (admittedly mint condition) tits?

So enraged was she by this apparent dismissal, that when Lydia got off the train back from Cambridge that evening, she turned, not left on the mile-long trudge back to Longbourn, but right, along the High Street and towards Denny's late-Victorian terrace. Fuck it, she wasn't just a pretty face, or a pair of pert and perfectly formed D-cups, she was a woman of substance, with facets, and depth, albeit packaged rather attractively.

By the time she reached Denny's front door, Lydia's cheeks were a shade that not even Nars would bring itself to mimic, and she had reached levels of self-righteousness of which Mary would have been proud. Needless to say, Denny was rather less appreciative when he answered the bell and Lydia launched herself past him.

'Come in, why don't you?' he muttered.

Lydia ignored him, springing along surprisingly attractive sanded oak floorboards. She'd assumed Denny would be all tacky laminate or war-crime lino and rag rugs, but these were original. Minimal. Not that Lydia cared, of course.

'So what is it?' she demanded, as she flung herself down on a mid-century-style sofa that definitely wasn't IKEA. 'I wouldn't put out so you won't put in?' It had made more sense in her head – had even sounded catchy. But Denny looked more confused than ever. 'You're avoiding me!' Lydia spelled it out. 'Because I said no to… to a fling.'

Denny, who had seated himself on an occasional chair (seriously, what straight man has occasional chairs?), stared at her, disbelief painted in broad strokes over his face. 'Are you for shitting real?'

Lydia flinched, then feigned indignation to cover it. 'So you're swearing at me now?'

Again, he looked baffled. 'What do you want me to do? Lay down a red carpet? Or just swipe right, HotGirl85?'

'What?' It was Lydia's turn to look confused. 'Are you having some sort of breakdown? Did you come off your meds?'

Denny, to his credit, did not rise to this, though would have had every right to, given all that he knew – or thought he did. 'Jesus, Lydia. You're on one of those apps,' he explained to her slowly, as if she were a toddler or moron. 'Looking for – what is it? – Oh yeah, "no-strings adult fun".'

Lydia's insides slipped. 'But I'm not,' she insisted. 'Why would I?'

'Really? Because you're quite the talk in the post room.'

And in the lavs, which is where Gareth Hoskins (who was admittedly ten per cent football talk and ninety per cent dick joke) had first shown him the photos.

'I thought that bird you liked was off limits,' he said, emerging from Trap 2, with a look that suggested it wasn't a shit he'd been needing.

Denny, at the sink, shook his hands quick. 'What bird— woman?'

'Nice rack and all,' said Gareth. Then, proving Denny's wank theory, held out his phone screen, which was sitting on a tit pic.

'Fuck's sake,' said Denny. 'I don't want to see your Julie's breasts.'

'Not Julie's,' he explained. 'Scroll up.'

'You're all right,' he tried.

'Seriously, mate, scroll up.'

Denny, making a mental reminder to rewash his hands in a second, caved in and did so. And then instantly regretted it, not least because of the dick pic that slid into his view.

'Jesus wept.'

'That's what they all say. I meant further up.'

Denny scrolled again, desperate to get whatever idiocy this was over with. Instead he got a full face of Lydia in a bikini, winking over one shoulder, tiny triangle bottoms barely covering her bum.

'Sorry,' said Gareth. 'I assumed you knew.'

He'd assumed no such thing and Denny knew it. It was currency, one-upmanship, a literal dick contest, which, judging by the shot he'd just seen, he would lose. 'None of my business.' He handed the phone back, turned on the tap. 'I'm sure she and Julie'll get on like a house on fire.'

'Fuck off. It's just a bit of sexting. I'll send you some screenshots.'

'Please don't.'

But, too late, Gareth already had, then walked back to the sorting room floor with, Denny assumed, jizz still on his fingers.

And Denny had been going to delete them, he really had. But it was like picking a scab – every so often he needed to remind himself what an idiot he'd been. And what a piece of work Lydia was.

'There.' He opened his phone and showed Lydia the bikini shot. 'Don't tell me that's not you.'

'What the…' began Lydia, snatching the phone.

'What I don't get is, why lie to me? I'm a big boy. I can take it.'

'So I see,' snapped Lydia, who had flicked through to the dick pic, held it up to him.

'That isn't…' Denny tried to grab it back. 'Look, I swear that's not me. Some dickhead at work was the one sexting you.'

'What the fuck, Denny? I'm not sexting anyone!' Lydia flicked on, yelled a silent but triumphant 'bingo'. 'See?' She held the phone out. 'These are definitely not my tits. Mine are way bigger, and the nipples aren't weird.'

This time Denny managed to grapple the phone off her. 'Forget it. I'm deleting them. I just… seriously, why lie?'

'For the millionth time, I'm not!' insisted Lydia, never one to hedge when it came to exaggeration. Only how could she prove it? That was definitely her in the pink bikini – Ibiza, 2010, maybe? But the tits, no way were they hers. 'Hang on.' She yanked up her T-shirt, pulled down the lace bralette. 'See?'

'Jesus!' Denny shielded his eyes. 'I mean, objectively, great. Just... I wasn't after—'

'But you see what I mean?'

'I... I don't know,' he admitted. 'I didn't look for long enough.'

'Open your eyes, then.'

'No...'

'In the name of science,' yelled Lydia. 'Look at my tits!'

Denny wasn't sure it was *science*, exactly, but he also didn't want to argue with Lydia, who seemed in danger of some sort of breakdown. So he looked. Then he looked at the photo. Then he thought very hard about the 1998 Liverpool line-up. 'Those aren't your tits.'

'Thank you.' Lydia dropped her top.

'So...' Denny brushed his nose, effecting 'casual'. 'You're saying... what are you saying?'

'I'm saying...' What *was* she saying? She flopped back onto the sofa, which was not the most-floppable, being slimline and – God, yes – original G-Plan. 'I'm saying someone's stolen my identity and is using it for sex work. Or something. Probably some six-foot Nigerian bloke. Or—' Fuck, that sounded totally racist. Possibly sexist. 'Or some... some plain Jane like Mary—'

Hang on...

'Omigod,' she blurted. 'I think it *is* Mary. She wasn't getting anywhere with her own pictures so she's lifted mine. The absolute b—'

Hang on again. This modus operandi was so *not* Mary. But it was, very definitely, within the wheelhouse of another sister.

'Show me those tits again,' she said, and held out her hand.

Denny handed over the phone, confirming in seconds what Lydia had feared, which was backed up again by the username. She shook her head as she lobbed him the phone back. 'I was born in eighty-seven.'

Denny frowned. 'What?'

'HotGirl85,' she said. 'Don't you get it? It isn't me. Those aren't my tits.' She couldn't believe she was about to say it, but it was the obvious answer. The *only* answer.

'They're Kitty's.'

★ ★ ★

Having made the momentous decision to embark upon 'research', when it came to adding pictures to her profile, Kitty had panicked. And so, she had done what, surely, any sibling would have done in the circumstances: she had exploited her little sister. If you squinted, and ignored the haircuts, she and Lydia were almost twins, so it wouldn't be actual catfishing, she had reasoned. And if anything, Kitty was the prettier one, and less addicted to things, so it would be win-win as far as any date was concerned. Not that she had dated anyone yet, and nor was she planning on it. She had been right: the 'likes' were the thing. Well, that and the sexting. Who knew the tradesmen of Meryton could be quite so elaborate in their fantasies? She had been wrong to dismiss brickies, really. And as for scaffolders... Besides, if anything it had revived her sex life with Dave. So intoxicated was she after half an hour in the bathroom talking dirty to Scaffman211 that, by the time she got into bed with Dave, it was like the early days of their relationship all over again: intricate positions, filthy whispers, the reopening of the 'gadget' drawer. If anything, Dave should be grateful.

So high was Kitty on the illicit thrill and the endorphins from almost nightly orgasms, that she had conveniently forgotten that it was, as far as Scaffman211 and several others were concerned, actually Lydia they were talking to. And even if she hadn't banished reality, hadn't she and Lyds once switched outfits in Ministry of Sound, the better for Lydia to get off with the inebriated C-lister who had latched on to her sister? So frankly, Lyds owed her one.

Such were the myriad justifications she could have mustered had she been better prepared for a confrontation; had she practised an answer in the manner she used to when confronted, for example, at two in the morning by a livid Mr Bennet, who had been woken by what he assumed was an armed intruder, only to discover Kitty and two of the Meryton Grammar hockey team semi-naked in the drawing room. 'We fell into a ditch,' she told him. 'And had to take off our clothes. We're just waiting for the wash to finish.' The fact that the washing machine was, indeed, on spin cycle had seemingly sealed her innocence. Although the rest of their session had to be conducted in the 'jumble bag' her father had fetched for them.

As it was, she was entirely ill-prepared when she walked into the Longbourn kitchen to find not Bridget, but an incandescent Lydia, whose opening gambit was, 'Show me your tits.'

Mrs Bennet, long used to this sort of ridiculousness, assumed it was some sort of ongoing peeve over cup size, or a borrowed bra, and vacated the room before it got physical, leaving Kitty to whatever fate her sister might mete out to her.

'I said, show me your tits!' Lydia repeated.

Kitty pulled a face, and her top down unconsciously. 'Why would I do that?'

This only incensed her sister further, who, in a surprise move, lunged for the T-shirt and yanked it up, and was about to wrestle down the cups of Kitty's M&S balconette when Kitty managed to grab hold of a spatula (Mrs Bennet and Bridget had been making salmon and caper fishcakes) and thwack her sister in the face.

'Bitch!' yelled Lydia, temporarily blinded by tinned fish, and gagging.

Kitty, who had retreated to the far side of the island, held the weapon out in front of her, fending off any reprise attack. 'What the fuck are you on? Glue?'

'Oh, so *I'm* livid and it must be because *I'm* high. It couldn't possibly be because *you've* actually done something so monumentally' – she paused, while she retrieved a caper from her left nostril – 'batshit as steal my pictures so you could go on Tinder and cheat on your husband?'

'He's not my husband!' Kitty snapped back automatically, still clutching the spatula as if it were a lightsaber not a sticky kitchen utensil.

'Husband, boyfriend, whatever,' Lydia, who was never one for semantics, batted back. 'What the fuck, Kitty?' At that she wiped her face on her own T-shirt, and slumped onto a bar stool, apparently defeated.

Kitty, whose own blistering rage at being assaulted had segued (as it usually did) into self-pity, slumped onto another stool, albeit on the other side of the island. 'It… isn't what you think,' she tried.

'No? So you're not exploiting me to get off with… with Meryton sex pests?' It wasn't her finest description, but it would have to do.

'I haven't got off with anyone!' Kitty insisted. 'And… and I didn't use any nudes. Those are literally my tits. It's just… your face on the homepage thing.'

'Oh, well, in that case, have at it,' replied Lydia.

'Really?' asked Kitty.

'No! You absolute… spanner. Delete the account.'

Kitty, who had been clutching her phone in her spare hand the whole time, flinched, and gripped it tighter. 'But it's only research,' she tried, finally remembering what she'd told herself previously. 'It's… a bit of a kick, that's all. Harmless.' That last one was stretching it, but as Dave didn't know about it, and had got a blow job out of it only this morning, was arguable at least.

Lydia, though, was unconvinced. 'Delete it, or I'll do it for you.'

'I—'

Before her sister could muster another excuse, Lydia had snatched over the counter, missing the phone, but at least succeeding in thwacking the spatula into the window.

Kitty, sensing impending defeat, physically, if not morally, did as Lydia had bidden. 'Happy now?' she snapped as she showed her the 'account closed' notification.

'Not really,' said Lydia. 'Fuck, I stink of fish.' She took the top off and lobbed it in the vague direction of the utility room. 'What were you thinking? What if Dave had found out?'

'But he didn't,' said Kitty. 'He couldn't have because it was...'

'Because it was me? A severed head on your grainy tits? Please tell me you didn't send any minky?'

Kitty winced. 'No!' she lied (she had sent an artfully blurred crotch shot to a film extra in Hitchin). 'And don't call it that! You know I hate it. It makes it sound like it's mouldy.'

'Minky,' Lydia repeated out of habit more than malice, then sighed. 'Seriously, Kits. Just... get some marriage counselling if it's that bad.'

'We're not *married*!' Kitty snapped again. But her brief revival declined into a sigh of her own. 'That's the problem. Dave says if I don't want to marry him, then why am I with him? And' – she paused, trying to corral her thoughts, which were, at that minute, as scattered as Bridget's, as Lydia's – 'I don't know why. Except, you know, patriarchy and all that.'

Lydia went to the fridge, fetched two disappointingly own-brand diet colas (Mrs Bennet was on one of her intermittent economy drives) and opened them both before sliding one to her sister. 'Bullshit,' she said. 'You got married before and it wasn't just because you were drunk. This is the "same penis" thing again, isn't it. And yeah, maybe Gareth Hoskins has got an inch on Dave but he's married, by the way, and also, according to Denny, an absolute twat.'

'Who the fuck's Gareth?' Then it clicked. Gazza81. The one with the thing about spanking. Whom she'd sent her self-pummelled butt-cheeks to. Which, oh fuck, had probably also been seen by Denny. 'Oh shit.'

'Bingo,' said Lydia.

'He hasn't told Dave, has he?'

'No,' admitted Lydia, 'and not because I begged him not to. But because he's a decent human.'

The wave of nausea that had threatened to wreck Kitty receded into more of a swell. 'Thank you,' she said, and reached to clutch Lydia's hand. 'I mean it.'

Lydia pulled her fingers back. 'Jesus, though, Kitty.'

This was the point at which Mrs Bennet bustled back in. 'Why is there fish on the window?' she shrieked. 'Why are you only wearing a bra? Honestly, Lydia, I can't leave you alone for a minute, still. You're worse than Bridget.'

This was a little harsh, as Bridget, who had traipsed in behind her grandmother, may have been sporting wellies and a riding helmet, but she at least had a top on for once. 'Hello, Aunt Lyds,' she said. 'Been sexing again?'

Lydia, to her credit, said nothing, but made a mental note that Kitty now owed her for both that, and the whole Tinder travesty. 'I'm going to my room,' she announced. 'Kitty will clean up the window.'

'It's dealt with,' she texted Denny later. 'Just Kitty pissing about. It's a sister thing. Sorry you got involved.'

The three dots appeared instantly. 'No problem,' he messaged back. 'Sorry I judged you. None of my business anyway.'

At that, Lydia felt her insides dip. No, it wasn't Denny's business. And yet somehow, that niggled her. Not that she wanted Denny, exactly – she'd made that perfectly plain – but that didn't mean Lydia didn't want Denny to want her. Yes, that was hypocritical. But hypocrisy had long been Lydia's calling card.

Still, she didn't apprise him of this, which in itself was clear evidence of progress. 'Thanks though,' she replied. 'Not all heroes wear capes.'

Denny, for his part, ignored the twinge of disappointment, deleted the message he had been going to send next, and replaced it with an emoji of a postman instead.

★ ★ ★

Lizzy, who was oblivious to the Kitty nonsense, and still very much imbued with the sort of enthusiasm Lydia could conjure in that narrow gap she inhabited between incapacity and chaos, set off for Pemberley in a quite remarkable mood. *This will be good for me*, she told her husband (ex-husband? No, she could not get used to that idea at all). *And good for the twins*, she added, *to spend a night apart from me.*

Actually she wasn't at all sure that last part was true, but if she put it down, in black ink on pale vellum, then perhaps it would manifest itself despite her misgivings. And to be fair to Lydia, she had proved herself more than capable of entertaining three year olds, so as long as there wasn't an emergency then all would be fine. Besides, she'd be home in, what, thirty-six hours? What could go wrong in that time?

No sooner had she asked that, of course, than her efficient mind began to list the possibilities: everyone struck down with a vomiting bug; an infestation of rats; a fox trying to run off with one of them; a ladder absent-mindedly left up, which Milo might climb and then perilously teeter atop before falling ten feet onto solid concrete—

She stopped herself. There was no floor surface in the

house made of concrete, she didn't own a ten-foot ladder, and a fox would find itself at a serious handicap against Milo and Arden. No, no, Lydia would manage it all splendidly. If anyone understood the tangential brains of toddlers, it was her sister. It was herself she should be worrying about, she realised, as she turned off the A1 (none of the Bennets would ever use the M1 again) and began to head west. The closer she drew to Pemberley, the more the butterflies in her stomach fluttered their wings. Or perhaps they were moths, she thought, scattering their – what did Milo call it? Anxious dust? Scattering their anxious dust as they flapped distractedly.

By the time she had neared the village, she was regretting the whole kit and caboodle. She could have got Mrs Briggs to manage the lot – *should* have. This was nonsense, wasn't it? And, not for the first time, she swore at Fitz for precipitating the situation. *I should go home*, she wittered to him. *Shouldn't I?*

But Fitz, as he might have done even in life when Lizzy was in one of her spirals, remained silent. And when Lizzy tried to picture herself slinking back to Lydia, and getting the sort of telling off more often warranted by her youngest sister, or Kitty, she nettled, and pressed on. It would be fine, she told herself. She would go straight to the hotel, save the house for the morning. Yes, it meant she wouldn't get a look at it before the agent, have a chance to tidy or hide things, but so be it. If it took a couple of thousand off the asking price, it would be worth it to preserve her previously solid, even jolly, mood. And so it was she checked into The Hawden at three in the afternoon, with no intention of leaving until check-out the next day.

The thing about hotel rooms, she thought, as she eyed the crisp white linen, the complimentary Aesop toiletries, the twin robes folded on the end of the four-poster, was that they were so very redolent of sex. Not that there was any trace of any previous occupants precisely, more that they invited it, were used to it, might even be disappointed if they didn't witness it. She and Fitz had always obliged. If not in the evening, when one or the other might well declare themselves 'too fat to fuck' after an indulgent dinner, then the next morning, in the dim light, and the fust of each other – unwashed and uncaring, revelling in the very human-ness of each other's bodies, the folds, the creases, the secrets only they knew.

Lizzy shook herself. Well, that was out of the question, wasn't it. But she could have a sauna and swim, read the Maggie O'Farrell novel she'd been given two Christmases ago and brought with her, determined to get past the first two pages this time, order something ludicrous from room service, not worrying about getting crumbs in the sheets because it wouldn't be up to her to wash them come morning. Yes, that was a plan – a plan always helped – and, buoyed, she unpacked her overnight bag, pulled on her Seafolly one-piece – the one that Fitz said made her look like a starlet – and headed down to the spa.

Afterwards, she would blame the steam room for mellowing her so heavily, the half-bottle of Chablis she had ordered to go with the bream, the glass of Sauternes to go with the clafoutis. It was they who had compelled her to pick up the phone and send the message, not to Lydia this time, who had threatened to block her number, but to Saul from her dance class.

She should still be furious with him. She *had been* a week ago when they found themselves partnered again for Gloria's wife swap, or rather he cornered her, and it was him or a short man called Gibbons with onion breath and too many hands, but Jane had claimed him (of course she had) and so Saul it was.

'You've been avoiding me,' he had told her.

She didn't dissuade him. 'My good opinion,' she replied, 'once lost, is lost forever.' It was something Fitz had once said to her in the early days, in a spat about God knows what, and had so successfully enraged her, she hadn't spoken to him for a week.

No such luck now. 'Forever?' he challenged. 'That's an awfully long time. May I ask why?'

Having to explain someone's mistakes to them was always painful. More so, when she shouldn't actually care. So she didn't.

'Shame,' Saul had gone on. 'I was going to ask you to be my plus one at Luella's wedding.'

In her startlement, Lizzy's ankle turned and she had stumbled, rendering their American Smooth considerably less so. 'I don't need your help,' she snapped, righting herself.

'So I see,' he said, in a voice that she was sure came with a smirk.

But to find out would mean having to look at him, which she was not going to do. Besides, what was he playing at? He'd made it perfectly clear he had no interest in her. 'Why ask?' she had blurted. 'I mean, why me?'

It was his turn to misstep. 'I... well, you're good company. You *were* good company,' he corrected.

'Ask Gloria,' she had hissed.

The penny still didn't drop. 'Why would I do that?'

This time she pulled back to glare at him. 'I believe she's more your *type*.'

She'd been right, he was smiling. But to this he added a frown. 'No, still baffled.'

For God's sake. 'Fine. I heard you. A while ago. In the corridor, talking? You said I wasn't your type.'

There was a pause. Then, 'Ah, that.'

'Exactly.' She looked away. The ping of triumph was less pleasing than she'd expected.

'In my defence, I was fending her off,' he said. 'I said I wasn't interested in anyone at all.' He paused. 'Have you never lied to get rid of someone?'

She had stiffened, perturbed that that possibility hadn't crossed her mind. More perturbed at the relief that had flooded her. 'I'm...' she tried.

'Sorry for eavesdropping?'

That smirk again. 'Well, if you will have conversations outside public lavatories, what do you expect? It's an occupational hazard.'

He laughed, and she felt his body jerk against hers, not unpleasantly. 'I'm going to ask you again,' he said. 'Would you like to come to Luella's wedding with me? No strings,' he added. 'Just for fun. For the company. You'd be doing me a huge favour, if that helps.'

Lizzy had found herself smiling. 'You want me to be your escort?' she checked.

'Yes,' he said. 'In a non-sex-worker sense.'

She smiled again. 'I'll think about it.'

'Take your time,' he replied. 'The wedding's not until November. I believe the theme is "pumpkin spice".' He shuddered.

Lizzy tried not to smile. 'Oh, I shall. And I warn you, it will probably be a no. So you might want to rope Gloria in as backup.'

'No thanks.' He dipped her down lightly, despite it very much not being a prescribed move, then grinned at her. 'I'll risk it.'

And it *had* been a no. Had been all the way home, and every day since, and the entire three-hour drive from Cambridge.

But now, wine-sleepy and spa-softened, she opened a thread he'd set up on WhatsApp – its single message so far a question mark – and finally she answered him.

'Yes.'

★ ★ ★

To do:
- ~~Timon – shoes~~
- Grace – shoes
- Caterers

What, meanwhile, of her older sister?

Jane's refusal to help when it came to Pemberley was, as Lizzy suspected, only partly bound up in the business of GCSEs, and overwhelmingly to do with Jane's absolute refusal to be, well, overwhelmed.

What good would it do her, she reasoned, to relive a single step of the mess of three years ago? What gain could be made by 'facing her demons', as Mrs Bennet, high on a cocktail of gin and *Queer Eye*, once named it? She knew exactly what she had lost – her first love, her best life – but she had dealt with it in her own swift, efficient way. Chiefly by grieving on George's enormous shoulder, and then, with his help, stripping Netherfield of anything that might remind her too much of Before Times. Let Lizzy wallow— no, not wallow, that was unfair. Let Lizzy steep herself in memory, and this time, perhaps, emerge able to face facts. Able to embrace the idea that there might be a life after Darcy after all.

And so it was, while her sister snored on at The Hawden, Jane pulled up her Golightly eye mask to find her bedroom at Netherfield invaded by Kitty, Bridget and, inexplicably, a pigeon in a crisp box (beef & onion, Dave had noted – hard to come by these days).

'Oh God.' George recoiled, pulling the sheet over his chest, lest the bird make a flap for it. 'Why is there vermin in here? Why is *everyone* in here? What's happening?'

'Bridget picked it up outside the flat,' explained Kitty. 'And I'm not dealing with it.'

'So you brought it here?' demanded George.

'Yes I brought it here.' She turned to Jane. 'And you know why, Dr Doolittle.'

At this, Jane winced. The name was a pet one of Charley's, from the days when Netherfield had been a semi-rescue centre. Mrs Bennet had a theory it all boiled down to the hysterectomy, but here her memory was selectively short. Jane was barely seven when she had brought home a minorly injured chicken (it had been hit by Dane Clayborne's scooter), begging Mr Bennet to find a box so she could nurse it back to health. The bird, under her excess of attention, did indeed recover and spent the summer merrily defecating on the Persian runner before Mrs Bennet put it in the back of the Passat and drove it to Turleigh Farm whence it had probably wandered in the first place.

Next came a cat who had managed to stagger into next-door's garage to have kittens (these were farmed out easily, the semi-feral progenitor less so). This was swiftly followed by another feline (this one with fleas, a tick and a lazy eye), Dane Clayborne's hamster (the family were emigrating to Spain) and a duck whom, she claimed, had followed her home from the pond, so there was nothing she could do about it. At which point, Mr Bennet declared that any further attempts to expand her menagerie would be met with his newly introduced 'humane extermination policy'. Thus came a hiatus until she met Charley, who shared her excess of empathy when it came to the unloved or misshapen and who, while still at Cambridge, had adopted a three-legged Manx called Andy, and then, upon their move to Netherfield, took on a series of retired greyhounds, the most recent being the forlorn Socrates, whose racing days had left him with corns and a perpetual air of melancholy – a sort of hobbled Morrissey without the latent racism.

George, though, had made it perfectly clear that, while he tolerated Socrates, he was indifferent to dogs in the main, and actively antagonistic to cats. And as for pigeons, well, they were all very well with a jus and a decent Merlot, but in a bedroom? As a pet?

'Get it out of here,' he begged.

'It's got a scabby foot,' explained Bridget. 'I want to heal it and keep it as a pet.'

'So keep it,' snapped George.

'I will when it's fixed,' said Bridget. 'And it's not vermin. It's just a sad boy. Look.' She thrust the box under George's nose.

'Oh God.'

'I'll take it,' Jane said quickly, jumping out of bed, grateful George had bid her wear the oyster silk pyjamas last night.

'Him,' said Bridget.

'Take it— *him* where?' George checked. 'Not just... downstairs.'

'I don't know,' admitted Jane. 'But I promise you won't have to deal with him.'

She took him to Hindon Lydiard.

It was her mother's suggestion, having exhausted the animal shelter (domestic mammals only), the Hertfordshire Pigeon Club (racing birds only) and the emergency vet (unmanned on a Saturday during cricket season).

'I can't go to his house,' Jane declared.

'Why not? I'm always popping in with things. He seems ever so grateful.'

'He's being kind,' said Mr Bennet from behind the Saturday *Times*.

'He is not,' his wife insisted. She turned back to Jane. 'He'll be pleased to see you. Poor man, all on his own. Of course, it's a shame it's not Lizzy with the whatnot.' She gestured at the pigeon ('Geoff', according to Bridget). 'You'll be wasted on him.'

Jane tried to smile. 'I don't think that's relevant' she began.

'You could just wring its neck,' suggested Mr Bennet.

At which point, peeved with the pair of them, Jane stomped off with her box in the direction of the Nugents' old cottage on Frog Lane. Where Hindon was, it seemed, pleased to see her, and to meet Geoff.

'Poor chap,' he said, as he inspected the bird on the kitchen table (Jane having laid down an old towel she had brought for the purpose).

'Is he fixable?' Jane asked. 'Only my niece is keen to keep him. God knows where, as her mother won't allow it. And I would, but, well, my fiancé…' She trailed off, still unused to the word, her thoughts drawn to the mix of belligerence and terror on his face not an hour ago.

'Oh totally fixable. It's hair,' he explained. 'Human hair. They like it for nests but tend to get tangled in it. And he can stay here for now. And later, well, we'll think of something. He might be releasable. Not sure your niece will be pleased, but it'll be better for him, I think. Oh, and it is a him. She did well, sexing him.'

'Bigger head, thicker neck,' said Jane.

Lindon looked up at her, a smile creasing ruddy cheeks. 'Quite so,' he said. 'Clever girl.'

'Actually, she just made a lucky guess,' admitted Jane. 'I helped her check.'

'I meant you.' Hindon grinned, then flushed. 'But, well, woman, not girl, obviously.'

'Oh, I…' Jane pinked with him – a shrimp on a skillet. 'Well, thank you. Animals are… *were* a passion of mine.'

'Were?'

'Long story. Can I help?' She pivoted quickly.

Together, she and Hindon unravelled several lengths of box-dyed blonde from Geoff's leg, pasted on some sort of salve, and settled him in a crate on a shelf in the sitting room, out of the way of Dorothy, who was unlikely to eat him, he explained, but would pester him into friendship, when what he needed was rest.

'You don't want a job, I suppose?' he checked, pouring peppermint tea from a kettle that had seen better days. 'Only we're after a veterinary nurse. I mean, I know you're a barrister by trade, and then there's your daughter. How old is she? Fifteen?'

'Sixteen,' said Jane. 'Last week. But' – she shook herself – 'how do you know I have a daughter? How do you know about… about the Bar?'

'Your mother?' Hindon looked sheepish.

Of course. If there was an Olympic medal for gossip she would take gold every time. 'I'm sorry,' she offered.

'Not at all. She does like to talk, and I'm happy to listen. I'd offer *her* the job but she should be retiring as it is.'

'Oh she wouldn't do it anyway,' said Jane. 'She's completely squeamish. She's only there for the drama.'

'Good to know.' Hindon laughed. 'So what about you? No chance of going back to the Bar?'

'God, no,' Jane replied. 'I hated it even back then. All too… testicular. Citizens Advice is bad enough. You're trying to fix things but mostly it feels as though you're meddling at the edges, or trying to stick a plaster on a broken leg. And I couldn't leave Grace. It's a difficult age, sixteen. You think the toddler years are the worst of it, when you're just trying to keep them alive. But protecting them against TikTok and toxic – what are they called? Frenemies? Well, that's far harder.'

'Oh, Lord,' said Hindon. 'I have all that to come. Though I suppose it's different with boys. Easier perhaps.'

Jane grimaced, thinking of Grace's grammar compatriots. 'I wish I could say yes,' she told him. 'But either you have the same problems or you have to stop them being the toxic ones. How old are yours?'

'Seven and ten,' he said. 'And currently living in Switzerland.'

'Oh, gosh.' Jane's heart twinged. 'You must miss them.'

'I do,' he said. 'But, their stepdad works at the Hadron Collider, and I think that beats being a village vet, don't you? Besides, I saw them at Easter and I'll see them again in a few weeks. It could be worse.'

Jane knew chivvying when she saw it, but she knew too that an excess of empathy right now could tip him towards maudlin. Besides, he was right: there *was* always a bright side.

'More tea?' he asked her. 'And I might have a shortbread finger somewhere.'

Jane should get back, she knew. George would have left by now for… whatever he did on these odd weekends without her, and Grace would be up and studying. Or moaning about studying. Or not studying and having a conniption about the fact. And yet, this was just so very… easy. Here, in the mishmash of a living room, with a pigeon asleep next to a porcelain Wally Dog, and Dorothy sprawled across her lap.

'Actually,' she said, 'yes please. A shortbread finger would be lovely.'

★ ★ ★

It is a difficult thing, being a teenage girl. It is infinitely more difficult being a teenage girl with acne, back-ne and hair the colour of a gerbil, who also happens to be the daughter of a woman considered practically perfect in every way. 'Mary fucking Poppins,' Grace was wont to mutter to herself when Jane produced a wipe, a Chapstick, an annotated *Romeo and Juliet* from her capacious Mulberry Bayswater. And it wasn't just the level of preparation, it was the way her mother would materialise at every opportune and inopportune moment, in a cloud of Byredo Gypsy Water, like a manicured phantom.

Gypsy Water. Who the fuck called a perfume that anyway? It was cultural appropriation. And maybe even racist. Which Grace would have pointed out, if she could have been arsed, which she couldn't. Besides, she needed her mother on side. Needed her to agree that a morning off from revision was essential to her mental health and if she didn't get one, she'd probably have a panic attack or self-harm and end up in a psych unit like Emily Kester. Grace also needed her mother for a lift to Cambridge, or, at worst, the station, because if she had to walk all the way to fucking Meryton, then she'd get sweaty and Jemima would be, like, totally revolted and post on her story that Grace was a minger and then she'd be back to having to eat lunch with the Ukrainians.

The Snap said Scudamores at midday for punting, so she had – Grace flicked her eyes to the top right of her iPhone, which had been glued to her hand since before she'd even opened her eyes – two hours to get there. And her mother was – where the fuck was she? Oh God, was she going to have to talk to The Knob? She shivered deliberately, imaginary cameras tracking the way her hair, despite using up half her mother's Aveda conditioner, still didn't shine, and the narrator in her head declaring that her existence was, indeed, pitiful.

Fine. The Knob it was. At least she might prise twenty quid out of him. Fifty if she could catch him on TikTok again, ogling Arianna Grande like some sadsack paedo. And, with an Oscar-worthy sigh, she slammed her bedroom door, and stamped down the stairs to the kitchen, where Wickham was, irritatingly, not on his phone, but fiddling with the De'Longhi coffee machine, which was, like, literally a penis extension.

'Figuratively, darling,' said the Jane in her head.

'Fuck off,' replied her reliable narrator, as Grace dug out her 'try me' face – a combination of latent rage and the ever-present threat of tears.

'Can you drop me in Cambridge?' she asked. 'It's, like, an emergency that I get there by twelve.'

Wickham glanced up from the filter thing. Grace swore he flinched. 'Station,' he said. 'Ten minutes. I've got things to do.'

'Where's my mother?'

'Fuck knows— Sorry. I mean I don't know. No, that's not true. I do know. She's taken a pigeon to the vet. Something to do with Bridget. Filthy fucking thing— Sorry.'

Typical. God, her mother was such a pushover. It was pathetic, really. She didn't know how Dad could stand it...

Could have stood it. She corrected herself with the familiar sinking that accompanied every reminder that her chief ally in life – he of the mediocre hair, the mediocre legs, the mediocre most things except personality – was gone. She should, by rights, blame him for... well, everything. But he wasn't there, and Jane was, and she was just... so infuriating. Even the way she breathed was stupid. And as for her and The Knob.

Still, at least he had wheels. And this way she didn't have to explain anything.

'Fine,' she conceded. 'I'll wait in the car.'

* * *

It was three hours later when Lydia, who had taken the twins on a long walk across Lammas Land in the hope of exhausting them, happened upon her niece on the wall next to Scudamores, her eyeliner smudged, but not artfully, her cheeks mascara-streaked.

'Grace? Oh shit! Sorry.'

The twins had immediately launched themselves on their cousin, oblivious to the fact she had a phone in her hand. A phone that had immediately been flung heavenward and was now floating slowly downriver, towards the Mathematical Bridge.

'Fuck!' yelled Grace, oblivious herself to small ears.

'Fuck!' agreed Milo.

'Jesus wept,' said Lydia. 'We say "flapjack", Milo. "Flapjack".' She hauled him off Grace. 'I'm really sorry. But it'll be insured.' Jane insured everything, sometimes twice.

'You don't understand,' wailed Grace staring in vain at the shallow but soup-thick Cam. 'They're running late. Now how will they meet me?'

After persuading her the phone was as good as dead, Lydia managed to ascertain through the sobs that 'they' were someone called Jemima Hollinrake and two of her minions, both called Sophie (of course they fucking were). They'd invited Grace punting at twelve, but none of them had shown up, and their Snap Maps suggested they were all still at Jemima's.

'I hate to say it,' said Lydia, as she tried to keep an eye on the twins, whilst also digging in the double buggy for a wet wipe to deal with the mascara. 'But do you think you've been stood up?'

Grace's already pale face turned to whey.

'Fuck them,' said Lydia then, ignoring Milo's gleeful repeat. 'Seriously, fuck them. You don't need friends like that. You need...' What did her niece need? Lydia plunged her hand in her metaphorical box of cheer-up delights, passed over 'getting obliterated' and 'a shag' and pulled out the next best thing.

'Come with me,' she said. 'You're getting a makeover.'

Of course salons on Saturdays in the summer in Cambridge tend to be fully booked, but Lydia, being Lydia, knew someone who knew someone at Scruffs, the very same place that had shaved in Lydia's undercut some time around 2003, who had had a cancellation ('Cystitis,' he said. 'She's been shagging a manchild.') for a full head of foils so had three hours to kill.

'Can I go wild, Mum?' he asked.

Lydia went to correct him, then thought better of it. Fuck it, she'd be Mum if it meant Grace got what she wanted. Her eyes met her niece's in the artfully flyblown mirror.

Grace nodded. 'Go wild.'

On the walk over, Lydia had further managed to wheedle from her niece that Jane's mere existence was painful to her at times. Something, of course, she could sympathise with.

'She's like a doll!' Grace complained.

'Do Mattel make middle-class Barbie?'

This raised a vestige of a smile, but it quickly slipped. 'If she's Barbie,' Grace replied. 'What am I? Not even "just Ken". I'm nothing.'

'You're not nothing.' Lydia nudged her, both hands still on the buggy. 'My God, I should know. I grew up in Jane's shadow. Take it from me, there's no point in trying to compete. We all learned that early on. Stop trying to be like her. Be... be different. As different as you bloody well can be.'

After Darcy

Two and a half hours later, Grace was different all right. Her formerly waist-length hair barely grazed her chin, and instead of mediocre rodent, it was a dazzling platinum.

She turned her head side to side in the mirror and, for the first time in Lydia's memory, grinned. 'I love it,' she said. 'Can I get my nose pierced now?'

Well, what other answer to that could there be but an emphatic 'yes!'?

★ ★ ★

Lizzy had woken that morning at The Hawden in the sudden flush of an orgasm – an unsolicited one, but an orgasm all the same.

Or rather, not the same. This one – the first since… everything – was nothing to do with her former husband, with the familiar whisper of 'shall we?' at eight on a Saturday, with the nudge of him, hard against her already; her half-laugh as she'd touch herself to check she was wet enough, then guide him inside. No, this bliss bore not a trace of Fitz.

This one was all Saul.

The dream was mostly a blur – and too boring to even think about, let alone relate, as other people's dreams always are – but it was his name she called as she came, his face above her, his hips she'd straddled…

Oh God.

She sat bolt upright, her head thumping unpleasantly – the Sauternes, she realised, at which idiocy she wanted to thwack herself. What had she been thinking – swilling around in a spa like some latter-day Cleopatra, drinking ridiculously priced wine, and then, yes, messaging her Anthony? No, not her *anything*, she chastised herself. And she snatched at her phone and went to delete the message before he could see it. It had been gone eleven after all when she'd sent it – past bedtime for anyone over the age of fifty. But, no, there they were – two blue ticks, and a 'last seen at 01:34' status. Of course, she thought, insomnia, also the province of the middle-aged.

Fuck it, she'd deal with that later. Right now, she needed to get to Pemberley and get... whatever it would turn out to be, out of the way.

And with that, she flung off the feather duvet, and stumbled to the rainfall dual shower, which she promptly told to fuck off.

Pemberley was everything and nothing she imagined.

Every turn on the staircase came with a flash of him. Every corniced ceiling with an image of something they'd done: that first Christmas, aged, what? Nineteen? Twenty? When they'd had sex in every room, just because they could; summer on their honeymoon, when he'd jumped in the duck pond still clothed from the drive up, and emerged, his white linen shirt clinging to every August-bronzed inch of him; the Christmas before it all, when she'd collapsed on the Chesterfield, and admitted she might actually be pregnant this time. Even the smell of damp when she opened the pantry brought with it a wash of nostalgia so swift and thick it was giddying.

'Bit gloomy.'

Lizzy was yanked from her reverie for the second time that day.

'Pardon?' She frowned at the shiny-suited twenty-something in the pointy shoes who had the audacity to call himself an estate agent.

'I mean, it'd be better if you painted it white.'

'The pantry?'

He pulled a face. 'The whole house. Blank canvas. Better for buyers' imaginations. It's all very... twentieth century in here. Knocks a bit off the price.'

For someone who was barely born in the noughties, this was a bold, and also wildly inaccurate claim. They'd last painted it in 2017, with the leftover Down Pipe (an elephant grey) from Ledbury Road. It was, admittedly, a bit dim, though Lizzy preferred 'cosy'.

'I don't care,' she said. 'I just want it sold.'

'Well, if you just—'

She held up a hand. 'I'm going to stop you there,' she said. 'I've told you I want it gone and I mean it. Put it on the market for what we agreed and you can accept anything up to fifty grand under. When it's sold, telephone me. You keep the keys.'

She left within seconds, the car already filled with petrol, a sad, garage sandwich on the front seat to save her too many pitstops. Jane had it right after all. There was no gain in facing it. In fact the whole trip had been a fool's errand. Look at what had happened with Saul—

No, not *with*, but… She shook herself. This just wasn't like her. None of this was. Leaving the twins with Lydia for an entire night, for God's sake. What had she been thinking? It would be a miracle if they'd made it through with all ten digits intact, let alone without learning at least ten new swearwords and a new and diabolical way to mess up the computer.

These thoughts kept her company all the way back down the A1, round the ring road, and right at the station, where, having swept into the brick-laid hard-standing at number twenty-seven in a state of almost religious relief, she found Milo, quite alone, and urinating voluminously against the front door.

'For God's sake,' she muttered, but let him finish, before yanking him back – she'd made that mistake before. It was only then that the full significance hit her. 'Wait, where's Lydia? And your sister?'

Milo shrugged. 'With Grace,' he said. 'She got a ring in her nose.'

★ ★ ★

Lydia, in her defence, had noticed Milo's absence quite rapidly – the time it took for her to argue with Arden as to whether or not a Fruit Shoot counted as one of your five a day, and if foxes were real. They'd made it back to Ledbury Road only minutes after Lizzy – admittedly enough time for Milo to get run over or even kidnapped. But he hadn't been. He'd just peed somewhere he shouldn't.

'He was desperate,' she said. 'And I told him he couldn't very well wee in Mill Road Co-op, and then the next thing I know, he's bloody stomped off, and you can't run with one of these things.' She rattled the ridiculous double-width Bugaboo. 'You try it!'

'I just—' Lizzy stopped herself. That could wait for later, when the children were out of earshot. 'Get inside now,' she told all of them. 'I'm going to call Jane.'

To say Jane was not pleased was an understatement. This was worse than the time Grace had cut her own fringe with the kitchen scissors. Worse, even, than when Charley had tried to remedy it. Now she took one look at her daughter and told her to get in the car.

'But Muuuuuuum—' tried Grace.

'I said, get in the car.'

Grace sighed as if her life depended on it and, door slammed pointedly behind her, slunk to the Range Rover parked surprisingly skewiff on the drive.

'How did you even afford it?' asked Lizzy, while Jane trailed Grace to have words about the door.

Lydia shrugged. 'You left money.'

For God's sake. 'That was for emergencies.'

'It *was* an emergency,' insisted Lydia. 'She'd been stood up by some Plastic and then your son drowned her iPhone in the bloody Cam.'

Lizzy did not take the bait. 'I guess we have different opinions on what constitutes an emergency.'

Jane was now back in the hallway, her full attention on Lydia. 'I can't believe you. She looks like… like a… a—'

'Teenager?' suggested Lydia, whose snark was always at its most potent in the presence of more than one Bennet. 'She's not a… a "mini-me", Jane. A little clone for you to play with. So stop trying to make her into one.'

'Well she's not one for you either,' Jane scoffed. 'Get your own child if you want to dress her like a— like a Spice Girl.'

'Fuck you.' Lydia threw back.

Jane didn't repeat the insult, though she was, for once, sorely tempted. Instead, she lobbed the worst possible thing she could say without swearing. 'You might as well still drink if this is what happens.' And with that mic drop, she left.

Lydia, though, being Lydia, had to have the last word. 'And I did not dress like a Spice Girl,' she yelled after her. 'That was Kitty.'

'I think you should go now.'

Lydia turned to face her next eldest sister, whose face was, if not quite as red, at least as steely. 'I can make tea, if you want?' she tried. 'We got fishfingers. You must be fucked— sorry, knackered after that journey.'

Lizzy winced. 'No thank you,' she said. 'That'll be it.'

Lydia frowned. 'For today?' she checked. 'I mean, I'll see you on Monday, yeah?'

But Lizzy shook her head. 'It's probably best if you don't. For the moment, anyway.'

'But, how—'

'I'll manage,' Lizzy insisted. 'The crèche has got places.'

'And nits,' reminded Lydia, who was verging on blistering.

But nits were preferable to neglect, even Lydia knew that. And in an act she decided was yet more evidence of how much she'd grown, she didn't call her sister a 'bitch' or an 'idiot', or kick at the wall. She just slammed the door for a third time in almost as many minutes, and set off for home.

Lydia had imagined that, when she did start drinking again – because this was never going to be a forever thing, was it; she wasn't one of *those* drinkers, not an *actual* alcoholic – it would be a wrench, a wrestle, a 'will I/won't I?' tug-of-war that might take, well, anything up to a day to come to terms with. It took less than five minutes – the time for her to trudge from the station in Meryton down the High Street into the Dragon and order a double G&T. Fuck them, she said to herself as she downed the first heady gulp. Fuck Lizzy and Jane, with their stiff upper lips and noses in the fucking air at all times. Like they'd never messed up? Jane and her impossible expectations were the reason Grace was falling apart in the first place and if Lizzy had dealt with Pemberley years ago, like everyone had begged, well, she wouldn't have had to go away and Lydia wouldn't be playing Nanny flaming McPhee (a remake, obviously, with the ugly sister vibe ditched, probably starring Lily Collins or that one out of *Game of Thrones*). Yes, that would possibly have diddled her out of a job that, it turned out, she actually loved, but whatever. At least she wouldn't have made herself a pariah for the umpteenth time. And over what? A haircut? A nose ring, which was barely noticeable by the way? A wayward piss? It wasn't as if anyone had died. If anything, she'd saved Grace from the mortification of being stood up in public and Milo from peeing in the pet food aisle. If anything, Lizzy and Jane should be grateful.

Lydia ordered another double. The first had barely lifted her mood an inch.

And another thing—

Four double gins and a shot of something blue later, Lydia decided it was high time she made some changes. Ever since she'd come back from Paris, she'd been made to feel like a broken doll. As if nothing about her functioned in the right way anymore — if it ever had. She'd been forced into giving up all the things she loved — drink, drugs, sex — when it wasn't as if they'd landed her in rehab or prison or sex jail (was there a sex jail?). So, fuck it, she was going to have a shag. A shag always fixed things. She scanned the lounge bar for likely targets, but it was all teenagers, pissheads — the kind with bulbous noses and perpetual sweat and some awful story about the time they were nearly in Led Zeppelin — and Ron Watkins from the golf club, who wasn't an alky, but was old enough to be her father (as well as knowing her father). God, Meryton was a desert when it came to men.

Except...

God, it was obvious. He already fancied Lydia. That time at the — where was it? Well, location was unimportant. The point was he had wanted Lydia and Lydia definitely wanted him. It was only this stupid sex ban that had been stopping her. And they were young — well, youngish — single, and, most of all, kindred spirits! Both cruelly outcast for... What had he been outcast for? Well, something minor, anyway. Something that had definitely chimed with her at the time.

That was it. She slipped off her bar stool, swayed gently, then swept out of the Dragon, only returning briefly to retrieve the bag she'd dropped on the floor, and then again for the phone she'd left on the bar in a small pool of blue liqueur and peanut dust. Then she turned right down the High Street and headed straight — well, straightish; she wouldn't have passed a police check — to Denny's terrace.

★ ★ ★

The first thing Denny had said when he'd opened the door had been 'Oh, Jesus', but Lydia had chosen to read that as a mark of awe, rather than shock, and, having trailed a hand suggestively down his face and neck, had lurched past him, marched upstairs, and thrown herself on the closest available bed.

In the moment, it had struck her as archly seductive: a sex-positive boldness and want that had served her well in the past.

But now, with Denny hunched in the door frame, hands in his pockets, backlit like a really pissed-off angel, it seemed to have missed its mark, was altogether less impressive.

'What are you doing, Lydia?' he asked.

'Carpeing the fucking diem,' she said, pulling off her top to prove it.

'Please put that back on,' Denny told her.

But Lydia was not one to lose at this, or any, game, and proceeded to take off her bra instead. 'I know you want it,' she said. 'And I've decided you can have it— me, I mean. It's sexy… sex time.' Not her smoothest seduction, she had to admit, but come on, he was a postman, not a fucking… poet or whatever. And Lydia was a sure thing.

Denny did not move. 'How many have you had to drink?'

Lydia shrugged. Her breasts jiggled pleasingly. 'I don't know. Some?'

Denny closed his eyes. Or perhaps Lydia closed her own? 'I'm calling Dave,' he said. 'He can take you home. Or back to his.'

'I want to stay here,' Lydia slurred, proving her point by beginning to unbutton her jeans.

Denny pulled his phone out of his pocket.

Oh my God. He was serious? He was turning her down? 'Don't!' Lydia lurched out of bed, throwing herself at Denny in a bid to pinch the phone. She missed, but the phone slid out of his hand and onto the floor, where she managed to stamp on it – accidentally, but unfortunately for Denny, still wearing Hasbeens.

'For fuck's sake,' he muttered.

Lydia shrugged. 'He's busy anyway,' she said. 'Him and Kitty are…' – what were they doing? Oh yes – 'It's sex night.'

To his credit, Denny didn't go to pick the phone up. Instead, he peeled Lydia off his body, and her top thing off the iron bedstead, and managed to wrestle Lydia back into it. The bra, he stuffed into Lydia's bag – they were hard enough to undo, he reasoned, let alone do up when the subject was highly resistant and writhing like a drunk moray eel. 'I'll take you then,' he told her, grasping her hand. 'Come on.'

But Lydia was having none of it. 'Get off,' she insisted. 'This is… assault!' Was it assault? Probably not, but it would serve her purpose right now. What was her purpose? Oh yes. Getting out. She snatched her bag from Denny's other hand. 'I know when I'm not wanted.'

'For God's sake, Lydia—' Denny began.

But before he could finish whatever it was he was going to say – probably something else insulting – Lydia was down the stairs and out the door, and halfway back down the High Street where she sat on a bench outside Abrakebabra and weighed up her options.

Going home would involve possibly her parents and definitely Mary calling her all sorts of names and probably thieving her Wi-Fi again. Kitty would be less judgemental but was probably tied to the bed with a vibrator in one or several orifices right now.

Sex. There it was again. That was what she was missing. That was what she wanted.

Fuck it. If she couldn't have sex with Denny, she'd get the next best thing. There was one person left in Meryton who might oblige. And he owed her – she wasn't quite sure for what, precisely, but she knew it all added up to a metric fucktonne of bargaining chips – so she opened her phone, clicked on his name, and prayed he wasn't already at Jane's.

He answered after a torturous seven rings.

'Wickham,' she drawled. 'Can I come over?'

JULY

As children, July meant the Bennet girls were decamped to a rambling pile on the North Cornish coast – the second home of Mr Bennet's hedge-fund-manager brother Norman. Summers, back then, had been a happy cavalcade of days spent crabbing in Padstow or gadding through tamarisk before tumbling down dunes to the white-crested waves at Treyarnon and Constantine – a veritable Betjeman poem complete with sand in jam sandwiches. Until the inevitable summer jobs got in the way for Jane and Lizzy, or, in Kitty's and Lydia's cases, they made it clear their preference was to linger around the centre of Meryton looking for boys, or take the train up to London to fritter their money on dayglo tat from Camden Town.

This, then, left Mary, who barely noticed her surroundings unless they were excessively wet or otherwise intemperate to a point that interfered with her reading, but who still managed to be a slight damp blanket on proceedings. And so, Mr and Mrs Bennet had declared their intention to holiday without their daughters, a habit that had stuck for at least a decade, with Mary 'holding the fort', a job she undertook with her usual muted enthusiasm but absolute pedantry, watering the borders like clockwork and reporting no less than forty-seven 'suspicious incidents' to Neighbourhood Watch. Then came grandchildren, and the vacations 'en famille' recommenced. Until, last summer, when the Bennets senior had leased an Airbnb via a mutual friend of the Lucases, a holiday that had been largely marked by all four grandchildren contracting norovirus from an errant Mr Whippy (an eventuality Mary had warned against, and was almost jubilant when proven right) resulting in a tag-team vomiting event that had blighted the entire fortnight. As a result, the plan had been that this year everyone would holiday, or not, in their own ways. Instead, however, no one had planned anything, the bulk of them too busy stewing to do so.

So it was that Mrs Bennet, mildly irate at the fact that climate change meant July in southern England was rather more akin to Benidorm, sat under the garden umbrella with Bad Karen and a large glass of Pimm's, fanning herself with *The Times* 'Style' section and pondering the state of play. Something was most certainly 'up' with the Bennets. This in itself was nothing new; with five daughters, one expected there to be a sort of perpetual roulette or whack-a-mole where their moods were concerned, solving one child's crisis only for another to spring up elsewhere (gin-sodden and with crocodile tears in Kitty's and Lydia's cases). This time, however, all five had contrived to be miserable about something.

'Mary's mooning about over heaven knows what,' Mrs Bennet began, 'and Lizzy went to Pemberley and won't say a single word about it, not even whether The Hawden's toiletries are all that, and if she brought them home.'

'I bet she didn't,' remarked Bad Karen from behind her rhinestone-studded sunglasses. 'Too good for her own good, that one.'

'Well, quite,' agreed Mrs Bennet. 'Then Lydia's livid with Kitty and I don't know what over, and everyone else is livid with Lydia.'

'Business as usual,' pointed out Bad Karen.

'True, true,' conceded Mrs Bennet. 'But this feels more… pointed. And the only thing I can think of is Grace's nose ring, which is, admittedly, hideous. Hideous! And the hair is... well, the less said about that the better, but it will grow out, and she'll grow out of the other.'

Honestly, why didn't people just tell her things? Didn't they realise information, preferably of the privileged kind, was a tonic to her? A pill? It might even be the very vitamin keeping her alive! In fact – she opened her mouth to try that as an argument, but Bad Karen had started in on Laurence's refusal to get hair plugs.

Perhaps that was what was wrong with her own husband? Was he reeling from her casual comment on the fact he needed to start factor-fifty-ing the top of his head these days? At sixty-seven this was hardly devastation, was it? And at six foot two, few really noticed it unless he was seated, which she had added in a bid to cheer him. Vanity notwithstanding, he was most certainly up to something though – had been creeping around at all hours, locking himself in the lavatory, with nothing to show for it – not even a courtesy flush – and had disappeared into Meryton this very morning with not so much as a by-your-leave. She'd suspect him of having an affair if—

She stopped herself. If what? If he'd been the type? Who *was* the type? Philippa Baxendale's Derek was hardly a silver fox, nor was he minted by any standards, and he'd been caught with his trousers down (quite literally) on the nanny-cam he'd set up himself when Philippa had had an inkling the cleaner had been filching her Crème de la Mer. She hadn't; it had been Derek, but she'd been sacked anyway, given it was her receiving Derek's 'full attention' on the spare room mattress, also since removed from the property. Hoist by his own petard indeed.

'Hester?'

She snapped to, sickness sweeping over her in a veritable tsunami. 'Sorry, I... sunstroke, I think.' Well, she could hardly tell Bad Karen, could she? It would be all over Meryton within minutes, and gossip may have been Mrs Bennet's lifeblood but being the root of it, unless it shed her in good light... No, she would talk to Jane. Jane was sensible. Jane refused to jump to conclusions, and was good at talking everyone else out of them, albeit to her own detriment at times. But rose-tinted spectacles or, better, sense, was what Mrs Bennet needed right now. Yes, she would call Jane pronto. Well, once she'd got the latest from Bad Karen about Carole Burghley's lip-filler incident. And persuaded Lydia out of bed. God knows what had got into her, but she'd been in a pit of self-pity ever since that hangover – worse than when she'd got back from Paris in January. Giving up drinking was never going to stick, Mrs Bennet could have told anyone that. No willpower, that one. It was like gymnastics, the guitar, and hip-hop dancing all over again. Still, at least there hadn't been a married man involved this time. That sort of scandal was the last thing they needed sweeping Meryton. Especially when the vet was still very much on the market and Lizzy still very much single.

* * *

Mrs Bennet was right: three weeks later, Lydia was still swimming in self-pity, reeling as she was from the events of that fateful Saturday in June. For a couple of days – while she sweated-out, and self-medicated her way through, the world's worst hangover (with bacon and full-fat Pepsi. Mr Bennet had been left to do the shopping and had made a grave brand error, but she was in no position to complain or request an exchange) – she'd felt sorry for herself. She'd been sacked, hadn't she, and sent to sodding Coventry, so what did everyone expect to happen? But as time went on, and her memory offered up more grim flashes – like overexposed Polaroids – guilt began to build in her, ballooning to such a size it rendered her incapable of leaving the bedroom, let alone the house.

She'd woken up naked in bed – back at Longbourn, at least.

But still, naked; not even in her knickers, which had since disappeared – lost, she assumed in the pits of Wickham's digs, or stolen, perhaps as collateral. And, though there was no specific evidence she'd slept with him – she wasn't sore anywhere; there were no love bites or bruises of the kind one might sustain from a little light bondage (one of his specialities in the past) – some of the mental snapshots that had latterly emerged were disturbing beyond the slightly upmarket crack den she'd imagined. Oh the flat itself was exactly as she'd pictured – bachelor central, with too much chrome and aggressive Scandinavian chairs – but the sheer quantity of cocaine they'd managed to get through was obscene, as was the fact that she'd had no cash on her, so how had she paid him?

At that, another snapshot flashed in front of her – her fumbling with his belt; oh, Jesus! – and she felt a fresh surge of nausea and her legs almost buckle. God, what *had* she done?

What had *he*? Because if she was guilty, then so was he. Perhaps more so?

For a second, she entertained the idea of exploiting it – whatever it was – in the ongoing Save Jane campaign. Except that no one but she seemed to be waging that particular war anymore. Even Lizzy, who detested Wickham, appeared to have conceded, agreeing to be maid of honour – a role that really should have been Lydia's, given she'd never been married and Mary wouldn't wear taffeta because of the rustling. And besides, Lydia realised with another lurch, if she had dirt on Wickham, his on her was certainly worse.

She could ring him, of course, ask for the facts, just so she knew what she was dealing with. Was it a blow job (less of a betrayal – only around five points on her hastily made scale from groping to anal) or full penetration (eight)? But Wickham, she knew, would likely deny the whole thing and what gain was there in reliving it? It was hard enough as it was, what with her mother finding her vomiting in the bathtub the next morning.

Kitty knew something was up as well – Denny had made good on his promise and phoned Dave to tell him to tell Kitty that Lydia was obliterated. But it had gone through to voicemail, which Kitty rarely checked, so it wasn't until three days later, by which point Lydia was in full regret mode, complete with Nutribullet smoothies and her mother's copy of *Eat, Pray, Love*, that she rang to ask what the fuck had Lydia done. To which Lydia replied, 'Pot, kettle,' and hung up.

She sighed. There had to be another way to fix this, other than wheatgrass shots and woo-woo books, hadn't there? Oh, sure, the drinking had stopped again, and this time she meant it – *really* meant it, whatever her mother said. But she needed to make it up to her sisters. Well, Jane anyway. (Lizzy probably wouldn't speak to her even if she prostrated herself at her feet and offered herself up as a doormat.) But how? An extravagant wedding present? She was broke again, thanks to Lizzy. (Well, thanks to herself, but, really, was one absconding and some mild public urination a sackable offence when it came to childcare?) And she could hardly offer to babysit Grace; she'd been barred from aunt duties there as well. Only Bridget was still willingly left in her vicinity, and probably on the grounds that she was already fairly strange. It was criminal, really, when you thought about how much she'd loved childminding. Criminal that they all derided her as selfish when actually she'd make a great mother.

She stopped, shimmered – as strongly as she did with a first kiss or a first sip of Cristal. That was it, wasn't it? The surrogacy. If she said yes to that, it would fix everything. She would absolve herself of any guilt over Wickham, allay Jane's dismay over Grace's makeover, and give herself something to focus on. What better reason for sobriety than pregnancy, after all? Plus it would prove she could be selfless, dedicated to something other than her own aggrandisement or instant gratification. And Denny… well. She'd come to Denny next.

First, she had to see Jane, and this very second.

To do:
- ~~Timon – who fetching?~~
- ~~Grace – dentist~~.
- Hen do?
- Socrates – worms again?

As GCSEs eased their precocious grip on Netherfield, so slipped Jane's ire over Grace's transformation from Mini Boden catalogue model to walking Bratz doll. 'It's just a phase,' Jane repeated frequently, echoing the very words her mother, Lizzy and George had placated her with – all of them ignoring the fact that Kitty's phase had lasted into her early thirties and Lydia was seemingly not done with hers at thirty-seven. But Grace was Jane's child, not theirs; she would have inherited common sense, respect for her elders, a penchant for cashmere and camel. And despite daily bag, pocket and bedroom sweeps, Jane had not yet uncovered any of the accoutrements of heroin or crack cocaine use, of which Google had warned her, nor even a disposable vape. Oh, she wasn't proud of her paranoia – kept her timings to Grace's interminable showers, for once not scolding her for the lack of concern for the environment. Polar bears, be damned! Her child's entire future was at stake! Actually, even thinking that caused a needle of guilt so sharp she had to apologise in her head to the bears, and promise to get one of those timers. At least once the GCSE results were in, the hair would be dyed back to a more human colour (the rule at Meryton Grammar, even in sixth form), and the nose ring likely consigned to the figurative 'cringe' bin, in which thankfully lurked Jojo bows, Kylie lip kits, and Justin Bieber.

It was during one of her habitual sweeps – she was in the laundry wondering whether or not a half-eaten Oreo buried in a jeans pocket might be a sign of an eating disorder – when the back door was flung open and an out-of-breath Lydia flew past the utility room in the sort of state of high excitement unseen since she got the letter for that wretched television show.

'Jane?' came the shriek from the kitchen. 'Jane? I need you!'

Jane's stomach swooped. Had she mistaken that look? Was this an emergency? Had something happened to one of their parents? But she dismissed it quickly. Her phone hadn't buzzed; the landline hadn't rung. No, this was just Lydia being Lydia, wasn't it? Flailing for attention, again.

She sighed, shoved the jeans in the washing machine, and the Oreo in the bin before Socrates got at it, and emerged.

'Can I help you?'

Lydia yelped and swung round. 'Jesus, you shouldn't creep up on people.'

And you shouldn't waltz into people's houses uninvited, thought Jane, but managed to stop herself saying it. Instead she went to the kettle — a tic she had acquired from her mother, whose frantic call of 'tea?' when faced with anything uncomfortable was infamous, although Mrs Bennet had admittedly progressed to gin in more recent years.

'Tea?' she asked now.

'No— yes, actually,' Lydia corrected herself. 'Two sugars— Actually one sugar. I've put on a stone since I gave up drinking. How does that even work?' Lydia plopped onto a bar stool at the island.

Jane refrained from mentioning the recent relapse, which had been relayed via their mother in a tone of feigned horror mixed with a hefty dose of 'I told you so'. 'Here.' She handed Lydia an Emma Bridgewater coronation mug, trying not to enjoy the wince with which her republican sister greeted any association with the royals.

'So...' Jane sat at a right angle — opposite would be far too much eye contact. Plus the Quooker tap was at an irritating eye level. 'To what do I owe this visit?'

She had fully expected an apology at last – it was three weeks now and Lydia still hadn't said so much as a 'sorry' for kidnapping her daughter and subjecting her to what equated to mutilation. So what came from Lydia's babbling mouth was, at first, a profound disappointment, until she realised what, exactly, Lydia was telling her. 'Pardon?' she asked. 'You want to—'

'Have the baby!' repeated Lydia. 'I had an epiphany, you see. After the' – she flapped her hand – 'drink thingy. I think I needed to go through that, to see how selfish I was being. Like, a long dark night of the soul – all the best films have one. Anyway, I saw the light – not in a God way, just metaphorically – and I want to go through with the surrogacy. It's a waste of my capable body otherwise, given I don't want any myself. I mean, I love other people's. Well, some other people's. But I don't think I can do the sheer quantity of vomit. And anyway I've been reading up on birth and there's this woman who says it was actually orgasmic…'

Thankfully, for everyone's sake, Jane had stopped hearing anything after the word surrogacy, and was gripping the granite countertop in a bid to steady herself. 'Really?' she checked once Lydia's monologue had petered to a close. 'And this isn't one of your whims? Like when you were going to take up the oboe?'

'God no,' said Lydia. 'What was I thinking? That would never have worked. And anyway, this isn't about me, this is about you. This is…' She paused, seeming to dig deep into her psyche for something. 'Well, this *is* about me, but me doing something for others. I don't mean simply proving I can do it, because I could just, like, pick up some dog shit with my bare hands or something and that would be a lot quicker and less painful.'

'Right,' agreed Jane, though in truth she was unsure this was a valid analogy.

'This is about being genuinely selfless. And…' At this, Lydia's eyes welled with tears – an act Jane knew both Lydia and Kitty had practised, but which now seemed suddenly genuine. 'I love you, Jane. I want you to be happy.'

Jane's heart and head filled, and her own eyes too. This *was* genuine, she was sure of it. Her little sister was going to carry a child for her. And in a snap, any residual bitterness over Grace dissipated, any doubts over George – who had been behaving a little strangely of late – vanished in a wonderful puff of colour. 'Oh God, Lyds.' She slipped off the stool and flung her arms round her sister. 'Thank you. Thank you!'

It was in this embrace that their mother found them, not five minutes later.

'Oh, well, that solves one problem then,' she announced as she marched to the Aga and put the kettle back on. 'You're speaking again.'

'Not just speaking,' began Lydia. 'I'm going to be a surrogate! I'm going to carry Jane's baby.'

Jane sighed. Dear Lydia. Of course, if she was going to do something selfless, she'd want the world to know about it.

* * *

Lydia was on a roll. Being sorry felt good. Being good felt good. Better than good: each time she thought of how happy she was making Jane, she got a little fizz of thrill inside her – a guilt-free shot of vodka or something stronger, even, with no comedown, no hangover, no risk of damaging her cartilage and ending up like thingummy off *Eastenders*. Why hadn't she done this before? Not the surrogacy, obviously. Just the… being kind.

So high was she on kindness, in fact, that not even her mother's frantic interrogation on the ride back, accompanied by a bleak forecast of piles, cankles and vaginal massacre could dissuade her.

'I'm not saying it's irreparable,' she went on, 'but there were times I didn't know what was going to come out of which hole.'

'Oh, I'll be having a C-section,' replied Lydia breezily. 'Lizzy will see to it.'

'I don't think it works like—' Mrs Bennet cut herself off as the Passat swerved to avoid a thuggish tabby that had sauntered across the Longbourn road. 'Should have hit it really,' she declared. 'More business for Hindon.'

Lydia gritted her teeth and rose above it. She would stay on this cloud, she *would*. 'Could you drop me off on the High Street?' she asked. 'There's something I need to do.'

She wasn't sure Denny would be in. On a Saturday he would still have a postal round and then there was band practice, and whatever else Denny got up to. Walking? He'd mentioned that, hadn't he? And obviously scouring salvage yards and retro markets – you couldn't just pick up doors like that or an original Ercol at Homesense. The very thought would have bored Lydia once but, perhaps as an after-effect of the selflessness, or the first inklings of a nesting instinct, it actually sounded rather darling, spending a weekend at a flea market. Somewhere in Somerset. A night at Babington first, then a meander along cobbled streets, perhaps with a whippet in a quilted jacket—

'Lydia?'

Lydia was snapped from her reverie about Denny by the very subject itself, who leaned on the door jamb in a pair of black, barrel-leg trousers. Which was all so very confusing. Where were the sadsack skinny jeans? Where the 'zany' man shirts? She shuddered at the very word. Anything that could be described as 'zany' should be barred on principle, frankly—

'Can I help you?'

Lydia snapped to once again. It was definitely baby brain. Already! See, she was born to be pregnant. 'Sorry, can I come in?'

'I don't think—'

'I'm sober,' she insisted. 'Smell me.' She breathed hard on Denny's face.

Denny grimaced.

'What?' Lydia slapped a hand over her mouth. 'Do I smell?'

'Only of bacon,' said Denny. 'And coffee. I'm starving.'

'Does that mean...'

Denny said nothing, but held the door open, and Lydia walked inside.

'So...' Lydia sat upright on the sofa, a mug of ginseng and hibiscus tea cradled in her hands. 'About that night.'

'You were a mess.' Denny eyed her from an occasional chair (the question of for which 'occasion' it was designed did cross her mind, but she managed to swat that thought away). He was rather too far away, but it was understandable, given... everything.

'I was!' admitted Lydia. 'But the thing is I think I needed it. I needed the epiphany! And it won't happen again, I promise. That's why I'm here. To apologise. So, yeah, sorry.'

'Okay...' said Denny.

That was it? Just an 'okay'? That was easier than she'd thought. If she'd known that, she'd have apologised a lot more in the past, as well as been selfless.

It was not it. 'And...?' prompted Denny, pushing his unkempt locks off his forehead.

Lydia felt her cheeks pink. God, it really did work, didn't it? That just-got-out-of-bed hair thing. 'And what?'

Denny rolled his eyes, which rather spoiled the whole effect. 'And how are you going to stop it happening again. Are you going to start therapy? Coming to meetings?'

'No!'

'I really think—'

Lydia cut him off. 'It was a one-off. You've seen me – I sat in a fucking pub listening to Listless Pigeons—'

'Biscuits,' corrected Denny.

'Listless *Biscuits* murder "Murder on the Dancefloor". So I have willpower. Besides,' she went on, 'I'm not an *actual* addict. I don't need to sit around with all the middle-aged saddoes in their polyester Sta-Prest.'

'Right.' Denny raised an eyebrow. 'What does that make me?'

Lydia flinched, and glanced again at his trousers. 'You're an anomaly.'

'You can still be an addict in… in Givenchy, you know.'

'Nice reference,' said Lydia. 'And fair, but the answer's still no. Anyway, I won't need it.' She steeled herself. 'I'm going to be pregnant.'

Whatever Denny had been expecting – and with Lydia, it really could have been anything – it was not that. 'You're pregnant?' he checked.

'No! Not yet. When would that have happened?' Lydia forced a chiming laugh, prayed it didn't sound fake. 'But I will be. I'm going to be Jane's surrogate. She can't have any more children – hasn't got a womb, and, well, I have, and so I'm being *selfless*!'

That word, though, did not seem to be the cure-all Lydia had imagined when it came to Denny.

'Jesus. Well, good luck, I suppose.'

'That's it?' Lydia was indignant now. 'Good luck?'

'What do you want me to say?'

Lydia bristled. She hadn't expected sex on the settee. Nor even a weeping festival of forgiveness. But she'd thought there'd be… well, more than this. 'I don't know. "Well done"?'

'Well done, then,' Denny conceded. 'I think you're in no state to do this. Even without the alcoholism. But yeah, well done.'

Unbelievable. 'I'm not a fucking alcoholic!' she yelled. 'Also, there's no need to be sarky.' Lydia slumped. 'I thought… I thought you'd be pleased,' she admitted.

'Pleased? Why would I be pleased?'

Lydia frowned. 'I don't know. That I was doing something *selfless*.' She emphasised the word again. 'Something *good* for me.'

'Well, that's hardly selfless then, is it?'

Lydia opened her mouth to protest, but Denny went on.

'And I'm not sure it *will* be good for you. I'm worried it'll mess with your head even more. I'm worried—'

'Well, don't!' Lydia stood, her undrunk tea slopping across the floorboards. 'Don't worry about me. My head's fine. I'll be fine. It will all be just… *fine*. You'll see.'

And then she swept – as well as one can in platform clogs – out of the terrace, and, she added dramatically to herself, out of Denny's life forever!

Or at least until Denny saw sense.

★ ★ ★

'What's up with her?' asked Mr Bennet when Lydia stomped through the kitchen on her way to her room, pausing only to open the fridge and take out an eight-pack of Diet Coke.

'Pre-natal blues,' sighed Mrs Bennet. 'I was exactly the same.'

Mr Bennet made a sound, which was perhaps the prelude to a question about his youngest daughter, but Mrs Bennet would never know, as she had sequestered herself in the drawing room with her mobile phone and a French Fancy. Having a lesbian in the family was one thing, but a surrogate surely topped that, and Meryton Women's Guild deserved to be apprised of this as swiftly as feasible.

'What in God's name is going on?' Her husband asked when he dared venture in, half an hour later. 'Has someone died?'

Mrs Bennet eyed her phone, which was pinging every few seconds. Which was impressive, given she had only messaged Bad Karen. But Bad Karen had WhatsApped Philippa Baxendale and Philippa Baxendale had Snapped Barbara Clyde and Barbara had just blurted it all out on the Prosecco O'Clock group chat. That's when the messages started rolling in, and Mrs Bennet felt the spotlight truly fall on her, and warm her pleasingly. It wasn't until she climbed into bed later that evening, Mr Bennet back in the study glued to his laptop, that she realised she'd clean forgotten the reason she'd gone to see Jane in the first place.

Sister Act
Jane, Lizzy, Mary, Kitty, Lydia

Jane Bingley added Lizzy Darcy-Bennet to the group.

~Jane Bingley
I've booked a hen do. Last weekend in August. Paris. You're all coming.
11:03

~Kitty Miller
Isn't Lizzy supposed to be in charge of that sort of thing? Does it have to be Paris? It's dead in August. Everyone will have left. Nothing will be open.
11:04

~Lydia Bennet
what kitty said. times eleventy. i don't want to go to paris.
11:04

~Jane Bingley
Lizzy is in charge from hereon in. But she's very busy with the twins (!) so I booked the apartment, and the trains. We get the Eurostar on the Friday. Back bank holiday Monday. And I've checked with Mum and none of you have mentioned anything so no excuses. Dave's already agreed to h
11:05

~Jane Bingley
AAGH. Dave's already agreed to have Bridget, obviously.

Charlotte and her partner are coming to sit the twins. Colin is checking in on Dad.
11:05

~Lydia Bennet
mum's coming?!
11:06

~Jane Bingley
Of course she's coming. And if you say anything else I shall add her to this chat.
11:06

Mary Bennet
There might be bedbugs.
11:07

~Lydia Bennet
fuck me! mary's here!
11:07

~Jane Bingley
Unnecessary. And **@Mary** it's a £500 a night apartment off the Place des Vosges. It does not have bedbugs.
11:08

~Jane Bingley
Also, while we're here, could you please all stop telling everyone about the surrogacy. There's a lot of details to be worked out and George is worried people will think the fertility issue lies with him.
11:09

~Lydia Bennet
i only told denny. mum told the rest of meryton.
11:09

~Kitty Miller
I thought Denny wasn't speaking to you?
11:09

~Lydia Bennet
he isn't.
11:09

~Kitty Miller
Sliding into your DMs…
11:10

~Jane Bennet
Last Friday in August. Please put it in your diaries now. It's going to be wonderful. The Clemenceau and the Curie are closed, but everything else is open **@Kitty**. I've already booked the d'Orsay and the Dior, as well as lunch at La Coupole and supper at Le Dome. **@Mary** I will send you the full itinerary so you can check the menus ahead. Au revoir!

AUGUST

A few years ago, perhaps even a few months ago for some Bennets, three days in Paris would have been the highlight of the annual calendar, a smörgåsbord of opportunities to feast, quite literally, as well as feast one's eyes on delights from the sublime Salle des Fêtes at the Musée d'Orsay with its ornate cornicing and glut of gilt to the somehow ridiculous pendulum at the Pantheon – a scientific marvel that had enchanted both Jane and Mary as children and terrified their mother, who was quite sure it was possessed. Then there were the opportunities to overspend – a favourite pastime of at least three Bennets – at the Galeries Lafayette on Hausmann, complete with knowing glass ceiling; in the art deco glory of Le Bon Marché at Sèvres-Babylone with its Instagrammable escalators and a food hall that would put Fortnum's to shame; in the signature mint green hush of Ladurée on Rue Jacob – Lydia's chosen corner shop once upon a time, until a particularly catastrophic hangover had seen her vomit up an entire box of pastel macarons onto her own lap, and she'd been effectively barred.

Perhaps, then, it would be understandable that Lydia, with her... colourful history, should be antagonistic towards the trip. She was returning to the scene of the macaron vomit, as well as her unforgiveable crime with Mme Perlot's husband, was she not? A fact that had nagged at her ever since Jane's decree. And yet it wasn't just Lydia who was having second and indeed third thoughts about the visit. Every Bennet, in their own way, was reticent.

Mrs Bennet was increasingly wary about abandoning Mr Bennet, whose secretive behaviour had not lessened in recent weeks. This in spite of her denying him any reasonable opportunity to be alone — insisting on accompanying him every time he left the house, bar golf, and only then because Bridget was caddying and could be trusted to report back any shenanigans. This, she told her husband, was not 'sudden cupboard love', but rather a manifestation of adult separation anxiety, which she'd read about in *Good Housekeeping*, and was all the rage amongst the newly retired. Thus, she said, he would do well to humour her. Mr Bennet wisely did not argue, but drew the line at her accompanying him into the en suite, whence Mrs Bennet could hear him (there was a substantial gap between the door and the bedroom carpet) tapping away on his phone. No doubt to his fancy woman. Of course, she could have confronted him and had it all out, there and then, but having watched enough Jeremy Kyle in her time, she knew accusations would not wash without a lie detector, or cold, hard evidence, and these she lacked, despite having gone through all files on the laptop twice. So it was that she had instructed Colin to 'drop in' over the weekend, preferably at odd times and with no warning, luring him with a lurid tale of a lonely pensioner too proud to ask for company. Colin, being Colin, suggested he just move in for the duration, bringing with him his portable supplements case, packets of flaxseed, and box set of David Starkey DVDs. Mrs Bennet could not have been happier if he'd proposed to Lizzy, or even Mary, then and there.

★ ★ ★

Mary, meanwhile, could not have been less thrilled to give up the chance to spend an entire weekend in the company of Colin.

For so it was, after years of confusion, of wondering if she was, indeed, asexual, or one of those unfortunate people who could only be truly fulfilled by the sort of porn that involved donkeys or dinosaurs (she hadn't tried it, you understand; rather she had just worried it existed and decided she'd rather die chaste) Mary had discovered someone who wasn't a Jeremy or in any way a celebrity, whose company not only didn't make her want to shut herself in a cupboard for a week, but who aroused in her feelings she had hitherto only experienced while masturbating, or during an episode of *The Fall* featuring Gillian Anderson in a particularly well-cut silk shirt. Choir, and the ride there and back, had thus become both the most thrilling and frustrating two hours twenty-seven minutes (thirty, if they caught the lights on the High Street at the wrong time) of her week, as she hung on his every word, from the benefits of chicory to the validity of the Richard III car park discovery, which he still contested. And as for his baritone solos – more frequent now, given the diminished ranks (a large contingent had followed through on their threats and were boycotting choral anything until he brought back Ed Sheeran) – she could barely contain herself, and more than once had had to retreat to the ladies and blast her underarms with the hand dryer.

★ ★ ★

For once, Mary shared more than just a few hapless strands of DNA with her sister Kitty, whose sexual frustration had reached a peak not seen since she'd gone through a nylon thong phase and given herself thrush for a month. It wasn't that she and Dave weren't doing it – they were doing it more than they had in the first weeks they got together, and in every conceivable position, orifice and time of the day. It was more that none of it seemed to placate her, as if she were perpetually chasing a sexual adventure just beyond the horizon. Dave wasn't complaining, but he was, he told her, a bit worried she was trying to fuck him into forgetting the whole wedding thing.

'That isn't it,' she said. 'I just… like sex.'

'Lydia likes sex,' he pointed out. 'It's called addiction.'

'Not like that,' she insisted. 'I don't want sex with anyone. I want… you,' she finished. As if saying it might make it so.

The truth was, she didn't know who or what she wanted anymore, just that if she didn't find it soon, she would die a small-town hairdresser whose ambitions had been abandoned along with her handbag in San Rafael sometime around 2016. Paris, she was worried, would only make this lack starker, would only open the chasm between the brilliant Kitty she'd dreamed of being, and the disappointing Kitty she was. Easier to just stay home and hope that a vibrating butt plug might, well, plug that gap for her.

★ ★ ★

Lizzy was similarly irritable, though unlikely to try to resolve it with sex toys. Sex was, though, at the heart of it, or at least the promise — or not — of sex. Since the whole Pemberley mess she'd put Saul firmly in a figurative corner, ignoring his intermittent messages, and grateful both that dance classes had disbanded for the summer, and the wedding was still months away. She was almost grateful for Lydia's 'mishap' as well, as the added chaos of trying to get two toddlers dressed and ready for crèche every day, and then remembering to collect them, took up a large sector of headspace that might otherwise have been looping itself furiously as to what, exactly, she was feeling these days. As it was, her evenings, once Milo and Arden had been ushered reluctantly to bed — so thankfully only an hour or two — were spent in a spiral of what the wet dream (God, so adolescent!) meant. Was it some sort of portent? Or no more significant than the time she'd had a nightmare about a horse eating her feet? And who to discuss it with? She couldn't very well tell Jane, who had inherited their mother's tendency to make a mountain out of molehill where romance was concerned, and would likely immediately start shopping for hats. And the one person with whom she had always discussed any pickle – still discussed them now – well, she could hardly confess everything to... him. Oh, she was still writing in the diary – Milo blah blah blah; Arden this that and the other – but the entries were blander by the day, and in truth, if Fitz had managed to read any of it, he would have known without hesitation that something was up by sheer dint of omission. Paris, then, instead of offering a sop – a welcome break from the everyday, from the drudgery of packed lunches and potty training and Milo's endless questioning: 'why don't chickens have willies?'; 'when I die will my eyes be shut?'; 'what even is blood?' – was a yawning maw that threatened to engulf her in the one thing she didn't need right now: free time.

★ ★ ★

Jane, while welcoming the idea in principle of time away from Grace, whose moods were mercurial at best, found herself in somewhat of a quandary, worried that even a day away from Netherfield might seal her redundancy as a mother for good, last week's GCSE results having precipitated a debacle that not even she, in a rare pessimistic moment, could have conceived. The fact was that, despite attending East Anglia's top-ranking grammar and an expensive if minor public school, neither Timon nor Grace had got any higher than a seven in anything. While Timon had arguably done worse – failing Triple Science and Latin outright – Grace had only managed a five in English, in which both Jane and Charley could boast an A★. Even Wickham had scraped an A. This injury though, wasn't the worst of it; the insult was that both were now refusing to return to their schools, insisting they would be better off at Mill Road Sixth, which was academically average, had a lax attitude to dress code (i.e. it didn't have one), and a reputation for accepting those students for whom education was merely a stop-off point on the way to a lucrative career in drug dealing or petty crime. Jane's argument – that neither of them had a place there, and so the whole thing was moot – had already been smacked out of her hands by the acceptance letters they both brandished, having applied on the sly back in May. Apparently at that point they were working entirely separately, but now operated a two-prong, co-ordinated attack that either kept them in cahoots in the den, or saw the pair of them slinking off to God knows where to do God knows what at God knows what hour, and both dressed in clothes that could best be described as 'lost property'.

And so it was that the atmosphere on coach C (premier) of the 12:31 Eurostar was considerably less jubilant than it might have been. Though that did not stop Mrs Bennet's attempts to rally her troops.

'We could have a pamper party at the flat!' she hooted (two proseccos down; when in doubt, drink). 'Kitty can do our hair and nails. You could get a vajazzle, Jane!'

Jane sighed, leaving Kitty to intervene.

'Christ alive, mother. It's not 2001.'

Mrs Bennet pulled a face. 'Susan Clopman got one!' Susan being an early adopter of all things by Meryton Women's Guild standards. She did not mention the fact that Ron Clopman, already well into his seventies, had suffered a seizure on the big reveal. 'At least let's go up the Eiffel Tower,' she tried.

'Under no circumstances,' said Lydia. 'I'm not queuing with tourists in August to climb what might as well be in Blackpool.'

Jane agreed. 'There's a perfectly serviceable view from the Tour Montparnasse or Sacré-Cœur, though I wouldn't try that either. The pickpocketing is rife this time of year. Anyway, I've already drawn up a packed itinerary. It's on the email.'

'You know I won't be able to find that,' huffed her mother. 'My phone has a mind of its own.'

Mary smiled. 'I printed out six copies. They're in with the insurance documents and the Metro map and a helpful phrase guide. You can have one when we get to Gare du Nord.'

At which point, Mrs Bennet joined her daughters in their preferred hen celebration of staring vacantly out of the smeared window at the flat, bland expanse of northern France.

★ ★ ★

Jane's itinerary was, indeed, packed, and planned to the letter, leaving room neither for Lydia and Kitty's habitual lingering in bed nor their mother's traditional whimsy, and already catering for Mary's dietary requirements and Lizzy's desire to see the tomb of Marie Curie (Milo was in a phase of being fascinated by death and she had stupidly advised him of its existence and had now agreed to touch it for him to see if she could 'feel a ghost', as well as photograph the moment). In the sixteenth arrondissement they visited the Fondation Louis Vuitton where they took in Rothkos they'd seen in the Tate fifteen years previously, and which Lydia had dismissed at the time as 'childish' (a fact of which Mary reminded her) but was now surprised to find she appreciated, a sure sign, she decided, that she was, contrary to popular opinion, grown-up. Which would have been fine, had she kept the revelation private, but this was Lydia, who struggled to keep a single thought to herself, and so inevitably it descended into an argument as to what constituted adulthood, which ended in Kitty declaring Mary's ankle socks a 'war crime'.

The Musée d'Orsay was no less fraught with tension, as Lydia, having totted up the number of paintings of nude women versus the number of paintings *by* women, declared the entire art world (bar Rothko; her newfound muse) to be misogynistic and hypocritical, and said she was boycotting any further gallery visits unless she was allowed to walk around topless. Kitty then dismissed Lydia as being 'tit-narcissistic', and it could have ended in tears had Mrs Bennet not then set off an alarm by trying to polish a smudge off a mahogany art nouveau bed, happily distracting everyone for long enough to prevent some sort of breast-off.

Day two was similarly rigidly timetabled, with petit-déjeuner at half eight (croissants and pain de campagne, which Jane rose at seven to fetch from the Rue des Quatre Fils), whistlestop tours of the Louvre and the Pompidou, and everything else scheduled down to aperitifs (half an hour maximum) so that there was barely any time to enjoy the apartment on the Rue de Turenne, with its double-aspect salon, state-of-the-art cuisine, and absolute lack of bedbugs (Mary had conducted a twice-nightly inspection with a torch and a look of grim resignation).

By the final day, dissension had burgeoned beyond mere complaint. Mary had point blank refused to eat any more gluten, Kitty said she'd rather die than look at any more 'stuff by dead people' and Lydia had bought a set of ear plugs from Monoprix, so that not even Mrs Bennet yelping at the water pressure (again) could have woken her before ten. By the time her youngest sister finally emerged, Jane was pacing with a frenetic energy not seen since the day of Grace's eleven plus.

'You realise we're two hours behind schedule!' she exploded. 'This morning's tickets will be invalid now and we'll have to queue.'

'Oh, God,' mocked Lydia, 'not queueing.'

Jane, whose forward planning had been in no small part to avoid the indignity and waste that came with a queue, looked to be on the verge of tears.

'Well, we've missed the Dior, so why don't we all just… do our own thing today?' suggested Lizzy. 'I'll take Mum to the Pantheon and you can all do… well, whatever it is you want to do.'

'Hoo-fucking-rah,' declared Kitty, and feigned fainting onto a beige chaise longue, before opening her phone and a packet of Pringles.

'Budge up,' said Lydia, snatching a handful of crisps (even she was sick of pastries by this point).

Mary, also quietly relieved, retreated to her room, and, after another bed check, got out the copy of *Ultra Processed People* that Colin had given her to 'read on the train' and began to happily terrify herself about margarine, all the while wondering whether anything could be construed from the 'To Mary from Colin' he'd inscribed on the fly leaf.

'What if I don't want to go to the Pantheon?' said Mrs Bennet, already wearing enormous sunglasses that, along with her tendency to flap, rendered her more fly-like than ever.

Lizzy set her jaw. 'Then you can also do... something else,' she said.

'By myself?' she wailed. 'What if I get kidnapped? Or manhandled? Or... or sold into slavery?'

Lizzy smiled through gritted teeth. 'Then come to the Pantheon.'

'No thank you,' snapped Mrs Bennet. 'I know when I'm not wanted.'

There was no winning with their mother when she was in one of her moods, so no one tried. Instead, Lizzy left to 'feel ghosts', Mrs Bennet left for wherever it was she was convinced she'd get kidnapped, and Jane, determined to make good on their picnic lunch in the Tuileries (13:30–14:15) set off to buy herself an individual quiche from a boulangerie on Rue Vieille-du-Temple, having informed everyone that 'Last Supper' was at eight, and that if anyone was late they would pay for it themselves – the only surefire way to move Kitty or Lydia to do anything.

★ ★ ★

As it was, the pair fell into a state of blissful fiddling on the internet, until, around two, having exhausted the Pringles and Lu biscuits, Kitty declared she was going out for lunch.

'I'll come,' sighed Lydia, as if the very suggestion was an imposition.

'Really?' said Kitty quickly. 'But... we're supposed to be doing our own thing.'

Lydia frowned, but briefly (she was attempting to frown less until she had the money for Botox again). 'That wasn't a, like, dictat,' she insisted. Then, suspicious, she frowned more deeply, cursing herself as she did so. 'Wait, you're not back on the apps, are you. You haven't set up a thing with some Jean-Paul, or... or a Gaston?'

Kitty reddened. 'Fuck off! No. And what about you?' She segued quickly. 'You're the one with the history here. Surprised you haven't snuck off for a quickie.'

It was Lydia's turn to crimson. 'As if. Anyway, they'll be away in August.'

Kitty, despite her injury, felt a brief flicker of sympathy. 'You could fetch your stuff,' she said. 'From the old flat, I mean.'

Lydia shook her head. 'No key,' she said. 'If it's even still there. And anyway,' she smiled brightly, 'like you say, it's history.'

Kitty nodded, swallowed. 'Sorry, Lyds,' she said. 'You *can* come, if you want. I'm only going to, you know, flâneur about.'

But Lydia, to her sister's relief, shook her head. 'Feeling a bit meh, anyway,' she said. 'That folic acid is disgusting.'

Kitty's embarrassment burgeoned further. 'I really am sorry, Lyds. That's an amazing thing you're doing for Jane. I couldn't begin—'

'It's nothing,' lied Lydia quickly. 'Go on, go... flân.'

Kitty smiled thinly, and did as she was told, slipping down the ornate wooden staircase, through a courtyard worthy of an *Emily in Paris*-themed Insta shoot, and out onto the Rue de Turenne, where she headed, not west into the Marais – flâneur central – but south, straight to the Metro, where she took Ligne 1 towards Défense, changing at Châtelet for Saint-Germain-des-Prés.

* * *

If Lydia had been less wrapped up in her own drama, she might have noticed Kitty's fidgeting, the jolt of promise when she saw the notification pop up, the sharp intake of breath as she read it. She might have delved deeper into why it was that Kitty, usually happy to dine on things from packets, was so eager to 'go out for lunch', particularly as it had begun to drizzle and Kitty's hair was prone to humidity issues. She might have enquired beyond the 'apps', and got to the bottom of just what, exactly, Kitty was up to.

Kitty, in her defence, hadn't lied. She wasn't on the apps. Well, not the ones Lydia meant. The message had come via Facebook, following a photo she'd posted of herself looking cute (definitely won't delete later) in front of a lavender macaron tower at the Palais-Royale branch of Ladurée.

Three words: 'You're in Paris?'

Her reply, the same: 'Yes. Are you?'

There had then followed some hasty arrangements – a quick kir at a 'great little place' on the corner of Rue Jacques Callot. A place, she ascertained from Snapmaps, must be mere feet from his apartment. That or he lived in the bar itself. And yes, it was likely a little foolhardy, and smacked of Lydia at her very worst. But, as Kitty told herself repeatedly on the way there: it was one drink, and not with a new prospect but with an ex. And not just any old ex – the sort with unfinished business – but her ex-husband, whom she had, in the end, been glad to see the back of. Which, she reasoned, she might be going to explain to him. And, then there was the fact that he was Bridget's ex-father, who had resigned all parental rights when he moved back to

Australia, but who, she could argue, might be looking to resume a few of them now he was older, wiser, less likely to cheat on her with her best friend while pilled off his tits at an all-nighter. She told herself this, in the measured way she might explain it to Dave later. As the obvious solution to a sort of mathematical problem. But as she walked through the fairy-lit entrance to La Palette, she knew that not one element made sense, not a single number added up.

'Kitty Bennet!' He stood as she walked towards him, a dick move, she knew, but a good one, given he was six-four, and all of it as tanned as it ever had been, though the blond hair was flecked with grey now, the eyes lined from all the squinting into the Brisbane sun.

'Miller,' she corrected him, allowing him to kiss her on each cheek (how long had he been here? He was practically native.) 'I kept it for Bridget's sake.'

'Bridget. Shit.' He lounged back on the wooden banquette. 'How is she? Did you get the card?'

'I did,' replied Kitty, failing to mention it had gone straight in the bin. As far as Bridget was concerned, her father was stranded in the outback with no phone or Wi-Fi, in sole charge of two thousand sheep – a job Bridget had briefly considered ideal, and had begged to join him, until Kitty told her the sheep all had scabies (did sheep get scabies?) and were highly contagious.

This could go two ways, Kitty realised then. One: she could take issue with him – catalogue the litany of things he'd done, or rather not done, in the nigh on nine years since Bridget had seen him, and demand back-pay of alimony and child maintenance. Two: she could drink the kir that was already waiting for her, condensation blooming on the glass, order another, and then do whatever it was they both knew they'd really come here to do. Was it even cheating when it was back catalogue? Wasn't it more… a final act? A sort of last rinse to get him out of her system? It wasn't as if it could kindle into anything else. Paris was, admittedly, closer than Australia, but even so, bi-monthly Eurostar tickets might take a bit of explaining to Dave. That's if Shane even lived here.

'Can't believe your timing,' he told her. 'I'm only in town for two nights.'

He didn't live here. Even better. 'You interrailing again?' She snorted at her own quick wit.

Shane squinted. 'I'm doing a shoot for *Vogue Australia*,' he said. 'You didn't see the pics?'

Vogue? Okay, so this was interesting. Kitty shook her head, picked up the kir, and finished it in one long gulp. 'Another?' she said. She was suddenly really bloody thirsty.

* * *

Kitty was not the only Bennet with 'history' in the city. After her sister's impromptu departure, Lydia had huffed around the apartment, intermittently picking up things and putting them down, and then trying to persuade Mary into a game of Spit or Shithead, which Mary, being sensible, and painfully aware of the absence of a suitable referee, declined. And so, having reached the same self-brutalising heights as a bluebottle repeatedly banging its head against the walls of a glass jar, she burst out onto the Rue de Turenne and headed towards the Metro with the same intent as her sister: closure.

She chose to walk from Abbesses – the long way, but a familiar route. One she'd taken every day in her first year in the city, from the garret overlooking the Église Saint-Jean de Montmartre (even 'garret' was pushing it – it was half a room, and shared a filthy shower and kitchen with four other bedsits, but who ate in, in Paris?) turning right at the tip of the Rue des Martyrs, then following its chameleon tail among the bustle of boulangeries and fishmongers at the northern end, through the red lights of Pigalle, across the dogshit-littered promenade (central reservation, really) in the middle of the perpetually jammed Boulevard de Clichy, and then down into the tree-lined ninth arrondissement. Here respectability crept up once again, as the street petered its way towards the splendour of Notre Dame de Lorette, where she had spent one pleasant afternoon of truanting, kissing in the chill of the pews. Her lover, you see, worked only two blocks beyond. Their 'office' taking up all four storeys of a Hausmannian terrace next to the Traiteur Grec. A lover whom she knew was not in the south for the summer – couldn't bear the tourist hordes. And besides, the design calendar, like a truculent teen, refused to align with the civilian one, and, with fashion week beckoning in September, they'd be bent over hems in their atelier. So when Lydia rang the bell for the workroom, she knew who would answer it. And she knew, too, that she would be let in, would scurry up the wooden stairs, which would get thicker with pilling, with pins, with the discard from overlockers, the higher she climbed (the cleaner would have taken his three weeks off, even if his employer couldn't spare them). She knew, finally, that when she reached the machine room, the door would be open and, framed in it, would be the real reason she'd had to leave Paris, immaculately dressed in a camisole and capri pants, and her hair in a French (naturellement) bob.

'Madame Perlot,' said Lydia.

The older woman rolled her eyes. 'Celine,' she sighed. 'It's Celine. How many times?'

★ ★ ★

What, then, of the rest of the Bennets? Were they similarly insinuating themselves into the lives of old lovers? Resolving or absolving or entwining themselves yet again?

In a way, perhaps they were.

Jane had taken herself to the Tuileries, where she ate her (exquisite) quiche, feeding half of it to the starlings, who sang frantically at her until she despatched crumbs of buttery pastry and yellow egg custard their way, an act she knew Charley would have found charming but at which George, whose tolerance of birds outside of a menu was on a par with that of cats anywhere, would have pulled a face, at best; at worst, he would have stayed her hand long enough for her to understand that she was to stop it. Stop it right now.

And that had done it. By feeding the birds, a modern-day Mary Poppins, it was as if she had (albeit unwittingly, and decidedly unwillingly) prised open a door to a dark room marked 'Charley' and the sliver of light she had succeeding in ignoring for almost four years suddenly flooded her, a wave of *him* taking her and sending her swerving, so that it was all she could do to stay on the green metal seat. Her head filled and swam, hallucinating in the manner of Disney's *Fantasia* – memories of them together dancing in line like those hollow-eyed elephants: the pair of them summer-drunk at twenty-one in the Crazy Horse cabaret, a laughing Charley having to pull her down from the table on which she had decided to can-can; an autumn walk along the Coulée Verte, as they dissected the egotistical mess that was Ethan Hawke as Jesse from *Before Sunset* and tried to fathom Julie Delpy's intentions; then one spring, her unwittingly pregnant with Grace, being sick into the Seine after one glass of Chablis – his grinning realisation before hers, leaving her to wait on a bench while he ran to the pharmacy on Rue Mazarine; him shredding a beer mat while she peed on a plastic stick in the grotty toilet of the Bar du Marché. Memory followed memory followed memory, and every single one starring Charley.

It was this city, of course. She could have hit herself – what had she been thinking? Paris was too full of him. On every corner she saw him now, dressed in his trench coat, looking over his shoulder at her and, seeing her, smiling. In every bar she heard him order 'deux bières, s'il vous plaît' in his godawful accent (Bingleys studied German, not French – the language of business). Along every cobbled side street she watched him ahead of her, beckoning as he tried to dance backwards, before tripping and making a fool of himself but not for a second caring. He never worried about anything like that – what others thought of him – as long as he did the right thing, the kind thing. And then more memories marched – not just Paris now, but Netherfield; Cambridge, where they'd met; Meryton, where they'd married; Pemberley where they'd stayed with Fitz and her sister during college holidays and beyond. Charley was everywhere. Because he was still in her, and always would be.

And if she'd met someone who measured up to him – not who matched him exactly, because one couldn't match another human, but who was *as* good, *as* kind, *as* delightful – well, then it wouldn't have mattered. She could have lived with her memories and her new life side by side. But when the man she was marrying was... well, so much less, Charley seemed to eye her from the sidelines, saying nothing, but his piqued expression asking 'really?'

Of course, Jane felt this only dimly so far. And right now, all she truly knew was that she needed to buck up. To muster. She had the Last Supper to get through, and then the Eurostar home, and once she was back at Netherfield, well, then she could work out how to deal with it. Therapy again, perhaps. Or a new colourway in the bedroom and a good Marie-Kondo-ing of the den. Or... or perhaps George had been right and a move to London was the obvious problem-solver for both of them. Yes, she told herself, she had options (though none of which, her sisters would be disappointed to hear, was to end it with Wickham). And so, having dabbed away tears, and said a grateful prayer to Charlotte Tilbury for her waterproof Full Fat Lashes, she collected herself, and her litter, and dropping the latter into a bin, took the former back towards Rue de Turenne for a cup of tea (she had brought her own bags, of course – Yorkshire Hard Water) and a nice little lie down.

★ ★ ★

The lie down was moot in the end, as Lizzy was seated at the wide table in front of the double French windows (how did the French refer to them, one wondered), the voiles shifting gently in the late afternoon breeze, though this did little to dissipate the heat (an apartment of this stature, and price, should really have aircon, and at least one of the Bennets would be suggesting this in an online review, which would also gently mention a small encrustation of *something* on one of the hand towels and a dead beetle [not a cockroach – Mary had spent a good hour on Google to verify this – but still: a *thing*] on the wet-room floor). Nor did it do anything to dissipate Lizzy's apparent distress.

'What is it?' asked Jane, relieved to push her own minor crisis to the back of the neatly ordered (and labelled) recesses of her mind and do what she was best at: empathy.

Lizzy, who had swiftly snapped shut the cover of whatever it was she was writing, muttered a 'nothing'.

Jane, however, was not persuaded. 'I'll put the kettle on, shall I?'

To which Lizzy nodded. Perhaps tea might… clarify things, she decided. Or at least distract her from the mess of her head, as the landscape of Paris, it seemed, was not benign in its beauty, was not a safe escape. For, though the streets were not paved with memories as they were for her sister, Fitz was both with her – and not – wherever she walked; she could not shake the habit of wondering what he might have made of things, of imagining his scorn. Only where, in the past, this imaginary friend had been something of a comfort, now it was more akin to the feeling she had suffered, aged twelve, when a much younger

Lydia had taken to dogging her every step, repeating her words like a malevolent parrot.

At the Pantheon, he had stood next to her in the queue for tickets, rolling his eyes at the ham-fisted attempts at French from an American couple in front of them. 'Jesus,' he had whispered. 'Absolute MAGA wankers.' Which might have been true – they did have the air of Trump voter about them – but was hardly the point. On the detour to Shakespeare & Company, he had sneered at the British taking pictures of themselves on the stairs, and had referred to the popularity of a Douglas Stuart novel as 'middle-class hand-wringing', to which Lizzy took umbrage, as she had picked out the same for Jane's birthday only the previous week. The final straw was the walk back across the river, at which he dismissed the lovers who attached locks to the bridges as 'idiots' who, quite frankly, should be 'imprisoned, or shot'.

And so it was, Lizzy had come to understand, that instead of a gentle, angelic presence, Fitz had morphed – entirely her fault – into some sort of devil's advocate, squatting on her shoulder and voicing the very worst of his opinions, and hers (and possibly Piers Morgan's) and spoiling what could have been a pleasant day by herself, without the endless press of Arden's twice-hourly loo visits because 'I think I can feel a wee deciding to come out'; or Milo's barrage of questions about coffins. She would rather, she realised, if she weren't with the twins, be entirely alone. Or – and this was the terrible thought – with Saul, whose thoughts on everything, from which cheese might be overrated to the point of invisible socks, she did not yet know. And, while the idea of that time-acquired shared knowledge might once have been a comfort – a 'thank God I don't have to get to know someone again' – it was now little more than torment.

Not that she told Jane any of this beyond, 'It's just all rather… exhausting, isn't it? Life, I mean.' And, having then reassured her sister this wasn't a cry for help, and that, no, she didn't have suicidal tendencies, they had settled back into a dissection of the French tendency to serve tea at eighty degrees centigrade, when it really wasn't like coffee, and so wouldn't scorch if the water was allowed to actually boil, but rather taste of something beyond vaguely brown water.

'No wonder Mary insisted on bringing her own kettle,' said Jane. 'And for that, I thank her.'

'Oh, God' – Lizzy shot to a stand – 'Mary! I said I'd take her to Monoprix at four.'

'For knickers again?' (Mary was on a perpetual quest for the perfect underwear, which was neither too small nor voluminous, which didn't chafe, had a breathable gusset, and – and here lay the evasive holy grail – came in a specific shade of beige known only to Mary.)

Lizzy nodded. 'She's probably seething. You know how she feels about lateness.'

And she shot down the corridor to the end bedroom that Mary shared with their mother, only to walk in on her far from seething, but rather semi-naked, and vigorously masturbating whilst watching something on her phone.

'Oh God!' Lizzy yelped. 'I'm sorry.' And she made to retreat, but Mary was having none of it.

'It's not what you think!' she yelled. 'I'm not watching porn.'

'I don't need to know!' begged Lizzy, still inexplicably in the room, albeit averting her eyes. 'It's all… it's perfectly natural.'

'But it isn't porn. Look!' And she held out her phone.

Lizzy, bracing herself, lifted her eyes to find being thrust at her a video, not of improbably hairless people having sex, but of Colin, giving a lecture on Saint Thomas Becket.

Was that better? Or worse? And why was she still staring at it?

'I… Fine,' she mumbled. And finally, her mind suitably boggling, bolted for the bathroom, where she stayed for the next hour and a half wondering what Colin – or, more crucially, their mother – would make of it.

As for their mother, Mrs Bennet had headed, in the end, to the Eiffel Tower, despite the queues she knew she would face. She had heady memories, you see, of the landmark from the school trip on which she'd met their father, including their first kiss on the second platform of the tower, just seconds before she vomited, having suffered not an allergic reaction to oysters (as she claimed) but the after effects of a night on the pastis, which, to this day, she still could not stomach. While that episode itself (the poor people below her!) was best forgotten, she dearly wanted to relive the rest of the climb while she still had the legs for it. She might be dead by this time next year, after all. Or Mr Bennet might have left her for Marjory Pence or Barbara Clyde or whoever it was he was messaging at all hours.

That, though, was really the least of her worries right now. Rather, the journey itself – all alone, in a foreign country, surrounded by strangers – was pressing in on her like polyester two sizes too small. Mrs Bennet's queendom, after all, was Longbourn. The intricacies of Wi-Fi and the unfathomable DVD player aside, there and in Meryton she enjoyed full reign, and knew herself to be capable, if not the very fabric from which the town was woven. Travel, on the other hand, was, well, foreign. In her adolescence, Hester's parents had chaperoned her to every restaurant on their annual fortnight in Lanzarote, a job swiftly taken on by her husband and only recently and intermittently relinquished to Jane and Mary, who were both capable and keen to do the organising, the chivvying, the translating of menus, the reading of maps, the conversion of euros to pounds and back again. Thus, she was more than a little surprised when she managed to get herself to Champ de Mars without being kidnapped, manhandled or sold into slavery. In fact she'd had a perfectly bearable Metro journey exchanging Franglais pleasantries with a sturdy woman carrying a dachshund with the improbable name of 'Napoleon' (the dog, not the woman, though it had taken her two goes to ascertain this, because one never knew, with the French, did one?) She had then suffered the queue as only the English know how – with rigid adherence, a portable fan and a tin of boiled sweets, which she offered around, endearing herself further to a family from Antwerp, whose English was thankfully better than Mrs Bennet's Belgian. (Or was it Dutch? So tricky, these continentals!)

By the time she had finished her visit, and settled back into the velveteen seat of Ligne C again she considered herself quite the seasoned traveller, a feeling only briefly dented when she realised she was heading in the wrong direction and had to perform a swift platform change at Issy, to the cheers of the three banquette friends with whom she had shared her last barley sugar. Why hadn't she done this before? she asked herself, as she decided – with all the bravado of a gap year student summiting Machu Picchu – to eschew changing trains at St-Michel Notre-Dame in favour of following the crowds along the left bank and across Île Saint-Louis, where she paused, for once able to push down the thought of possible people traffickers and probable phone thieves, and take a photograph of herself against the glimmering city, which she sent to the Meryton Women's Guild WhatsApp with the caption 'Gay Paris!' If they read that as her consorting with homosexuals, so much the better.

And as she stood on the Pont Louis-Phillipe, under the gaze of the Seine, she thought for a moment of sending her husband the selfie, rather than the daily reminder to take his tablets and rinse out the washing-up sponge properly and lock the back door. But the thought of his reaction being less than giddy – and yes, she knew in her heart that 'giddiness' was not what one expected after so many years, but she had just been up the Eiffel Tower, remember, and was now friends with a large part of Paris – was a slosh of cold water. Besides, he was probably feverishly admiring selfies of, well, someone much younger, and even if not, he'd made it perfectly obvious he wasn't going to forgive her for the Colin thing for a long time, and so she put her phone back in its zip-up pocket, resolved to 'jolly well sort it all out' once she got home, and set off for the so-called Last Supper. Perhaps her daughters would be in improved moods since this morning. True happiness – and marriage, for all bar Jane – seemed further away than ever. But not snapping at each other was, at least, something to look forward to.

★ ★ ★

The dinner – at the cheap-as-chips Bouillon Chartier, one of Charley's favourites, with its down-to-earth menu and out-of-this-world decor – had begun, understandably, given everyone's circumstances, in a subdued mood. Kitty contemplated her latest betrayal of Dave; Lydia the truth of her affair with Celine: that her employer would never, ever leave her husband, still less admit to her bisexuality to anyone outside the bedroom; Jane the fact that she still missed her dead husband despite being engaged; Lizzy that she didn't miss hers as much as she thought; Mary that her latest pointless 'fixation', as Mrs Bennet tended to refer to them, was now likely to become public; and Mrs Bennet the truth that her husband had been right: she was overly focused on Longbourn and her daughters, and had, thus, entirely neglected him.

Unsurprising, then, that all parties, bar Lydia, decided to drink their way through it. As such, conversation, which might otherwise have been stilted, flowed as erratically but enthusiastically as the Cab Sav and Viognier that was accompanying their pork terrine and duck confit. Until, that is, Kitty felt something leak from her ladyparts, and for a brief, hideous moment thought it might be Shane's sperm, before remembering they had, in fact, used a condom, and that he hadn't, in any case, ejaculated.

The whole thing hadn't been at all what she'd imagined. Where she'd seen, in her mind's filthiest eye, an afternoon of lingering kisses, of blissful intimacy with a man whose body she already knew as well as her own, and whose talent in the in-between years had only expanded, the reality was he still wasn't that big on foreplay, the way he pronounced 'pasta' made her want to do actual bodily harm, and she was having sex, doggy style, in front of a mirror (which really wasn't that flattering to either of them) with a man she remembered now, only too clearly, had never once measured up to Dave. She had stared at her reflection for only another grunting second before pushing him off and pulling her clothes on. So no, this wasn't his spunk, it was her fucking period, two days early, and she'd not come prepared.

'Lyds?' she said, holding out her hand. 'Tampon.'

'I… Oh.' Lydia frowned. 'I haven't got any.'

'Don't be a pain. I know you're on this week. You're always on the week before me, isn't she, Mum?'

Mrs Bennet, who knew her daughters' cycles like clockwork (it paid to be prepared), whether or not they were under the same roof, nodded.

'Lyds?' Kitty thrust her hand out again. 'Don't be stingy. You know Mary only uses those towels the size of nappies and the others are past it. Sorry,' she added to Jane and Lizzy, 'but it's true.'

But Lydia wasn't being stingy. Instead, having done the sums in her head, she paled. She was late. Not just days, but weeks. In fact, she'd not had a period since—

Fuck.

'Lydia?' asked Jane. 'What is it?'

'I think…' Lydia began, as full realisation hit her. 'Shit. I think I'm pregnant.'

Mrs Bennet could have cheered (but didn't, given the company) and yelped instead. The others were, predictably, about as thrilled at the prospect of becoming aunts as Lydia was at becoming a mother.

'Jesus, Lydia,' said Kitty. 'How the fuck did you manage that?'

'The same way as everyone else,' said Mary, genuinely confused as to why anyone would ask such a stupid question.

'Unless it's Wickham's,' said Mrs Bennet. 'Oooh, *is* it Wickham's?'

Lydia felt her cheeks heat. 'God, no!' she protested. 'Why would it be Wickham's?'

'The surrogacy?' said her mother.

Lydia caught Jane's eyes, felt a swerve of nausea that she was sure was morning sickness. 'That hasn't… We haven't…' Oh God this was awful. Being pregnant was bad enough, but by him? And having promised Jane— 'Jane, I'm sorry, I didn't mean for this to happen. I don't know how…'

'For fuck's sake, Lyds,' snapped Kitty, still revelling in not being the worst Bennet again. 'You must know *how*. A boy and a girl—'

'Fuck off!' Lydia snapped back. 'I don't mean that. You know what I mean.'

'Can everyone just stop fucking swearing!' said Jane.

For a second the table, unused to Jane raising her voice, let alone using a word that would warrant a pound in the swear jar, fell silent, while Mary, who had put her hands over her ears (to little avail) said a silent 'hear hear'. But there were too many questions, and wild accusations for that peace to hold.

'What about your resolution?' demanded Kitty. 'You were supposed to be celibate! For a year!'

'And I am… I was… I just…' Lydia petered out, before rounding on her sister (deflection being prime amongst the younger Bennets' weapons). 'Anyway, what about you? You've been up to stuff, and I don't mean with Dave.'

'What?' asked Mrs Bennet.

'What?' repeated Kitty. Could Lydia know about Shane?

Already? Or was this just the idiocy with the apps? Oh God, please let it just be the apps.

It was moot, anyway, as Lydia wasn't finished. 'You're all hypocrites. None of you have stuck to anything. Mary hasn't been on a date since that twat from the hospital with the hands. Mum's barely halfway through *Complete Delia* and she gave up Zumba after three weeks. Oh, and Lizzy's still mooning around after Darcy.'

'What?' said Lizzy abruptly. 'No I'm not.'

'Well, you are rather, darling,' said Jane, whose fourth glass of red had loosened the usually firmly shut valve that read 'don't say that out loud'. 'I mean, come on. "Dear Darcy, blah blah blah". It isn't healthy.'

'What is she talking about?' asked their mother. 'Lizzy, what is this?'

'Nothing, Mother,' snapped Lizzy. 'Jane's just drunk.'

But she wasn't. Or not 'just'. Because during that brief, appalling interlude, when Lizzy had walked in on the Colin porno scenario, Jane, telling herself (and truly believing) it would be an act of kindness, had lifted the leather-bound flap of Lizzy's journal, and seen to whom – and more importantly about what – Lizzy was writing. Scorched, she had dropped it, but she had read enough to know Lizzy's musings on her own sisters were far from the benign she tried to project. And as for her thoughts on George. Well, at least now Jane knew the truth.

'"Dear Darcy",' Jane went on. '"You won't believe what Lydia's done. And Kitty, well, she's a complete bitch. And as for my mother, Jesus Christ on a stick."' She was slurring her words now, as well as making them up, but that didn't stop Jane. '"And Wickham's such a pitiful little weasel. Whereas you, Darcy, are a god amongst men."' She paused, having run out of steam. Added only a half-hearted, 'Et cetera, et cetera.'

Lizzy rarely swore at her sisters, and never at Jane. But this torrent was unwarranted. 'Fuck you,' she snapped. 'Just because you've moved on at the pace of a freight train. Or… or been dragged. And…' She paused, steeling herself against the pinch in her stomach, the prick of saltwater at her eyes, and reminded herself that she wasn't the sneaky one. 'And you shouldn't have been snooping. Who gave you the right?'

'I…' tried Jane. But nothing more came out and the party fell to silence.

Now, the Bennets were not unused to fraught dinner tables, but this was more taut than any since Bridget had asked how 'lesbian ladies' had sex. And this situation did not come with a useful 'let's do the washing-up' option.

It was Kitty who spoke first. '*Do* you think I'm a bitch, Lizzy?' she asked.

'No,' said Lizzy quickly. 'I don't.' Or rather, perhaps the Lizzy who wanted to entertain Fitz might have written such a thing, even thought it fleetingly, but Lizzy herself, right now, truly didn't.

'And what had *I* done?' asked Lydia.

'Take your pick,' said Kitty.

'Fuck off,' batted back Lydia.

'And what about *me*?' yelled Mrs Bennet. 'What's wrong with *me*?'

'Nothing,' insisted Lizzy. 'Just, all of you, stop it. It was a stupid… I just needed to vent and it was… I was just trying to keep something alive that, well, wasn't.' Her face, which had reddened with the snap of embarrassment, was now ashen. 'I know I need to move on. I know I do, and I don't need any of you to tell me. And I'm trying, I am. I just… need to do better. That's what selling Pemberley's about. And I was trying to find a way to tell him that today – which I know sounds… mad, and maybe I am, but so be it. And so I'm sorry about' – she flapped her hand – 'all that. But can we move on and talk about something else now?'

'So you don't think I should marry George then?' asked Jane.

Lizzy, now in a truthful mood, but not unkind, did not answer.

Jane, who had expected to be placated, instead found herself flailing. Her next move was even less sensible. 'Who thinks I should marry George?' she demanded. 'Put up your hands.'

Mrs Bennet dutifully put up her hand. No one else moved. Not even Mary, who was usually quite biddable on this topic, on the grounds that marriage 'made sense'. Mrs Bennet, seeing this, grabbed Mary's hand and raised it as well.

'Mary?' checked Lizzy. 'Really?'

Mary looked at her sisters, and muttering an apology to Jane, as well as her mother, lowered her arm.

'Really? Just Mum? Well, thank you for being honest, I suppose.' Jane was beyond deflated. 'Though I note you were all happy to have this weekend paid for to celebrate a wedding you didn't actually believe in.'

'Oh, Jane,' said Lizzy. 'We—'

'No, no!' Jane held up a hand. 'Please don't try to soften it now. It's perfectly clear what you all think. But just so you know…'

She paused, as the clarity of it snapped at her. Wickham *had* been right all along: her sisters were a coven, and Meryton was hell. And, no she didn't love him like she loved Charley, but he didn't deserve… this. He'd been ridiculed his entire life for being less than well-bred, for never wearing quite the right tie, the right brand of loafers. He was a pigeon to everyone else's peacocks, and, well, everyone knew how she felt about pigeons.

'I'm marrying him anyway,' she announced. 'And we're moving to London.'

★ ★ ★

The train journey home was largely civilised, and mercifully quiet, punctuated only by the popping of ibuprofen packets, and the frequent trips to the carriage lavatory for one or other of the sisters to heave up some bile. The Last Supper, though (which, now that Jane was vacating East Anglia, was more aptly named than one might previously have assumed, though who, exactly, was Judas in this scenario, no one could decide) had left everyone in a state of mild despair and quite major estrangement. No one was really on speaking terms beyond checking who had the tickets, and which sandwich everyone wanted from the Liverpool Street Marks. A state they might have stayed in had Colin not been prompted (by his online following of the 14:31's journey through Harlow and Sawbridgeworth) to drive to the station in his aunt's BMW X7 to fetch everybody.

'What is it?' asked Mrs Bennet, as she heaved her weekend bag (weekend requiring eight changes of clothes and a full cabinet of toiletries) into the boot. 'You look like someone's died.'

'Well… that is to say… they have,' said Colin. 'Or rather they might.'

'Oh gosh,' said Jane. 'I'm so sorry. Who? God, not your aunt?'

'Not her.' Colin mustered his best bedside manner (which was not really saying anything, but, as he told himself, it was the effort that counted). 'Your father's in hospital,' he said. 'The outlook's not good.'

AUTUMN

SEPTEMBER

Colin Burghley was not a man prone to underplaying, well, anything. As a child, if a single Lego piece was lost, a Bourbon biscuit snapped accidentally, or a doll (his mother, Lorna, had been a progressive type, and had bought dolls with realistic genitalia for both her children, an act that had cemented her status as family 'black sheep' as far as her sister Carole was concerned) wetted in the rain so that her hair hung lank and matted, then his wails of indignation could be heard across the entirety of Meryton Goughs. As an adult, his wails may have been contained, but his tendency to doom-monger had not, manifesting in a potent mix of hypochondria, and the transformation of any routine hospital visit or minor trip to A&E into a life-threatening spectacle. So it was that, while Mr Bennet was, indeed, 'in hospital', he was not quite as close to death's morbid door as Colin's station pronouncement might have suggested. In fact, he was really only at the hospital in the first place on Colin's insistence, and possibly instigation.

The 'bachelors' weekend (as Mrs Bennet had taken to calling it) had begun exactly as uncomfortably as Mr Bennet, and anyone, could have imagined, with Colin taking over meal planning, the television remote control and, the very cherry on the cake of menace, bedtime. It was, he repeatedly told Mr Bennet, 'no trouble at all', as if he were doing the older man a favour. In fact it was the reverse, with the whole weekend lending Colin the sort of purpose he had only previously enjoyed on his mother's deathbed, during his aunt's hysterectomy, and in the run-up to the collapse of his marriage during which Charlotte had taken to the attic declaring that if she had to listen to him bleating another 'I told you so' about Covid-19 she might die of spite.

He mustered up low-GI meals with the zeal of a teenage vegan; he scheduled the watching of documentaries on Cromwell, the Crimean war and the prospective extinction of pangolins; he prepared a nightly tincture of ginger and turmeric to aid both digestion and sleep, and a morning bowl of prunes to 'move things along'. It was the latter that Mr Bennet fingered as directly responsible for the apparent collapse of his bowels at half eight on Monday. Though, as Colin pointed out, the bleeding (which had been on and off for months) and the agonising cramps were unlikely to be induced by either prunes or the herbal tea, unless that tea were raspberry leaf and he were pregnant, which it and he were not.

Given the severity of the pain, and the fact the GP was closed for bank holiday Monday (and in any case, in the absence of Dr Ogden, for whom a replacement was yet to be found, was currently only the practice nurse, Mrs Trickett, whose cup of sympathy operated on a permanently half-empty level) Colin decided the best course of action was an emergency trip to the A&E in Cambridge, where, as the Paris contingent's train pulled into Meryton station, Mr Bennet remained in a cubicle in the sort of paper-thin backless gown that can only be described as 'undignified'.

'Drive faster! He'll be dead by the time we get there!' his wife had pleaded (not unlike Colin in her ability to turn a medical molehill into a mountain). 'I should never have left!'

'I'm driving at the speed limit,' Colin had replied (to the mile, in fact). 'Although when I left, he was looking terribly pale, so one can only hope.'

After Darcy

The sisters, meanwhile, had said little, each apparently absorbed by their own morbid thoughts, or perhaps quietly saying the thank you to Colin — for being there to rescue their father, and indeed them — that they had singularly failed to utter out loud. Although Mary had checked that her father had got *The Times* crossword to keep him occupied (he had) and said she hoped the attic had not been too hot for Colin (it had, which he told her, but he had set himself up on a camp bed in the study, which suited him very well as it had easy access to books and the downstairs lavatory, which, he added, he had descaled, and not before time).

Given the ominous tone in which Colin had delivered his news, one might be able to see why the scene that greeted the rest of the Bennets when they finally arrived at Addenbrooke's was somewhat of a relief, at least to Mrs Bennet, who (having watched every season of both *House* and *Grey's Anatomy*) had imagined visible bleeding, a lolling of the tongue, and a quorum of medical students poring over his unfathomable rash. Not that she showed it.

'Will he die?' she wailed to nobody in particular.

'Not today,' said Mr Bennet, wondering how on earth all seven of them had got past the ward sister (sturdy, air of Zac Efron as a 1970s wrestler), before remembering that this was, in fact, Lizzy's place of work.

'He's being referred for colonoscopy,' she said, having checked with the nurse station. 'And a possible biopsy.'

'A biopsy!' yelled Mrs Bennet. 'So it *is* cancer! So he *is* dying!'

'God willing,' Mr Bennet might have uttered at that precise moment, had Lydia and Kitty not been clinging to him like monkeys, and Mary dabbing him with a damp flannel (Colin had brought this along with spare socks, pants and two bottles of hand sanitiser).

'We don't know that yet,' said Lizzy, adopting her hospital voice. 'It might be nothing. Or rather, just nothing that sinister.'

'It's not nothing!' protested Mrs Bennet. 'It's retribution is what it is. For me thinking he was having an affair, when all along he was in agony!' (The logic of this did not bear scrutiny, but the narcissism made perfect sense to everyone.) 'With cancer!' she added, before collapsing back into the pleather chair at the side of the bed, where she wafted herself with a month-old *Women's Realm*.

'Who had an affair?' demanded Lydia.

'Daddy,' said Kitty, delighted to be apparently only the third most terrible Bennet in the room.

'Nobody!' yelled their father. 'Why would I have an affair?'

'Bondage,' said Mrs Bennet knowingly.

'Oh dear,' said Jane.

Mary put her hands over her ears again. Masturbating to Colin and Saint Thomas Becket was one thing, but her parents even owning genitalia was questionable.

'Oh, it's all the rage,' went on Mrs Bennet. 'Susan Clopman says her Ron came home one day with a pair of crotchless knickers from a charity raffle, and now they own two kinds of lube, a vibrator and a set of nipple clamps.'

'How in God's name do you know that?' Mr Bennet asked. 'Actually, I don't want to know. And no, I don't want an affair or... or nipple clamps. I don't have the energy or the inclination. I just want to shit more than once every four days.'

Mary, who had foolishly uncovered her ears, shuddered.

'And you will, Daddy,' insisted Lizzy. 'It's probably just constipation.'

'Cancer!' moaned Mrs Bennet from the chair. 'It's cancer.'

It was Colin – blessed Colin – who calmed the situation. 'I think we should probably let your father and mother have some privacy,' he told the girls. 'We could pop past Papworth to Hobson's Park if you like, or I can drive you all to Lammas Land.'

'Actually, I should be getting home,' said Jane. 'Grace and Timon start sixth form tomorrow and there's probably some sort of crisis afoot. I'm really sorry, Dad.'

'Not at all,' he replied, not even trying to disguise his relief. 'Needs must. Send her my good luck. And Timon – I assume they're camped out at yours, not at their father's.'

Jane assumed too, and found she was rather relieved. Somehow their presence, albeit unnerving – a sort of black-clad golem who slipped in and out of rooms with the air of a disgraced cat – softened the edges of Grace, and they made her smile, which was more than Jane could claim lately.

'I should go too,' said Lizzy, whose need to see the twins had reached pathological status. 'But I'll pop back later and check what's what.'

'And me,' said Kitty quickly. If Paris had taught her anything, it was that Dave was a good egg – the best egg, in fact. And, at last, she missed him almost as much as she missed Bridget. Which, in her head, justified the illicit sex entirely.

'So, Colin Taxis all round!' Colin seemed entirely delighted by the prospect of ferrying several people across several counties, 'good to be useful' being one of his mottos.

And so it was that, having driven around Cambridge and the back roads of Hertfordshire dropping off various Bennets, it was only Mary who took him up on the prospect of a walk.

'Interesting fact,' began Colin, as they strode past the children's paddling pool, still replete with shrieks and bedecked in armbands in every garish shade, 'Lammas Land is so-called because it was private until Lammas Day—'

'August the first,' said Mary, a glimmer of something prickling her skin, like goose pimples, but wished for.

'Precisely.' Colin beamed back at her. 'When it became public pasture until Spring.'

'Lammas comes from Loaf Mass,' added Mary. 'Because of the harvest.'

Colin stopped and turned to her. 'I had no idea you were so interested in history.'

'Oh, it's the etymology.' Mary flushed under his gaze. 'I like to understand words.'

'Quite,' Colin replied. 'Quite so.'

They walked on for a mile, discussing the roots of 'nightmare' (not a horse but a homunculus), 'sandwich' (the Earl, of course) and 'quarantine' (the forty days of isolation for those on board ships) before Mary brought up crabs, and the fact that cancer was said to resemble them.

'Do you think it *is* cancer?' she asked.

Again Colin stopped. 'If it is,' he said, touching her arm, briefly and awkwardly, but touching it all the same, 'I will be there for you.'

That was enough for Mary. And on they walked, back to the car, and thence to Addenbrooke's to collect Mrs Bennet.

★ ★ ★

If there was one thing Mrs Bennet lived for, it was a crisis. Preferably, though, someone else's (and if she was honest, ideally Carole Burghley's) – the sort that can be observed from a discreet distance, and then regaled in lurid detail over the Meryton Women's Guild WhatsApp and picked apart, like vultures at a carcass. Still, a crisis was a crisis, and cancer was cancer, and so it was that, by five o'clock, Mrs Bennet having only left his side to fetch a plastic-wrapped sandwich from Costa, most of Meryton and the extended area believed her husband to be riddled with tumours and lucky to be alive at all.

'Why is Lucas calling me?' he demanded, as she handed him not the ham and cheese on white he'd requested, but some sort of falafel-based monstrosity. 'And what the hell is this?'

'I couldn't say,' Mrs Bennet lied, regarding the Lucas query. His former employer (and Charlotte's father) was obviously calling him because he got it off Mrs Lucas who got it off Bad Karen. 'But red meat's a terrible carcinogen. And white bread. And dairy, I expect. You need to eat healthily from now on if we're to have a chance of saving you!'

Mr Bennet, who had already endured a weekend of unpronounceable vegetable matter, sighed. 'We don't even know what's going on,' he protested. 'And if it *is* my deathbed, which it isn't, but if it is, well, I don't want my last meal to be' – he grimaced – 'macerated chickpeas.'

Mrs Bennet, as was her wont, ignored him. 'Cancer!' she continued. 'It'll be all those fancy lunches at the bank! And that time your mother had four kinds of pork on Boxing Day. *Four!*'

The conversation, if it could be called that, as it was rather more a monologue with interjections of sighs, continued in this vein for several hours until a cheery consultant from the Antipodes (at least judging by his accent, which somehow turned everything into a question) told them Mr Bennet could go home and await a phone call telling him when and where to attend to have the colonoscopy.

'It's just a tube?' the consultant told him, grinning. 'Nothing sinister? Slides up nicely? Bit of a wiggle? Nothing to be worried about? Done in a jiffy?'

Mr Bennet, though wincing, thanked him kindly. Mrs Bennet told him her husband could well be dead before anything got inserted anywhere, and she would hold him personally responsible if he was. At which point Colin and Mary reappeared and the latter began to explain the etymology of 'colon' (in both senses) and Mr Bennet sighed again, and prayed silently for death to come quickly.

Sister Act
Jane, Lizzy, Mary, Kitty, Lydia

Lizzy Darcy-Bennet joined the group

~Lizzy Darcy-Bennet
Dad's got his op scheduled for next Wednesday. Obviously I'll be there. It's day surgery so no visiting hours.
10:23

~Lydia Bennet
mum says he's not 'been' for two days so god knows how they'll get it up there
10:24

~Lizzy Darcy-Bennet
They'll give him something to clear him out.
10:24

~Kitty Miller
Bum cancer is the worst kind. It would be easier if it were breast.
10:24

~Lydia Bennet
men don't get breast cancer
10:24

~Kitty Miller
They actually do. Google it.
10:24

~Lydia Bennet
i still don't think it's the worst kind. what about wee-hole? eyeball? bellend?
10:27

~Lizzy Darcy-Bennet
It isn't actually 'bum' cancer, it's bowel. Very different. It's like

confusing vulvas and vaginas. Not that we even know he has it.
10:28

~Jane Bingley
If you don't stop, all of you, I will disband this group.
10:29

★ ★ ★

Lydia didn't like to admit it, but her father being the centre of attention was a timely relief. Oh, the thought of him ill, possibly with cancer, was too appalling to consider, but her mother's clucking around him, and Mary's endless googling for potential alternative medicine, plus the sudden semi-permanent presence of Colin, meant that her own pregnancy was going largely unremarked upon, even unnoticed, except of course by Lydia herself.

Now, of course, every symptom made sense; every aspect of her health, mental and otherwise, could be attributed to the alien life form squatting unwanted in her belly: her weight gain, which she'd attached to the lapse in her antagonism towards carbs (a necessary character trait in the industry); her mood, which admittedly tended to ricochet at the best of times, but now verged on almost permanent tears; the overheating at night – and not just in Paris at the height of summer, but now, at Longbourn, where the temperature had dropped a good ten degrees; the desire to do bloody murder to anyone who questioned her – again, not entirely new, but definitely at a level only ever previously reached at the peak of PMT.

No surprise then, given her discomfort, that the first thing she did the morning after they arrived home was book herself an appointment to have the thing… rinsed out ('terminated' reminded her too much of Schwarzenegger, and 'rinsed' made it sound pleasant and easy – like spring cleaning, or mouthwash).

Kitty had been strong-armed into accompanying her, despite complaining she'd 'done' the last two, and surely it was Lizzy's turn, and ideal, given she was 'in the business'. But Lydia had pointed out that this was like claiming pet shops were in the same business as abattoirs, and besides, Lizzy came with more disapproving looks and likely a lecture on condoms, which was all rather horse/stable door/bolted.

'Only if you tell me whose it is,' Kitty had said in the end.

Lydia had flinched, but was surprisingly quick-witted. 'I'll tell you when it's done,' she promised.

And so Kitty had relented, albeit reluctantly, booking the morning off work and having to reschedule Bad Karen's lowlights – a fact that did not go down well with Bad Karen, who telephoned Mrs Bennet to complain that she was going to have to attend the Golf Club Charity Pancake Brunch with unsightly regrowth (another reason to be grateful for the current star status of their father, as the conversation was deftly segued within seconds from hair to the potential state of his colon).

Only now, as they sat in Dave's Volkswagen Polo, outside the Marie Stopes on Bateman Street in Cambridge, Lydia's mood began pitching again and her conviction – that this was the only feasible solution to pregnancy, ever – waned.

'Tell me again about how much the birth hurt,' she begged Kitty.

Kitty obliged. 'It was like being shagged in reverse by a cantaloupe melon. With stabby hands. In a non-sexy way.'

Lydia nodded. 'Go on. And afterwards?'

'Afterwards, I couldn't piss without wincing for about three weeks.'

That was barely scratching the surface of it. Lizzy had warned Kitty not to look, under any circumstances, but Kitty, who was firmly of the belief one should be au fait with one's genitals, got out the hand mirror after only three days. The result was a fit of hysterical sobbing, which probably contributed to Shane's swift exit. That and the apparent massacre in her underpants.

'But I heard of a woman who actually shat through her vagina,' she added. 'So I got off lightly.'

That should have done it. That should have propelled Lydia to the front door of the clinic quicker than if she were being hunted by swivel-eyed pro-lifers. What could possibly be worse, after all, than shit in your minky? Except... something was off. Something was stopping her. An odd, warm feeling that she'd not experienced before except when high, or in the first flush of a love affair, only less frantic, less potentially momentary.

'And then, there's the vomit,' Kitty went on. 'Endless fucking vomit. Theirs and then yours, because there's no way you're not catching noro once they've sodding got it. And the accidents. And the never shutting up about stuff. There's barely any room in your head for a thought of your own for at least four years. And then they go to school, and the *Mean Girls* fuckwittery begins. No, you're better off without them. I mean, obviously I love Bridge to death, and I don't regret her for a second— Well, maybe only for a second. But I definitely wouldn't go through it again if I had the choice.'

'Definitely?' checked Lydia.

Kitty paused, caught between truth and useful anecdote. Would she really not pick Bridget over a child-free life? I mean, she'd definitely not pick other people's kids. Other people's kids were hideous. But Bridget was... Bridget. And how small Kitty's life might have been without her, she realised. How watercolour. 'Actually no,' she said. 'Of course I would have her. She's brilliant. But you're not me. You're even less... mumsy.'

That did it. It was the box splits, the cup song, fitting twenty marshmallows in her mouth without throwing up all over again. Told she couldn't, she bloody well proved everyone wrong. And then there was the feeling, the warm buzzy feeling – that was her being maternal, wasn't it? It had to be. 'I'm keeping it,' she announced. 'I just… I'm keeping it.'

'Jesus,' said Kitty. As well she might. 'Seriously? You're not going to just… you know, have it and give it to Jane anyway?'

Lydia flushed scarlet. 'Y–you know what Wickham thinks of adoption,' she stammered. 'It might have two heads. Or be a murderer.'

'Or a socialist,' offered Kitty, oblivious to Lydia's slip in conviction.

'Exactly.'

Kitty snorted. 'Fuck me. Mum's going to love this. I mean, genuinely.'

Lydia shrugged, conscious of her hand on her stomach. 'Might be nice to be in her good books for once.'

'I wouldn't go that far.' Kitty snorted. 'But now you *have* to tell me who the father is. *Before* you tell her. Or him. Unless you already have?'

Lydia shook her head. 'I'm not telling him,' she replied. 'I'm not telling anyone. It's too messy. That's if it's even his,' she added quickly.

It wasn't like Lydia to belittle herself. But there were advantages to people thinking she put it about. Of being perceived as a 'slut'. And this way, Wickham would never guess; she wouldn't even need to confront him, to confess all to Jane. Let them think this was someone from Bumble, from down the pub, or up at a club in London. Never mind she'd barely been out for nine months; she was Lydia Bennet, this was just what she *did*.

'But you can tell *me*?' insisted Kitty.

'I can't,' said Lydia. 'I really can't.' And quietly hoped that the baby, when it did come out, did not resemble its father a jot. Better two heads or a murderer, she decided, than that.

★ ★ ★

After Darcy

For once, Lydia, a born blabbermouth, who would have confessed the identity of anyone who'd confided in her for the price of a pint, managed to keep to her word. Neither her mother nor her sisters (the ones who asked – Kitty because she was also a gossip and Mary because she wanted to assess genetic inheritance probability) could wheedle any details from her other than that the sex itself was a mistake, and in any case the likely culprit had left the country (only a white lie, as Wickham had actually popped to Krakow a month ago for his stag do). Jane and Lizzy kept well out of it, other than to offer her cast-off baby clothes and the Bugaboo, once the twins were finished with it – Jane surprisingly generous given that this child meant the loss of her own. And God knows what their mother had told her cronies, but the rest of Meryton, who had, naturally, known within days, looked at Lydia anew – and not through the sly eyes of the outwardly morally outraged (and inwardly thrilled), but with something bordering on respect. It was a pleasant change, she decided, to finally fit in.

There was, though, someone for whom the news was less than a pleasure.

Lydia had, since the catastrophe of the last encounter, made good on her promise to stay out of Denny's life forever. Only Denny, of course, was a postal worker, and there is only so much say they have in their allocated rounds, and so it was that he was back on the Longbourn walk in September, and back at Lydia's door.

'Congratulations,' he said, holding out a parcel clearly marked JoJo Maman Bébé.

Lydia pinked – another recent addition to her litany of symptoms was the heat that lurked never far from the surface, along with hurt feelings. So what if she was already shopping? If someone had told her how satisfying buying small things might be, she'd have probably got pregnant a long time ago. Plus her father was more easily persuadable as far as an allowance was concerned these days. And the matinée jacket was in a neutral colour, given she was yet to have a scan. Not that she believed in gendered anything, but there was something so charming about baby-pink pinafores and matching over-knickers. 'Thanks,' she said eventually.

'Feeling selfless then?' added Denny, one eyebrow raised. 'Glowing with it yet?'

She didn't say 'Oh, fuck off' (so very un-Lydia, she thought with delight; pregnancy was definitely changing her). Instead she pinked further. 'It isn't... it's not...' How to explain this without rendering herself the OG selfish version? She couldn't, she realised. And perhaps honesty *was* the new her. 'It isn't Jane's,' she said. 'I fucked up.'

'Oh.' Denny's face was unreadable, but the lack of words a veritable novel. 'Right. Well, see you, then.'

And that was how Lydia knew that any vestige of friendship she might have wrestled from the mess of the situation was now no more than a figment of her wild and rose-tinted imagination.

★ ★ ★

If Mrs Bennet thought that a dying husband and a pregnant, destitute daughter were the highlights of her autumn calendar, she was about to add a third, thrilling string to her bow of Meryton Women's Guild fame, when Kitty arrived on the doorstep of Longbourn, on an otherwise innocuous Wednesday afternoon, with two large suitcases, a binbag and Bridget.

'What on earth is happening?' Mrs Bennet demanded.

'Ask Bridge,' replied Kitty, taking herself, one suitcase and the binbag up to Lydia's room and shutting herself in before her mother could take umbrage.

Bridget's explanation to Mrs Bennet was this: 'A man who is my actual dad is back from the sheep and loves Mum because of the sex in Paris.'

Kitty's explanation to her sister, while interspersed with snot and sobbing, was marginally more comprehensive: 'I fucked up,' she wailed. 'And I didn't even enjoy it!' This, to Kitty, was the ultimate insult. 'It was like I was on the ceiling watching really shite porn – here I am, having sex with my ex-husband—'

'You had sex with Shane?'

Kitty nodded.

'Where? When?'

'Paris,' admitted Kitty, wiping her nose on Lydia's gingham linen oversheet.

Lydia, to her credit, did not flinch at what was, effectively, sacrilege. The whereabouts of the sex, however, were a little more concerning. 'How? I mean... when did you have the—oh.'

Lydia's memory flashed vividly with an image of herself in the loft on Rue des Martyrs, pulling away from Celine's embrace, swiftly followed by one of Wickham's digs. She slapped them both away, grateful for someone else's convenient shame. 'God, Kitty. What were you thinking? I mean, I thought you were over all this... last fling business? And with Shane of all people?'

'I know!'

'This is a man, can I remind you, who I've seen snort Nurofen in the hope of a high.'

'"Whom"! And he's not that bad anymore,' Kitty replied, before adding, with as much aplomb as she could muster. 'He's working for *Vogue*. I mean, the Australian one, but still. *Vogue*!'

Time was when Lydia would have squished down any vestige of morals, and begged Kitty to put her in touch in case there was a job in the offing. Pregnancy had definitely changed her. 'You're defending him? Seriously?'

'No, I... I don't know.' Kitty wiped her nose on the Piglet in Bed linen again.

'Oh my God, use a fucking tissue!' Lydia exploded, handing

her not the tissue in question, but an American Vintage T-shirt she'd picked up from the floor. 'So how did Dave find out?'

Kitty blew her nose. 'He showed up. Shane, I mean. Flew to Stansted, got a taxi to the flat and proclaimed true love and half-ownership of Bridget.'

'Jesus.'

'Exactly.'

'How's Bridge?'

'Better than Dave.'

Lydia pulled a face. 'How's Dave?'

'Well, he ended it.' Kitty held up her hands in defeat. 'Said Bridge could stay if it made things easier but that I needed to leave.'

'Well...' – Lydia clutched at a straw – 'at least Bridge chose you.'

Kitty sighed. 'She didn't. She chose Longbourn because she thinks Dad will let her have a fucking duck here. She doesn't understand that this is it. That this means no more Dave.'

At those words, Kitty's insides lurched as the implications charged at her, bull-like, for the first time: no more arguing over whether it was better to take the side of the bed near the door or the toilet in a hotel; no more someone to make her a cup of tea when she felt, well, like this; no more someone telling her she was the 'a-star, number-one, cherry on the cake of my life'. She wailed loudly and long.

'Wait, where's Shane?' asked Lydia then, looking around her, as if he might manifest from her wardrobe at any moment like Drop Dead Fred or Dobby – the Byron Bay version.

'Birchanger Travelodge,' Kitty confessed. 'Dave dropped him off.'

'Dave is a saint,' said Lydia without thinking.

'I know!' wailed Kitty, and recommenced sobbing in the demonstrative, cacophonic way only the younger Bennets knew how.

Lydia, meanwhile, went to see Bridget.

Bridge was, of course, not fine. Believing your father to be a renegade sheep farmer in the mould of Hugh Jackman was one thing, but being confronted with a sort of red-eyed, regretful budget Matthew McConaghey, asking you to come and live in Sydney, was another kettle of bees entirely. Sydney, Bridget knew, was very far away. Further than even Puckeridge, or Brent Pelham, which were probably eighty miles. And Dave didn't live in Sydney. And nor did her grandparents, or Aunt Lyds, or any of her aunts, and even though some of them, e.g. Lizzy, were a bit grumpy, she didn't want to leave them. Not now and probably not ever. Mary hadn't left home, so why should Bridget?

'You could just live here?' she had suggested to Shane when he had arrived at the flat. 'We've got a sofa bed.'

But not even Dave, who was the kindest man in the world bar Grandpa, would agree to that. And so Longbourn it was for Kitty and Bridget, and the Travelodge for Shane, while Dave – poor saintly Dave – stayed in the flat above Ladbrokes, trying to work out how his entire world could be so thoroughly upended by one stupid fuck.

★ ★ ★

Though Mrs Bennet complained, loudly and frequently, it was rather a treat having Kitty and Bridget back permanently. And it distracted so very well from the tragedy of her husband, as she pointed out, also loudly and frequently, to Bad Karen and anyone else who would listen.

'It's as if the universe knew,' she intoned solemnly. 'It knew Longbourn would soon be bereft. Its dim corridors ringing with silence.' They weren't dim – she had put 100-watt bulbs in – but she had taken to switching the lights off for the drama.

'Has he actually had his scan?' asked Bad Karen, as she stirred stevia into her full-fat mochaccino, before making a gesture that was clearly supposed to resemble a colonoscopy, but which could have feasibly been murder.

'Well, no,' admitted Mrs Bennet. 'Not until Friday. But that's just a... a formality scan. I mean, the signs are all there.'

Bad Karen did not argue – in truth the drama took her mind off Laurence and his nose hair, which was getting out of control. Other people's problems were always a boon, and Meryton was replete with them. At that very moment in fact, as Mrs Bennet and her friend sat on the green velveteen settee at the Meryton Kettle, with its faint patina of latte and croissant grease, Jane was hurrying out of Nesbitt and Nesbitt Estate Agents at the far end of the High Street, a sheaf of details clutched in one hand, and her heart seemingly in the other, having just signed an agreement to put her precious Netherfield on the market.

The anger that had blistered in her – admittedly drink-bidden – in Paris, simmered still, now she was sober and back in the Hertfordshire countryside. How dare her sisters dictate to her like this? How dare they not trust her judgement? Only Jane herself was conceded that privilege, and she had already realised the doubts she had entertained must have been placed there deliberately by one sister or another – most probably Lizzy or Lydia, given their... history.

No, she was doing the right thing, Jane told herself. Whatever her mother said – and she had said plenty. Her father was on her side, anyway. Or at least he hadn't said anything. Admittedly he had other things on his mind, but this showed that her moving to London was at least not as bad as bowel cancer. It was this vivid image that distracted her as she swung round the corner past the kebab house (there for ten years but still regarded as a down-market incomer and the general harbinger of the End of Days) and bumped – quite literally – into someone hurrying the other way, causing her heart to leap and the agreement details to scatter across a pavement that was, for once, not stippled with sick.

'Oh, God,' she said. 'I'm so sorry.' She reached to help gather the papers, though her opponent was already head down, doing an enthusiastic job.

'Not at all,' he said from somewhere under a checked flannel shirt. 'I was rushing and wasn't looking where I was going. Here.'

He stood and handed her a dusty bundle, and she saw for the first time who it was she'd almost knocked for six.

'Hindon,' she said, as a sudden calm settled over her, any embarrassment evaporating like water off an Aga plate. 'Oh, I really am sorry.'

'Jane.' He smiled. 'Well, I've been meaning to run into you. Although possibly not quite as literally as this.'

'You have?' She frowned.

'Geoff?' he said. And, when she remained in a clear state of confusion, he added, 'Bridget's pigeon. He's, well, he's doing rather well. I mean, he won't leave the house, so it's lucky I've grown fond of him. As have the boys. Dorothy less so, but she mucks along.'

Jane shook herself. How could she have forgotten? That poor darling bird. 'I'm so sorry,' she said again. 'I should have checked. Well, I'll...' What would she do? What *could* she do, now? 'I'll let Bridget know?'

'Tell her she's welcome to pop round.' Hindon grinned. 'Anytime. You too, of course.'

'I, well... that might be tricky.' She waved the papers sheepishly.

Hindon's face fell a little. 'You're moving? Not far though, I trust? Or Grace would have something to say about that!' It was a pot shot, flung in the sort of happy abandon one can embrace when one knows the truth couldn't possibly be even in that vague direction.

But the shot hit its mark and Jane felt her back stiffen. 'Well, yes, actually. London. And Grace is… Grace will learn to love it. There's… so much for young people to do there.' Drugs, she thought. Guns—

'Oh. Oh, heavens. Well, that's a shame.' Hindon had pinked. 'I was going to float that job again. But no matter.' He stuck his hands in the pockets of his corduroys, apparently casually. 'Anyway, got to be off.'

'I…' began Jane. 'I'll call in before I go? To see Geoff, I mean.' Hindon nodded. 'Of course. Well, goodbye, then.'

'Goodbye,' replied Jane, but it was to the back of his worn jacket, as he hurried past Abrakebabra and off down the road.

As she returned to the Range Rover, Jane's stomach whirled with the finality of what she'd done. Grace would be livid. Timon, perhaps less so – they'd half grown up there, after all – but they'd back Grace up, she had no doubt about that now.

And with the sort of nauseated lurch that she'd not experienced since morning sickness, she clunked open the car door and braced herself to head home.

Livid didn't cover it.

'I, like, literally hate you,' were Grace's exact words. 'I hate you and I hate Wickham. No offence.' She turned to Timon, who was, of course, by her side.

'Well, I'm not sure you mean "literally"…' began Jane.

'I'm not an idiot,' Grace slapped back. 'I know the difference between figuratively and literally.'

'I didn't say…' Jane stopped herself, reassembled. 'You don't even like it here,' she tried. 'You're always moaning about how boring it is in the provinces.' Grace hadn't said 'provinces', she'd said 'bumfuck nowhere', but Jane was not wont to repeat that out loud.

Grace flinched, but was not beaten. Timon had prepped her, after all. Years of Wickham and Silly Calypso had wised them up to every trick in the book. 'I know what you're doing,' she replied. 'And it won't work. We're not moving and that's that.' And the pair of them swept from the room looking like a sightly overdressed Kurt Cobain and Courtney Love, if Kurt and Courtney were from the home counties and spent most of their spare time watching *Sex Education* and playing Animal Crossing.

Jane sighed. They *would* come to like London in time.

And, more to the point, so would she.

* * *

While Jane strong-armed herself into the conviction that moving on was what she wanted – decluttering work surfaces and touching up skirting boards and attempting the sort of 'staging' that could barely be maintained for a minute with teenagers living in the house, let alone an untrained greyhound – Lizzy found herself, for the first time, itching to do something different.

She hadn't actually ditched the journal. That was, well… that would come when she was ready. But she'd not written to Fitz since Paris; hadn't invoked him when the twins had caught nits from the crèche for the second time in as many months and kindly given them to her; hadn't taken his name in vain when the handle came off the bathroom door with Arden trapped inside and she had had to call out the fire brigade, who, far from their general publicity, were four small, thin men, one of whom was called Clive, and all of whom rolled their eyes at the state of the hinges. Though Milo had been delighted – both at his sister's entrapment, and the opportunity to grill 'danger men'.

'Is the dead people very burned?'

'Is their eyes shut?'

'Is you fireproof?'

No, it was not Fitz to whom she recounted any of this, on paper or in any flight of fancy.

It was Saul.

She hadn't planned on seeing him so soon after… everything. But he had messaged to ask why she wasn't in class, and she had had to explain about the rift with her sister – she winced at the memory; it was still unthinkable, and needed to be dealt with, but later – and he had said, 'Well, Jane didn't show up either last week and I know how much you love being shouted at by Gloria.'

'But Luella…' she had begun.

'She's doing polefit apparently. I don't even want to know why.'

Nor did Lizzy. 'Well—'

'Go on,' he had urged her. 'One more term. Just until the wedding and then you're free to, I don't know, take up woodwork or… conversational Mandarin.'

And, well, she had.

Of course, she'd had to suck up to Lydia to beg babysitting favours. Well, not favours – she was paying her. But she had had to practically prostrate herself as well, which was a little rich given Lydia had no alternative income. And on the walk to Gwydir Street she had turned back twice, asking herself what the hell she was playing at, when she'd been the one complaining about coming in the first place, and also Gloria *was* awful. Of course, it would have been so easy to back out. To text him some feeble excuse – an illness, a lost tooth, Lydia being late (which, unbelievably, she hadn't been). And yet, here she was, in the familiar hall, being spun, albeit clunkily, to what sounded worryingly like Bon Jovi.

'So what happened in Paris?' he asked. 'Between you and Jane?'

'Long story,' she had replied.

'Well, I'm not going anywhere,' he said. 'Not until "wife swap".'

'God help me,' she said, aware that Saul was, frankly, the best of a very bad bunch.

But was he just that? Or was he better anyway? For the first time, she let herself feel his hands on her – *really* feel them: the heft of them, the strength, the gentleness as well. Could smell his cologne – that was a first; he'd not worn that before, surely? But then, nor had she worn any perfume. Nor quite so much lipstick.

'I messed up,' she confessed eventually. And then went on to explain the entire history of Wickham, of Bingley – of Fitz as well, which she found herself able to articulate without flinching or feeling a needle of guilt. It was a relief to unburden to someone who hadn't known him, who didn't dip their head in that ridiculous imitation of sympathy, and then try to outdo her with their own woes (which, given his wife, Saul would be entitled to do) but instead listened, and squeezed her when she got on to Pemberley and, well, death.

By the time she was describing what happened in Paris, they were wandering back towards Ledbury Road – his car was parked that way, he'd told her, so it made sense to walk her to the door.

'So un-mess it?' he suggested as they passed the vast Salvation Army shop. 'Be the bigger person. I can tell you want to be.'

'I have,' she said. 'I mean, I've tried. And she said she accepts it, but I know she doesn't. She doesn't at all. She's just... not Jane anymore. And the whole moving thing is... well, how can I stop her? It's not my decision. And perhaps it *will* be good for her, getting out of Netherfield, getting away from Meryton and Mum and—'

She stopped herself abruptly as they reached the door of number twenty-seven. 'Well... this is me,' she said.

She watched him take in the front door – faded and chipped, but the stained glass original – the carvings on the surrounding stone. 'Arts and crafts,' he said. 'Have you seen the David Parr house? Opposite the hall?'

'Yes, but... a long time ago.' She and Fitz had been, in fact, in the run-up to the twins' arrival. But she'd felt heavy and sweating, trapped in the tiny, heavily wallpapered and painted terrace, and had had to come outside after only five minutes. 'I'd like to go again.'

'Perhaps we can find a time?' he tried.

She smiled, wide and genuine. 'I'd like that.'

If he was angling for coffee, metaphorical or real, he didn't show it; didn't push her for an invitation to see any 'etchings'. Didn't even need to wait to be told it was a no. 'I'll message you,' he said. 'With some times.'

She nodded, suddenly awkward – a floundering fifteen year old on the doorstep of Longbourn, unsure of the etiquette. And then, as she seized the urge that burned in her, and went to hug him, found herself stumble on the pathway tiles, because he was already heading back to the car that was, in fact, parked a hundred yards away at the Salisbury Arms. She shook herself. Foolish woman, she chided. Not yet. But perhaps sometime?

Oh, she had tried to dislike him – back in the spring – but every time she had dug up an excuse not to get to know him, Fitz's own words echoed: 'How very misfortunate to find a man agreeable whom you seem so determined to hate.' And the thing was, she *did* find him agreeable. More than – she *liked* him. Liked the promise of him. Not in the sense of a vague ideal she was imagining, but more what a new friend – or whatever he would turn out to be – might bring into her life. Jane may have sprinted too quickly after the accident, but Lizzy had allowed herself to get stale, in the same way dust had collected on the shelves in the study, or the tap in the utility continued to drip. She needed to do new things; she needed a spring clean of her very existence. Not in a horrible Marie Kondo way – that woman was a soulless zealot – just, more of a sprucing up, a binning of things that no longer served her. And a welcoming in of those objects – and people – who might spark joy.

And so it was she turned the key in the lock, and burst into her own hallway with the sort of vigour and determination usually only mustered by Mrs Bennet on Twelfth Night when the extensive decorations, she claimed, threatened to curse her (she always imagined it would be with gout), only to be greeted by a whey-faced Lydia standing sentinel outside the downstairs lavatory.

'God, what's happened?' asked Lizzy, as the rush of whatever it had been was flushed away with a sudden wash of cold 'I told you so'. 'Is it Milo? Arden?'

Lydia shook her head, her bottom lip wobbling as if she were the child. 'It's me, Liz,' she said. 'I'm bleeding.'

Lizzy frowned. 'Bleeding where?' she asked. Then, as she realised, 'Oh.'

It took her barely ten seconds to run down the road, thank God Saul had been distracted by a cat, and beg him for the favour. 'I'll be a couple of hours,' she promised. 'I'd call my mum but she'll lose her shit and she's already got my dad to deal with. And Kitty.' Bloody Kitty.

Saul didn't take much persuading. 'What shall I do if they wake up?' he questioned.

'Call me and I'll FaceTime them. Oh, and tell them some facts about rabbits, pencils or death.'

And so, as Saul settled himself on Fitz's favourite green chair with last Saturday's *Guardian*, Lizzy drove Lydia the mile and half to Addenbrooke's, and took her straight into gynae, where, after a lot of persuading, a call-in of more favours, and several promises of weekend and bank holiday cover, Lydia was given an ultrasound.

And Lizzy's heart sank.

'Lyds.' She grasped her sister's hand. 'I'm so sorry, but there's nothing there.'

Lydia, who had been willingly placated by the 'this happens all the time' and 'honestly, there's probably nothing to worry about', felt her insides pitch. 'What do you mean, there's nothing there?'

Lizzy turned the screen around for her sister to see.

Lydia set her jaw as she felt the sudden slump in her, trying to head off tears with anger. 'So I've already miscarried, then,' she snapped.

It seemed the obvious answer, and yet to Lizzy, it made no sense, unless… She took a breath, then barrelled in with the question. 'Lyds, how much did you say you've been bleeding?'

'Just spotting,' said Lydia, with a worrying gusto that suggested she might think Lizzy had got it wrong. That the baby was hiding behind… well, whatever else was in there. What *was* in there? Where did placenta even come from? Her cascading thoughts were interrupted by Lizzy's decisive 'no'.

'You haven't miscarried,' her sister assured her. 'But, Lyds, I don't… I don't think you ever were pregnant.'

'What?'

'I just… there's not enough blood for you to have miscarried at two months. There just… isn't.'

'But…' Lydia trailed off, as the brutal truth hit both sisters at once.

'Did you do any pregnancy tests?' asked Lizzy carefully. 'When we got back from Paris?'

Lydia, resigned now, shook her head. 'I didn't think I needed to. I've been there before, remember? And I had the same… feeling. I just *knew*. I was craving carbs. My mood was batshit – and yes, I know my mood's always batshit.'

Lizzy held up her hands – she had not been about to say it, but she had been thinking it.

'But this,' continued Lydia, 'was – *is* – different.'

Lizzy wiped the gel from Lydia's admittedly distended belly, gestured at her to pull up her trousers and pull down her top. 'I'm going to run some tests,' she said.

'What sort of tests?' asked Lydia.

'Nothing invasive,' Lizzy replied. 'Just… some hormonal checks.'
'Like PMT?' Lydia sighed.
'Like PMT,' lied her sister. 'Just like PMT.'

OCTOBER

Over the years, medical tests had been, to Mrs Bennet, a source of unending delight, tending, as they did, to be accompanied by high drama, which in turn lent itself well to gossip. Thus, two sets arriving within an hour of each other, should have been truly a boon. Instead, she found herself floundering, not sure whether to laugh or cry or take herself off to Ragdale spa for three days of recuperation and a facial.

The first set belonged to Mr Bennet, who, after that grim fifteen minutes with what amounted to a hosepipe-mounted camera, and the swift clipping of several polyps and a small fraction of bowel for biopsy, was given the all-clear by proctology as far as cancer was concerned, and details of a diet more suited to someone with severe IBS.

'The bloody mung beans,' he railed at Mrs Bennet, Mary and Colin as they stood, mute (a first) in the kitchen, the chickpeas Colin had been about to turn into some sort of hummus forlorn on the counter behind them. 'It was the bloody mung beans! And the falafel. And all that Delia!'

Well that was it for Mrs Bennet. Not only had her stock at Meryton Women's Guild already crashed, but now her husband was blaming the high priestess of twentieth-century home cooking. 'Now, you can stop right there,' she said. 'I'm not having you take this out on Delia.'

But Mr Bennet was on a roll. 'Meat and potatoes!' he yelled. 'Meat and potatoes and nice white rice, not brown.' He looked pointedly at Colin. 'They're all on the menu as of now. So I'm having steak and chips for dinner,' he announced. 'And that is, frankly, that.'

'Well, yes, but there's still cholesterol—' began Colin.

'Meat and potatoes!' repeated Mr Bennet, and stormed into the study to eat a packet of Hula Hoops as if they might be the elixir of life itself.

'I suppose one of us will have to ring your sisters.' Mrs Bennet sighed and eyed Mary.

'I will ring everyone,' said Bridget, who had appeared at the promise of potatoes. '*Everyone.*'

And so it was that Kitty and Jane – and Dave, and various people listed in Mrs Bennet's telephone book, including the dentist, found out from a nine-year-old that Mr Bennet 'is alive' and 'must eat crisps forever but not cheesy or beefy ones because of the onion'. Lizzy and Lydia's versions, however, went straight to voicemail, being, as they were, in Lizzy's office at the hospital, dealing with results of their own.

★ ★ ★

'The menopause?' Lydia snapped. 'You've got to be kidding? I'm thirty-seven. Thirty-fucking-seven.'

'Perimenopause,' corrected Lizzy. 'And it's not the end of the world. We can get you straight onto HRT. That will sort out your moods, any vaginal atrophy—'

'What the actual *what* now?'

Menopause had seemed unthinkable enough to Lydia when their mother had gone through it, with her endless fanning and threats to leave their father over the same minor infractions that she'd lived with for thirty years. But now her vagina was going to die as well? And then there was the bigger issue. Or possibly equal, in Lydia's eyes. 'So I can't ever… have a kid?'

Lizzy tilted her head.

'Don't fucking do that. I'm not your patient.'

Lizzy, unaware she'd been habitually guilty of the very gesture she hated, untilted. 'Not… well, not easily. I mean, there's a slim chance, but…'

She paused; something was awry. Lizzy had assumed that by keeping the pregnancy – well, the phantom pregnancy – Lydia was just being bloody-minded, or making hay from a tricky situation. But there was more to it, clearly. 'Are you disappointed?' she asked. 'Is this about… feeling old or did you actually want a child?'

Lydia wilted. 'I… I don't know. I think… I think perhaps I did. That I *do*. Oh fuck.'

Oh fuck indeed. Lizzy handed her the box of Kleenex that rested on her desk for the sort of joy and devastation that pregnancy and birth tended to wreak. Lydia ignored it – she had always preferred the drama of mascara rivulets to polite wiping.

'Had you told the father?' Lizzy tried. 'Well, the… whoever you had sex with?'

Lydia shrugged. 'To be honest I don't even know if I had sex.'

Lizzy had held off well throughout the entire duration of Lydia's return to Longbourn, but this was the limit of 'Lydianess', and now she gave in and rolled her eyes. 'For God's sake, Lydia.'

'What?' her sister protested. 'You'd just sacked me. Jane hated me because of Grace's hair and the nose ring. I was upset. So I drank, and then… well I phoned Wickham.'

'Wickham?' God, it only got worse. *Lydia* only got worse.

'I know, okay?' Lydia held up her hands. 'I am an awful human being. But it's the truth. And as I said, I don't even know if we did anything. I went to his and I remember there was cocaine. And more drink. And then the next thing I knew I'd woken up at Longbourn naked.'

Lizzy was about to blurt something out, then stopped herself. This *wasn't* Lydia's fault. At least not all of it. Wickham knew how vulnerable she was. He knew why she was trying not to drink. God, what a knob he was. 'You're not awful, Lyds,' she said, pushing the Kleenex again. 'You need to give up drinking, but you're not awful.'

Lydia pushed the box back. 'I have given up drinking. Again.'

'Yes, but...' Lizzy braced herself for an argument. 'I think you need help. You need to start AA meetings.'

Lydia's instinct at this was to slap it down, just as she had done Denny when he suggested it. But despite all previous wars when she had fought to the bitter end, long after any battle was effectively lost, she understood that this time she was defeated. 'I know,' she said. 'I'll find one this week.' She watched as a Maximum Black teardrop fell onto the taupe pleats of her & Other Stories midi kilt, then lifted her head up. 'Will you tell Jane?'

Lizzy thought hard. Of course, it was tempting to cash in when it had the potential to end things for her sister and Wickham. But what would that do to Lydia and Jane, whose relationship was already strained at best? 'No,' she said eventually. 'But one of us has to find a way to stop that nonsense.'

'I will,' promised Lydia. 'I'll find a way.'

* * *

Three days later, Lydia was greeted by a torrent of blood – the first of several erratic periods that would blight the next few months until the oestrogen gel and progesterone tablet regime settled. And each time, Lydia would mourn her fertility as strongly as if it *were* a life she was losing.

Perhaps, to her, it was. But perhaps it was this, as well as Lizzy's unanticipated fidelity to her, that fuelled her determination to deal with the whole Wickham situation. Because on the very same day she began to bleed, she decided to talk to her father.

He was, as was his recent wont, sitting in his study with a plate of ham slices and a decaffeinated tea (Colin was, in this one minor factor, jubilant, with all forms of coffee now strictly verboten – 'it's not just the caffeine; it's the histamine!'), and regarded his child's entrance – with its familiar grimace – with a frown, and a reluctant relinquishing of *The Times* crossword. 'Go on then,' he said, patting the threadworn chair next to him. 'What idiocy have you committed this time?' His policy had always been that if his children were determined to be fools, he would rather know about it.

Lydia seated herself, took a deep breath, and began to explain.

'I see,' he said eventually, when she had detailed not merely the Wickham thing, but her alcoholism in general, a possible addiction to sex, the whole Denny debacle, and, inexplicably, the time she was sick in Scott Auger's mouth at a sixth-form disco. 'But you can't tell Jane because it paints you in a terrible light? About Wickham, I mean. Not the Scott whatsisname thing. Although that is truly disgusting.'

'Obviously,' replied Lydia. 'And she hates me as it is.'

'She doesn't hate you,' her father corrected her. 'She took you to Paris.'

'No, but—'

'She's worried about you,' he went on. 'We all have been, a little. But you've come out right in the end.' He smiled. 'Leave it with me. But Lydia, this drinking thing. I think you need some help with it.'

'I know,' she said, not even a little snippy. 'I mean it. I know.'

Denny had been right. Lizzy was right. Her dad was right. Lydia couldn't do this – all of this – on her own. And so, on the very next Tuesday, she took herself to the upstairs room at St Saviour's church hall, the sounds of Colin and Mary preparing for harvest festival with an unlikely rendition of 'Strawberry Fields Forever' (Colin had bowed to pressure – a threatened defection to Meryton Operatic Society – and popular songs were back on the roster) wending up the stairs.

In the end, it hadn't been all that dreadful, deciding to sign up. As her mother pointed out, there was gossip to be had in who among their neighbours was a raging alcoholic.

'*Recovering*, Mum,' she had said.

'Yes, yes,' Mrs Bennet had replied. 'I wonder if Carole Burghley is there. I mean, I've never seen even a Baileys pass her lips but she's got a pair of leggings that she can only have bought drunk, so you never know.'

Carole Burghley was not there. Nor was anyone Lydia recognised from her years at Meryton Grammar, or even the last eight months at home. Well, except – shit – for one person.

'Denny?'

The postie lifted his head from the Paul Murray he'd been reading, and, to Lydia's relief, did not swear, yell, or roll his eyes. Instead, his lips lifted into a half-smile. 'You took your time.'

'I can leave,' she offered then. 'Find another group if you want. It was a toss-up anyway. Between here and NA, I mean. I only picked this because NA's at the ATC hut and the toilets are fucking freezing.'

But Denny shook his head, then nodded at the wooden chair next to him. 'It's all right. I'm a grown-up.'

'I'm not, but I'm trying. And thanks.' She sat down, took the Starburst he offered her. 'Do you believe I can do this?' she asked as she unwrapped it.

'Do you?' Denny questioned.

She smiled, popped the sweet in her mouth. Lime. Nice. 'I do.'

'Good,' he replied. 'Because that's all that matters.' He let a beat fall, then added, 'But for what it's worth, I know you can too. And you know, the baby—'

'I'm not pregnant,' she blurted. 'It was a mistake.'

Denny nodded slowly, as if processing this. 'Okay,' he said eventually. 'Okay then.'

That was all they said to each other that day.

But it was enough. For now, it was enough.

★ ★ ★

It is a cliché to state that escaping cancer may lend one a new lease on life, but clichés are only thus because they are so often true, and being released from the clutches both of bowel tumours – albeit imagined – and of Delia Smith, had renewed Mr Bennet's vigour in a way he had not felt since the early days of his retirement. On top of that, he had a mission, and that mission was Wickham.

He had never warmed to the man, not when he had dogged Lizzy like a sullen toddler, not when Lydia flitted about him like a drunk butterfly, and not even when Jane had taken him on (though she was unlikely to admit to it) as one of her projects, no more worthy than those cats she dragged in as a child, or that ridiculous pigeon. Yes, the man had had a bad hand dealt to him by dint of inheritance – his parents hadn't been well-off, and his mother had done a runner when he was still young; he'd only ended up at prep because Fitz's father had felt sorry for the boy – the son of some lower-rung colleague – and swung him a scholarship. Or was it Charley's dad? No matter. The point was, several of Mr Bennet's old colleagues at the bank had hardly been to the manner born, and not one of them had gone about attempting to rectify it by being a land-grabbing, drug-addled cad. Oh, Jane had claimed he'd mended his ways as far as cocaine was concerned, but clearly that was a load of old poppycock, which meant he was probably still a gambler, and therefore still in terrible debt. And *that* – he almost rubbed his hands in glee – was where Mr Bennet came in. No, he could not hack bank records any more than he could waltz into his old branch and riffle through the contents of the deposit boxes, but he had been schooled in the art of obtaining salacious information by the very best, and, contrary to popular opinion on women and trivia versus men and their focus on subjects of substance, if there was one thing the Golf Club was good for, it was gossip.

From Robert Goldsmith, he had ascertained that Wickham's bank balance was so deep in the red as to be a practical bloodbath. However, being merely poor wouldn't be good enough for Jane to get rid of him, might do the reverse and deepen her pity; no, it was what, exactly, the cash had been squandered on. And from Dick Wilkins, whose daughter was a barmaid at the Dragon, he established that Wickham was well-acquainted with one Maudsley Mick, so-called because of his notorious reputation as both a madman and a gangster, whose poker games came with plentiful 'marching powder' (Dick's term, and one he was clearly over the moon to get to use) and who was reputed to own a gun. Still that might not persuade his overly empathic daughter. So it was from Malcolm Nesbitt (the elder) that he had secured his next hand: that Wickham had, three years before Jane had walked through the door of their estate agents, and less than twelve months after the death of Charley, got Len Nesbitt (the younger) to value Netherfield. And it was with that and one more trump card in his back pocket (along with contraband Rolos and half a Twix) that he went to call on Jane on a day when he knew, from the ultra-efficient grapevine that was his wife, that Grace and Timon were at a new friend's in Cambridge, and Wickham had gone to watch rugby.

'Dad?' Jane ushered him in past Socrates, who had realised that, since his all-clear, Mr Bennet was now the likeliest source of illicit snacks and bounded with expansive happiness whenever they were in the same vicinity. Until today, though, those vicinities tended to include the chief denier of snacks: Mrs Bennet, who was now conspicuous by her absence. A fact that, while it delighted her dog, played on Jane's mind as she led her father through to the kitchen, where she seated him on a bar stool, popped the kettle on for tea, and produced a plate of walnut shortbread, all with the brisk efficiency of a silver service waitress and the grace of a ballerina. 'Is everything okay?' she asked him. 'Is something up with Mum?'

'Your mother is fine,' he replied. 'She and Bridget have gone to Linton Zoo. With Shane of all people.' Shane having made several appearances at Longbourn since his first return, ostensibly to see Bridget, but more likely to pester her mother.

'Poor Kitty,' said Jane.

'Well, I'd say poor Shane,' said Mr Bennet, 'given Bridget's encyclopaedic knowledge of otters. But it's Dave I feel most sorry for. I just hope he can forgive your sister. She's been a bloody idiot.'

'Quite.' Jane perched on the stool opposite him, a mug of hibiscus tea clutched in her delicate fingers.

She had lost weight lately, he had noticed. No doubt that was down to Wickham as well. 'So, look,' he began, 'it's not your mother or Kitty I'm worried about really.'

'No?'

Jane frowned, and he felt a twinge of guilt then, that her innocence, the delightful, guileless way she danced through the world, was about to get kneecapped. But needs must. Needs *really* must, with the wedding only weeks away now and a move soon after. 'It's you,' he continued. 'I'm worried about you and, well, George.'

Jane stiffened, but said nothing, so he went on.

'I've stayed out of it until now, but... some things were brought to my attention, and I've done some digging, and, well, it's not good news. He's in debt, Jane. To the tune of tens of thousands.'

Jane did not question the source of this snippet, but her pale face reddened, suggesting this was not actually news after all.

'It's... it's not as bad as that. Not *tens*, anyway. And that's only at the bank. It's prudent to have debt in one place and move money to another. He's probably got it in something offshore or... or a trust.'

Mr Bennet paused before ploughing on. 'He owes money left, right and centre. The only cash he has – *had* – was his salary...' – another pause – 'from a job I am reliably told he was fired from a month ago.'

That, clearly, was fresh information, as Jane's crimson cheeks fell back to ashen. 'No, I... I would know. He... he would have said—'

'There *is* no money,' her father interrupted. 'Just yours and Charley's. Why do you think he's so keen to sell up?' He placed his hand over Jane's trembling one.

She withdrew it. 'Because he's tired of the jibes,' she tried quietly.

But her father could hear in her voice that she was beginning to doubt it. 'I wish it were that,' he said. 'And I know others haven't been fair to him. But he's not being fair to you. I think he's doing it – getting you to sell Netherfield – because he needs the equity. He got it valued years ago, before you two were even a thing. God knows how he had access to keys but, well, he did.'

Something flickered in Jane's memory – the day Socrates had gone missing and she had gone on a long search with Grace and he had offered to stay at the house in case he came home. And when they had returned, Len Nesbitt had been pulling out of the drive. George had told her he'd come to help in the hunt, and not an hour after that, George himself had found Socrates in the shed – the shed that was never locked – and she had never questioned, until now, who had shut him in...

But no. No! This was unthinkable. He wouldn't lie to her like this. And as for the job, perhaps he'd been taking a stand against the 'wankers' as he referred to his bosses. But before she could argue this, her father had reprised his argument.

'But all of this is beside the point,' he went on. 'The thing is, my darling, he isn't right for you.' This, he realised now, was his real trump card. This, above all, was what mattered. 'He's not a patch on Charley, but, worse, he's not a patch on *you*. You are far too good for him, and yes I know I'm biased but I wouldn't even wish him on Lydia. And I know it's none of my business as to whom you choose to spend your time with or… or share your bed, but when it risks ruining your life and my granddaughter's – financially and otherwise – I'm afraid I can't hold my tongue any longer.'

The room, aside from Socrates' persistent sniffles around Mr Bennet's back pocket and the solid tock of the railway clock above the Aga, fell into a tight silence. It was several minutes before Jane stood, cleared away the cups and swept the crumbs from the counter – a signal, Mr Bennet assumed, that it was time for him to go, to leave her to contemplate these brutal truths and then act on them, to rip that Wickham-shaped plaster off the wound Charley's death had left and get on with her life. Yes, she'd probably equivocate for a day or two, but then, this had to be it. Wickham would be gone in a week, he knew it.

But as Jane stood in the hallway, watching him shrug on his worn Barbour, her words were precise, decisive.

'You're right,' she said. 'It *is* none of your business.'

And when she closed the door to Netherfield, he feared it was not Wickham who might be ripped out of Jane's life, but him.

★ ★ ★

With Bridget off bothering otters with Mrs Bennet and the now semi-constant presence that was Shane, Kitty and Lydia decided to replay their favourite adolescent Saturday, sprawling on the living-room floor with their duvets and a bowl of dry Cheerios, binge-watching *The OC* (Kitty on Team Seth, and Lydia very much Team Ryan, Team Sandy [total DILF], and also Team

Marissa, on whom she had modelled some of the best of her outfits and the very worst of her behaviour).

'What the fuck did I ever see in him?' Kitty asked, as she shovelled another handful of hoops into her mouth.

The question was probably rhetorical, but Lydia chose to take it otherwise. 'God knows. He's such a dork,' she replied. 'That whole Captain Oats toy horse thing with Summer was the sort of weird shit Colin would pull.'

'Not Seth off the telly.' Kitty sighed. 'Shane.'

'Oh.' Lydia frowned. 'I don't know. He was different?'

'He was an idiot,' argued Kitty.

'Well, yes, but so were...' Lydia trailed off.

'So was I?' Kitty marched in where her sister feared to tread.

Lydia shrugged. 'We both were. Idiots I mean. Always...' She paused. 'Always contorting ourselves around boys. Remember when you met that diving instructor – the one who looked like a sort of homeless Lewis Hamilton – and decided you were going to move to Cornwall and haul fucking oxygen tanks around in a van and wear, I don't know, wetsuits all day?'

'Rory,' Kitty said with evident self-disgust. 'God, as if. I wouldn't have survived five minutes. Saltwater ruins your hair.'

'And the time you got into football. And were going to learn Mixed Martial Arts. And take up yoga.'

Kitty shuddered. 'Point made.'

Lydia, who hadn't been making one, merely enjoying the mental equivalent of a Burn Book, suddenly saw with clarity that there was, actually, a point, but that it had not been fully pushed home. 'You don't do that with Dave,' she said, as if she was just realising it – because, in fact, she was. 'With him you're just... Kitty.'

Kitty, who had flinched with guilt, initially, at the very mention of Dave's name, now seized an opportunity to snap. 'Exactly. Boring. Who wants to be "Just Kitty"?'

'But it isn't boring. *You're* not boring. You're brilliant, Kits. And...' – Lydia paused, aware as well that this could be said about herself – 'your life is brilliant. Here in Meryton. You don't need Ibiza or Paris or anywhere else. And if you want to do different things, or do things differently, then *do* them. You don't need to shag someone else to make that happen.'

There was a truncated lull as, onscreen, Sandy Cohen brought out the bagel slicer as if presenting the ark of the covenant, and offscreen the sisters contemplated their respective eight months of fuck-ups.

'You've watched too much daytime TV,' said Kitty eventually.

'*Just Seventeen*,' replied Lydia. '"Ask Anita". Actually, I should be an agony aunt. I would excel at that.'

Kitty didn't argue. And so the seed Lydia had sown flippantly, instead of being blown away by a snide comment, fell onto the fertile ground of sobriety, and was watered by Lydia's not insubstantial ambition. She was busy imagining herself as a hotter *Dear Deidre,* or even a female Dennis Plemons, complete with primetime TV slot and two self-help guides in *The Sunday Times* top ten, when the episode ended and her sister flicked off the television.

'Where are you going?' asked Lydia, all instant belligerence. 'I thought we were going to do gel nails?'

'I don't know,' Kitty admitted. 'I just need... to think.'

Lydia wilted. 'But what shall *I* do?' This had been an oft-repeated refrain from their younger days, when the older Bennets were off at various clubs, their parents were busy ferrying them, and Kitty decided for once that she wanted to do something alone.

Kitty shrugged. 'I don't know. Mary's somewhere. Mum and Bridge will be back in a bit. Probably with a half-dead penguin. And Dad. Unless he's at golf. God, if I decide to take up golf, you have permission to shoot me.'

And with that, Kitty disappeared upstairs to think and think hard. About what she'd done. About what she wanted. About, just as importantly, what Dave wanted, and whether he would ever let her close enough again to give it to him. Jesus, she really had fucked up, hadn't she? Still, there was one small saving grace: even given the bed she had made, and was now lying in miserably, she still wasn't Lydia.

* * *

In this, Kitty was harsh, but fair. After all, Lydia didn't even know how she had nearly ended up pregnant, a fact that she pondered on as she lay in the nest finishing the last of the dry cereal.

None of it made sense. How had she got home? Who had put her to bed if not Wickham? Why had she been naked if they hadn't had sex? And, more importantly, who could she ask, if not Wickham himself?

Then it came to her. Her parents had, according to her mother, been spark out by whatever time she came back in, having watched their favoured soporific, *Call the Midwife*, so there was only one other person who might have seen something. And that person was, to Lydia's delight, entirely incapable of lying.

'Mary,' said Lydia, as she sat down at the kitchen table, where her sister was eating oxtail soup and doing the quick crossword (cryptic clues were baffling to her; she left that to their father).

'You remember that night after the hoohah with Grace?' Lydia asked her.

Mary nodded as she filled in 'ALBERT' (the first animal in space) with a sense of smug satisfaction, knowing that most people would try to stretch 'LAIKA' into the gaps, not realising that the dog had been preceded by an ill-fated monkey. 'Obviously,' she replied.

Lydia went to sigh, before reminding herself that with Mary, questions had to be direct rather than merely suggestive. 'So can you tell me what happened? I mean, specifically, how did I end up naked in bed the next day when I'd been… in Meryton?'

Mary looked up, frowned. 'You came home in an Uber. You'd been sick on yourself. And the taxi. So I paid him a hundred pounds to get it cleaned and then I undressed you, washed you, and put you to bed. I tried to put pyjamas on you but you punched me in the left breast.'

'Oh God.' Lydia winced. There was no point even contesting it. It was obviously true. 'Mary, I'm so sorry. Why didn't you tell me?'

'You never asked,' her sister replied. Then sighed heavily. 'No one asks me anything.'

Old Lydia would have noticed nothing in Mary's casual addition, or demeanour. Old Lydia would have merely protested that a hundred pounds was too much to wash a taxi and she could have done it herself in the morning, or paid some teenager twenty quid. And Old Lydia was still there – and would always be so, even without the drink and the drugs. She would continue to flit from project to project; would still plunge across the road without checking both ways; might even die one day in some idiotic adrenalin-fuelled incident with a hot-air balloon. But she would also, from now on, consider people's feelings other than her own.

She framed her question as simply as she could. 'What do you want to tell me, Mary?'

Mary put down her spoon and her pen, and took an enervating breath. 'I think I love Colin,' she said. Then, to clarify, 'Burghley. From choir. He lives at Rosings with his Aunt Carole and—'

'I know who Colin is,' Lydia blurted. 'Mary, when you say "think" do you mean "probably"? I mean, statistically, how likely is it that you actually love him?'

Mary considered. 'Ninety-seven per cent,' she said.

Lydia, already brimming with the possibility of a new career as an agony aunt, tacked on 'matchmaker' to her curriculum vitae. 'Then you must tell him, and you must tell him now.'

'Must I?' checked Mary. 'I haven't finished my soup.'

'Fuck soup,' said Lydia. 'Oxtail can wait. This is love! Now go on. Get to Rosings and tell him, for God's sake. Before I tell Mum and she does it for you.' Chief amongst Lydia's epiphanies since starting AA was how much she enjoyed honesty.

'Very well,' said Mary, standing. 'I suppose I should get my coat.'

★ ★ ★

One might imagine Mary would have managed more than a 'very well' given the circumstances, but the middle Bennet had never been one to gush, and pragmatism always won out over plunging headlong into something she might regret. In fact, it would be safe to say Mary had not plunged into anything in her life – not even Kelsey Kerridge swimming pool, which she entered sensibly, backing down the steps, because that was, after all, what they were there for. No, this would be the biggest and swiftest commitment Mary had ever made to anything or anyone, and so she would do it with a level head, a cagoule (it had threatened to spit around two) and decent shoes.

Still, her breath hitched as she knocked on the door of the imposing Rosings, with its flint infill and double front. And, as she waited for Colin to clip down the passage – she could hear by the tread it was him, not his aunt – and open the door, her heart almost jigged. Because this man understood her. This man was kind. This man made her happy, and in turn was happy for her to be as Mary as she could possibly be, and that, she knew (unlike several of her sisters), was a rare thing indeed.

'Colin,' she said as he (of course, he) opened the door, 'I have something to tell you.'

'Mary.' He smiled thinly. 'I am so glad to see you. I have something to tell you as well.'

Mary's heart did jig this time. 'You first,' she said, having read on a blog somewhere that this was the polite thing to do.

But as Mary awaited – even prayed to a secular god for – a confession of the same giddy feelings she had recently experienced, she was about to be horribly disappointed.

'It's my aunt,' Colin told her. 'She's dead.'

NOVEMBER

If there was one Meryton event Mrs Bennet relished more than any other – and this included the dizzy heights of the Women's Guild 'Christmas Craft-a-thon', the Golf Club 'Pimms and Divots' party, and the Amateur Dramatic Society's woefully un-woke annual panto – it was a good funeral. Not only was it a chance to tally up who, amongst her peers, was still living, but above all it offered – once the eulogies had been sat through, the warm wine downed rapidly, the vol-au-vents tolerated – the chance to dissect the life of the recently deceased for every slight, every minor infraction, every petty snub. And Carole Burghley, with her holier-than-God airs and ambitious graces (that extraneous 'e' on the end of her name was frippery itself), was prime meat.

'Of course, this leaves the casting for *Streetcar* wide open,' observed Bad Karen, over an insipid blini. 'And Barbara Clyde's going in for her you-know-what, so she's out of the running.'

That both women were in their sixties should, of course, have put them well out of the running to play Blanche Dubois, but status tends to trump age, and talent, in amateur circles, a fact that should have energised Mrs Bennet, who had been looking for ways to oust Carole from her perch for several decades. Other things, however, played on her mind, chief among them Colin, sole heir to the substantial Rosings, with its coveted walled garden and – it transpired – one of those taps like Jane's that dispensed boiling water in an instant. And now, apparently, prime meat himself.

'I don't know *what* Julia Gibbons thinks she's playing at,' she complained, as she watched Hertfordshire's foremost mobile waxing technician corner Colin by the teak credenza. 'He's a decade younger than her *and* he's a professor. A professor! She can't even spell the word.'

'I would,' said Bad Karen. 'I mean, he's a bit Benedict whatsisname to look at but I bet he's a devil in bed. The quiet ones always are.'

'Laurence still not performing?'

'Not a twitch since the night Geraint Thomas won Sports Personality of the Year,' lamented Bad Karen. 'He couldn't get over him beating Harry Kane.'

Mrs Bennet would have said this was a blessed relief, but each to their own. But as for Julia Gibbons, Lizzy's absence was yet more insult to injury; this was an opportunity to move on, and straight into Rosings with its four en-suites (she had checked), stone gazebo, and useful proximity to Longbourn. And what was she doing? Messing with wretched Pemberley. Of course, selling it was progress, but she could have waited a day to traipse up there. Or she could have if it weren't for this alleged wedding at the weekend – about which Mrs Bennet had yet to wheedle any details, but the whole thing stank, frankly. And God knows what was up with Jane, who had not deigned to grace Longbourn for weeks now. Mr Bennet had told his wife not to fret, but he might as well have told her to give up breathing.

'Mary's quiet,' Bad Karen said then. 'I mean, quieter than usual.'

Mrs Bennet glanced at her middle daughter, sitting awkwardly on a pouffe reading the bill of service for the umpteenth time – standard Mary. But Bad Karen was right – there was a new… tetchy air to her. She had been the one to burst into the house bearing the bad tidings – an honour Mrs Bennet was livid to have missed, but better her than either Bad Karen or, God forbid, Maureen Gyp – had helped Colin with all the funeral arrangements, had taken an hour to get ready this morning (not that one could tell, though at least the Hogwart's scarf had been put back on the peg), and had practically bounded through the door of St Saviour's to take her place in the front pews. But now she was back at Rosings, Mary was as recalcitrant as a cat, or indeed as Kitty and Lydia, both of whom were conspicuous by their absences – Kitty insisting she couldn't take time off work, and Lydia being roped in to sit the twins – a slight Mrs Bennet would take a while to forgive Lizzy for, despite having turned it down in favour of attending the funeral unencumbered by a child likely to try to climb into the coffin. It was all very vexing, very vexing indeed. The joy of daughters was that one should be able to read their like-minds, and yet she had no idea what went on in any of their heads at any given minute. And with this thought ruining what should have been a jolly good funeral, she bit into another listless canapé and went back to dissecting the choice of soft furnishings.

★ ★ ★

Lizzy, for her part, had felt not a single needle of guilt at missing the funeral. Gravesides were not her favourite place, for obvious reasons, but more than that, it would be churlish to mourn a woman who had been, at best, a thorn in the side of the Bennets, and indeed most of Meryton, for the larger part of her sixty-nine years. It was awful for Colin, of course, but now he would be free to leave, or at least turn that behemoth of a house – the majority of its bedrooms laying empty, wasted – into something that might earn its keep.

It was this that had been egging her on with Pemberley. Even when Fitz was still with them, it had been a vain luxury – a clutching on to something none of them needed, not really. They had Ledbury Road; why not just rent a place for holidays like any other couple? Or stay with Georgie, who had a perfectly nice house in the area, which, she recalled now, Georgie had suggested a decade ago, only Fitz had refused to listen. But Fitz was gone – she could accept that now – and this was Lizzy's decision, and hers only. Contracts were about to be exchanged – tomorrow, if all went well – and then completed by the weekend. Hence the need to pop up to do what she couldn't in June, thus having a more useful excuse to avoid Rosings than 'I'm not a fan of death'. And so Lydia had been roped in, saving her from the dim proceedings as well.

'One night,' Lizzy promised. 'I'll be back first thing and then if you can stay until eightish? I'll not be long at the wedding. One dance and then I shall hightail it out. Like a middle-aged Cinderella! And for God's sake don't let Milo out of your sight this time. And neither of them are to piss on the doorstep, understand?'

'Back garden?' checked Lydia.

'Only if next-door is watching.' Lizzy laughed. 'Thank you. Really, Lydia, I mean it. I should never have… I panicked and—'

'No,' Lydia insisted. 'I mean, obvs, that was the catalyst for me almost shagging that twat and not getting pregnant and realising too late that I can't be a mother—'

'Lyds—'

'Wait! I'm not finished.' Lydia held up a finger. 'If it hadn't happened then it would have done sooner or later. And the sooner the better.'

'How many days now?'

'A hundred and thirty-seven.'

'I'm so proud of you.' Lizzy pulled her little sister into a swift hug.

'Me too,' Lydia said into the thick knit of a Toast crewneck. 'Though Jane's wedding might push me over the edge.'

Lizzy extricated herself. 'You know she hasn't spoken to me since Paris? Not properly.'

Lydia shrugged. 'That makes none of us then. But at least we're not disinvited?'

Perhaps that would actually be easier? Lizzy thought to herself as she bundled her overnight case into the boot of the BMW (which was another thing; she'd be trading the wasteful 5 series in for something smaller and preferably electric the second she had time). Better that than having to sit on their hands when the Reverend asked if anyone objected.

But, as she cruised down Station Road, heading towards the Fen Causeway, it picked at her, niggled. This was ridiculous – she and Jane not even on speaking terms. And fine, her sister had made up her mind about Wickham (and whatever Dad had said had made not a jot of difference, clearly), but she at least needed to know that Lizzy was there for her when... *if* it all went wrong. Besides which (a plan was beginning to take shape) there was a stack of Charley's things still to deal with up in Derbyshire, and it was unfair on Lizzy to have to attend to two sets of dead men's wellies and whatever else they'd left. This was Jane's responsibility and she was shirking it.

Well, that did it – Lizzy was sick of being responsible. She'd been responsible for far too bloody long and for too many bloody things. So if she was going to Pemberley, then Jane was coming too. And instead of turning right at the end of the Fen Causeway, northbound up the M11, she swung left towards the Essex borders and Netherfield.

★ ★ ★

Thus far, Jane's Friday had not gone to plan.

Grace had casually dropped into conversation over breakfast bagels that she needed some TCP because her belly button piercing was a 'bit green' and the ensuing hoohah had meant both she and Timon had missed their train. Timon had asked their father to drive them in but George – who had still not admitted to being 'between jobs' – had conjured an early meeting in the city and was gone before the coffee machine had finished its hissing. And so Jane, who was still brimming with guilt over the impending move, had had to drive the pair of them to Mill Road, and in their haste she'd forgotten to walk Socrates who had been forced (poor Socrates) to relieve his bowels on the doormat. Which, one might have argued, was preferable to the living-room carpet, but wool was at least washable and did not come with inch-long bristles.

She was still trying to rinse out the ick when the doorbell went, sighing to herself as she trudged to answer it in her Marigolds and apron.

The sigh hitched, along with her insides, the minute she saw who was on the doorstep. 'I... I don't think there's much to say,' she said swiftly. Meaning there was nothing she wished to listen to, a nuance her sister must surely have known.

'I'm not here to fight,' said Lizzy. 'You and Wickham, well, that's your business. But before all that you need to come somewhere with me.'

Jane pulled a face. 'Come where? I'm busy.'

This was a sticking point Lizzy had anticipated. But with no immediate solutions, had decided she'd wing it when she came to it. 'You'll see,' she said. 'Just get in the car.'

'I'm not... getting in the car,' Jane replied. 'I told you, I'm busy. Socrates needs walking for a start.'

Think. Think! 'Bring him,' said Lizzy quickly. 'We can do that on the way.'

'Way *where*?' demanded Jane. 'I can't just go abandoning... *things* on a whim. I've got the florist calling at eleven and... and caterers to chase and—'

'Bring your phone then, for fuck's sake!' snapped Lizzy,

unable to bear it any longer. 'I need to talk to you. I need you to… to *help* me with something.'

That emphasis found the chink Lizzy had been looking for. Jane could resist any temptation except when it came to helping someone. Empathy was her heroin, after all. She steeled herself. 'Fine,' she said. 'Fifteen minutes. I'll get the dog.'

Lizzy grimaced. 'It might be a little longer than that,' she admitted.

But Jane didn't hear her. She was already back in the bowels of Netherfield, shucking off gloves and stuffing Socrates' lead into the pocket of her Didriksons parka. Whatever it was had better be quick. She was already teetering on the brink of something she couldn't name; couldn't even think about for fear of having some sort of mental collapse. But perhaps a favour for Lizzy might buoy her, if adding to the tally of favours her sister owed in return.

It wasn't until they had circumvented Cambridge and were firmly on the A14 heading towards what was surely the A1(M) that Jane realised she'd been had. 'Stop the car,' she said.

'Can't,' said Lizzy. 'Too dangerous on this bit of road.'

Jane's face was red. 'Pull into a petrol station then!'

'Tank's full,' said Lizzy. 'No need.'

Jane's tender frame fired with a blistering electricity. 'I don't mean… Just let me out!'

'Not until you agree to help me with Pemberley.'

So Jane was right. 'No,' she snapped. 'I said I didn't want to go and I don't. I don't want to see it. I don't want to even think about it. I don't want to have to… to have to pick through those things.'

'Well nor do I,' said Lizzy. 'But Pemberley will be gone in the morning, so just woman up and help me.'

She could have done a runner at the Grantham North services. Well, she could have called an Uber – or George – and paid them to fetch her. The fact she would inevitably have to compensate her fiancé was not as galling as it should be, but of course it was habit now, a fact she did recognise, but did her best to tamp down. She was so very good at that – tamping things down. But Lizzy was right: it was unfair on her to have to sift through... everything, alone.

'I don't know what Grace will say,' she said pointedly, as they wended their way into the dales.

'She'll say, "thank God, a night off" and eat filthy takeaway,' said Lizzy. 'And so she should. She's sixteen not six.'

'George will worry, then,' tried Jane.

'Will he?' Lizzy, despite her efforts, did not sound convinced.

'Of course,' Jane said snippily.

'About you?' Lizzy checked. 'Or himself?'

'What on earth do you mean? He's quite capable of making his own dinner.' Well, he was. He just chose not to. And Jane liked to cook, so why not oblige?

'I didn't mean like that,' said Lizzy. 'I just... He'll worry for the same reason you're worrying now.'

'Oh?' demanded Jane. 'And why, precisely, am I worried?'

Lizzy gripped the steering wheel, thankful for the quiet, occasionally farting, presence of Socrates, whose dislike of loud noises meant, at least, Jane was unlikely to scream. 'You're scared you'll remember too much of Charley, and realise just how short George falls.'

The rest of the journey continued in silence. Lizzy trying not to regret saying it. Jane wishing she hadn't heard it.

Because the thing was, it was true.

★ ★ ★

The 'sold' sign had been a jolt for them both – though at least for Lizzy it came with the ring of an imaginary till that might now stretch to fixing the roof on Ledbury Road before she decided what to do with their home (she had been pondering 'something', only the specifics, as they tended to do, eluded her), and plump up the twins' university funds. For Jane, who had not seen the mottled taupe of the stones, the twelve-paned sashes, the etched-glass of the porch for almost four years, it was more of a wake-up call. It was time, the sign said, in its bold black on orange print, to face up to things. To pull off the veil, the rose-tinted spectacles, and take a look at her life in stark, harsh light. Thus, it had taken her less than ten minutes in the damp depths of Pemberley to collapse onto a Chesterfield (the new owners were keeping the larger furnishings) and confess: that she wasn't sure at all about George; that she was having second and third and even fourth thoughts about the wedding; that, aside from the sex, she wasn't sure they had anything in common at all.

'Is that it?' Lizzy tried as she handed Jane another few sheets of toilet paper. 'The sex? Is Wickham better?'

Jane crimsoned as she dabbed her eyes.

'That's a yes, then.'

'No! Well, technically perhaps. If we're being mathematical about these things. But…'

And that 'but' was the thing. The connection – the soul connection – that she assumed would be kindled by George's tinder of tricks, and built on a pyre of their shared grief for Charley and Fitz, remained conspicuous by its absence. She'd tried several times to will it into existence; had thought she'd caught it once, in a look he'd given her over a lamb casserole, but it turned out he had indigestion, and so she was left with this slackness in the air between them – a gap where a taut string should have kept them close.

And then there was everything her father had told her. Oh, she had railed at the time – not to him, but to herself, later, and then a little to George, when he asked why the wine was already open when he got in. But she hadn't asked him about any of it – if there was a truth to it. At the time, she'd told herself it was because she didn't need to, because of course George's answers would be viable. But now, she realised, it was because she hadn't wanted to listen to his excuses, knowing them to be as fabricated as his feelings for her in the first place.

God, what an idiot she'd been. What a silly little fool.

'You're not,' said Lizzy. 'Whatever it is you're blaming yourself for' – she held up a hand – 'and I know you are so don't argue, I can tell you it isn't your fault. He knew you were vulnerable and he knew you were kind and he took a punt. And maybe he does love you, in his own way, but that isn't good enough. It isn't good enough for you. You are five times more beautiful, five times more kind than anyone in any room and you need to be with someone who knows it. Not someone who sees you as… as—'

'A meal ticket,' Jane finished. 'And I know. I just…' She petered out, was in danger of letting herself give in to sobbing, when she remembered she still had her Marigolds – she'd pushed them into the pockets of the coat in her hurry. 'Shall we make a start, then?' she asked, as she pulled them out, mustering the sort of briskness and efficiency with which she approached most tasks in life.

Lizzy nodded, picking up the roll of black rubble bags she'd brought along. 'A bag to keep,' she said handing one to Jane, 'a bag for charity' – she ripped off another – 'and a bag for landfill.'

'Or we could burn it?' suggested Jane, that sliver of Lydia that lived buried inside her – that was taken with the romance, with dramatics – making itself known.

'Tempting,' admitted Lizzy. 'But I'm not having a Manderley on my conscience. And I don't think the insurers will take too kindly either. There's a skip in the village – Mrs Briggs said old Heathcote's having his bathroom done – and we can leave it in that.'

And with that, they set to work.

For charity, they bagged up coats and boots and books – stacks of them, foxed and mottled with patches of damp, the spines cracked, and emerging every now and then a silverfish, irritated at being disturbed after almost four years of blissful solitude. They kept a copy of an old Brontë that Charley had bought Jane for their paper anniversary, a 'Best Dad' mug Lizzy had given Fitz to let him know she was pregnant, Pyrex breakfast bowls in shades of 1950s kitchen: pale green, duck-egg blue, a faded red that Jane remembered was Grace's favourite.

'When will you tell him?'

Jane started. 'Pardon?'

Lizzy smiled faintly. 'George – when will you let him know?'

Jane's insides slipped again. 'I... not tonight. I can't face him. Not yet.'

Lizzy's lips quirked firmly upwards. 'I was rather hoping you'd say that. There's this wonderful little place called The Hawden. The room's booked. And yes they take dogs. We'd need to top and tail, obviously, and you'll have to borrow some of my things, but—'

'Yes,' said Jane, taken with it. 'Oh God, yes please.'

They swam (Jane in her underwear); they ate good food, or a little of it (Jane's stomach was as unhappy as Socrates', who did not take well to steak and had to be walked four times between seven and ten) and drank fine wine; they talked until late in the king-sized bed, and then fell into a fitful sleep for what few hours they could manage before they had to leave to get Lizzy back in time for the wedding – or at least the reception.

'So, Saul then?' questioned Jane as they approached the familiar stretch of road where the A14 becomes the M11 again, signalling to both that they were nearly home. 'Is he rich?'

'Not especially,' said Lizzy.

'Is he kind?'

'Horribly.'

'Then I like him,' said Jane.

So do I, thought Lizzy, decisively. So do I.

✦ ✦ ✦

Longbourn, meanwhile, was oblivious to proceedings, taken up as it was with a drama all of its own, involving Lydia (of course, Lydia, who, on her mother's insistence, had brought the twins for a post-funeral visit with Bridget) and some vitamins.

As a toddler, everyone had thought Bridget pleasingly oddball, each idiosyncrasy an inheritance from her mother or aunts: her refusal to wear wool, to take off her coat, to eat anything wet, were all dismissed as 'a bit Lydia'; 'like Kitty', the tendency to get into scrapes that had ended, more than a few times, in A&E. The staring into the middle distance, the failed efforts at friendship, were no different to Mary's; the fixation on pigeons, the preference for the misshapen when it came to Jellycat animals, were not unlike Jane's empathy for the bruised in both man and beast; when her Reception Year report came home declaring her obstinate, headstrong, it was to Lizzy they all looked before acknowledging that all five sisters, and indeed Mrs Bennet, were Bridget-like in this respect. It wasn't until a clued-up classroom assistant had taken Kitty aside at parents' evening and explained that narrating the class gerbil for an hour wasn't very—

'Normal,' Kitty had finished. 'Sorry, I know.'

'I was going to say neurotypical,' the assistant (an enthusiastic woman, with appalling taste in muumuus) corrected her. 'Have you thought about autism? Or perhaps ADHD?'

Her tone had been as matter of fact as asking if Kitty had thought about enrolling Bridget for gymnastics, or taking her bowling. And in that blithe spirit she had made an appointment with Dr Ogden, who said, 'ah, yes' a lot, went through a lengthy questionnaire, and referred her straight on to the specialist, who, on their first meeting, had declared Bridget 'off the scale'. 'Frankly,' she said, 'I'm amazed you've not picked it up until now.'

After Darcy

Mrs Bennet had initially been embarrassed at a diagnosis that was more than just 'a bit Bennet' and, according to several tabloids, possibly made up. But Kitty had persuaded her that it a) was real and b) might actually be beneficial, not least to Bridget herself, and so Mrs Bennet had determined to embrace it, quite vocally, becoming quite the star turn of Meryton Women's Guild for at least a fortnight until someone's niece contracted measles. It was she, now, who took charge of Bridget's medication, doling it out daily alongside her own collagen, cod liver oil, and vague 'lady' tablets, as well as Mr Bennet's litany of vitamin D, zinc, and flaxseed capsules, and Lydia's myriad skin-conditioning supplements to which she insisted she was not addicted, merely embracing as part of a new, healthy lifestyle.

No one knows quite how it was that Bridget's pill got mixed into one of the other old Gü pots (Mrs Bennet's receptacle of choice for pills and peanuts alike). Lydia and Mr Bennet blamed Mrs Bennet; she blamed everyone else. But when Mrs Bennet, who had taken all three grandchildren to the park, returned to Longbourn at lunchtime, she was in a blistering mood.

'Where is Bridget's pill?' she demanded, scouring the kitchen counter for the leftover receptacle. '*Someone* forgot to give it to her, and I've had two solid hours of duck commentary.'

Someone being, one assumes, Kitty, whose own brain had been increasingly vague of late. 'You said you'd do it!' she protested.

'I did. And I definitely left it here.' Mrs Bennet turned to her husband, who had been buried, surprisingly, in *Style* magazine, and Lydia, who was, inexplicably, cleaning the oven. 'One of you must have had it!'

'Don't look at me,' said Mr Bennet. 'It's bad enough taking the ones you insist on giving me. Why would I pilfer someone else's?'

'You'd know anyway,' said Kitty. 'He'd be like the sodding Road Runner. Unless he's got ADHD, obvs.'

'I do not,' said Mr Bennet decisively. 'IBS is enough acronym for one man.'

'Lydia?' tried Mrs Bennet then.

But Lydia was busy. Very, very busy.

'Lydia!' repeated her mother.

'What?' Lydia reluctantly lifted her head.

'Have you done something with Bridget's pill?' her mother snapped. 'And what in God's name possessed you to clean the range? You haven't so much as hoovered your own room in eleven months.'

'I don't know,' admitted Lydia. 'I just sort of… felt the urge. And once I'd done the bathroom and the downstairs lav, this seemed like the obvious next step?'

There was a tight silence as the room held its breath, waiting for the enormous penny to drop.

One…

Two…

'Fuck,' said Lydia.

'Fuck,' said Kitty.

'Fuck,' repeated Milo with delight.

'What?' demanded Mrs Bennet. 'What's going on? And don't say that word, Milo. Say "flapjack".'

'Lyds has got ADHD,' said Kitty.

'Has she?' asked Mrs Bennet. 'Since when?'

'Since forever,' Kitty filled in for her sister, who was still crouching gape-mouthed on the floor clutching a tin of Mr Muscle. 'I mean, it's so f—flapjacking obvious. How did none of us see it? I mean, it explains *everything*. Everything!'

'If anyone had asked me—' began Mary. But, of course, no one had, and nor did they then.

'Lydia?' urged Mrs Bennet. 'Lydia!'

Lydia snapped to for the second time. 'What?'

'Well, *have* you?'

'I…'

Lydia thought about it. I mean, Kitty had perhaps over-egged it; it might not explain *everything*. But it did tally, from what little she knew of it – the lack of ability to stick to one thing, the short-lived but profound passions, the fidgeting, the restlessness, the – what had someone called it? That was it – the lack of object permanence, which came across as indifference but was merely the fact that he hadn't been in her brain at that point because she'd got into roller-blading—

Lydia sprang to her feet, threw her filthy gloves onto the counter and ran from the room.

'*Now* where are you going?' her mother called after her.

But Lydia didn't have time to answer, because she needed to speak to someone and speak to them now.

She was about to head into Meryton when she realised he'd still be on his round – probably up towards Bad Karen's by now – and so she marched, still wearing her indoor Uggs and her father's barbecue apron, up towards Pig Lane, where, yes, she saw the red van parked half on the pavement, and Denny sauntering towards it.

'Denny!' she yelled. 'Denny!'

Denny, who had been happily contemplating an afternoon of sanding down the bathroom sash, looked up and curbed the instinct to grin. The fact that, despite everything, Lydia instilled something verging on giddiness in him was a constant source of irritation. And one that needed forceful restraint. He pasted on what he hoped was indifference. 'Lydia.'

'I need to talk to you,' she panted as she came to a dramatic halt in front of Reg Hemmings' gnomes, wearing – was that an apron?

Oh God, she wasn't drunk again, was she? It was only just gone lunch. 'You could do that at group?' Denny tried.

'Too late,' she managed. 'Now. I need to do this now.'

'Lyd—' he began to protest.

'No,' she insisted. 'Just listen.'

Denny braced himself. Whatever it was, he was not going to agree to it, he decided. Just… no. He didn't need the drama, not at this age. Not without alcohol to damp it. And with Lydia, that was the risk.

'So, I have ADHD,' she announced. 'Or at least I'm pretty sure I do. I accidentally took Bridget's meds and I cleaned the whole house. I even nearly read a book. I haven't read a book since I was in school.'

Denny frowned. This was… not anything he had expected, and yet… well, it made sense. 'Okay? And you need to tell me because?'

Lydia looked at him as if he was mad. 'So, you can, like, absolve me? Before the meeting? For taking drugs, I mean.'

The laugh was unforced. 'I don't think—'

'I'm serious,' Lydia pleaded. 'I've done a hundred and thirty… eight days and this utterly fucks it. I don't want to start again.'

Again, he laughed. 'Lydia, you don't need to start again. It was an accident. And besides, if the drugs do work, then… well, maybe you should be taking them anyway?'

'That is…' Lydia paused. The drugs *had* worked: it had been as if something inside her had clicked and pulled focus and the eight million things in her head competing for attention all slid under cupboards. Procrastination – and the almost physical pain of having to do something she didn't relish – was suddenly a distant memory, and the need to achieve something was champing at the bit. 'I, yes. Right then. Well, thanks… I guess.'

And before she said anything else she might regret (although the urge to blurt out every single thought was distinctly less pressing than usual), she turned and walked back down Pig Lane towards home leaving Denny oddly discombobulated, and not a little bereft.

★ ★ ★

After Darcy

Lizzy, who might have been a little perturbed at both the abandonment of the twins to her mother, and their childminder's consumption of a controlled substance (albeit accidental and eventually beneficial), missed all this. She had arrived back at Ledbury Road to find a note from Lydia as to their whereabouts, and her dress laid out on the bed, a condom atop it. And at this, Lizzy surprised herself, because instead of flinching, or wishing ill on her idiot of a sister, she laughed. Though rather than her clutch bag, the thing was ushered into the bedside cupboard, where it nestled next to her progesterone capsules, oestrogen gel and pessaries and a bottle of amitriptyline that she'd been prescribed in the wake of Fitz's death and had used only intermittently since, preferring to remain sharp, if horribly short on sleep.

The dress was new – a deep green that shone like the carapace of a pleasing beetle when she swished its full, ankle-length skirts – and hadn't been cheap, but it was the first item of clothing she'd bought in four years that wasn't for someone under three feet tall, and, frankly, bugger it: she earned a decent enough salary, the mortgage had been paid off by life insurance, and she deserved to dress up once in a while. Besides, the shoes were more than well-worn – the same pair of Pied a Terre heels she'd sported since the early 2000s, and which she knew would not pinch or cause a blister, which was key, given dancing was the thing – the whole point of today's engagement.

Or was it? Because as she clacked cautiously across the marble floor of the University Arms Hotel into the warm-lit, dark-panelled ballroom (she had been spared the church service, the wedding breakfast with its inevitable chicken something or other, the speeches, either drunk or self-conscious, or both) she began to wonder if it wasn't just 'company'. It had been so long since she'd accepted an invitation to any sort of social engagement that wasn't in some way Bennet-related and thus compulsory that she'd forgotten how much she actually enjoyed meeting people – well, decent people: clever, empathetic, the sort who scrubbed up well in a tux…

'Are you sure this is okay?' she asked. 'With Luella I mean, given her mother?'

'Lizzy.' Saul grasped her arms and kissed her on each cheek, his woody cologne sending a frisson through her that she would neither deny nor attempt to curtail. 'You look' – he stood back, admired her – 'bloody incredible.' His grin was infectious. 'And yes, it's more than okay. Come on, let's go and meet her, get that bit over with.'

And he bustled her towards the top table, where the bride sat in ivory resplendence, drinking a bottle of Stella Artois.

'She'll probably remember you anyway,' he said. 'From dance class, I mean. You're not easy to forget.'

It was a line that might otherwise, from another man, have smacked of twattishness, but from Saul was not a line at all, but mere statement of fact. And when he introduced her as his 'friend', this, too, was precisely the truth, and yet Lizzy found it fell somehow short of her feelings towards him. Not that she knew, exactly, what those feelings were. But over the last month or so, since that flit with Lydia and the apparent miscarriage and him sitting the twins, they'd talked almost every day and something had been kindled in her again. There had been no more adolescent wet dreams, admittedly, but it was his image she had kept in her head when she climbed into bed and thought she would just 'check it was all working' (which it was). And after she'd watched him take to the floor with his daughter for a wildly improvised foxtrot, she found herself electric with want. Happily, the band – a local jack-of-all-trades combo – segued effortlessly from 'Cheek to Cheek' to a gliding three-time she recognised as the waltz to which she and Saul had danced in the decidedly less dappled surroundings of Gwydir Street.

'May I?' he asked, holding out an arm for her.

She arched an eyebrow, smiled. 'You definitely may,' she replied.

And with this continued politesse (and a level of consent that would tick every box in one of Grace's Sex Ed classes), they danced through eleven more songs before she said she'd better get home.

'Already?' checked Saul, appalled. 'It's not even nine.'

She laughed. 'I know. But I said I'd be there at eight. I'm already a terrible stop-out.'

'Your carriage will turn back into a pumpkin, I assume.'

'Oh, the horses are mere mice already,' she replied. 'I'm resigned to walking.'

'Across Parker's Piece? In heels?' He nodded at her scuffed satin pumps.

'Oh, I've done worse in these shoes,' she told him. 'They'll be just fine.'

'At least let me walk you,' he pleaded.

'But Luella—'

'But nothing. I've done my bit – danced with her and paid for it all. Besides, she's so drunk it'll be a miracle if she even notices. She's already had a tactical chunder.'

'Oh, to be young!' Lizzy declaimed.

'Thank God we're not,' replied Saul, and held out his arm again.

Then they donned coats – his a smart grey wool, hers a soft Cos faux fur – and walked out of the hotel and left towards Ledbury Road, their feet keeping up a steady one-two, but their hearts scattered as rabbits', dancing to the delicious frenzy in their heads.

★ ★ ★

Ten miles away, it was a no less frenzied, if far less thrilling, scene as Wickham arrived back from wherever the hell he had been, and Jane finally got the chance to tell him everything she'd waited on tenterhooks all day to say.

'Call off the wedding?' he sputtered. 'What the fuck?'

'There's no need to swear,' she replied, pouring the coffee she'd insisted he drink to take the edge off whatever it was he was on. 'And yes. It's… well, I think you know this whole thing is a sham, isn't it.'

'A what? A sham? Are you mad?'

'Not in the least,' she said. 'I was, but actually' – she sat herself down – 'I can see clearly everything that happened now. I was fragile and you saw that, and now here we are. Only you don't really love me—'

'Oh, come on—' Wickham protested.

'No,' Jane stopped him. 'You don't really love me, and that is fine, it really is. It's important for you to know I'm okay with that. That I don't blame you for, well, taking advantage of a beneficial situation. But I am not okay with some of the other things. Specifically the drugs, not with teenagers around. And, well, selling Netherfield to pay off your debts.'

There, she had said it. Or most of it. The bits that mattered anyway.

Wickham, whose face had turned puce not two moments ago, was suddenly whey. 'This is Lydia, isn't it? Did she tell you we had sex? Because if she did, it's bullshit. I just let her believe that to teach her a lesson.'

Jane's flinch was only momentary. And in its wake came a second wave of disappointment in the utter inevitability of it all. 'God, poor Lydia,' she said. 'No wonder she's been so upset.'

Wickham pulled a face, one that turned his faded charm into pantomime villain. 'You're siding with her?'

'She's my sister.'

'I'm your fiancé, for fuck's sake!' he railed. Then rallied. 'You've always looked down on me, haven't you. Had it in for me from the beginning because I'm not in fucking Debrett's like your precious Charley.'

Jane had expected this, was ready. 'He wasn't in Debrett's, as well you know, and I don't—'

But Wickham was on a roll. 'Which is rich, considering. I mean, have you looked at your family? A drunkard, a weirdo, a small-town hairdresser, a… a stuck-up jumped-up midwife and a mother who's a walking fucking embarrassment.'

Jane closed her eyes for a moment, gathered herself.

When she opened them, her thoughts were clear again. 'Lizzy's an obstetrician,' she corrected him. 'Lydia's not a drunkard, she's a recovering alcoholic. Kitty's a bloody good hairdresser. Mary is… well, Mary, but we love her. And as for Mum, you'd have been lucky to have her as a mother-in-law. As it is, I'd like you to clear your things out by the end of next week,' she said, mentally ticking off a box on her list. 'I'll deal with the wedding arrangements.'

Wickham floundered, then righted himself. 'What about Timon?' he demanded, needling a weak spot. 'Going to throw him out as well, are you? Abandon him?'

But Jane had already made arrangements for this as well, at least in her head. '*They*'ll stay here,' she told him. 'With Grace and me.'

It hadn't even been a question. Grace had bloomed under Timon's tutelage. It was as if the brittle, beige chrysalis had opened and out emerged, perhaps not a butterfly, but a hawkmoth – mesmerising and not a little scary. Lydia's initial efforts had been aided by a sixth form that actively encouraged individualism, a growth spurt that had seen her shoot up three inches in as many months, and Timon's eye as a stylist, who augmented their Mill Road charity shop finds with judicious Vinted buys and some pieces from Calypso's wardrobe, that Timon had begged on their last custodial visit.

'And what if he wants to come with me?' demanded Wickham then.

'*They*,' said a voice. 'How many fucking times? And I don't.'

Jane swung round to see her children framed in the doorway, both wearing sequins and smirks.

'I mean it,' said Timon. 'I'm staying here.'

Wickham shook his head. 'You look… ridiculous,' he said. 'And you'll do what I bloody say.'

'I'm sixteen,' said Timon. 'Nearly seventeen. I'll do what I want.'

'And they look f–fucking fabulous,' added Grace, the stumble over the swearword not detracting from the impact of her back-up.

Jane, who had known herself to be on the verge of wavering as soon as she knew she had an audience, felt her daughter's words like a shot of vodka – hot and emboldening. She turned back to Wickham. 'You can leave your keys on the hallway table,' she said. 'Your stuff is in the garage in boxes so you won't need them again. And there's five hundred in cash in this envelope.' She handed him a thickly wadded A4 vellum.

'I… You…' But Wickham was defeated, and he knew it.

He made one final parasitic gesture – taking Charley's 1963 Armagnac from the rack and opening it on the doorstep while he called himself an Uber (the keys had not included the one to the Range Rover, and the Audi was not packed up at all, rather sold for cocaine). But to all intents and purposes, and to Jane, Grace and Timon's entire delight, Wickham left Netherfield for Meryton, where he would stay for two nights before doing a runner on his rent and holing up in a cheap B&B on St Leonard's seafront with what little he had left from the cash he'd wangled from Jane. A month later he was arrested for drug offences and debt, and took up his new residence in HMP Lewes, where he shared a cell with a man with congenital body odour and a vocal tic that led Wickham to punch him, adding several more months to his sentence.

    And Jane? Jane was free.

WINTER

DECEMBER

Sister Act
Jane, Lizzy, Mary, Kitty, Lydia

~Lydia Bennet
how are you doing **@Jane**?
10:23

~Kitty Miller
God, Lyds. Time and place!
10:24

~Lydia Bennet
what? i'm being supportive. that's literally what this group is for.
10:24

~Kitty Miller
I don't think it is literally for that. It's mainly for hearsay and gossip, isn't it?
10:24

~Lydia Bennet
well mum saw wickham moving his shit out of the meryton flat so...
10:25

~Kitty Miller
Good. But also OMG. Was Timon with him? I hope not. I wouldn't wish Wickham on anyone.
10:25

~Lizzy Darcy-Bennet
Jane is in this group you know.
10:26

~Jane Bingley
It's fine. Timon is at Netherfield. I am here. And you can be supportive face to face later anyway. I'll be at the funeral.
10:26

~Lydia Bennet
can't believe it's finally happening. mum's beside herself. she's wearing a hat AND a fascinator
10:27

~Kitty Miller
Wait til you see Bridget. She's got a hooded cloak.
10:27

~Lydia Bennet
is dave coming?
10:27

~Kitty Miller
Apparently. And Shane FFS. Mum invited them. Actually I don't know anyone who isn't coming.
10:28

~Lydia Bennet
she does love a funeral. oh, did kitty tell you? I think I have

ADHD.
10:28

~Lizzy Darcy-Bennet
Tell me something I don't know.
10:29

~Lydia Bennet
why didn't you say?
10:29

~Lizzy Darcy-Bennet
you'd have told us to fuck off.
10:30

~Lydia Bennet
i wouldn't!
10:30

~Lydia Bennet
actually i would. sorry. anyway I'm on a waiting list for diagnosis. three years.
10:30

~Lizzy Darcy-Bennet
I can pay.
10:31

~Lydia Bennet
you don't need to.
10:31

~Lizzy Darcy-Bennet
But I want to. Let me. Pemberley can do something useful for

once. Anyway got to go. Milo wants to wear a bloody policeman's helmet and Arden's trying to bring a cat to the funeral.
10:31

~Jane Bingley
What cat? You don't have a cat.
10:32

~Lizzy Darcy-Bennet
Precisely.
10:32

★ ★ ★

It had been the same with Mrs Bennet's own mother, Beryl, whose ashes had sat on the mantel in an Alpen box (there'd been an incident with the urn and some overenthusiastic hoovering) for eight years before she and her own sisters could settle on a place – the Birchanger services, which was almost equidistant between them and convenient for Costa. So it was with Arthur, the Bennets' old Alsatian-cross, who had languished in the chest freezer for nigh on five years, with Mrs Bennet undecided what, exactly, to do with him. Should he be returned to the village near Hinxton where he'd been born? Perhaps cremated and his ashes scattered at Wandlebury woods where he'd fling himself in happy abandon every Sunday? Perhaps, even, laid to rest in Meryton, next to Charley and Fitz, where he could share their flowers and be next to the only men, bar Mr Bennet, he'd ever taken to? Meanwhile, every protest about cleanliness had been met with a wail and a reminder that she'd given him a bath only the day before he'd died (having rolled in fox excrement on the Meryton rec), and gradually Mr Bennet and Mary had realised they would not die of lysteria, dysentery or, indeed, plague, and his presence had gone largely unnoticed until Lydia's return.

Now, though, Mrs Bennet was in the mood for renewal. To wit, she had bid Mr Bennet dig a pit behind the larger of their two sycamores and Mary write a eulogy, and requisitioned Hindon to deal with the corpse, given his experience in these areas.

Contrary to Mr Bennet's suggestion, Hindon was delighted to be invited. 'I can read some sort of rites, if you like,' he offered.

'Oh, yes,' said Mrs Bennet. 'A professional, I like that.' She couldn't have been happier if the vicar himself had agreed to supervise the service and internment.

'Not a churchy person,' Hindon went on, 'but I've been to a fair few funerals. I know what I'm doing.'

'Ooh, anyone I know?' checked Mrs Bennet, before Hindon assured her that, with the exception of Carole Burghley, whose cat, Agatha, he had been dealing with, these had all been elsewhere, and no, none of them had been celebrities, not even minor ones.

And so it was that poor Arthur was finally entombed in a jerry-built coffin of bits of fruit crate nailed together, carried down the garden path by the men present – Mr Bennet himself, Dave, Shane (much to Kitty's indignation), Colin, Hindon and Denny, who had been on his round and happened into the garden to deliver an Amazon package at decidedly the wrong (or possibly right) time – and then lowered into a somewhat wonky hole in the Bennets' own back garden (Bridget had insisted on 'helping' with the dig, and then the twins had caught sight of it that morning and immediately tried to bury each other in it, necessitating showers all round and a fair bit of emergency re-digging).

Hindon's belated last rites and Mary's eulogy were solemn and strange by turns, and the latter curtailed by rain that ushered everyone back into the house for a wake catered as if it were for one of the Bennets themselves, two bottles of sherry emptied within the hour and Bad Karen having to be driven home by Laurence, having been sick into the very pit in which Arthur was trying to finally rest in peace. Mrs Bennet, meanwhile, was pleased as punch, and considering marketing herself out as a funeral planner as she regarded the scene with glee: Jane and Hindon chatting happily by the fireplace – the first time she had seen Jane smile in weeks, if not months; Mary and Colin (having both had a single sherry, which while seeming parsimonious to some, was the most alcohol either had imbibed in a while) singing 'Ave Maria' with a passible harmony; Lydia and the postman (he'd come back after finishing his round) on the chaise in the corner, both looking earnest. Admittedly Kitty was letting the side down a little, refusing to engage with either Dave or Shane – who had been circling each other like trapped cats – and instead busying herself with Lizzy and the twins. But give her time. Give them all time.

'Will you get another dog now?' asked Norman Fazackerley (two doors down, unfortunate moustache).

'Oh no,' she replied, then added, with a deliberate air of mystery. 'I shan't have the time.'

'Daughters enough trouble on their own?' asked Norman, before guffawing in a manner that felt like nails down a chalkboard.

The urge to blurt the truth was as strong in Mrs Bennet as the one that forced her to seek out gossip, yet for once she managed to swallow it down and trot out the line everyone expected. 'I'd say,' she replied. 'Never a minute's rest.'

Norman Fazackerley, who had been privy to myriad comings and goings over the years, nodded in a conspiratorial manner, eyeing Lydia, whom he considered chief offender among the younger Bennets.

And yet Lydia was, at that precise moment, not causing bother at all. Hadn't, actually, for a few weeks now, since the meetings. Rather, she and Denny were conducting some sort of confessional, outdoing each other with past misdemeanours, scoring it in the manner of Eurovision, which, it would be fair to say, Lydia was currently winning, thanks to the legendary *Love Shack* blow job. Not even Denny's almost choking on someone else's vomit after an all-nighter in Hanoi could match up to that level of public humiliation.

'Anything else?' he challenged her. 'Better out than in, you know.'

Lydia, who was rather enjoying the Great Unburdening, nodded. 'About four months ago I drank so much and took so much cocaine I actually thought I'd slept with someone and got pregnant and it turns out I hadn't slept with anyone at all.'

There was a pause, before Denny said, 'Cinq points.'

'Cinq? Is that it?' Lydia faux-bristled. 'Fine. But I haven't told you about Paris yet.'

'You shagged your boss's husband,' Denny said. 'Impressive. Dix points. But we had that already – after *Love Shack* and before the thing with Scott Auger.'

'Oh, hold your horses.' Lydia lifted her drink – a cup of turmeric tea. 'I didn't just sleep with her husband. I slept...' She waited – like her mother, Lydia was a fan of the dramatic pause.

'With *her*,' Denny realised. 'You were sleeping with her and – what? She wouldn't commit, or you wouldn't?'

Lydia felt a sudden slump, as she heard it prattled out in someone else's words: sounding quotidian suddenly, sad. 'A bit of both, perhaps,' she admitted. 'Committing has never really been my thing. Not in the past anyway,' she added swiftly, though suspecting it was already too late. 'And I wasn't sure I was ready for... for love. I mean, the sex is all very well – who hasn't got off with a woman, after all?'

'Well, I suspect that's what porn wants you to think,' said Denny.

Lydia shrugged. 'Anyway, I was falling for her – or I thought so, anyway – so I fucked her husband.'

Denny shrugged. 'And do you still love her?'

Lydia paused again, then shook her head. 'I think I was more in love with the idea of it – that it would be simpler, with a woman. But, well, turns out we're just as sodding complicated. And then of course I have a horrible addiction to dick.'

Denny – thank God – laughed, as intended. 'Dix points for sure.'

But Lydia wasn't finished. 'There's more. I can't be pregnant. Ever, I mean. So the joke was on me the entire time. Turns out I'm already perimenopausal. I'm a withered old woman at thirty-seven.' She tried to laugh, but it came out as more of a strangled sob.

'Lydia,' Denny put his hand on her arm. 'You don't need to tell me all this. It's clearly difficult.'

'I do need to,' she insisted. 'I fucked up. I mean, I've fucked up a lot in my life but upsetting you was the worst because I liked you. I mean, *really* liked you. I… still do. And I think you like me. And so I need to tell you everything. Full disclosure. So now you know – I'm a fuck-up. But I'm going to get better. I already am.'

'Lydia…'

She shrank. 'Oh God. You're going to say that's never going to happen, aren't you?'

'I…' began Denny.

But that sentence was never finished. Because from the other side of the living room commenced the sort of ruckus that tended, in the Bennet household, to be accompanied by concerns of impending death and a stampede to A&E. But for once, it was not Lydia, nor even Bridget or the twins at the centre of it. But rather, Mary.

What had happened was this: after 'Ave Maria', Colin, high on the Harvey's Bristol Cream, and demob-happy in the wake of his aunt's demise, had suggested they try harmonising on 'Islands in the Stream' – not a traditional funeral tune, but a recent addition to the St Saviour's choir repertoire following the narrowly averted coup. Mary had, initially, demurred, but Colin had grasped her hand and implored her, singing the opening Kenny Rogers' lines as encouragement. Well, with that, Mary found herself transformed into Dolly – brown eyes bright and gazing into his as she responded with a higher-than-usual soprano harmony. The pair swooped and soared through two verses and choruses, then, as they approached the final peak, found themselves quite overwhelmed with the enormity of it all – the music, the drink, the proximity – that Colin broke away, compelled to tell Mary exactly what he thought.

'You are a marvel,' he said. 'An absolute marvel.'

Mary's heart – a tight, guarded thing, but which, she now realised, had beat quietly and steadily for this man for the last eleven months, if not her entire life – billowed, and suddenly she could not stop herself any longer, and grabbing his cheeks, kissed him. And for three intense seconds, it was as if the heavens themselves applauded, so bright did they burn for each other.

It was only when Colin began to sputter that Mary reluctantly pulled away.

'What is it?' she asked him. 'Does my breath smell?' She breathed hard into her hands, sniffed, but could detect nothing but alcohol and possibly the sandwich she'd stolen from the wake spread and had eaten during the ceremony.

'Peanuts!' choked out Colin. 'Have you eaten peanuts recently?'

Mary paled as it dawned on her. The sandwich had been on the plate intended for Bridget and the twins (who could not be persuaded to eat either cucumber or fish paste). It had contained jam (apricot), and, yes, a dollop of SunPat. To which Colin was deeply, fatally allergic.

The realisation was as awful as it was swift: she had murdered Colin. With her sordid tongue.

Mary, though, even under the influence of drink, was rendered sensible immediately, and knew exactly what to do. And so it was that, having experienced true love's kiss, and almost killing her lover, she saved his life as well, rescuing him with the EpiPen that Hindon carried as a matter of course in his vet bag, which he also carried as a matter of course, because, as he told Jane later, one never knew when one would come across an injured kitten, or crow, or even a forty-four-year-old theology professor.

'Quite,' said Jane as she watched Mary fanning Colin gently on the settee. 'So, I was wondering... I'm having a party on New Year's Eve at Netherfield. The wedding reception...' She paused. It sounded so mercenary out loud, and yet it wasn't intended that way, not at all. 'Everything was booked and it seemed a shame to waste it. So would you—'

'I would love to come,' he said, then hesitated. 'Though I've got the boys...'

'The more the merrier,' said Jane, and meant it. 'Lizzy's bringing the twins, and Bridget will be there. And my two.' Yes, two. Timon might not be hers by birth, but they were, like so many strays she had taken in over the years, hers through happenstance, and she loved them no less for it.

So, while Lydia's feelings may have been thwarted, Kitty's ignored, and Lizzy's... well, who knew what was going on in her head, two of the Bennet women felt their embers decidedly kindled that day.

And that, Mrs Bennet, thought to herself, as she settled in bed next to Mr Bennet that evening, would be the best Christmas present she could get.

★ ★ ★

Christmas Day itself passed in the Bennet household, as it tended to: in a surfeit of good humour and food, and a deficit of well-thought-out presents, Mrs Bennet's mantra being 'more is better, no matter the relevance', and Mr Bennet's 'whatever is left on the shelf on Christmas Eve'. And so Lydia received both a full set of monogrammed towels, and a Homer Simpson Pez dispenser (which, to be fair, had been intended for Bridget, but the parcels had got muddled somehow and she refused to relinquish her Gillette Venus razor, with which she had already shaved two bears and a stuffed monkey). Only Colin and Mary had gone out of their way to think hard about their gifts' intended recipients, with a range of vitamin and mineral supplements individually chosen to do everything from reduce flatulence (Mrs Bennet) to restore sexual function (Lydia, who had complained to Mary that actually, she hadn't missed the shagging as much as she thought she would and was worried the menopause would rob her of that outlet of satisfaction even as the New Year, and thus her liberation, dawned).

It was, though she might deny it, with that in mind that she texted Denny to check when he was coming back from his mother's.

'New Year's Eve Eve,' he replied. 'But we're rehearsing that night. Don't want to let your sister down.'

'She'd forgive anything,' texted Lydia truthfully, hiding her own disappointment. 'But I guess I'll see you at the party then.'

'You will,' he replied. A pause followed, the three dots pulsing, then, 'How's your first sober Christmas?'

She smiled. 'NGL,' she typed. 'If I can get through this I can get through anything.'

Actually, it wasn't as terrible as Denny or she or anyone might have imagined. She wasn't going to get pious about it, that was Mary's area. Nor was she going to suddenly embrace healthy everything, which, she'd noted, tended to be the way with women in groups; no, wild swimming was about as appealing as church, if apparently an endorphin rush that came close to the first sip of fizz. Besides, Lydia didn't need it. That snap of clarity was becoming an addiction in itself, waking with only the blur of ageing eyesight rather than seven pornstar martinis and countless bumps of something. And she could see writ large now the ADHD that had managed to go undetected for thirty-seven years. And which, in combination with drink, she blamed for, well, a lot.

But not everything. Even sober, and what she considered thought out carefully, she had made some poor decisions. This, though, was not going to be one of them.

She braced herself, messaged again. 'I wish you were here.'

The three anxiety-inducing dots began to bounce again, then subside, bringing with it the trip of Lydia's insides. But then, just when she thought she'd fucked up, a reply materialised with no run-up. 'Me too,' it said. 'The food here's fecking terrible.'

'Oh ha fucking ha,' she replied. Then, panicking, '(Jokes. Not actually cross with you.)'

His reply this time was swift. 'Jokes too. I miss you, Lyds.'

* * *

New Year's Eve dawned bright and sharp, fitting for a day that was, for the first time in four years, replete with optimism, with sheer, giddy possibility. Yes, the Bennets – all of them, including myriad children – had walked to the graves in the morning, but then they'd left Jane and Lizzy to pay respects in peace, and walked back to Longbourn the long way, across the soft crunch of frost on the common, and via the rec, where Milo and Arden insisted on the swings, and Bridget on being spun on the roundabout to see if she could make herself sick, while the adults stood around, clapping their hands and breathing out great huffs of fog into the air.

'I'm thinking of going to uni,' said Lydia, out of seemingly nowhere. 'That's my resolution I mean, to apply.'

'Where? Cambridge?' clucked Mrs Bennet. 'I always said you

were clever, didn't I?' She nudged her husband. 'Quite the little brainbox under all that' – she flapped a hand dramatically – 'shenanigans.'

'Maybe not Cambridge,' said Lydia. 'I'm not Jane or Lizzy after all.'

'To do what?' asked Mary, who had managed to refrain from the temptation to point out several obvious problems, and was relieved that Lydia had already nixed them anyway. 'Fashion?'

'Media studies?' offered Colin, squeezing Mary's hand. 'That might be nice.'

'Honestly, I don't know yet,' Lydia replied. 'Nothing sciencey though. I can't wear lab coats. White—'

'Drains you,' finished Kitty. 'I'm going to train as a tattooist,' she added, unprompted, and if she was honest, entirely on a whim. 'And open my own salon.'

'I could get a tattoo!' yelled Mrs Bennet. 'That could be my resolution.'

'Oh please, God, no,' said Mr Bennet. 'I don't think my heart will take it.'

'You're probably right,' she sighed. 'Anyway, there's something else. I've been meaning to tell you all and I was going to do it tonight, but while we're on the subject…'

The seed had been sown in Paris, and the tense weeks afterwards, when she'd been convinced poor Gordon was on his way out. His resurrection, and then, conversely, the burial of Arthur, had sealed the deal.

'Yes,' she had said at the wake to Mr Bennet.

Mr Bennet frowned. 'Yes to what? Another sherry.'

'No,' she said. 'To Australia. Let's do it in the new year. We're not getting any younger after all, and if there's anything your bowels have taught me, it's that I might die tomorrow.'

Mr Bennet was unsure that it was his bowels that had taught her this, given she had been threatening it ever since they'd met, but he was not going to look this particular gift horse in the mouth, and brushed his teeth twice before bed that night, just as Mrs Bennet had shaved her legs.

Today, though, the announcement of their imminent departure had not gone out with quite such a bang.

'You're what?' demanded Kitty. 'Why, for God's sake?'

'Well, it's been five years since we saw Phil and Sue and, well, then there's your dad's cancer—'

'He didn't *have* cancer,' pointed out Lydia.

Mrs Bennet, however, was not to be dissuaded. 'Still, it made me think. And they have kangaroos in the back garden that eat from your hand. Your *hand*! Imagine!'

Bridget could indeed. 'Can I come?' she asked. 'Shane can come with us. And see his sheep!' (Shane's recent bleakness put down to missing his ovine friends, rather than Kitty's refusal to even consider his presence in her bed or the loss of his contract with *Vogue* while he pursued his ex-wife to no avail.)

'No,' said Mr Bennet, before his wife could contemplate it, and then turn it into some sort of Bennets Abroad circus. 'Just us. Six months. And when we get back, we're downsizing the house.'

If the trip had lain the rockets and set the Catherine wheels spinning, this had lit the blue touchpaper.

'What?' yelled Lydia. 'But where will I live?'

'At university,' said Mr Bennet. 'You already said it.'

Lydia bristled. Damn it. 'Where will Mary live then?' she tried.

'At Rosings,' said Mary. 'It's already arranged.' She beamed at Colin, who beamed right back, and not only because he was remembering the quite filthy sex they'd had only that morning – a side of him that, though he'd known existed, certainly hadn't reared its head with Charlotte, who, bedroom-wise was all bleak efficiency, and yet with Mary, well... He shivered with the frisson that caught Mary as well, who giggled.

'You knew?' Lydia wheeled on her sister.

'No one knew,' placated their mother. 'Except Lizzy and Jane, and only them because they're sensible. And because I needed a favour.'

'What favour?'

'We're going to rent at first, to check we're not going lala,' admitted Mr Bennet. 'And so Lizzy will move in. She's selling Ledbury Road and it seemed the best with everything. You doing childcare and whatnot.'

Lydia's indignation retreated a little. Nannying was rather a calling, she had decided. Perhaps she could even keep it up while studying – go to Anglia Ruskin for Child Psychology or something.

Kitty's ire, meanwhile, seemed to brim. 'She only just sold Pemberley,' she said, seething and green at the myriad fresh starts, when hers had been meant to trump everyone.

'And apparently it felt transformative,' said Mrs Bennet. 'Transformative! You know she's bringing someone to Jane's later. A gentleman she says, and someone I don't even know. A gentleman *and* a stranger! Imagine!'

'But where will the twins go to school?' Kitty whinged on. 'They're on the doorstep of preps!'

'With Bridget,' said Mrs Bennet. 'About which I should think you'd be pleased. She won't be the only oddball anymore.'

She was nothing if not honest, and Kitty appreciated that, at least. Particularly given Bridget was, at that very moment, being spun by Timon and Grace into a veritable frenzy.

Lydia frowned. 'Can we redecorate?' she asked, her mind suddenly a cavalcade of Farrow & Ball palettes and Heals catalogues. 'If you're moving out?'

'No one is touching my sconces!' shrieked Mrs Bennet.

And that was the last word on the subject, as, at that point, Bridget did indeed, to her absolute delight, throw up.

★ ★ ★

The move, too, had been the subject of much discussion back at St Saviour's graveyard, as Lizzy and Jane, their arms linked, stared down at the headstones of their respective beloveds.

'I miss him,' admitted Jane, for the first time since Wickham's appearance, and subsequent scuttling away. 'I couldn't say it because I thought it might break me. But it doesn't, does it?'

Lizzy shook her head. 'And missing someone doesn't mean you can't also live,' she said. 'I realise that now.'

Jane squeezed her sister's arm. 'I'm going to ask Hindon about a job,' said Jane resolutely. 'If Mum's going, you know?'

'Good,' said her sister. 'And I hope he'll let you train up as well. You'd be wasted on the reception desk.'

'Would I?' said Jane, thinking of all the dogs that might come in, needing comfort, the cats requiring a kind word – the sort of calm Jane excelled at.

'Actually, no,' said Lizzy, picturing it as well. 'You'll be brilliant whatever you do.'

They turned to catch up with the others. 'Am I doing the right thing?' Jane asked then. 'About tonight,' I mean. 'You don't think it too ghoulish?'

Lizzy shook her head. 'It's perfect,' she said. 'Everyone is going to love it.'

Not least she and Saul.

They had already kissed – a blissful six minutes on the doorstep of Ledbury Road, before she politely told him she wasn't inviting him in, but only because he had a wedding to get back to, and that this was 'to be continued'.

And continue it, she thought, they probably would, at midnight, if not before. As long as the twins were in bed, and Grace and Timon not too drunk to mind them for the night. He'd booked into the White Hart in Meryton, he'd told her, no pressure.

'None felt,' she'd said.

And it was true. But want? Want was another thing. And

as she trod back towards Longbourn, she knew she had a final letter to write.

★ ★ ★

In her defence, Kitty's action had been prompted only in part by her inbuilt need to outdo her sisters as far as fresh starts were concerned. But it was something that, as with Mrs Bennet's epiphany, had come to her in Paris, and only been derailed by the reappearance of Shane. Also in her defence, she hadn't intended to do it in public, but he hadn't been answering his phone, and had refused to come to the door when she'd called round that morning, so Jane's party was the first chance she had. And at least she waited until he was off-stage – or almost – to do it. Not that anyone had advised her; none of them knew. Not even Lydia, who had been mesmerised by Denny – every cell of her suddenly alive to the sheer perfection of him, in all his messiness – and didn't realise what was happening until Kitty was down on one knee.

'What the… hell are you doing?' asked Dave. 'Kitty, get up.'

She shook her head. 'I've got a speech,' she said, 'and I need to say it, whatever your answer.'

The room – or rather, tent – by this point, had fallen silent, all eyes on the decking square where Listless Biscuits had been playing, and where Timon was now DJing, and not too badly either, if PJ Harvey was your thing.

'I have fucked up,' began Kitty, 'like, a tonne. And I'm not proud of the way I've been since, well, Lydia came back home.' She glanced at her sister. 'Not that I'm blaming you, Lyds. Just that your' – she waved in Lydia's direction – 'chaos is sort of infectious.'

'None taken,' said Lydia.

'The thing is' – Kitty turned back to Dave – 'I love you. I have loved you since we met, and no I might not have shown it.

And yes I did get into bed with my ex-husband. And that was a big mistake. Huge.'

Shane, to his credit, said nothing.

Kitty braced herself. 'But not as big as the one I made when I said no to you.' She pulled a small circular object from her pocket, held it out to him. 'Dave Pickens, will you please marry me?'

The tent held its breath. What would he say?

Dave blinked, opened his mouth. 'Is that a glow-in-the-dark Disney Princess ring?' he asked.

'Yes,' said Kitty. Then whispered, 'It was this or a cock ring, and, well…' She gestured to the crowd.

'Well, that's something.' Dave rolled his eyes.

Oh God, the build up was bad enough, but the stringing it out was unbearable. No wonder he'd hated her in the wake of his own proposal. 'Come on?' she willed him, aloud (he wasn't that good at reading her mind, except in the bedroom). 'Just say it. If it's no then, well, I'll be devastated.' She had been going to bring up Bridget at that point, but decided against blackmail. 'But I'll accept it and… and move on. But I will always regret not making this work. You are… you are the best person I've ever met. And' – fuck it – 'the best father as well.'

'Hang on—' began Shane, but Mrs Bennet thwacked him.

Dave put his hand over his eyes. Was he crying? Or deciding how best to let her down.

He let the hand drop; Kitty saw – thank fuck! – tears.

And then, 'Yes,' he said. 'Yes, Kitty Miller, I will.'

★ ★ ★

'Do you think they're mad?' asked Lydia, not an hour later, as she and Denny sat huddled in a Welsh blanket (Jane had thought of everything) on a bench under the willow.

'Yes?' said Denny. 'But in a good way.' He handed her a glass of the Nosecco they'd been given in the run-up to midnight, which Lydia, out of habit, had downed in one, hence the sharing now. 'So, university?'

'I never went,' she said. 'And maybe I'll be shit at it, but I don't want to regret not trying. It's my resolution,' she added. 'Now that I've ticked off giving up drink.' She didn't mention the sex. That would be too obvious, wouldn't it. And she was trying to be slightly less so. Less emotionally incontinent. Less impulsive. That was what the university was about, as she tried some long-term thinking, until she got meds, which, she hoped, would make all that easier.

'Well you never really "tick off" drink. You do know that?' checked Denny.

Lydia grinned. 'Jokes,' she said. 'I knew you'd rise to it. Anyway, what's yours? Resolution, I mean.'

'I don't know. Record some stuff with Dave maybe. Finally find an original G-Plan sideboard.'

Lydia sighed. 'Seriously? That's it?'

'If you'd let me finish.' He smiled, that dimple – be still, Lydia's heart – pitting his left cheek. 'See as much of this woman I fancy before she buggers off to college.'

The words hung in the air between them as if neon-lit and tangible. Then, Lydia surprised them both by asking for his consent.

'You may,' he said. 'You very much fucking may.'

And their kiss, when it came, was every bit as good as either of them had imagined (and oh God, they had imagined). And the sex, which followed not half an hour later (in their defence, it had been more than a year for Lydia, three times that for Denny) was that glorious combination of awkward (would he be able to get an erection on meds? Would she get wet enough without the lubrication of several sambucas and a gram of cocaine?) and easy ('Yes, there and – oh God, there!') and very much to be repeated. Again.

And again.

And again.

Not everyone was as quick to get to bed, though bed was certainly in the minds of Lizzy and Saul as they danced an imperfect jive to the delight of everyone assembled (particularly Timon, who had put on Pharrell Williams' 'Happy' as an ironic nod to Grace, who had bet them a pound they wouldn't be able to lower themself to play it).

'He's excessively handsome,' said Mrs Bennet as she watched her daughter spin quite professionally, given those heels, and the drinking.

'You said that about Fitz,' observed Mr Bennet.

'And I was right,' his wife pointed out. 'I know a good horse when I see one. And Saul's a good horse. An underdog one. Like Dream Alliance.'

Mr Bennet had the good sense to let that lie, and Mrs Bennet carried on watching them then, her girls: Lizzy with her fancy man, Mary with Colin, Kitty with Dave, Lydia with the postman (who could blame her? He looked like a young Sean Bean but with more lip), Jane with Grace, the vet and his two boys, all cooing over Socrates, who had managed to eat an entire asparagus quiche and was feeling rather sorry for himself. And it struck her then: they were happy. They were all, actually, happy. And she knew it was a precarious state, held together like a secondhand car with duct tape and faith. She knew that, by morning, at least one would have suffered some minor catastrophe. And she knew, too, that that catastrophe would, in turn, be patched up, because they were all adults now, and surprisingly capable of fending for themselves. And as for her hankering for marriage, to get them off her hands – if Kitty and Lizzy and Jane had taught her anything, it was that marriage didn't mean the end of one's worrying. One never got rid of one's children, not really. They vexed you until your dying day.

But they brought you joy too. So much joy.

After Darcy

★ ★ ★

Dear Darcy

It's been four years, my love. And I have to stop now. I have to stop these letters, I have to stop talking to you as if you are still in the room. And above all I have to stop comparing. For too long I only remembered the best of you. And then only the worst. And it's not that I wish to forget. Til death us do part was not long enough, and I will love you until my dying breath, but I have to let you go. I have to make room for someone. Or the possibility of someone.

I think you'd like him. Actually, that's a lie. You'd protest that his trousers were 'obvious' and his choice of car 'suspect' and that anyone who thinks Columbo *outdoes* Inspector Morse *is a fool. But that doesn't matter. Because he'd feel the same about your suits, and your shoes and the civil war obsession.*

And besides, you would have something, I know, in common.
Me.

I am who I am, in part, down to you – Milo and Arden more so – and I will make sure they know that and celebrate it, just as I celebrate our two decades together. Those first days in Cambridge. The months running up to the wedding when we thought I was pregnant. The years after when we knew I was not. I can't have been easy – obstinate, headstrong girl that I am. But not once did you think of leaving me, and nor I you.

Until now. Now we both have to move on.

So goodbye, my darling Fitz, and thank you – for the twins, for the wonderful life you gave me, and for everything yet to come.
xxx

Sister Act
Jane, Lizzy, Mary, Kitty, Lydia

~Lydia Bennet
happy new year!
09:23

~Jane Bingley
Happy New Year, Lyds!
09:23

~Lydia Bennet
also denny says hi (!)
09:23

~Jane Bingley
Hello, Denny (!)
09:24

~Lydia Bennet
where is everyone? no offence but i was hoping for a bit more impact than just you. isn't lizzy up with the twins?
09:40

~Jane Bingley
Lizzy didn't stay (!)
09:40

~Lydia Bennet
!!!!!
09:40

~Lydia Bennet
fine. duck you all, you bunch of drunkards. see you at lunch.
10:10

~Lydia Bennet
no. duck you all
10:10

~Lydia Bennet
oh duck it
10:10

Acknowledgements

While writing is a solo and often lonely pursuit, publishing a book is, thankfully, a team sport, and I am lucky to have so many excellent people on my team. First and foremost, my agent Jenny Savill who believed in both me and that bedraggled Lydia who stumbled through the door of Longbourn on New Year's Eve. Likewise, my publisher Carolyn Mays and everyone at Bedford Square who have so enthusiastically brought a new generation of Bennets to life.

The Friday Writers' Club (mostly meeting on a Monday now because, as every woman knows, even without a pram in the hall, life tends to get in the way) – Hana Tooke, Lou Abercrombie, Catherine Bruton and Clare Furniss – who have shared every up and down of drafting this novel. The Boskenna writers – Anna Wilson, Natasha Farrant, Elen Caldecott, Lucy Coats and Wendy Meddour – who restore my belief in the power of words (and women) every midsummer.

My virtual water-cooler writer friends, The Placers, who do the same every day, and are an antidote to any slight on social media. I grew up without sisters, and while my little brother was occasionally willing to dress up as Cinderella, there were limits to his capacity for indulgence, and I envied my friends who had living Girls Worlds to plait, and paint, and confess their secrets to. Sisterhood, though, comes in many forms, and so, in addition to all the above, and my brilliant sister-in-law Helen Nadin, I am grateful to Henny Stringfellow, Rosh Cornford, Lucy Cuthew, Lucy Christopher, Rachel Davis, Ruth Pelling, Ruth Cook, Jude Savill, Nic Watkins, Karen Sheairs, Jo Holbek, Leona Dean, Annika Bluhm, Rachel Delahaye and Dandy Butler-Smith, who have (figuratively), at various points in my life, held back my hair and allowed me to smear them with Rimmel.

About the Author

Photo courtesy of Joanna Nadin

Joanna Nadin is a former broadcast journalist, political speechwriter and special adviser to the Prime Minister. Since leaving politics she has written numerous books for children and adults, including an adaptation of Jane Austen's *Sense and Sensibility* for younger readers, the Carnegie Medal-nominated *Joe All Alone*, which is now a BAFTA-winning and Emmy-nominated BBC drama, and the *Flying Fergus* series with Sir Chris Hoy. Originally from Essex, she now lives in Bath, and is Associate Professor in Creative Writing at University of Bristol.

Bedford Square Publishers is an independent publisher of fiction and non-fiction, founded in 2022 in the historic streets of Bedford Square London and the sea mist shrouded green of Bedford Square Brighton.

Our goal is to discover irresistible stories and voices that illuminate our world.

We are passionate about connecting our authors to readers across the globe and our independence allows us to do this in original and nimble ways.

The team at Bedford Square Publishers has years of experience and we aim to use that knowledge and creative insight, alongside evolving technology, to reach the right readers for our books. From the ones who read a lot, to the ones who don't consider themselves readers, we aim to find those who will love our books and talk about them as much as we do.

We are hunting for vital new voices from all backgrounds – with books that take the reader to new places and transform perceptions of the world we live in.

Follow us on social media for the latest Bedford Square Publishers news.

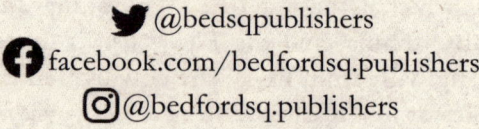

bedfordsquarepublishers.co.uk